Ambai

A Kitchen in the Corner
of the House

TRANSLATED FROM THE TAMIL

BY LAKSHMI HOLMSTRÖM

archipelago books

"Fish in a Dwindling Lake," "The Calf that Frolicked in the Hall," "A Thousand Words," "One Life," and "Journey 4" are reproduced with permission from Penguin Random House India © 2012.

"Journey 1," "Parasakti and Others in a Plastic Box," "In a Forest, a Deer," "Wrestling," "A Rat, A Sparrow," "Journey 3," "Forest," and "A Movement, a Folder, Some Tears" are reproduced with permission of Oxford University Press India © Oxford University Press 2006.

"My Mother, Her Crime," "Some Deaths," "Yellow Fish," "A Kitchen in the Corner of the House," "Trisanku," "Once Again," "A Fable," "River," and "Wheelchair" appeared in *A Purple Sea*, published by EastWest Books (Madras) Pvt. Ltd. 1992.

Archipelago Books
232 3rd Street #A111
Brooklyn, NY 11215
www.archipelagobooks.org

Library of Congress Cataloging-in-Publication Data available upon request

Distributed by Penguin Random House
www.penguinrandomhouse.com

Cover art: Arun Prem
Book Design: Zoe Guttenplan

This book was made possible by the New York State Council on the Arts
with the support of Governor Andrew M. Cuomo and the New York State Legislature.

Archipelago Books also gratefully acknowledges the generous support from Aditi: Foundation for the Arts,
Lannan Foundation, the Carl Lesnor Family Foundation, the Nimick Forbesway Foundation,
and the New York City Department of Cultural Affairs.

Contents

A Kitchen in the Corner of the House

In a Forest, a Deer

It is difficult to forget those nights. Nights when we listened to all those stories. Thangam Athai, it was, who told them to us. They were not tales of the fox and the crow, nor of the hare and the tortoise. No, these were stories she herself had made up. Some were like fragments of poetry. Others were like songs which would never end. Stories which developed in all sorts of ways, without beginning, middle, or end. At times, at night, she would create many images in our minds. Even the gods and demons would alter in her stories. She would speak most movingly about Mandara. Surpanaka, Tadaka, and the rest would no longer remain as rakshasis, female demons, but be transformed into real people with impulses and feelings. She brought into the light characters which had seemed only to cling to the pages of the epics. As if she were stroking a bird with broken wings, with such gentleness she would portray them in words. I don't know what it was about them – the night-time, or the central hall of that old house where we lay, or the nearness of all the cousins – but those stories still keep circling and sounding somewhere in my mind, like the buzzing of bees.

In that house with its old pillars and central hall, I see Thangam Athai in several frames. Leaning against the heavy wooden door. Carrying a small lamp which she has shaded with the end of her sari; placing it within its niche. Serving a meal to her husband, Ekambaram. Pulling on a rope, one foot firmly placed upon the small parapet surrounding the well. Feeding the plants with manure.

Thangam Athai had beautiful dark skin. A face without a single wrinkle, as if it had been ironed smooth. Plenty of silver in her hair. There was an old-fashioned harmonium in Athai's house, worked by pressing a pedal. Athai used to play it. She would play different tunes, from the *tevaram* "Vadaname chandrabimbamo" to the popular "Vannaan vandaana," singing softly at the same time. Her long fingers which looked like the dark beaks of birds would fly over the keys of the harmonium as if they were black butterflies.

A shell of mystery surrounded Thangam Athai. There seemed to be a deep pity for her in the way the others looked at her with tenderness, or stroked her gently; it was there in the compassion flowing from their eyes. Ekambaram Maama had another wife. He always treated Athai as if she were a flower. Nobody had overheard him address her as "di." He would always call her Thangamma. All the same, Athai seemed, somehow, as if she stood a long distance away, behind a smokescreen. It was Muthu Maama's daughter, Valli, who pierced the mystery. What she found out was both comprehensible to us, and yet totally incomprehensible. According to Valli's mother, Athai had never "blossomed."

"What does that mean?" several of us wanted to know.

Valli was old enough to wear a half-sari. "Well, it means that she never came of age."

"But her hair is all white, isn't it?"

"That's different."

After that we watched Athai's body carefully. We discussed among ourselves how a body that hadn't "blossomed" would be. We couldn't understand in what way her body wasn't complete. Athai looked just like everyone else when she appeared in her wet clothes, after her bath. When she stood there in her knotted red choli and her green sari, she didn't look at all unusual. Valli's mother had said to Valli, "It's just a hollow body." We couldn't make out where the gap could be. We wondered if it was like the broken wing of a sparrow, a hollow that wasn't overtly discernible.

One evening they cut down a huge tree in the garden, which had died. At the last blow of the hatchet, it suddenly slid down to the ground amidst a rustling of leaves. When it was split across, there was a mere hole within. Valli nudged me at the waist and said, "That's it, that's hollow." But it was impossible to compare Athai's shining dark form with this tree, lying there facing the sky, exposing itself utterly, nothing inside.

What secret did that form hide? In what way was her body so different? In the hot summer afternoons, Athai would remove her tight choli and lie down in the storeroom. When we went and snuggled close to her, laying our heads against her breast, freed now from its confining choli, she would gather us up in a light embrace. Held within the protection of her breast, her waist, her arms, it was difficult to perceive any hollow. Hers was a temperately warm body.

She seemed like one steeped in feelings and emotions. Like a ripe fruit full of juice, a life-spring flowed through her body. And often those vitalizing drops fell upon our own selves. Through her touch, through her caress, through the firm pressure with which she massaged us with oil, a life-force sprang towards us from her body, like a river breaking past its own banks. It was at the touch of her hands that cows would yield their milk. The seeds that she planted always sprouted. My mother always said she had an auspicious hand.

Athai was there when my little sister was born. "Akka, stay by my side. Keep holding on to me. Only then will I not feel any pain," Amma muttered, as we children were being swept out of the room. When we came to the threshold and looked back from the doorway, Thangam Athai was softly stroking Amma's swollen belly.

"Nothing will happen. Don't be frightened," she said quietly.

"Oh, Akka, if only you too could. . ." my mother sobbed, unable to finish what she began.

"What do I need? I'm like a queen. My house is full of children," said Athai. Ekambaram Maama's younger wife had seven children.

"Your body has not opened. . ." Amma wept the louder.

"Why, what's wrong with my body? Don't I feel hungry at the right times? Don't I sleep well? The same properties that all bodies have, this one has, too. It feels pain when it is hurt. Its blood clots. If its wounds go septic, it gathers pus. It digests the food it eats. What more do you want?" asked Athai.

Amma took her hand and laid it against her cheek.

"They turned your body into a bloody battlefield. . ." she moaned, holding that hand tight.

Valli's mother had told Valli that there was no medicine left that they had not tried on Athai's body. If any physician came to town, most definitely he would be asked to prescribe for Athai. It seems they even tried English medicine on her. It seems that at times she would take these medicines and fall into such a deep and heavy sleep. It seems that for a few months they made puja with neem leaves and the sound of the *udukku* drum. In the hope that something might happen if she were suddenly startled, a dark figure wrapped in a black cloth once sprang on her when she was alone in the backyard. Screaming with the shock, Athai fell down, hitting her head against the washing-stone. The scar is still there, on the edge of her forehead. When the next physician came to her, it seems Athai cried out, "Leave me alone. Leave me alone." The evening after they had been to see a prospective second wife for Ekambaram, it seems Athai swallowed a mixture of ground arali seeds. They gave her an antidote, and somehow managed to resuscitate her. After that, Ekambaram had wept and said, "I don't want anything for myself that will cause you pain." Then Athai herself sought out a bride for him. And that was how Senkamalam came to live in that house. All these were details collected by Valli.

Without removing her hand from Amma's clasp, Athai stroked her head with her other hand. "Leave it. Leave it now. Let it all go. Why think of my story at this time when you are giving birth?" she said. It was that very night that my little sister was born.

It was some time later, on one occasion when we were visiting her house, that she told us the story.

It was the rainy season. On one side of the living room, the *jamukkalams* had been spread and a few pillows encased in pillow-cases with stubborn hair-oil stains were scattered about. And there were some pillows without pillowcases. These were made of heavy cotton in dark colours, stuffed with cottonwool. Here and there the cottonwool had knotted into lumps. These were not the pillows in daily use. They were kept for the use of the children of occasional visitors. Were the lumps and knots going to matter, after all, to children who played all day long and went to sleep with full bellies?

We could hear the sound of the kitchen being washed down. Then we heard the clang of the brass pot, the creaking of the door, the soft thump of the coconut-frond broom being banked against it. A tin box clinked. That would be the tin in which the kolam powder was kept. The kolam would now be traced upon the hearth. After that, having shut the kitchen door, Athai must come this way through the living-room. Not one of us was asleep. We waited.

As soon as she came by us, Somu began.

"Athai, won't you tell us a story. . . Athai?"

"Aren't you asleep, any of you?"

She stood there and watched us awhile, then she came closer and sat down. Kamakshi and Somu crept up to her immediately, put their heads upon her lap and lay on either side of her, gazing up at her. The rest of us leaned our elbows against our pillows.

Athai was tired. The sweat gleamed upon her forehead. She shut her eyes and thought for a moment.

"It was a huge forest," she began.

"In that forest, all the animals lived together, happily. There were lots of fruit trees there. A small stream ran through it, to one side.

If ever they felt thirsty, they would drink from it. Whatever any of the animals wanted, it was all there, exactly as they wished, in that forest. In that forest, they never feared the hunter. All those animals roamed about freely, never afraid that a sudden arrow might pierce them, or that they might lose their lives. Like any other forest, it was not without such things as forest fires, or trespassers coming from elsewhere to cut down the trees, or to steal the fruit, or even to shoot at the birds, or to strike at the fleeing wild pig. All the same, it was a forest to which the birds and animals had become accustomed. Indeed, they knew it well. They knew on which tree the owl would alight, and how it would hoot at nights when the entire forest lay silent; they knew on which stone the frog would sit and make its sudden croaking noise as if it were lapping water; they knew the places where the peacock danced.

"Everything went on like this until one day when a herd of deer went to drink water. As they walked on, following the water, one of the deer was separated from the rest. Suddenly it found itself in a different forest. It seemed to be a forest which had no pathways at all through it. There were marks on all the trees where arrows had penetrated them. Within the forest, a waterfall sounded with a loud flourish. The place wore a desolate look, as if there wasn't a soul about. The deer felt its whole body shudder with fear. Crying out loudly that this was not the place it knew, it wandered the entire forest, leaping about in its panic. It grew dark. The deer couldn't bear the terror of it. The waterfall's sound was frightening. In the distance, a hunter had lit a fire and was eating the roasted flesh of the animal he had killed. The deer could see the sparks from that fire.

It hid itself. It sank down, exhausted from having gone round and round that forest, all alone.

"It wandered about in this way for many days. And then it was the night of the full moon. Moonlight filled the forest. Spread with moonlight, the waterfall had taken on a different form. A form that was no longer frightening. The moonlight touched everything softly, gently. Suddenly, as if a magic rod had been laid upon it, the deer's terror disappeared entirely. It began to like this forest. It began to learn all its nooks and crannies. Even though it was a different place, this forest, too, contained everything. There was the waterfall. There were all the trees and plants. Slowly, gradually, its eyes discerned all the animals and birds. It could see the beehives hanging from the trees. It saw the freshness of the green grass. The deer understood all the secrets of this new forest. And after that it walked around the entire forest without fear. The deer's terror had all gone and it was at peace."

Athai finished her story. All the rest of the living room was in darkness. Only this part was lit up. As we children listened to the story, we imagined that the dark parts of the room were the forest; we made friends with the deer, and now we too were at peace. Hugging our pillows, we fell asleep. As I fell back against my pillow with its rough cover of dark blue and yellow and black, and opening a single eye, looked upwards, half-asleep, I saw Thangam Athai sitting in our midst, leaning forward with her knees drawn up, her arms across her chest, and her hands clasping her shoulders.

Once Again

Two were created.
    Lokidas.
    Sabari.

Loku, what will you do when you are grown up?
    I'm going to eat all the lollipops I want.
    Idiot, talk sensibly. Tell this uncle and aunty.
    I'll buy myself a puppy.
    Silly. Today he is not in the right mood. Come on, tell us what work you are going to do.
    I'll be an engineer.
    Correct. See how well he answers? He'll usually say it straight off. Today he's being stubborn.
    Loku, come here. Repeat the dialogue from *Sholay* for us.
    Won't.
    Tch. A clever child will always do as his parents tell him. Go on. Repeat the dialogue.
    I want to go out and play.

You can go out later. Give us the dialogue first. Otherwise I won't give you your ball.

"Arré, O Samba. . ."

Good.

The first piece that Lokidas wrote in school, entitled "My Parents":

"My mother's name is Kaveri. My father's name is Sankaran. My mother likes boys who listen to their parents. My father reads the paper. We have a TV in our house. When I grow up I won't be an engineer."

The teacher said this lacked logical order and gave it one out of ten.

In the drawing lesson, he wasn't able to do circular men with arms and legs as he was told to do. He made them all square.

"Is this the way to do it? Look how everybody else has done round men. Is this how people are?"

"Yes, that's how they are. They have square arms. Square heads. And they can fly. They fly up to the sky and play cricket there. Even the footballs they play with are square."

The teacher said it showed an unhealthy imagination and marked it zero. His mother scolded him. She said he should repeat every morning, as soon as he got up: People walk. A ball is round.

Loku, the boy who sits next to you is a Hindu isn't he?

Yes.

Then who is the boy who came with you yesterday?

Joseph.

Where did you go and play?

We didn't play. He showed me their church. There was an aunty there, holding a baby. That's Mother Mary.

I don't want you to go to such places hereafter. Understand?

Very well, Appa.

Loku, I think you should have a shave today.

No, Appa.

Kaveri, fetch him some hot water. Here's the brush and soap.

Appa, it hasn't grown that much.

Here comes the hot water. Finish it soon.

If you take up mathematics, you could apply for engineering later. After the initial training you'll earn a four-figure salary.

I like economics, Appa.

What will you do with that, after your B.A.? You'll get a job as a bank clerk.

No, Appa, I'd go into management.

Why all that? Just go in for engineering. Here's the form. Fill it. Here, write "Mathematics" in this space.

A man is one who earns. He who earns is a man.

Away the heroine runs. The hooligans give chase. The hero arrives. There's a hand-to-hand fight. He wins her. He is a man.

That yellow sari
who climbed into the bus –

13

in my imagination, I stripped her
and lay with her.

Doesn't matter. It was only your imagination. That's the way a man's mind is. There will be a woman in actual fact for you one day. For this reason. With a *tali* round her neck.

Aren't the puris good enough? There will be a woman to cook for you one day.

Wear our suits, your girlfriend will appreciate you.
Wear our shoes, the girls will turn round to look at you.
Wear our shirts, the lion in you will wake up.
Use our razor blades. She will stroke your cheek. Then. . .
Buy our toothpaste, her face can come near yours.
Drink this. Your boss will commend your energy.
Why wear crumpled clothes? Buy our crease-proof material.
You'll be praised for your efficiency.

You are the one who earns money
You go out to work
You are the one who has many rights
You are the one who casts the vote
You are the one who mustn't cry
You are strong
You make decisions
You can change the world

You have firmness of mind
You enjoy women
You are forceful in bed
You want to impress your boss
You are a man.

———

Sabari. . . Must you walk around like this without your knickers?
Naughty. It's only naughty little girls who stand about without their
clothes. Good little girls say, "Amma, put my knickers on."
    Amma, put my knickers on.

Sabari in the first class. Sabarikutti, who are you going to marry?
    Abdulla, who's in my class.
    No, no, you mustn't say that. That's wrong.

Sabari in the third class. Sabari, what happened to that Abdulla?
    Don't know.
    What do you mean you don't know? Wasn't he your friend?
    No, Appa. He was a Muslim, wasn't he?
    She has sense, this girl.

Mm. You're a big girl now. Why should you play with that Murali?
What do you mean, flying kites? Why these boys' games? Go and
read a book instead.

Why do you have to run in that noisy way?

———

Mm. That's quite enough eye make-up. And what sort of top is that?
Go and change at once.

What were you talking to Sita about? Did I hear you say "sex?"
Why should you girls chat about these bad things? Go and say your
prayers.

I bow at the feet of the Lord Ganesha
who gorged on handfuls of fruit and sweets.

Repeat it ten times. Good.

All those who work upon the land are the poor.
If they demand their rights, they are slandered
by the base rich, who aim their arrows upon
the wounded.
The wide heavens watch these scenes all day,
my brother,
And break out into pustulous stars, when it darkens.

Applause.

Where did you learn all this? Why were you participating in that
debate? What's all this talk about the rich and the poor? Is this the
sort of thing girls talk about? What students' association do you belong to?

Appa, I don't want to do history. I'll take up maths and physics.
Then I might go on to aeronautic engineering.

Take history. After all you'll end up blowing at the kitchen hearth.

Learn to cook. Nobody is going to marry a girl who can't produce tasty foods. Read *Femina*. Collect recipes from it.

. . . Put in a spoonful of dalda, or the equivalent amount of oil. Throw in the onion chopped fine. When it begins to brown, toss in the ground masala. Fry, roast, blend, grind, pound.

What have you dressed up like this for? Is anyone coming to "see" the bride, or what?

Get rid of unwanted hair. Here is our cream.

Wear our bra. It will enhance your youth.

This is our special sari season. People who buy our saris have good taste. He will be enticed by this sari.

When you have bathed with our soap, washed your hair with our shampoo, tipped our talcum powder on your shoulders, used our nail polish and our bindi, and when you open the door – there will be Cupid himself standing in front of you.

Those difficult days. . .

Use our cooking oil. Notice the difference in your household.

Amma, the food is terrific.
Terrific, Kamala.
My husband won't eat out hereafter.
Yes, she is a clever wife.
Use this to cleanse the toilets in your house. . .
Amma, our bathroom smells lovely.
Yes, she knows how to keep the toilets clean.

She is a receptionist. She has to be beautiful. She wears our saris.

Let us appoint a woman secretary. Whether she works well or not, the office will look good.

It's good for women to be teachers. It's a respectable job.

You look after the house
You know that beauty products are for your use
You are modest
You listen to decisions
You are a goddess
You are always helpful
You work outside the house only when in dire need
You need protection
You are a woman.

—•—

Hoping Nachiketan would be at home, he slipped through the

—

narrow gate into the huge garden, scratched at the wooden door with his fingernail and called out, "Nachiketa, Nachiketa."

Nachiketan's mother came to the door. She smiled. He must have told her to expect him.

She took him in, opened a small door and pointed.

Black and white and brown, they tumbled about, tugging and pulling at their mother's teats.

Nachiketan's mother went in quietly and picked up the little black one. She gave it to him. It moved in his hands, rubbing against the smooth skin and whimpering softly.

As he walked along, he bent to its ears, reciting into them, "Lucky, Lucky, Lucky," in a name-giving ritual.

The chain he brought was surely strong enough to stand up to Lucky's mischief. At the ironmonger's, he had allowed his eyes to wander from locks weighing all of two kilos, to "rocket" locks that came apart as soon as the key was turned. When the shopkeeper began to growl, he pointed to what he wanted, tested it by pulling at it, and finally bought it. When he woke up the next morning and hurried to the back of the house, the long chain was hanging loose, broken.

He could not call out Lucky's name, it stuck, tightly lodged in his throat. There would be half a foot of the chain still hanging from Lucky's neck. Dragging along the road, tangling with his legs, pressing against his stomach when he sat down, rolled up between his paws. Lucky's toy, to push about, to worry with his teeth, to bark at softly, and play with, in pretence anger.

Did it run away? Just as well. Making a mess all over the place.

Nachiketan came with him to the pound where the stray dogs were taken. As soon as the tin-plated doors were opened, fifty puppies came running to them, whimpering weakly. They looked at him with tragic eyes, licked his feet and said, "Free me." They were skinny, almost like mice. A cart was trundled in. A whole heap of dogs, their legs and tails spread out, hanging loose. At the top, there was a white dog, nose lifted, looking upwards, soundlessly. From its stomach, its burden hung in lumps.

He broke into loud sobs when he felt their tongues, wet against his legs. He said softly, "Lucky's not here." When the doors were closed, he could hear their tragic howling.

Should boys cry like this? Silly. Crying for the sake of a dog.

Lokidas turned over and looked at the skies.

Her grandmother's house in Coimbatore. R.S. Puram. She played with her cousins Shanta and Annalakshmi. Shanta was the proud one. So she was always made to be the patient when they played doctors and patients. The other two were the doctors. Even if it was only a cold, Shanta was made to lie down on Thatha's table, and given an "operation." Shanta was usually put down, but occasionally, after she had pleaded desperately, they would play hide and seek.

Once when she lifted the lid of the big laundry basket, she saw a litter of kittens, all curled up, like a bunch of flowers. As she stood there, lid in hand, the little world huddled together there seemed to expand before her. . . Caught you. . . Caught you. . .

Sabari placed her hands on his.

The old man had a deep voice, pure as bell metal. He was related in some way; a classificatory grandfather. Terribly keen on musical time-schemes.

He'd begin:

jamakkalam   to be spread out
and a pillow   to be slept on

then he'd demonstrate the syllable count:

jamakkalamtobe   spread out
andapillowtobe   slept on

once again:

jamak kalam tobe spread out
anda pillow tobe slept on

You'd actually hear the mridangam being struck. With his gnarled hands, the veins standing out, he'd tap out the rhythm and expound upon it. He was very much a part of evenings at Styamangalam. He came to Delhi, this grandfather. At evening times, he would sit on his string bed on the terrace, place the palm of his hand flat against his ear, and begin, most beautifully, "I shall never be rid of this cycle of birth, though countless years pass. . . When there was *rasam* spiked with cumin seed, and a relish of roasted gram, the most pleasurable sounds would emanate from upstairs. He would sing, "Maha sugirta rupa sundari. . ." with a sweep and toss of the head. He would conclude by repeating that "maha" ten times, the final "maha" vanishing away into the darkness. Suddenly he would lower his head upon the pillow, fling his arms and legs on to the bed like pieces of wood, and drop off to sleep.

Lokidas pressed Sabari's hand.

Against the first winter, she had a woolen coat. It was pink with narrow brown lines upon it. It had been made to withstand three winters. So the sleeves hung loose, like tongues, and were meant to be folded back. Each year the coat was let out, showing a difference in colour in half-inch-wide ribbons. By the third winter, the coat had bands of different colours along the edges of the sleeve and neck and hem. A pink coat. . .

Then there were those swivel chairs. . . There were four of them, named England, Japan, America, and Singapore. With the words, "Chalo, Singapore," she'd be lifted and spun around ten times.

Sabari stroked Lokidas's laughing mouth with her fingernails.

He loved the smell of books. The smell of new books; the smell of yellowing pages touched with mould; the smell of pages crumbling away into dust.

Lokidas touched the lids of her wide eyes.

The hair that the barber's knife scraped away was both black and white. The old lady who lived down their street had her head shaved once in three months. She had followed the barber to his three-foot-deep front room, a conversion from the verandah, with windows put in. When she reached up to the window and peered inside, the razor had just completed its first stroke. There was a strip running right down the middle of the bent head. Her drooping, wrinkled breasts covered with green veins showed through her white sari, jolting the spectator.

She was frightened at the thought of old age. What was it like, a woman's old age? How would it be?

Sabari looked into his eyes for a long time.

I have never talked about all these things.

Nor have I.

I feel as if I had been shut up in a trap all this time. I can actually begin to breathe now.

Yes. As if they had built a wall all around.

. . . It's like silk.

What is, Loku?

Your body. Didn't you know?

I didn't. It's only after you said that, that I can actually see myself.

I like it when you touch my shirt button.

If I undo them, and touch you like this?

That's good.

Don't men have hair on their chests?
Mm.
But you don't?
You'll just have to think I've come a long way from the time that
we were apes.

An outburst of laughter.

Aren't there bras with a fastening on the front?
Fool. Only for nursing mothers.
Really? Are these difficult to undo?
You try.
It won't come undone. Don't laugh. It really won't.

A waterfall of laughter.

I didn't know a man's body could be so beautiful.
What did you think?
How did I know. I thought it would be repulsive.
Idiot.
And you?
I didn't know that lips were so soft.

A dry leaf fell on her.

You are Eve.
But there's no apple?

I don't need an apple.

A squirrel leapt away.

These pebbles are poking me in the knee.

Laugher as they part and come together again.

Hey, you are making me want to laugh.
Don't laugh right now. . .
Hey, a drop of water fell on my nose. It's going to rain.
Let it.

One, two, three drops of rain. Like pearls on his back.

Sabari just touch my head.
Streaming wet.
You've got all this red clay in your hair.

The rain was like glass screens all about them. They spread their
arms and legs freely upon the earth, accepting the rain.

———•———

The rope fell upon the floor like a cobra's head, then wriggled and
retreated.
One.
It rose above her head and then hit the floor again.

25

Two.

It described an elongated circle above her head and then swung beneath her feet.

Three, four, five, six, seven.

The sweat dropped off her. Just above her lower belly, somewhere deep within, there was a churning.

Next she lifted her stomach and touched the floor without bending her knees. The potatoes she had eaten the previous evening seemed to give off a gas that entered her nipples, causing her acute discomfort. The sweat ran down her nose.

A spark of light fell on the balcony. The first light of dawn, like a tiny calf, leaping.

Vanamali opened her eyes, still in a drowse.

Sabari was reaching up, then touching the ground.

Reaching up again and touching the ground.

"Sabari. . ."

She stopped, holding in her stomach.

"What is this, first thing in the morning? First you were jumping up and down, making as much noise as if you were breaking up a gourd. Now this. What's it all about?"

"Nothing."

Sabari put on her tennis shoes and went out.

When Vanamali walked to the balcony, rubbing her eyes and looking about, she saw Sabari running in circles on the green lawn.

The water flowed smoothly. it was as dark as a cave. A covered basket came floating by.

That Marathi song.

Suddenly a sari *pallav* is moved to a side, revealing a big stomach. Sita speaks: "Lakshmana, look. I am pregnant. See for yourself. Make sure you tell your brother. Otherwise he might suspect me about this, too."

Jaa saang Lakshmana saang Rama rajala. . .

The song echoes.

The basket floats out of the cave's darkness and comes near. The covering is removed.

Ah. . . a loud scream.

"Sabari. . . hey, Sabari. . . What is it?"

"A weird dream."

Vanamali came to her bedside. She upturned the water pot, filled a tumbler and gave it to her.

"What's the matter, Sabari?"

"Shall we have a cup of tea?"

Vanamali looked at the time. Five o'clock. She turned on the heater. She filled a kettle of water and put in some cardamom shells.

Sabari looked on.

As soon as the water came to a boil, she put in the tea leaves. She added the milk. Then she poured the tea out into two glasses.

"Here."

The tea went down, fragrant with cardamom.

"Now what's the matter?"

"I'm pregnant."

Vanamali spilt her tea.

"Who is it?"

"Lokidas."

"So this was what was going on in Simla, was it? Didn't you tell me it was a Students Union Conference? Couldn't you have been more careful? Have you told him?"

"No. I tried. His mother picked up the phone. I put it down straight away."

"Will he come here?"

"How can he? He's got his exams."

Vanamali struck at her own forehead in anger.

———

They went there together, all three.

"How old are you?"

"Seventeen."

"Where are your parents?"

"They are away in Dubai for a year."

"And what about you, young man, how old are you?"

"Eighteen."

"Mm. Come in. I had better examine you."

Vanamali tried to go in as well.

"You please wait outside."

"No doctor, I'm her guardian."

"Oh, really? And how old might you be? Fifty?"

"I'm seventeen too."

He opened the door for all three of them and said, "Get out."

There was the stench of blood everywhere. Added to that, the smell of urine and faeces from the waterless lavatory filled one with nausea. The tongawallah's wife, Santoshkumari, who was sitting next to them, got up and left, full of fear. It was her fourth pregnancy. Sabari's fingers clung to Loku's, wet with sweat.

Santosh returned, looking as pale as if she had smeared sacred ash all over herself. Her legs giving way, she sat down, trembling.

"Sabari... Sabari Muthayya."

There were ten medical college students there.

"Lie down," said the doctor.

"Now look carefully. Unlike the previous case, this is past the twelfth week, therefore..."

The faces came closer. The voice faded.

A fork was scraping inside her. Roughly. Blindly. An extreme pain throbbed through her veins and shot to the very top of her head. The fine walls of her vagina began to break down

Loku... Loku... Loku... Loku...

Vanu... Vanu... Vanu... Vanu...

The doctor raised her hands. There was a formless thing between her fingers.

"Look well. Do you really want this a second time?"

She was speechless with horror.

She came out. Vanamali and Lokidas came running to her side.

———•———

They were watching an old film, *Amar*. Nimmi was tragic, her eyes three-quarters shut. Madhubala was flirting with Dilip Kumar, all crooked half-smiles. She had slammed the door in his face and had started on a song, "Janewale se mulakat na hone payee." At that instant she felt a sharp pain, as if a nail had been rammed through her vagina, twisting into her.

She tightened her thighs.

"O janewalese. . ." Madhubala leaned and swayed against the door.

Her womb filled with scorpion stings.

"Amma. . ."

Loku and Vanu held her tight. She was shuddering all over. Hot blood poured down her thighs.

The hot-tempered doctor who had ordered them out showed them a ball of flesh, small enough to be held in the palm of one's hand.

"Where? In that stinking hospital, was it? The doctor left her mark all right. If it had gone septic, that would have been the end of you. Didn't she frighten you? She'd make you feel like you never wanted sex again."

Vanamali sobbed. Sabari's breath came in deep gasps. Loku wept.

———•———

A cold December. On the ground stood a square container of charcoal on which lay skewers of fragrant kebabs. They were in an open-air canteen. Behind them, the aeroplanes were descending, their lights winking. They felt a sharp winter-evening hunger. Three plates of kebabs were on order. He would bring them in his own time. Vanamali was already relishing the moment when she would put out her right hand from the shawl, just long enough to dip a piece of kebab in the hot chutney and pop it into her mouth; how she would chew on it slowly, her hand back within the comfort of the shawl. Lokidas who had been leaning back in his chair, gazing into the distance, joined in with his anticipation of the hot spiced milk to follow, half an inch of cream floating on top, as good as *payasam*.

"December is a good month for babies to be born," said Sabari.

"It could have a rose-coloured cap, and jumper and socks. It could be tied to the back as with that Tibetan woman who sells noodles. . . only the eyes would show. Could be a blue jumper, but then it should have white flowers on it. I like those wooden cradles, the ones that stand on the floor in Gujarati houses. There'll be designs in different colours all over it. Dark green, yellow, red, blue. There'll be birds hanging from the top."

Silence.

"Underneath one's coat, a huge stomach. A niggling back pain. Now and then. Then the pains will come much closer together. You have to breathe properly, along with the pains. Suddenly, with the force of pushing a huge rolling stone, holding one's breath and straining and screaming and pushing. . . sensing something pushing out. . . and screaming again as it bumps its way out. . . It will fall out like a frog, slippery, with blood and slime all over it. . . and hang by the umbilical cord, crying out. . ." Sweat bloomed on Sabari's upper lip. She smiled.

Loku held her hand tightly.

In that cold late evening thickly spread with stars, a birth took place, true to its time.

A Kitchen in the Corner of the House

It seems that Kishan's father had bought the land at the rate of eight annas per square yard and built the house upon it. A row of rooms like railway carriages. Right at the end, the kitchen, stuck on in a careless manner. Two windows. Underneath one, the tap and basin. The latter was too small to place even a single plate in it. Underneath that, the drainage area, without any ledge. As soon as the taps above were opened, the feet standing beneath would begin to tingle. Within ten minutes there would be a small flood underfoot. Soles and heels would start cracking from that constant wetness. Kishan's mother—called Jiji by everyone—would present a soothing ointment for chapped heels on the very first day one entered the kitchen, cooked a meal and was given the traditional gold bangle.

There were green mountains outside the window that looked eastward from the kitchen. Somewhere on top of them there was a white dot of a temple. A temple to Ganesha. The cooking area was beneath this very window. The green mountains might have made one forget one's chapped heels. But since the clothesline was directly beyond this window, trousers, shirts, pajamas, saris, and petticoats spread out to obscure the view.

As one looked up from turning the pieces of meat which had been sprinkled with coriander, chilli powder and garam masala, spread with ground turmeric and ginger, and marinated in curd, what one encountered might well be a pair of pajamas with their drawstring hanging down. But nobody seemed to object to this.

Their style of life did indeed encompass the kitchen; was woven around the concept of the kitchen. The lineage had reputation for its love of food and drink. They were people who enjoyed the pleasures and experiences of life. In fact, at their wedding – Kishan's and hers – the one thing the Ajmer relations objected to was that no sort of alcoholic drink was served to anyone.

Even the prasad for their clan goddess, Amba, was spirits. Whatever was opened, whether it was Scotch whisky or country liquor, it was drunk only after first being sprinkled on the walls with the words, "Jai Ambé." The first thing to enter a new-born baby's mouth was a finger dipped in spirits. When such was the case, what sort of marriage celebration was this? Very well. Perhaps there was no need for rum, gin or whisky. But what about the orange-coloured kesar kasturi made in their own Ajmer? After all, it had a kick that went straight to one's head! Tch. Tch. How could you get married like this, they asked him, without the horse and the drink that is appropriate to a warrior, how can it be a wedding? Older women, whose heavily pleated and hugely flowered skirts in deep earth-brown, green, orange, and bright red flared and swayed from their wide and swollen hips, lifted silver-edged veils to ask him: Isn't there anything to drink?

In the days when Jiji could get about, she would start cooking pappads at the stroke of seven. Papaji would be ready and waiting in the outside verandah, having finished all his other business. Jiji would bring him pungent, spiced pappads stacked on a plate. As soon as the pappads were finished, there would be Bikaner sev, sharp upon the tongue. If they tired of that, then pakoras of sweetcorn. Or groundnuts dipped in chillies and besan and deep fried. They would sit opposite each other, and begin with, "Jai Ambé." If the sons and daughters were there, the entire family would join in. Jiji would sing country songs. "If you go to the fair, bring me tassels for my hair. . . and a bright-coloured *dupatta* for me to wear." Papaji would laugh. "Do you still care for these things?"

On a small stove, in the corner of the kitchen, there was always water boiling for tea. If anybody they knew appeared at the threshold of the house at meal times, first they received ice-cold water. Then, Papaji would begin.

"You must eat with us. Give chacha a plate."

"O no, thank you. I just dropped in"

"Yes, quite so. But what about a cup of tea?"

"No, thanks."

"Coffee, then?"

"This water is plenty"

"How can we allow you to drink plain water? At least have some sherbet."

"Very well."

Jiji would get up.

"Just put one or two kebabs for him on a plate to go with his cold drink."

Even before Jiji reached the kitchen, Papaji would remember the methi parathas which were made that morning. "Suniye ji," he would call to his wife, "warm up two of those methi parathas and butter them," he would say. "Let chacha just have a taste."

The visitor would be forced to accept defeat. "All right then. Let me eat my meal with you."

Jiji would go into the kitchen in any case, to fry up a couple of eggs, sprinkled with salt and pepper. Suppose there were not enough to go round?

All the same, the actual details, the concrete facts of the kitchen and its space didn't seem to matter to them. It was almost as if such things didn't actually exist. In their family houses, one crossed the wide stone-paved front courtyard and the main room before reaching the kitchen in a dark corner. A zero-watt light bulb hung there. The women appeared there like shadows, their heads covered, their deep-coloured skirts melting into the darkness of the room, slapping and kneading the chappati dough or stirring the fragrant, spicy dal. The kitchen was not a place; it was essentially a set of beliefs. It was really as if all that delicious food which enslaved the tongue appeared as from a magic carpet.

On one occasion, when they were eating, Minakshi raised the subject. Papaji was building a room above the garage at that time.

"Papaji, why don't you extend the verandah outside the kitchen?

If you widen it, we could have some chairs out there. If you then build a wash place to the left, you could have a really wide basin for cleaning the vessels. And then beyond that, you could put up some aluminium wire for drying the clothes."

Papaji looked for a moment as if he had been assaulted by the words expressing this opinion. Jiji in her turn looked at him, shocked. Daughters-in-law had not thus far offered their own opinions in that house. Radha Bhabhiji stared fixedly at her plate. Kusuma straightened her veil to hide her agitation. Papaji turned to Kishan. Kishan continued to eat calmly. At last Papaji cleared his throat and asked, "Why?"

"The basin in the kitchen is extremely small. And the drainage is poor. If the servant woman washes the vessels there, the whole kitchen gets flooded. And, Papaji, if you hang the clothes outside the window, the mountain is hidden."

Again he looked at Kishan. And that skilled architect agreed with his wife.

"What she says is right, Papaji. Why don't we do it?

"And when did you go near the kitchen?"

"When she cooked us that Mysore-style meal, it was he who sliced the onions and chillies for her," said Jiji.

"It seems we might as well present you with a gold bangle and be done with it."

"Never mind the bangle, Papaji. You could give me a ring, though." Papaji laughed.

The new room was completed. The state of the kitchen remained unchanged. Two more nylon lines were added, for drying clothes. Outside the window. Papaji's silent retort:

Woman, woman of Mysore, you who have not lived here for many generations, why do you need mountains? Why do you need their greenness? What possible connection is there between Rajasthani food customs, and the window, and the washing-up basin? Dark-skinned woman, you who refuse to cover your head, you who talk too much, you who have enticed my son. . .

———

At the first fading of the night, as early as three o'clock, the peacocks began to call. One after the other, with their harsh discordant voices; broken music. When she and Kishan came to the open terrace at five-thirty in the morning, a peacock in the tree opposite spread its tail, wide as Siva's spread locks. As it turned, there were sudden flashes of soft green, then dark blue, and then again, the deepest of deep green. Most unexpectedly it flew over to the terrace and sat upon the parapet wall, trailing its tail feathers. Then two more came, without extended tails. Before you could turn around there were another two, this time with tail feathers as long as whips. A gentleness and coolness spread within one, as of a weight being eased. Those dark-blue and green icicle-like feathers seemed instantly to calm all unruly passions. She ran her tongue along Kishan's mouth and kissed him very gently. A kiss like a snowflake, the passion contained within.

The door to the terrace creaked. Bari-Jiji had woken. She had come to collect charcoal from the big drum near the door, and to light the portable stove. Bari-Jiji was Papaji's stepmother. When Papaji was seventeen, his father had married a second time, a young girl who was also seventeen years old. In the following years five daughters were born to her. Papaji had been her mainstay and comfort. She was only Bari-Jiji in name. Between her and Jiji there was only a difference of two years. She was now completely toothless. She refused to have false teeth, claiming that she didn't need teeth any more, now that she had given up eating meat.

Bari-Jiji left, her heavy silver anklets clinking on the stone steps.

"Shall I bring us some tea, Mina?"

"Hm."

As soon as he had gone, she opened the tap of the water tank in the terrace, washed her face and cleaned her teeth.

Kishan brought the tea in a kettle, covered with a cosy. When he set it down and poured the tea into two cups, the delicate smell of ginger and basil rose from it. A single morning star shone in the sky. The peacock sprayed its green and blue. The tea descended, warm to the throat.

When they went downstairs, Bari-Jiji sat in the corner of the kitchen, blowing upon the hot tea which Kishan had poured for her, and holding the hot tumbler with the end of her dupatta. Radha Bhabhiji was pouring hot water into another large kettle with tea leaves in it.

"Shall I mix the dough for breakfast?" asked Bari-Jiji.

"Papaji has gone for a walk. He'll bring samosas and *jilebis*. We'll only need some toast. I'll do that in the toaster. What sort of cuisine shall it be today? Our style or Mysore style?"

"She and Kishan bought vegetables and coconut yesterday."

"What sort of bland food is that, with coconut. Just do one thing, Bari-Jiji. Grind up some turmeric and ginger. We'll do a mutton *pulao*. Grate some of the gourd for me. We'll make a few koftas. Then I want you to peel the colocasia. You must also pound some cardamom, pepper, cinnamon bark, coriander seeds and cloves. Really fine, please. I also want some coriander pounded separately for the alu-gobi tonight."

Radha Bhabhiji came out of the kitchen carrying a tray with the teapot and cups.

"Well, Mina, what are you going to cook today?"

"Nothing whatsoever. We are going to the Ganesh Mandir mountain."

"Very well."

Minakshi went into the kitchen to prepare another round of tea. Bari-Jiji opened her toothless mouth to smile. She held out her brass tumbler.

"I want some tea too. Shall I add some ginger, Bari-Jiji?"

"Yes, please. I love the tea you make."

A command was spoken from outside the kitchen, to everyone in general. "I've brought the samosas and jilebis. Put a few jilebis into hot milk." Minakshi took the packet of jilebis into the kitchen and began to open it.

"Sh... here... here."

Minakshi turned around.

"Give me four," said Bari-Jiji.

It was a food war. The protagonists were: Jiji, Bari-Jiji. When grandfather was alive, Bari-Jiji ruled absolutely and tyrannically. Jiji kneaded mountains of chappati dough. She sliced baskets of onions and kilos of meat. She roasted pappads in the evening while Bari-Jiji drank her kesar kasturi. She made the pakoras. She fried entrails. Then grandfather died. Within ten days Jiji was sworn into power. Bari-Jiji lost her rights to kumkum, betel leaves, meat, and spirits; she also lost in the matter of everyday meals. Every day there was meat cooked in the kitchen. In a democratic spirit, the vegetarians in the family (actually only Bari-Jiji) were served potatoes. Bari-Jiji celebrated her loss in the battlefield with loud belching all night long, by breaking wind as if her whole body was tearing apart, and then muttering in the toilet. Before she could be attacked again, she started a second offensive of her own. Once in six months, Bari-Jiji began to be possessed by Amba.

Amba always chose the moments when Jiji and Papaji were seated at evening times with their pappads and their drinks. At first there would be a deep "hé" sound which came from the pit of the stomach. When they came running to her panting with fear, she would yell in anger, "Have you forgotten me?" The instant Jiji bent low and asked reverently, "Command us, Ambé," the orders would come. "Give me the drink that is due to me. I want kesar kasturi. I want a kilo of barfi. I want fried meat. . . ah. . . ah." When she was given all these things, she would say, "Go away, all of you." And for a while there would be loud celebratory noises emerging from Bari-Jiji's room.

The next morning Bari-Jiji would appear in the kitchen lifting her alcohol-heavy eyelids with difficulty and smiling her toothless smile. "Amba tormented me very much," she would say.

It might have been possible to bandy words with Bari-Jiji, but Jiji did not have the courage to question Amba.

"Give me jilebis," said Bari-Jiji.

Minakshi gave her four jilebis. When the jilebis were served to all the family, Bari-Jiji would get her fair share. This was for pure greed. At first, Minakshi used to wonder where Bari-Jiji hid away these things. It was only later that she realized that there were a couple of secret pockets in the heavily pleated four-yard skirts that Bari-Jiji wore. She had shown them to Minakshi. She put the cover on the teapot.

"Give me the masala ingredients before you go," said Bari-Jiji. "And I need ghee as well. For the mutton pulao."

This was a recent thrust of the battle. Jiji's asthma and blood pressure had restricted her activities somewhat. Next to her bed was the wooden cabinet in which were kept cloves, saffron, cinnamon, peppercorns, raisins, cardamom, sugar, ghee, cashew nuts. You could not get to any of these things without going past her. Before that you were subjected to a severe catechism: Why do you need the ghee? What happened to the ghee I gave you yesterday? If there is half a katora left after spreading on the chappatis, a quarter katora should be sufficient now. Show me all the masala ingredients you have taken out before you go. That saffron was specially ordered from Kashmir. Don't dump it into the pulao. What are you cooking for the vegetarians today? Wasn't there anything left over for them from yesterday? What is the use of just eating and then going to the toilet?

From that dimly lit, narrow-windowed kitchen, there were hands reaching out to control, like the eight tentacles of the octopus that lives in the sea. They reached out to bind them, tightly, tightly; and the women accepted their bonds with joy. If their waists were bound, they called them jewelled belts; if their feet were held back, they called them anklets; if they touched their foreheads, they called them crowns. The women entered a world that was enclosed by wire on all four sides and reigned there proudly; it was their kingdom. They made earth-shaking decisions: today we'll have mutton pulao; to-morrow let it be puri-masala.

When the window was opened to gather in the mountain, the open air, the blue and the green, it was as if their strength was sucked out of them. Like Vina Mausi, Kishan's aunt. She was now fifty and had been a widow from the age of fifteen. She was a teacher in a village. She had a room and a kitchen at one end of the garden belonging to the owners of the school. An asoka tree stood in front of the house, and behind the kitchen, a champak tree, with its creamy flowers and yellow stems. Flower-laden creepers entered through her windows freely. In the evenings, all the neighbouring children would come to visit their teacher. Otherwise there was the koel song from the asoka tree. But Vina Mausi would still say, "I don't have any authority." The little ones surrounded her, calling out, "Teacher, Teacher." She had the entire responsibility for primary education at

43

the school. She could walk down to the bazaar at will. If she put a charpoy under the asoka tree, she could share the companionship of the koel and its calling voice until her longing ceased. In the early mornings the white flowers were at touching distance the minute she opened her door. But Vina Mausi's breath caught in her chest. As soon as she reached open spaces, something in her moved towards the earth. Her nipples and her womb became as stone. Heavy. Pulling her down. Descending, descending, descending to the earth in surrender. Forcing her to stand stock still, her feet buried deep.

———

From the edge of the lake white wings were raised, lowered and tilted as the birds began to move. Minakshi was shaken with astonishment on the very first instant that they came into view. As the birds circled over the entire spread of the lake, coming to rest upon its waters, their red beaks shone through the distance. Then they rose again, smoothly separating their wide wings, tilting to the left and then to the right, now gliding. . . the swish of their wings was very near, almost in one's face. Their coral beaks were flat and thrust forwards. Russian birds. They came to Anasagar Lake for a few months; sudden visitors.

The picnic to the lake had been decided upon only the previous evening. The plan was for all the relations to make a trip to the lake together. For twenty people: a hundred puris, with enough potato, and tomato chutney; a hundred sandwiches, things to munch, bottles of milk for the babies, hot water in flasks. A portable stove to cook hot pakoras in the evening. Oil, besan, onions, chilli powder, salt and green peppers for bhajias.

A light burned in the kitchen from four o'clock when dawn broke. On a large tray, Jiji began to mix the wheat flour into dough. Kusuma was heating oil in a pan, ready to cook the rolled-out puris. Radha Bhabhiji was spreading bread with butter and chutney, the packets of bread opened, surrounding her. Bari-Jiji was filling small plastic bags with things to nibble and rubber-banding them. Mina had not thought about this whole aspect of the trip to the lake.

"O, Mina, are you up?" said Radha Bhabhiji. Her hair was glued together with sweat. "Will you make some tea?"

Mina started to make tea for all of them. She put basil leaves into the hot water. Kishan, joining them after brushing his teeth, put out the cups on a tray.

Radha Bhabhiji was muttering to herself, "The children have to be bathed. It might be a good idea to take two or three extra pants in a plastic bag. Priya sometimes forgets to ask. I must roll up five or six rugs for spreading on the grass. How many tiny babies will there be? Four. Milk powder Glaxo for Minoo. Archana's baby takes Lactogen. Mustn't forget the packet of biscuits. Mine only likes salty ones. If there aren't any, we'll stop on the way. Otherwise the child won't stop crying. And he hates that. Sugar. Mustn't forget the spoon. Serving spoons. Plates. Kusuma, take that bottle of soap to wash the plates. There's a tap there. Bari-Jiji, please slice ten or fifteen onions. If we take them in a plastic bag, the pakoras will be done in minutes. Mina, please, will you bathe the children?"

"Bhabhiji, it's only six o'clock now. They'll cry if they are woken up. Why doesn't Gopal Bhaisaheb give them their baths later?"

"O yes, he'll bathe them. Keep thinking that."

Mina handed her the tea. She poured some tea into Bari-Jiji's brass tumbler. She understood Radha Bhabhiji's sarcasm. Radha was brilliant at maths. Because her family would not consent to her taking up further studies in this subject, she was working in a bank, in quite a high position. A few months before this, she and Gopal Bhaisaheb had invited Kishan and Minakshi to spend a few days with them in Jodhpur. Gopal Bhaisaheb was a doctor at the hospital there. It had been really hot at the time. The midday meal had not been ready.

"The heat in these parts absolutely burns you up. It's impossible to do anything. Radha was out of town recently for a couple of days, on her bank work. I was completely helpless. I couldn't so much as stand in the kitchen. And you can't even get servants over here. Can you imagine what it was like, Kishan. I couldn't even stand in the kitchen long enough to make a cup of tea." Kishan said quietly, "Isn't Radha Bhabhiji, who also has a job at the bank, cooking in the same kitchen at this very moment?"

"Certainly. So what? After all, women are used to it."

True. You could not expect Gopal Bhaisaheb to wake up early during his vacation in order to bathe his children.

"Radha Bhabhiji, what sari are you going to wear? asked Kusuma.

"My red silk. I pressed it last night, and then did his clothes and the children's."

"I was thinking of wearing my white sari with the black spots, but my choli needs ironing. Mina, will you lend me your black choli?"

"Why not? Do take it. But it is sleeveless."

"O dear. In that case please iron my choli for me, Mina. I cannot wear a sleeveless choli. I haven't shaved under my arms."

"Make sure you have left a long enough *pallav*, and just cover yourself with it. After all, who is going to come and peer under your arms?"

"Look here, Mina, don't try to be funny. Are you going to set up the iron?"

"All right, all right."

Jiji came in very slowly, holding on to the walls, and opened the large pickle jar.

"Whatever are you trying to do, Jiji? Go and lie down quietly," Radha Bhabhiji scolded.

"But they'll all enjoy some pickle. Let me put some out."

"What's all that racket in the kitchen? You are not allowing us to get any sleep," came a voice.

Immediate silence. Then, in hushed tones, "Mina, will you put the potatoes on to boil on the little stove?"

"Radha Bhabhiji, why don't you spice them and put them in the pressure cooker? Then you won't have to boil them first and then peel them."

"You do that then. Leave Bari-Jiji to fry the rest of the puris."

By the time eight o'clock struck, all necks and underarms were raining sweat. Cholis were stuck to bodies. Oil smoke irritated their eyes. Their eyelids were heavy from lack of sleep. Papaji peeped into the kitchen.

"As soon as the trip to the lake was mentioned, the lot of you began to leap with enthusiasm." He laughed aloud.

Chirping and clucking, the small birds floated on the water, yellow and black. All of a sudden, white wings swirled above, coral shadowed.

Upon the rugs, card games. A few of the women were playing too, until children tugged at them, clutching their backsides and pleading, "Mummyji, dirty." Then off they went with old newspaper in their hands. There would be a swift knock on the child's head, enough to hurt. When the mothers got up, the younger girls took their places. Every now and then they rose, offering the men water to drink.

Radha Bhabhiji and Kusuma washed the plates. Then the stove was lit to make pakoras.

"Arré, what a marvellous smell! Two for me please, with only green chillies."

Intermittently was conversation with the children:

"Raju, what are you going to be, when you grow up?"

"A pilot, z-o-i-n-g"

"You, Priya?"

"I. . . I. . . I'll make the thapatis in my house."

"How cleverly she talks," Jiji laughed.

"I've climbed all the mountains which surround Ajmer," said Papaji.

"Jiji, what about you?" asked Minakshi.

"Every time he climbed a mountain, I was carrying a child," Jiji laughed whole-heartedly. Everyone laughed with her. Jiji had borne fourteen children.

At last, they gathered up everything, firmly changed the minds of the children who were wondering whether they should go "dirty" one last time, and started homewards.

Kusuma lingered. "Mina, walk a bit slowly. I haven't even seen the birds properly yet."

"Shall I call Satish?"

"No, no. Let him go. Otherwise there will be trouble."

They walked on slowly.

"I was ten days late. Just as I was thinking of going to the doctor, it's come on."

"Did you come prepared? If you had said, we could have stopped by the shops."

"O yes, I came prepared. Even so, it's a white sari. Can you just have a look?

"It's all right. Nothing's happened."

"Should we walk a bit faster? There's no time to sit by the lake shore. I have to peel the garlic for the evening meal."

"Just come. Don't talk."

She silenced Kusuma and made her sit by the lake. She had asked Jiji once, "What sort of daughter-in-law would you like, when your third son marries?" Jiji had answered at once: educated, fair-skinned, quiet. "Well said," Papaji had agreed. Minakshi had refused to believe that such a girl existed. She had assumed that Jiji's answer had been a continuation of that afternoon's incident. A friend of Papaji had visited them, an expert in skin diseases. At that time, Minakshi had found a few whitish spots on her hand which gave her some discomfort. Papaji introduced her to the skin specialist. This is Kishan's wife. She never stops roaming the town. She always has a book in her hand. A chatterbox. Examine her hands.

The expert's advice: Just stay at home. Be like the other women. Everything will come out all right. If people live as they ought, why should anyone fall a prey to disease?

"Aha," said Papaji, in admiration.

She had thought that what Jiji said was a kind of joke, following upon this. But when Kusuma was found, she was like a fine illustration and commentary to Jiji's exposition.

An M.A. in politics. A diploma in French. It wasn't quite clear why she had studied French. It seemed that collecting a diploma in some language or the other was a necessary part of waiting for marriage. If the bridegroom had a job in foreign parts, then it seems the knowledge of a foreign language would come in useful. During this time of waiting, Kusuma had also embroidered cushions and pillow cases, handcrafted small objects, decorated saris with lace and embroidery. She had not missed out on classes in flower arrangement, bakery, sewing, and making jam, juice, and pickles. She had learnt all these skills. She was the perfect daughter-in-law.

As if they had remembered them suddenly, the white crowd that had gone a long distance rose high, wheeled about, and flew in towards their left. They came floating, at a moderate speed now, circling by them. Kusuma wept.

"That beak... what a red," she sobbed.

Winged coral floated against a reddening sky.

The unpeeled garlic. . .

Wings opened to the beat of another circle.

The unformed foetus. . .

One, two, three, four, five – in series they slid gracefully into the water and began to float. Kusuma sobbed quietly.

—◆—

Jiji's worst attack happened when they came to Ajmer for the Holi holidays. One afternoon she sorted out the ingredients needed for the cooking, tucked in her keys at her waist, and came walking slowly towards the fridge to check what was left there. Before she could reach it, her breath caught, and then came in loud, dragging sighs. Before the family could come rushing to her aid, her heavy body had fallen to the ground. She was streaming with sweat and was drenched in her own urine.

"I am going. . . I am going. . . My daughters-in-law are all elsewhere. . . That wretched Bari-Jiji will rule in the kitchen. . . Hé Bhagawan." She kept turning her head from one side to the other. The doctor who lived downstairs came in haste to give her an injection. At last, she began to breathe evenly once more; her eyelids drooped and she fell asleep.

When she opened her eyes again, she first made sure her keys were as usual at her waist. "What are you cooking for the evening meal?" she asked. When they answered, beans, she grumbled, "Why? Didn't I say cauliflower? Did she change it? Did she think I was going to die?"

"No, no, Jiji. It was just that there was no cauliflower available in the bazaar."

"My sari. . . give me. . . another sari," she said.

Kusuma opened Jiji's wardrobe and took out a green sari, a green underskirt and a pale yellow choli. She placed them by Jiji's bed. Jiji turned her head to see. She asked in a feeble voice, "Where are my bangles?" Minakshi opened the bangle box to take out some green glass bangles.

They closed the door and removed Jiji's clothes. Her body was like a fruit that has passed its full ruddy ripeness and is now wilting. Upon the backs of her wizened hands, the veins stood out. Heavy lines ran along the palms. There were scars of childbirth on her lower abdomen, as if she had been deeply ploughed there. Her pubic hair, whitened, hung in wisps. Buttocks and thighs, once rounded, now shrunken, hung loose with deep creases. The upper part of her inner thigh was like withered and blackened banana skin. Dry nipples hung low, like raisins. On her neck were dark lines caused by heavy gold chains. A wide, polished scar, as if she were going bald, shone at the lower edge of her centre parting, where the gold band with its heavy pendant had constantly pressed.

A body that had lived. A body that had expelled urine, faeces, blood, children. A body with so many imprints. As soon as the sari was on, Radha Bhabhiji combed Jiji's hair and plaited it with a dark string finished with coloured tassels. Kusuma tucked the cabinet keys at her waist. Jiji leaned back on her bed.

After the others had left, Minakshi sat by Jiji's side. Jiji's hands burrowed at her waist. The room was darkened, the curtains drawn.

Jiji began to speak. Because of the medicines, her tiredness, and the onset of sleep, her voice was deep, yet it seemed curiously weightless, as if it had roamed about in the wind and then returned.

"A red skirt."

"What is it, Jiji?"

"My wedding skirt. It was bright red, with gold and silver decorations all over. Twelve gold bangles. Two necklaces. Earstuds in pearls and red and green gemstones. Another set of earstuds in coral. Five sovereigns worth of centrepiece to the gold headband. A silver key-hook. I was just fifteen years old. At the time of my *bidai*, when my parents sent me to my new home, my mother spoke to me in my ears. The memory of that bidai is still heavy in my heart. With her head covered she leaned over me and held me to her. Her big nose-ring was sharp against my face. 'Take control over the kitchen. Never forget to make yourself attractive. Those two rules will give you all the strength and authority you will need.'"

"Let it be, Jiji. You sleep now."

"I. . . remember. . . everything. There were thirty people in the household. I used to mix five kilos of atta to make three hundred chappatis. On that first day, the palms of both my hands were blue with bruises. There were shooting pains in my shoulder blades. Papaji said. . . shabash. . . you are an excellent worker."

She let out a huge breath.

"We had a baby, a son, even before Gopal. Did you know that? He died at the age of one. There was a puja that day. Everyone was in the kitchen. The baby had climbed the airs and fallen off the parapet wall. He had crawled up thirty steps. . . I heard that huge scream just as I was putting the puris into the hot oil... It seemed to knock me in the pit of my stomach... The base of his skull was split... His brains were splattered all over the stone pavement, like white droppings... After all the men returned... I fried... Mina, are you listening... I fried the rest of the puris."

Minakshi stroked Jiji's forehead.

"After Father-in-law died, I slipped the keys onto my silver waist hook. Mina... see how much I gained. I am like a queen... Don't you think?" Jiji muttered. She was almost asleep.

Minakshi bent low to those withered earlobes wearing flower-shaped earstuds covered in pearls and brightly coloured gemstones. They were alone, Jiji and she; alone as Maha Vishnu on his serpent bed floating upon the widespread sea. In that darkened room, there was a feeling like that of the cutting of an umbilical cord. We cannot be certain whether this conversation was actually started by her, or whether it happened on its own, or whether it only seemed to her to have occurred because she had imagined it so often. It is not even certain whether that conversation was between the two of them alone.

Jiji, no strength comes to you from that kitchen; nor from that necklace nor bangle nor headband nor forehead jewel.

Authority cannot come to you from these things.

That authority is Papaji's.

From all that

be free

be free

be free.

54

But if I free myself. . . then. . . what is left?

You alone, having renounced your jewellery, your children and Papaji. Yourself, cut free. Just Dularibai. Dularibai alone. And from that, strength. Authority.

And when I have renounced all that, then who am I?

Find out. Dip in and see.

Dip into what?

Into your own inner well.

But there is nothing to hold on to. . . I'm frigh. . .

Dip in deeper, deeper. Find out the relationship between Dularibai and the world.

Had there not been those three hundred chapatis to cook every day, nor those fourteen children who once kicked in your womb

If your thoughts had not been confined to mutton pulao, masala, puri-alu, *dhania* powder, salt, sugar, milk, oil, ghee

If you had not had these constant cares: once every four days the wick to the stove has to be pulled up; whenever kerosene is available it has to be bought and stored; in the rainy season the rice has to be watched and the dal might be full of insects; pickles must be made in the mango season; when the fruit is ripe it will be time for sherbet, juice, and jam; old clothes can be bartered for new pots and pans; once a fortnight the drainage area in the kitchen must be spread with lime; if one's periods come it will be a worry; if they don't come it will be a worry

If all this clutter had not filled up the drawers of your mind

Perhaps you too might have seen the apple fall; the steam gathering at the kettle's spout; might have discovered new continents;

written a poem while sitting upon Mount Kailasam. Might have painted upon the walls of caves. Might have flown. Might have made a world without wars, prisons, gallows, chemical warfare.

Where did you go away, Jiji?
How could you think that
your strength came
from food that was given in the appropriate measure
and jewellery that weighs down ears and neck and forehead?

Sink deeper still
When you touch bottom you will reach the universal waters. You will connect yourself with the world that surrounds you.

Your womb and your breasts will fall away from you. The smell of cooking will vanish away. The sparkle of jewellery will disappear. And there will be you. Not trapped nor diminished by gender, but freed.

So touch the waters, Jiji
and rise
rise
rise.

Jiji turned, searched for and held fast to Minakshi's hand.

Journey 4

There was still some time before the bus would start. She had already demolished a paper packet of peanuts, following it with a ginger *murabha*, just to aid the digestion. Still no sign of the driver. Next to her, a pregnant woman, on a seat meant for three passengers. She looked as if she were five or six months gone. Wrists covered in bangles: red, yellow, green, and dark blue. Around her neck, chains, *tali*, mango-patterned necklace, etc. The middle-aged woman beside her – possibly her mother – kept blotting the sweat off her forehead, shoulders, and neck with a small towel. She touched the younger woman as gently as she would a bird. "How it's pouring off you! At least when the bus starts there will be a bit of a breeze," she said, fanning the girl with the newspaper she held in her hand. The pregnant girl accepted all her mother's attentions with quiet pride. At the same time, she was mindful of the young man who stood outside, beneath the window. He, for his part, continued to hand her, one after the other, a tender coconut, gram sweets, *murukku*, bananas, and so on.

"Come back soon. Don't stay on there," he said, standing solidly there. Firmly moulded arms and legs. A body like a rock.

"I've told Bakkiyam-anni to send you your meals. Eat properly. And don't go about in the heat, ayya. It's not good for you," she told him, again and again.

The same conversation might have been repeated ten times over, without change of tone. Yet it seemed to contain different meanings each time. The expressions on the speakers' faces kept changing too, showing in turn elation, fond reproof, playfulness, laughter, tenderness, yearning, and sadness at parting.

Now and then the mother intervened to say, "Why don't you let Thambi go home? He shouldn't have to stand there in the sun."

The driver jumped in and sat down. Noises preparatory to starting the journey ensued. All at once, the man standing beneath the window began to cry.

"Go and return safely. I'll be yearning for you," he said, sobbing hugely, and crying aloud.

The girl was shaken. Greatly anxious, she said, "Don't cry. I'll be back. I'll be back very soon." He wept the more. Broken words came from him, "The house, so lonely..."

The girl rose to her feet. "Ayya, should I just stay here? Will you go on your own?" she asked piteously, wiping her tears.

"No, no. It's a wedding in your relative's house. You must go. But come back quickly," he said.

The bus began to move slowly. The girl leaned forward and stretched out her hands to reach him. He touched her fingers, then laid his hands against his cheeks. "Go safely, Kamalam," he said, breaking down yet again.

The bus began to pick up speed. The words "careful," "heat," and "food" mingled with the wind and were lost. As the bus left the station and turned into the main street, when they looked back, they could see him standing in exactly the same place; his whole self shaken, his shoulders rising and falling soundlessly. The girl must have caught sight of him.

"He's still crying," she announced. "He's like an innocent child. He won't even realize when he's hungry," she said.

"Oh, really. It's not a year since you married. Did he stay hungry before that? He's his father's only son. After the woman of the house died, his father brought him up, didn't he? What are you talking about?" The mother snapped at her.

"You don't know anything, ayya. Within four months of arranging his son's marriage, my father-in-law went off on his countrywide pilgrimage. No, he'll be all alone at home. Only a wife knows what goes on inside a house." The girl's eyes filled with tears.

"As if he's the most fantastic husband around town! I've borne four children, remember? Are you trying to teach me?"

"Let's say he is a fantastic man. He's certainly better than the bridegroom you wanted to tie me to – the one who demanded another half sovereign's worth of gold and a motorcycle before he would put a tali on me."

"Why do you want to rake up that old story now? You just go to sleep," the mother consoled her, laying the girl's head against her shoulder.

The girl laid her head on her mother's shoulder and went to

sleep, her handloom sari of green with yellow checks tucked conveniently at her waist, her stomach slightly raised, her bangles jingling each time she moved.

When the bus stopped at Nagercoil, several people had arrived to meet mother and daughter. A small girl in a rose-coloured *paavaadai*, who wore butterfly-shaped slides studded with brightly coloured stones in her hair, hugged the young woman, calling her "Athe." A young boy who looked as if he had just begun to wear long trousers came and stood next to her. Love, sympathy, and contentment on all their faces.

When she had finished her work, her friend told her she must not leave Nagercoil without going to Kanyakumari. At Kanyakumari, waves like shoals of whales. Yet as they touched the feet they were as gentle as a kitten's tongue. The sun, smeared in liquid orange. When she turned her head to take in the full sweep of the sea, the girl came within her orbit. The pregnant girl on the bus. She was standing by the waves, at a little distance from her relatives. A round vessel with a lid in her hand. There was a tenderness in her expression as she gazed at the sea. Like a mother looking at her child. A softness played on her face, reminiscent of Balasaraswati when she mimed gazing at the Baby Krishna in his cradle, as she danced to the song Jagadhodharana aadisathalu Yasoda, "*Yasoda played with the saviour of the universe.*" Was she looking at the sea, or at some illusory form? Even as she gazed at her, the young woman turned sharply towards her, returned her look for a second, and recognized her. She came forward, smiling.

"Watching the sea?"

"Yes; I've never seen it before. How the waves beat against the shore! I want to watch it forever."

"Did the wedding go off well?"

"Mm. All of us are here together. We'll be leaving soon."

"You'll go back home soon, won't you? Your husband was in tears, wasn't he, poor man!"

She smiled. "Yes, he wept. He's got a heart as soft as cotton-wool, akka." She stopped, then repeated, "A heart as soft as cotton-wool." She looked at the sea.

"My family looked for a different bridegroom for me. That man worked in a government office. He seemed all right. But when we were about to buy the wedding clothes, he cut in, 'So you are going to spend two thousand rupees on her sari, but only eight hundred on my *vetti*? In that case I must have two vettis.' People in our town laughed amongst themselves, 'What's this! He's talking like a child!' But gradually the whole story changed. Before he would tie the tali, he claimed that the wedding jewellery was short by half a sovereign's worth, and demanded that it should be made good immediately, besides a promise of a motorbike within the month. It turned into quite a fracas. My sister held my brother-in-law's chin and pleaded, 'Let me give her the chain I'm wearing round my neck.' Something like a frenzy came over me, at that time, akka. I rose to my feet and rushed outside. I said, 'I don't want this bridegroom. I will not marry him. If there is a man here who is willing to marry me as I am, then let him come forward.' My voice was trembling. The base of my throat was hurting. Everyone was stunned. Their party said, 'How brazen of her to say all this!' My family worried, 'She's gone and thrown it all away by speaking out.' Our townsfolk meanwhile were wondering, 'Who will marry her now, when she does this at such a tender age?' But then, his father came forward, bringing his son, his hand on his shoulder. His face was as innocent as milk. His body well set and sturdy. He was smiling slightly.

"The older man said, 'This is my son. He is educated. He supervises my lands. There is no woman in our house; I have brought him up myself. He is willing to marry the girl. Ask her what she wishes.' I stood there in shock. I looked at my father and nodded assent. I bowed to the departing bridegroom's people and said, 'Stay and eat before you leave.'

"And that's how this tali came to me, akka. He has such a good heart. A child-like heart."

She stopped and looked at the sea. Then she continued, as if she were speaking to the sea. "He dotes on children. All the children in our town come to him if they need anything. To fly kites, play ball, produce a play, to be taken to cricket matches. But a senior doctor has said that he of all people can't have children. It seems he wasn't looked after properly when he had mumps as a child, and became infertile as a result. He doesn't know this. He would die if he knew."

Because of a short bus journey together, she was willing to take her entire life apart, and to share it. Responding to the glance at her slightly raised stomach, she said, "This belongs to his family, absolutely."

An image flashed through her mind of an older man on pilgrimage, dipping into and rising from many temple tanks.

"He's never seen the sea. If I catch the waves in this vessel, will they still be tossing when I show him, akka?"

She imagined a wave rising and falling within the small circular vessel. In the evening light, the pregnant girl who stood by the shore seemed one with the sea.

She could only touch her gently and say, "No, you cannot capture the rise and fall of the sea's waves."

My Mother, Her Crime

Whenever I think of my mother, certain incidents flash through my mind and stab my heart.

My elder sister Kalyani has frequent fainting fits. I am not of an age to understand, being only four years old.

I open my eyes at dawn. Something sounds in my ears like the rhythmic striking of a drum. I go to the door to see. They have seated Kalyani on a wooden plank. Someone stands in front of her with a switch of leaves in his hand. My baby brother, whose gurgling laugh was to delight us for only four months, is in his cradle in my room.

"Nirajatchi, go and bring it now," says someone.

I look at my mother.

I remember her dark blue sari. Her hair is gathered into a knot. Mother goes into the little room that is adjacent to mine. She removes the top part of her sari and collects breast milk into the little bowl that is in her hand. Tears spill from her eyes.

Every morning, while it is still dark, my mother lights the firewood under the big brass pot which is built into the bathroom, and heats the water.

I watch her one day. Her hair has come undone and hangs loose. She sits on her haunches, knees doubled. Her hair falls on her cheek and ears. As soon as the fire is alight, the red glow of the flames plays across my mother's lowered profile. That day she is wearing a red sari. Even as I am gazing at her, she quickly gets to her feet. Her hair falls down to her knees. Her sari has slipped and beneath her un-hooked choli, I can see the green veins on her pale breasts. Suddenly she seems to me like the daughter of Agni who has come flying down from elsewhere. Could this be my mother? Really my mother?

Kali Kali Mahakali Bhadrakali
Namostute.

Why does the sloka come to mind all at once?

"Amma."

My mother turns her head.

"What are you doing here, di?"

I cannot speak. My whole body is covered in sweat.

The sacred fire is lit in the house. It is the redness of my mother's lips, or the sharp *kumkumam* mark on her forehead that makes her seem the very image of those blazing flames? With long drawn out "Agniye swaahaa," they pour ghee on to the flames. And with each "swaaahaaa" my eyes dart from the fire to my mother.

My mother gives me an oil massage and bath. Her sari is lifted high and tucked up. I can see the smoothness of her light-skinned thighs.

When she bends down and then stretches up, a green vein throbs there.

"Amma, how is it that you are so fair? How come I am dark?"

She laughs. "Go on with you. Who can be as beautiful as you are."

There is no connection between all these incidents, except that my mother is queen in all of them. She was the purifying fire that burned away all impurities. With a single smile, she created a million beauties that seemed to hang like pennants in my mind. When I lay with my head on her lap, she would stroke me with her long, cool fingers and say quite ordinary things like, "I am going to send you to dance classes. You have a fine body." Or she would say, "Such lovely hair, di." Trivial things. But immediately something would flower in my heart.

Now I am not sure whether these feelings were of her instigation, or because of some quite independent imagination of my own. And I don't know what she intended to create for herself when she sowed these seeds in me.

I am thirteen. My *paavaadai* are all getting too short for me. My mother has to lengthen each one of them.

One evening, as I lie with my head on my mother's lap, some words I had read earlier, come to mind.

"Amma, what does 'puberty' mean?"

Silence.

A long silence.

Suddenly she says, "Always be as you are now, running about and playing, twirling your skirt..."

Some people are to visit my aunt's house, to "see" her daughter, Radhu, for a possible marriage. My mother too goes away there. So on this eventful day she is not at home: it is my sister who rubs me with oil and washes my hair. Through the bathroom window I can see the still dark sky.

"Kalloos, you've woken me up far too early. I can't even hear the sound of fireworks."

"After your oil massage and bath, I've got to do mine, haven't I? You are thirteen years old now. Can't even do your own hair. Lower your head, stupid."

Kalyani has no patience.

She rubs my head until it hurts, as if she is pulling away the fibers from a coconut shell.

For that particular Dipavali, my mother has made me a paavaadai of purple satin. How I had yearned for it as it slithered smoothly under the sewing machine! This time she had measured me carefully before she began.

"Come here child, I have to measure you. You've definitely grown taller." She measures me and then looks up. "This girl has grown taller by two inches."

This purple satin paavaadai was not going to be too short. It was sure to glide right down to reach the floor.

Abruptly Kalyani pulls me to my feet and rubs my hair dry. I pull on my chemise and run to the puja room. My father hands me my set of new clothes from the ones stacked on the plank.

"Here you are, dark girl." He always called me that.

Sometimes when my father said that, I would go and look at myself in the mirror hanging in the hall. Then it would seem to me that my mother was whispering to me, "You are beautiful."

The satin skirt slips and slides as smoothly as the fish in the glass case in Sarla's house. There is a velvet jacket to go with it too. I place kumkumam on my forehead and run to stand in front of my father.

"Not at all bad!" he says.

I take the bundle of fireworks, place them in the front room and then race out to climb the champakam tree.

It was my special job to climb the champakam tree every morning, for its flowers. Always when I handed the filled basket to my mother, she would say, "So many." Her eyes would widen, and her fingers, wandering among the flowers, would seem, petal-like, to disappear.

The satin skirt is slippery. I can't climb to the topmost branch. Besides, it is still very dark. Just as I am about to climb down, suddenly a firework explodes. Shaken, trembling all over, I leap off the tree. I dash to the house, still trembling, gasping for breath.

Somehow I pull myself together and run into the front room to light my share of the fireworks. It is only after that that I remember the flower basket.

Dawn has broken.

Holding up my paavaadai I bend down to pick up the flower basket. Some of the flowers lie scattered about. As I stoop well down to pick them up, my skirt spreads about me on the ground. Here and there I can see stains upon it. Perhaps from climbing the tree?

I go back inside, calling out to my sister, "Kalloos. . ." Basket in hand I stand in front of her saying, "I've gone and stained my new skirt all over. Will Amma scold me?"

Kalyani gives me a horrified stare for a full minute and then goes off screaming, "Appa!"

That look, and the way she runs off, without so much as taking the basket from me, send centipedes crawling in my mind. I glance at the satin skirt. I run my hand over the velvet jacket.

Nothing has happened, has it?

Good God, nothing has happened to me, has it? But even as I ask myself this, I realize that something has indeed happened. Everywhere about me there is the thunderous noise of exploding fireworks. I stand there, clutching the flower basket, my breath coming in gasps, lips trembling, shaking all over.

With a great sob the tears come.

I want my mother. I want to bury my head deep into the Chinnalampatti silk of her shoulder. I want, unashamed, to tell her, "I am frightened." I want her to comfort me and stroke my head. Because surely something very terrible has happened.

Kalyani brings along the shaven-headed old widow from next door who helps with jobs like making *murukku*. This old woman comes up to me.

"What are you crying about, you silly girl? What has happened after all? Nothing the whole world doesn't know about."

I cannot follow a word of what she is saying. Nothing seems to reach my understanding, although my instinct, half grasping something, freezes in fear. I feel a single desperate need from the depth of my being, like an unquenchable thirst. Amma...

I remember the time I was lost, when I was five years old. I am walking along a huge park, oblivious of the gathering darkness. Then all of a sudden, the darkening trees loom; the noises and the silences begin to frighten me. My father finds me, but it is not until I see my mother that the tears come bursting out.

My mother takes me to her side. She strokes me and says softly, "There! Nothing whatever has happened to you. Everything is all right now." Her lips are like blades of flame when she puts her face against mine.

Now too I am struck with that same fear, as if I am lost. I sink down, bury me head against my knees and weep. I feel as if something has ended for ever. As if I have left something behind, in the way one leaves the cinema after they show "The End" on the screen. It seems to me that in all human history I am alone in my sadness. I weep as if I carry all the world's sorrows on my own narrow velvet-clad shoulders.

I wonder why my mother never spoke to me of these things when we were together in the evenings.

My mind is pervaded with fear. It isn't even the kind of fright that grips one because of alien surroundings or unknown people.

No, this is like the absolute terror and confusion that assaults one at mid-scream, seconds after seeing a snake. Such terror hangs, like spiders' webs, from all corners of my mind.

I remember seeing a corpse with pale lips split apart. The head had smashed against a stone. A moment before, a bald pink head had been in front of me. Now it was split open like the mouth of a cave, and gushing dark red blood. Within minutes, the blood dripped to the ground. I stared at it. The redness spread everywhere and seemed to leap into my eyes. Now these repelling images return. So much blood. So much blood – but no sound comes from my mouth. A bed of blood. The older man opens his mouth. The eyes stare open. They bore into my heart. Blood is so frightful. . . enough to make lips pale and limbs freeze.

I need my mother. My heart yearns for her to free me from this fear and ugliness.

"Please, why don't you get up. How much longer will you keep crying?" Kalyani begs. She is sitting next to me and has been crying too.

"Amma. . ."

"But you know she's coming back next week. I've just written to her about all this. She'll come as soon as Radhu's 'viewing' is over. Get up now. This is becoming a real headache." Kalyani is getting angry.

"What has happened to me?"

"Nothing. Your skull. How many times do I have to tell you?"

"Am I not allowed to climb trees after this?"

She gives me a swift blow on the head.

"Fathead! Here I've been begging you for the last half hour to come and change your clothes, and you've got to be asking all these questions. Appa!" She calls out to my father, "She's being a terrible nuisance."

My father comes and says, "You mustn't be difficult now. You must do as Kalyani says."

And after he goes away, the old widow adds, "Why does she have to be so stubborn? This is every woman's destiny, after all."

Seven days. Seven days for Mother to come home after they have "seen" Radhu. Seven days of stumbling in the dark.

One day the women from the neighboring houses come to visit.

"Shouldn't she be wearing a davani now, Kalyani?"

"Only after my mother returns, Maami. She's terribly willful. She only listens to Amma."

"O, she'll be all right hereafter. Hereafter she'll be modest, she'll know what is proper."

Why?

What is going to happen hereafter?

Why should I wear a davani? Didn't Amma say, "Always be the same as you are now, twirling your skirt. . ." Why should I change?

Nobody explains. They make me sit here like a doll and gossip among themselves. When my father comes in, they draw their saris tightly about themselves and lower their voices.

On the fifth day, Kalyani gives me warmed oil in a bowl. "From now on, you had better do your own oil massage," she says.

Weeping, I battle with my waist-length hair, and then stand in front of the hall mirror in my chemise.

"Finish dressing in the bathroom hereafter. Understand?" says my father.

I close the door after him and remove my chemise. The mirror reflects to me my own dark body. My hands run by turns over my shoulders, arms, my chest, my waist and my soft thighs, all of them very slightly paler than my face. Then am I not the same girl as I was? What is my mother going to say? I put on my school uniform.

As soon as I open the door, Kalyani comes in. "What are you going to tell them at school when they ask you why you've been absent?"

I stare at her. I had been about to set off for school with the exultation of a bird that has just been released from its cage, but now my spirit is dashed.

"You don't have to say anything. Just keep quiet."

I don't join in during the games lesson. I hide behind a large tree. Once before I had done this and Miss Leela Menon asked us in class the next day, "Who are the fools who didn't play yesterday?"

I didn't stand up.

"And you? Why aren't you on your feet?" she asked.

"I am not a fool, Miss," I replied. She wrote in my progress report that I am impertinent.

But today I don't even fear Miss Leela Menon's scolding – it strikes me that nothing will ever be more important to me than this one thing that has happened to me now. I don't want to sit under the tree and read Enid Blyton as I usually do. I ask the dry leaves that have fallen into a hole by the tree, "What on earth has happened to me?"

I look forward to my mother's answer with the anxiety of an accused who waits upon the pronouncement of a judge.

Will Amma say, lowering her eyes and looking at me, "This thing that has happened to you is beautiful too?" I know that by the fiery spark of her smile she will get rid of all of them: the old woman who frightened me, Kalyani, all. My mother is different from all of them. Where she stands there is no place for unnecessary things. Everything is essentially beautiful to her.

I need her desperately. There is something yet to be explained. Someone has to explain to me gently why my whole body sweats and trembles at the mere thought of the purple satin skirt; why all of a sudden my tongue goes as dead as a piece of wood; why the world seems to darken and before I can turn to look I hear that terrible exploding noise and see streaming blood and a long corpse.

I sense that everyone has gone and I am alone. The gardener wakes me up. Slowly I go home.

"Why are you so late, girl? Where did you go?"

"Nowhere. I was sitting under the tree."

"Alone?"

"Mmm."

"What is the matter with you? Do you imagine you are still a little girl? Supposing something were to happen. . ."

I throw down my satchel. My face feels very hot. Putting my hands over my ears, I shriek, "Yes, I will sit there like that. Nothing is wrong with me."

It's a crazy shriek, each word drawn out into a scream. My father and Kalyani stand there, stunned.

In a great fury, I rush past them upstairs, and sit on the open terrace. I want to stay alone in the scent of the champakam. Neither Kalyani nor my father should ever come up here. This scent which is without words or touch is more comforting to me than the people of this house. How pleasant it would be if they never, never spoke. Why can't they just smile with that widening of the eyes, like my mother? When she smiles like that, something happens inside me. I want to break out into laughter. I want to sing. She is an artist, a creator. With a turn of the head and a smile she can summon joy, enthusiasm, beauty. Like magic.

Kalyani comes upstairs.

"Come and eat, your highness. Amma has spoilt you rotten and no mistake."

I stand up nonchalantly and look at her in scorn.

My mother comes home the next day. She opens the taxi door and walks into the house, her sari of dark green silk creased from the journey.

"What happened?" asks my father.

"He's refused, the rascal. Apparently the girl is too dark-skinned."

"What does your sister say?"

"She grieves, naturally. Poor thing."

"We too have a dark girl."

I dash down to stand in front of her. I want to explain everything to her myself, much better than Kalyani did in her letter. I want to tell her about all the creeping horrors. I want to pour it all out into the crook of her neck, quietly, with trembling mouth.

I look deeply in to her eyes, sure that now, at last, she is going to explain the mystery; the feelings that choke my throat at night, my distress at the changes in my own body. She is just about to take me into the circle of her arms. I know I shall weep out loud. I shall twist my fingers into her hair and let the loud sobs come bursting out.

She looks at me.

I don't know whether in that instant I am changed into another Radhu.

Her words are like a sting. "And what a time for this wretched business of yours! It's just one more burden for us now."

Whom is she accusing?

Noiseless sobs knock at my chest.

A blood-red glow spits out from my mother's lips and her nostrils and her kumkumam mark and her nose-drop and her eyes. In that fiery instant the divine image that covered her falls away to reveal the mere, the human mother. Her cold unfeeling words rise like swords blindly butchering all the beauties that she had hitherto tended. Endless fears will stay forever in my mind from now on; dark pictures.

Agniye swaa-haa. Not impurities alone are burnt in the fire. Buds and blossoms too are blackened.

Forest

It was not real forests that Chenthiru had in mind. Rather, forests from the poems of Ahanaanuuru. Forests where waterfalls fell sheer, like milk, flanked by granite rocks on either side from which beehives hung. She wanted to go away to a forest. To a forest far away, leaving behind the noise of traffic, the sounds of conversation, of people walking about, of electrical gadgets in the house.

There were those who teased her: Was this an attempt at vanaprastha? they asked. Others ridiculed her saying, "Oh Forest, come come! Oh Home, go away!" Brahmacharya, samsara, vanaprastha, and sannyasa – must all these happen at separate times and stages? Must one enter the next stage only on the completion of the one before? Why could they not all be mingled together?

Her father used to work on a coffee estate. He was chief accountant to the owner of a number of coffee estates. She and her younger brother normally stayed in Bangalore with their mother. When they went to their father during the school holidays, their afternoons were spent running about the coffee plantations, among the pepper

79

and cardamom plantations which lay along the densely forested mountain slopes.

The estate workers always warned them, "Watch out. These are places where bears roam about."

It seems when her mother started her labour pains, and they were taking her to the hospital which was some distance away, she actually had to get out of the car halfway. They had hurried her out, and brought her to sit under a tree with widely spreading branches; within ten minutes of their doing this, Chenthiru was born.

"As I was walking through the forest one day, I came upon you lying under a tree. So I picked you up and brought you home. Who told you that your mother gave birth to you?" It became a game for her father to tease and provoke her until she was in tears.

She would go to her mother each time, her eyes full of tears, asking, "Is it really true, Amma?"

"Oh yes; very true. You were just lying there; he picked you up and brought you home. He's the great Janaka-raja himself, don't you think?"

When her younger brother was a little older, he began to make fun of her as well. "Ei, you're a girl who was born under a tree!"

But by that time she had learned not to cry. "Why, the Buddha too was born under a tree, you know; didn't you know that?" she'd retort sharply.

"So, you'll also go off in search of a *Bodhi* tree, will you?" he'd mock in his turn.

She declared to Tirumalai that she was the selfsame girl who was born in the mountain woods and played there as a child. Tirumalai could not agree. He claimed she was building up an imaginary picture of herself as a huntress who lived in the forest. Given a chance, she'd start thinking of herself as Valli, singing *aalolam* songs in the mountains, he teased.

What had he said, after all, for her to want to run off to the forests as if she were venturing into a life of austerities? He certainly was prepared to accept her as a partner in his many-branched business. If he saw himself as king of all that, he certainly considered that she was his queen. If his other business partners couldn't quite see it that way, how could he be faulted? Surely, she must realize that he too regretted this state of affairs? Should she just bundle up her goods and set off? Run off to the forest? Quite true, during the years when he wandered here and there, struggling to leave behind a mundane life and to make some real progress, she gave him her unreserved support. Did he ever deny that? But the situation was different now, wasn't it? Just because she had been asked to distance herself a little from business matters, did she have to make these preparations as if she were renouncing everything? Besides, what sort of goal was the forest, anyway? Was it just waiting there, to be her sanctuary, did she imagine? Wasn't her behaviour like that of someone who dreams that she is in the ancient epic world?

Anyway, even in epic times, a woman only went to the forest meekly accompanying her husband. It was the epic men who went on their own, to hunt or to destroy demons. As for women, they could only be in the position of Sita, accompanying Rama who assented immediately when his father ordered him into exile in the forest. A woman's visit could only be like that of Damayanti, walking by the side of Nala. It was most appropriate for a woman to be a *rishi-pattini*, spouse of a sage, journeying along with her husband. If she did go there on her own, it could only be as the seductive Menaka, putting an end to a sage's meditation. For a woman, a forest is a place where she cannot find her way. Everything there – trees, deer, flowers – is bound to mislead her and make her lose her direction. For a woman, the forest is a means of punishment. To send her there is to cast her aside and make her destitute. So argued Tirumalai.

The time has come to re-write the epics, she replied, smiling. Is that why you are making this trip, he asked. For that as well, she said.

There had been a reply to her application to the official in the Forestry Department. She now had a letter which said she could stay at the government guest house in the forest. A letter of permission on cowdung-coloured paper. She showed it to him. He exclaimed in irritation. He complained that she had made all her decisions herself, informing him only at the end. He said she was behaving as if he had banished her, in some sort of way. Arguments and counter-arguments. Threats. Entreaties.

After all this, he said, "The bus-stand is very far from here. Let Annamalai drive you there in the car."

She agreed.

Annamalai went with her. While they were waiting for the bus, he said, "Anni, you don't think badly of me, do you?"

"*Che, che*, it's nothing like that, Annu. After all, you work with your brother. You have to do as he asks, don't you?"

She climbed in as soon as the bus arrived. She put her head out of the window, and waved goodbye.

She thought of the notebook with its camel-yellow covers and its blank white pages, lying there in her suitcase among her clothes. She had bought a dozen dark-leaded pencils. A pencil sharpener. An eraser.

The wind traced the first sentences as it went along its way.

—•—

The horses yoked to the chariot ran as if they were clashing against the wind. The opposing wind struck hard against their bodies. The trees on either side seemed to come running along with them. The journey had been decided upon all of a sudden. All these colours and sounds of the forest fill my mind as if they were bridal gifts from my parents' home, Sita said to Lakshmana. He did not answer. He merely folded his arms together, and faced windward. As soon as the chariot stopped and they climbed out, he told her of his brother's command. When Lakshmana told her that hereafter the forest was to be her dwelling place, Sita looked hard at him, and spoke up. This was not something new to Lakshmana, Sita said. It had become his brother's main duty to doubt other people's purity; to put them constantly to the test. He was suspicious of everything. He cross-questioned witnesses. He called upon the sun and questioned him. If Surya protested that he could bear witness only to the times when he was present, how could he speak for the times when he wasn't there, then Rama flung his barbed questions at the moon. And when Chandra said I can only give you a guarantee for the nights when I am in the sky, after all I am not in the sky on *Amavasya* night, Rama immediately summoned Fire as the final test of one's purity. Didn't Lakshmana himself experience this? How firm he, Lakshmana, had been in his celibacy! How radiant his body! The moment he touched the musical instrument known as *kingri* by the forest dwellers, who had not been enticed by the music which rose from it, gently at first, like a fine fragrance, then falling like an uncontrollable torrent? Did Lakshmana remember the Gandharva girl? Indrakamini, from the assembly of Indra himself? She who, having failed to arouse Lakshmana's lust, scattered her broken bangles and her earrings all over his bed in order to discredit and defame him? Was it not Sita herself who had seen them when she came to clean his room, and who then went running to tell Rama about it? The headman of the village was summoned and all the women living there were asked to try on the earrings and the repaired bangles. The ornaments did not fit a single woman there. Rama then asked whether there was anyone left among the women who did not partake in the test. The headman said, "The only one who has not done so is Sita Devi herself." When she tried them on, they were exactly right for her. It had been Indrakamini's plot all along. Surely, he must remember the reply he made to his brother's unjust accusation? Did he not dive into the fire with a newborn child of one of the forest dwellers, emerging unscathed, and thus establishing his purity? She was weary of these purity tests. This forest was not new to her. Nor was it a place she disliked. But before he left her, Lakshmana must look carefully at her lightly swelling stomach.

He must make sure to tell his brother she is with child. Otherwise, there will be preparations for yet another ordeal by fire. There are some whose minds cannot travel in a straight line. As for the king of Ayodhya, his mind was entirely warped.

The chariot began its return journey. The sound of the horses' hooves could be heard for a long time before silence reigned in the forest once more. She was alone. The gusting winds covered her body with dust. She was alone. Gazing at the stream that flowed in front of her. Thinking of herself. Thinking of her own birth.

As the stylus finished writing that last sentence on the palm-leaf, a shadow fell. Sita looked up. The sage Valmiki was standing in front of her.

"What are you writing, amma?"

She stood up and bowed to him. "A life-story," she said, "Sita's *ayanam*."

"Isn't the Ramayana that I wrote sufficient?" he asked.

"No. In the ages to come, there will be many Ramayanas. Many Ramas. Many Sitas."

He picked up the palm leaves in his hand and asked, "Is this not the same Sita I wrote about?"

"You were a poet of the king's court. You created history. But I experienced it. I absorbed into myself all manner of experiences. My language is different."

"And where will this story be launched?"

"In the forest. In the minds of forest-dwellers."

It was not a particularly large room. But it was arranged in such a way as to invite one to stay there. There was a sense of warm comfort about it, like the feel of a hot-water bottle that soothes away one's pain. A small bed, covered with a spread of handloomed material, bark-brown, scattered with deep red flowers. Next to it, a table and a chair. A bathroom with just the essentials. More important than anything else, that window. A window right in front of the table. It had shutters fitted with slats that moved up and down, and which opened outwards.

When the bus dropped her off, it was already the very last moments of dusk. They told her she would have to walk a little, to reach the government guest house. A small boy offered to carry her suitcase. In the fading light, she walked along a path through the trees, the boy showing her the way; by the time she arrived at the guest house, it was totally dark. As soon as she introduced herself, an attendant there opened the room for her. While she looked about her, the attendant leaned across the table, stretched out his arm, and pushed the window outwards. Suddenly, there in front of her was the forest, enshrouded in darkness. A wide forest, where the branches of trees hung in festoons like snakes, or stretched upwards like the necks of giraffes. Strange and unrecognizable noises. Right in the middle of the window, as if it were strung upon a fine thread, a moon – the colour of well-thickened milk. In her mind a song echoed, in Raghunath Panigrahi's voice, throbbing with life: When I look for you, must you run away? Why do you turn away from me, white moon?

The attendant went away, having asked her about her evening meal.

Still watching the moon, she sat down in her chair and leaned her arms on the table. Then she climbed on to the table and sat there, her legs hanging down sideways, and turned her head to watch the moon, and the forest spread with its light.

Before she went to sleep, the camel-yellow notebook found a place on the table, with the dozen pencils and the rest on its back. Through the slatted shutters of the window, now closed, the moon shone in many fragments.

———

A pond filled with lotuses. Each lotus as wide as a mother's lap. Each lotus made up of a thousand, thousand petals. As he walked past, surrounded by his retinue of soldiers and bodyguards, Ravana glanced at the pond with its floating lotuses. Their colour and form attracted him, enticing him to pluck one at least. Handing his bow and arrows to one of the soldiers standing by, he waded into the pond, his silk garments dragging in the water, when he heard a child's voice saying, "I will kill you. I will kill you." Thinking it must be a myna-bird, he looked about the pond to see if any were about. Not a single water-bird that spoke with a human voice was to be seen. Each time he touched a lotus, the same voice spoke up again. He couldn't make out from which lotus the voice actually came. He plucked all the lotuses he could reach, and gave them to Mandodari when he reached home, telling her about the voice that he had heard. The entire floor was covered in lotuses. Mandodari sat down and opened the lotuses one by one, gently smoothing them out, petal by petal. As she opened the innermost petals of the very last flower, there, right in the heart of it, she saw a girl baby. The baby looked up at Mandodari with her dark eyes, and said clearly, "I will kill Ravana"; but the next moment she smiled widely, and began to babble, lapsing into meaningless baby-noises. Mandodari's stomach churned. She placed the baby in a box made of bamboo. With two maidservants in attendance, she walked to the seashore. She waded in among the waves and put the box out to sea. It floated onwards, riding on the waves.

It went a long way and at last touched shore. The first person to open the box raised an outcry; others thronged about him, and the baby was handed over into the safe keeping of their headman. That headman was Janaka. He gave the baby the name Sita.

Sita came into being, in touch with flower and earth and water.

Rama, as soon as he was born, caused grief to a living creature. Kosalai determined that they would serve venison at the feast celebrating the child's birth. Under a green tree there rested a male and female deer. The doe looked troubled. "What has happened? Didn't you find any green leaves? Are you thirsty?" asked the buck. "No, I'm not thirsty. But I hear the sound of hunters coming near. You'd best run away," said the doe. Then, to the hunters who approached them, she offered, "You may kill me if you like." But they killed the buck instead, saying, "It is the flesh of the male that is the best." The doe then ran to Kosalai and pleaded with her, "Please at least give me the skin of my dear partner. I will gaze at it and assuage my sorrow." But Kosalai said, "I intend to make a beautiful *kanjira* with that skin and to give it to my baby boy to play with."

Each time Rama crawled up to the kanjira, tapped it with his hand, played with it and made it resound, the echo would make the doe's entire body quiver. Each time she wailed with grief, saying, "Kosalai, one day you too will suffer this pain of loss."

Sita tied the palm leaves together and looked up. Some distance away, Valmiki was telling Lava and Kusa about the *putrakameshti yagna* which Dasaratha performed for the begetting of children; and the births of Rama, Lakshmana, Bharata, and Shatrugna.

———

As soon as she woke up in the morning, she felt an urge to walk until her legs were weary. She put on some sturdy shoes. When she came out of her room, she happened to see the guest house attendant. She asked him to bring her some tea, and sat down outside on the verandah steps. Dark green, light green, and palest green stretched away in waves as far as the eye could see. In a cleft where two greens collided, light red rays of the sun played hide-and-seek, appearing and disappearing.

The tea arrived.

She took it and began to drink, blowing on it again and again. The scent and flavour of tulasi leaves were soothing to her. When she returned the cup, she questioned him about the extent of the forest, where the tracks began, and where they led. She decided upon an easterly direction, and began to walk as if she were hastening to greet the sun.

Many paths branched off, one from another. As she walked further and further along, the densely spreading trees spread out like a shadow above, completely hiding the sun. Sometimes, suddenly, a single ray of light sparkled like a diamond and sped along the leaves. And was hidden again.

Suddenly, something cool touched her. In front of her there was a stream. Before she could reach it, however, she was surprised by a peacock flying low, dripping its blue and green tail-feathers. And before she could recover from the shock of it, it touched the earth, walked about, and then, in an extraordinary instant, spread out the full extent of its tail, and began to dance, hopping from one foot to the next. A dance for her alone. The peacock danced, watching her, and moving about in a small circle. Beyond it, the stream.

She sank to her knees in front of the peacock and began to weep as she sat there. I don't understand, peacock. I don't know my goal. Is there a goal at all? I know how to overcome the obstacles that stand in my way. But I don't understand the quest. What do I seek? And how? Do I even seek? How much further is it going to be? Even though I have come so far, the burden has not eased from my body. I want to feel light. As soon as my toes press against the earth, as if I were propelling a swing forward, I want to feel myself rise up into the air.

The peacock continued to dance.

Oh peacock, peacock, peacock, peacock...

She heard voices coming towards her from a distance.

"Ayiga! *Tya morala bag*." Startled by the sight of the peacock, a group of women exclaimed in Marathi, "There will surely be a drop or two of rain at least, look at the peacock dancing!" As they approached, their bundles of food swung from their hands. They washed their faces in the stream. They shook out the cloths which were tied about their heads and wiped their faces. When they saw her, they showed their surprise. Opening their bundles, they invited her to join them.

She went and sat by them. Thick rotis made of millet flour. A bright red *thuvaiyal*, made of coarsely ground garlic and chillies, roasted groundnuts, desiccated coconut, and rock-salt. One woman broke off a piece of roti, put some of the thuvaiyal on it and gave it to her. Another took an onion between the palms of her hands, squashed it, and gave her half. Yet another laid four or five green chillies on her share of roti.

With the ease of long-familiar friends, they asked after her and told her about themselves. They told her their names: Minabai, Rukminibai, Savitabai. The millet-flour roti went down her throat to the savoury accompaniment of the thuvaiyal, between bites of on-ion and chilli. When they had finished eating, Minabai took some tobacco leaves out of the drawstring bag at her waist, placed them in the palm of her hand, and began to roll them with her thumb.

"Would you like one?" she asked Chenthiru.

"No, I'm not used to it. Do you know that it's not good for your health?" Chenthiru remarked.

"*Ravde Bai*. If it isn't good for the health, then why has that Dev put so much flavour there?" Minabai asked in her turn. She spat out the spittle that had gathered in her mouth.

Chenthiru's mother used to say exactly the same thing. Her

mother used to chew tobacco. Wherever they went, her eyes would rove in search of a betel-leaf and tobacco stall. "My mouth feels bland and numb," she'd say. If ever Chenthiru protested, "You don't need that," she would retort, "If I chew tobacco, why do you get so annoyed?" Chenthiru's father never said anything. He, after all, smoked cigarettes. "Call it quits," Amma used to say in Telugu. Amma had travelled about with her parents and lived in several places with them. She used to say she had acquired her tobacco habit in Kerala and her love of music in Andhra. Her father had said, "They say that in certain places in Andhra some women smoke great big cheroots. It's just as well, Chendu, that your mother didn't pick up that habit." Amma had returned, "It's not too late, you know. Just bring me a box of Havana cigars from Cuba, I'll smoke one and show you." In this, she and Tirumalai's mother were exactly the same. There was a period of time when Tirumalai's mother suffered from ill-health, and Chenthiru refused to allow her to buy tobacco. Tirumalai's mother would keep opening her betel-box, looking inside it and fretting. She'd take Chenthiru by the chin and plead with her, "Listen, princess. If you like you may starve me. Only don't punish me by keeping me away from tobacco."

Rukminibai lit her bidi and began to pull at it. "Ei, don't blow your smoke all over me," said Savitabai, moving away. She went a little further off and lay down, pillowing her head on her arm. A foot or two away from her, Chenthiru lay down as well.

Savitabai asked "Chendiyabai" what she was doing in these parts. When she replied that she had just come away on her own, Savitabai proceeded to ask her a series of questions: Was she married? Did she have children? Where was her husband?

Rukminibai, who had finished her bidi, scolded Savitabai. "Ei, Savitabai! Are you looking for a second wife for your husband or what? Firing off all these questions, one after another!"

"Oh yes, as if Chendiyabai is of an age to get married now! And as if all that drunkard needs is a second wife!" Savitabai sat up, loosened her hair, and tied it up again.

Chenthiru laughed and rose to her feet. She told them that her children were studying abroad and that she had left her husband and everyone, and come away just to be by herself.

"Is that so? Very well, then," they said, and made ready to go. They told her that if they were in the vicinity of the guest house, they would most certainly come and see her, and then they walked on at a swift pace.

The peacock had disappeared a long time ago. Only its dance continued to unfold in her mind, green and blue.

She began to walk in the direction of the guest house. Tirumalai's trademark was actually a peacock. A peacock in profile, spreading its tail on the ground. Tirumalai's father ran a small business in *vibhuti* and *kumkumam*. A *swamiyaar* who was like a guru to the family had given them the symbol. When she first met Tirumalai, he was carrying packets of vibhuti and small tins of kumkumam in a cloth bag, the colour of a peacock's neck. He had brought these materials which had been ordered by the members of the Women's Association who met regularly at her Periamma's house in Bombay. He must have travelled quite a distance on his motorbike. He was exhausted. He asked for some water to drink. She brought him a glass of cold water, and another of lime sherbet, just as her Periamma had told her to. Completely relaxed, smiling, he asked her, "Have you come on a sightseeing visit?"

"No, I'm here for my further studies."

"What will you be studying?"

"M.Sc. Textiles."

"Do that." He put his glass down.

"And what do you do?" she asked him.

"I'm in trade. With my father. I studied up to my B.Sc. But my father's health wasn't up to it. So I became involved in this business. My younger sister is studying for an MA degree."

"Where?"

"Oh, she is here too."

Her aunt came in and asked, "Well, Tirumalai, why couldn't you have brought your mother and sister with you?"

"Amma is not very well, you see."

"What do you mean, she's not well? It's a whole year since I saw her," she complained.

"She's just tired. I'll bring her one day," he promised.

"This is Chenthiru," said her aunt.

"Yes, we chatted," he said. Then he said goodbye and left.

It had only been a casual conversation. But the thought of him remained in her mind. A very tall figure. Dark skinned. The darkness of his pupils seemed to shine against the whites of his eyes. A moustache which very slightly hid his mouth. A finely sculpted body. His buttocks were modest, and didn't protrude or swell out. The back of his trousers did not bulge in an unseemly way, but fell somewhat loosely, with a fold. It was her opinion that a man's bottom should be tightly muscled and well-knit.

She wrote to her father about him. She said that she liked the fact that he worked independently, for his own business. She wrote that his unflashy, simple lifestyle really attracted her. Her father, surrounded by coffee blossoms that were bursting open, could not make any sense of vibhuti and kumkumam. He didn't see what was happening to her.

By the time she finished her M.Sc. she had become totally familiar with him and his family. She wrote to her father again. He immediately telephoned her.

"What Chendu, is this all about love?"

"Mm."

"Does he have a moustache, this man?"

"Mm."

"Tell him you have a great big bow in your house. Tell him unless he bends and breaks it he can't marry you."

"Go on, Appa."

"What does he look like?"

She sang softly, "His body is like the green mountains. . ."

Her father laughed.

The trees spread their shade above her, so she did not feel the excessive heat of mid-day. She walked on at a fast pace. Nowhere was the peacock to be seen.

Whenever she crawled in the courtyard, the baby Sita's eyes fell upon it. That huge and heavy bow. She first learnt to walk by leaning against it and holding on to it. Ever since her earliest memories, she knew of it as Shiva's bow.

All hours of her day were spent playing in the forest. She knew all its secret places: the mountain springs where the water was as sweet as honey, the ponds full of water-lily and lotus, the trees where ripe jackfruit lay, burst open, the streams where the deer came to drink, the rocks where the beehives hung, the best places to rest, where the trees gave their most dense shade.

One day she decided to stay at home and help her mother. While her mother was resting, she brought fresh cow-dung and began to pave the wide courtyard. When she came to the place where the great bow lay, she lifted it with one hand in order to spread the cow-dung underneath. She had just finished and was replacing the bow when her father came by. His eyes widened in surprise.

He lifted her to her feet, her hand still full of cow-dung, and held her close.

"With one hand, my daughter has lifted up the bow that no one else could carry. Only a man who can bend and break it shall be fit to marry her."

She turned around and gazed at the bow.

Of course, she married the man who alone could break the bow. But he was not someone who was unknown to her. One evening when she went to the orchard to pick fruit, she saw a young man standing among the fruit trees. They looked at each other, the two of them. When he opened his arms, she walked into his embrace, without even knowing what she was doing. Then she freed herself, exclaiming that if her bangles broke in his tight clasp, she would not know what explanation to give at home. After that she ran homewards. Her mother asked her why her eyes were red, why there was that drawn look on her face. She said that however angry her mother was going to be, she would accept it; take whatever punishment she thought fit to hand out, even if it went to the extent of driving her away from home. With complete honesty she said that she had met Rama in the orchard, and been embraced by him. Her mother consoled her, saying that it was certain that the very same Rama would break the bow and marry her.

He broke the bow. He married Sita.

It was time to light the lamps. Sita rose to her feet. Lava and Kusa came running in with their bows. Breathlessly they told her about chasing after a deer, far, far into the forest. They had been surprised, shocked, by the beauty of the deer, and the terror in its wide eyes. You must let the deer be; let it run, you don't have to chase it, said Sita.

———

The tea that arrived in the evening was fragrant with ginger. That morning's long walk had left her feeling pleasantly tired. The hot tea was as comforting as a poultice. The languor of her afternoon nap hadn't quite left her.

She found that she had to speak to Tirumalai almost immediately after she returned to the guest house. He said he had tried to reach her by telephone three times, and had been anxious when he was told she wasn't there.

"Why should you be anxious? I went out intending to walk a little while. But I found I had gone a long way."

"Why do you have to wander about like a ghost, a *pisaasu*? See if there is a tamarind tree close by you. That's the right place for you."

"So I am a tamarind-tree pisaasu, am I?"

"Yes, a stubborn pisaasu. A beautiful temptress of a pisaasu. Have you eaten?"

"Mm. I saw four or five men when I was out walking. I swallowed them up in one gulp."

"Yes, you're quite a one to do that. Isn't it enough that you've swallowed me?"

"I swallowed you, yes. But I couldn't digest you."

"And why's that?"

"Too much fat and impudence, you see."

He laughed. Then he said, "Valli and Kaarmegam both telephoned."

"What about?"

"Kaarmegam needs to go to Canada, he says, next week. He said he hoped to see his sister. Then Valli rang to say she's expecting him there. Both of them said they wanted to speak to you."

"Shall I put the receiver down, now?"

"Why?"

"It's getting too expensive, isn't it, this call?"

"So when do you plan to come home?"

"I don't know," she said. Once again she said, calling him by his name as she did when they were alone, "I don't know, Tirumalai." She could hear his sharp intake of breath at the other end.

"What on earth is going on in your mind?"

"I need to feel easy. I need to feel light."

"Come home. Come back, amma."

"No, I have to do it on my own. . ."

"On your own, in that forest?"

"Yes. *Even if it is a forest path, Even though it is beset by robbers.*"

Silence.

He would call every day. He would plead with her to go back. She put on her shoes and began to walk westwards. Apparently, she had begun to walk early, when she was only ten months old. When she was eleven months, and they were visiting her Periamma in Bombay, she had walked across the street and gone off to Shivaji Park all by herself. She could remember to this day the young boys dressed in khaki clothes, doing their drill. She had never forgotten how she stood on an ant-hill, how the ants had bitten her, how it had hurt. If ever anything happened, she always set off walking at a swift pace. The family teased her, "The ants are biting her feet. That's why she's off." On both occasions when her parents died, she had walked and walked until her feet were swollen. Tirumalai, and her younger brother who had come home from abroad, had caught up with her and insisted she return with them.

Everywhere she turned, there were ant-hills. If she went in a slightly different direction, or went away on her own, there were ants biting her feet. She wanted to roam at will in several cities and in desolate forest interiors. She wanted to sleep wherever a ledge was available to her. Watching the dark sky with its sparkling stars, she wanted to sing aloud, raising a voice from her very underbelly, without any particular aim, addressing no particular god, "Diamonds encrusted in an indigo sari are the stars you see at midnight, di." She wanted to sing, in the Kaavadichindhu *raagam*, just for the pleasure of the sound of the words, and for the sake of its rhythm, "In the forest of time, in the tree of the universe, a bee buzzed; calling itself *Kali-shakti*." She wanted to dive into whatever pond she chose, and rise from it.

Tirumalai's father used to sing:

His stomach dropping, his hair whitening,
his teeth rattling, his back bent,
his lip hanging down, one hand on his staff, he comes —
to the sound of women's laughter.

He'd go on, melting, melting as he sang,

When my woman weeps and wails, when Yama's messengers gather
around,
when the waters spill out of the body, when my life is ending,
come to me swiftly, upon your peacock.

All visions and all quests are allowed only to those who are old enough. And only to men. As for her, she had to give a thousand explanations. Make excuses. Or become a devotee of Kannan or Shiva. She must seek sanctuary, repeating, "*Mere to giridhara Gopala*," or the Varanamayiram, or the words, "She worshipped at the Lord's feet." Then she could reach liberation, mukti, at once. And become one with the light. Those journeys in flower chariots were only meant for male bhaktas. Tukaram could hope for it. Not Janabai. As for herself, she hoped for neither visions nor for heavenly chariots. She only hoped to achieve a sense of expansion. An expansion that knew no boundaries.

Tirumalai's father was a humane man. A man of integrity. If Tirumalai questioned something, he'd say, "I've given my word, Thambi." It was a sentence that came to his lips every day. Tirumalai's mother suited him, like a lid that fits a jar. It was under her supervision that the vibhuti was made. As soon as Chenthiru and Tirumalai were married, the father gave up his position as head of the business.

Tirumalai teased him, "Why, Appa, have you gone and given your word to anybody that you will give up all your responsibilities as soon as your son gets married?"

"Yes, I have," he said, "I promised your mother." Then he called Chenthiru to him and said, "Look, amma, people tell this story. One day, a thorn entered Dasaratha's hand. He felt a terrible throbbing pain. While he was suffering like this, Kaikeyi came to him and gently, very gently, drew out the thorn. At once he gave her his word: he would grant her wishes, whatever they might be. Just so, whenever your mother-in-law massaged my back, or rubbed oil into my head, or pressed my forehead when I had a headache, I too have given my word, I don't know how many times. Now she's nagging me to make good my promises. Now she wants to travel, and see the sights in Kodaikanal, Ooty, Kuttralam and all those places." And he laughed.

"Shameless man," said Tirumalai's mother, laughing along with him.

She worked tirelessly alongside Tirumalai as they gradually turned the business in the direction of masala powders, and then expanded it to include silk material and readymade garments. For fourteen years they struggled in the jungle of commerce, as if they were competing in a race, running to touch the boundary line. Now their business had reached as far as Canada. For the past eight years they had also gone into the totally unknown field of leather goods. She herself had seen to the expansion of their sales: suitcases, handbags, shoulder-bags, wallets, purses for holding small change. There was talk of making her an equal partner in the business. It didn't come to anything. At once she was seized by a frenzy to walk. To walk a long, long distance. The rejection was not a reason. Only the signal.

In front of her, the sunset unfolded like a silent drama, spreading different colours in the sky. The crimson ball which had been sinking very, very slowly was suddenly not to be seen anymore. Its remains were in the skies. She wasn't aware of the passage of time. Then she heard the sound of voices.

Rukminibai and Savitabai were approaching with their water-pots. They had no more drinking water left in their homes, they said. She walked along with them. Just nearby, there was a small water-hole full of water. The water was still and clear, almost as if it had been rained in. Moonbeams lay scattered upon it. Amidst the scattered light, the moon could be seen, clearly outlined. The water held it captive there. As soon as Rukminibai dipped her water-pot into the well, the moon dissolved into fragments and spilled all over the water. When the water-pot was held upright again, there was the moon, within its narrow mouth. Savitabai too lowered her water-pot and lifted it out. Again the moon floated in her water-pot. The water in the well became motionless once more, and lay there with the moon.

She began to walk back towards the guest house with Savitabai and Rukminibai. The moon accompanied them, floating in their water-pots. Along the way, she said she was thirsty, and at once Savitabai poured some water into her cupped hands; the moon remained within her hands for a moment, then partly slipped down her throat, and partly drained away through her fingers. When she looked at the moon within her cupped hands, drank the water, and then looked again, Savitabai laughed.

"It's gone, Bai. If there's no water, there's no Chandrama either."

True. In all the open courtyards of all the little houses of the forest, there must be innumerable moons in water-pots and little puddles of spilt water. Perhaps, if you put out a small vessel, a moon as big as a small coin would float there, who knew? Moons that float so long as there is water. Moons which approach with every scoop of water, and hurry off as the water drains away. A moon brought down from the skies. And then its extension. She felt a coolness pervade her body. She was a woman who had feasted upon the moon. She had eaten her fill, and returned the rest to the skies.

As soon as they reached the guest house, the other two said goodbye, and hastened away. In the dining room, her meal had been placed ready for her, under covers. After she had finished, she went to her room and switched on the light. Then she sat at her table.

The larger part of Sita's life was spent in the forest. The forest of her childhood where she had played, plucking fruit and flowers and leaves, was a miracle, hiding many, many secrets deep within itself. Later, it was a refuge and an asylum for her and her husband. A place where many experiences became possible. Sita was then an entirely innocent girl. When she saw herself in the clear water of the pond where she first went to bathe, she came running back to Rama, to tell him the moon and a swarm of bees were inside the water. Rama had to return with her and point out that it was her own face she saw; what she thought was a swarm of bees was her own long curly hair that flew about her. It happened another time too. On that occasion, the face she saw in the clear water was a radiant one. It was filled with grace. She went off in haste to pick a quarrel with Rama. She said that he lied when he spoke of his faithfulness to his only wife; she accused him of keeping another woman hidden somewhere. Once again, Rama went with her, and asked her to look in the water. Immediately she saw the beautiful woman. I will show you the woman's husband, he said, and came to stand next to her. When she saw Rama's reflection next to the woman's, she recognized herself. She was ashamed.

It was in a forest, too, that she was imprisoned. And now, it was a forest that was her sanctuary.

With what intensity, with what childlike obstinacy she had thought of Rama alone, in her forest-prison! And what was it that Rama had declared publicly, the very day the war ended? When he sent word through Hanuman that she should come to him, attired in her best clothes and ornaments, had she not replied that she would rather come in the clothes she had always worn in Ashokavanam? Even when they had insisted on adorning her, her heart had not been in any of it. There was a big stone beside her, where she sat under a tree. She had often thought, when her whole body felt shrivelled, when she longed for the day when she would be rescued, when she would at last be home in Ayodhya, how useful that stone might be, to grind sandalwood into paste. When she confided this to Hanuman, he tried to pull it out of the earth right away. But the elder statesman, Jambavan, intervened to say that one must never take back a gift. This land has been given over to Vibhishana, he said, and she must not take anything without requesting for it properly. She was a girl who had longed for a deer, and for fruits and flowers. She had given up the comforts of royalty. She had made the forest itself her companion. Out of all the kingdom of Lanka, she had only asked for a stone. She wondered whether he implied that she had not behaved with the dignity of a royal princess, and she felt ashamed.

At the great battlefield strewn with the dead, her legs entwined and buckled. She thought of the many who had died to rescue her sole self. It seemed to her that Rama was treating her like an exhibit in front of the crowd. She had been alone for so long in Ashokavanam, totally protected from public gaze; now she had to come out into the wide-open battleground, in the midst of all the men standing there, battle-stained and weary, and in front of the thrusting crowds who had gathered there to gaze upon her. She arrived in her best attire and ornaments, as if she had not suffered in the least, as if she were now proclaiming aloud, "Look, I am a redeemed woman." But it became apparent very soon that all that adornment had not been for the sake of delighting Rama. He told her that all eight points of the compass surrounded her, and that she was free to go in any direction, and with whoever she chose. The battle had been fought in order to defend his honour, he said, not to rescue her. She could choose to live with anyone: Lakshmana, Bharata, Vibhishana, Sugriva. The Jambavans who had reminded her to behave as a princess did not raise their voices then. He who was so aware of the pride of his lineage, did he forget that she too belonged to a proud clan? Had she not herself made it necessary for him to wage a battle, because she was so aware of his pride? Otherwise, would she not have sat on the shoulders of Hanuman, who thought of her as a mother, and left Lanka when she could?

Hanuman set fire to Lanka. All Rama could do was to light a fire in his wife's heart.

Her very first words to Lakshmana, who greeted her after those long days of parting, were, "Lakshmana, light the fire!"

Even after she finished writing about it, that moment was like a weight upon her heart. A little way off, Valmiki was telling Lava and Kusa the story of Ahalya and her deliverance from the curse that had been laid upon her. How many changes there are, while an event becomes gossip, and then turns into story! Ahalya's heart had hardened into stone. Only when she worshipped Rama's feet did it melt again and fill with the essential waters of the fountain of life. But, Sita thought to herself as she rose, there is even more miracle and drama in turning a stone into a woman.

East, west, north, and south, she had walked in all the directions, many times. As she walked and walked, she felt a prickling sensation at the base of her spine, as if something were trying to grow there. At night it spread all over her body, and rocked her to sleep. Eastwards, past the stream, they told her, was a small waterfall. One day she set off to meet the waterfall. It was a restrained little cascade. Like washed hair, left loose to dry. As she sat down to look at it closely, she discerned a face at the edge of the water. Its body glowing like gold in the sunlight, a deer was drinking. It drank some water, then shook its head, and looked all around. It stooped to drink again. The next time it lifted its head, it spied her. It leapt, startled. Then, like a yellow whirlwind, it was gone.

She went quietly to the edge of the waterfall, and lay face down at the place where the deer had drunk. Holding in her stomach, she reached out and drank, just as the deer had done. The water trickled through her, in some hitherto unknown path. As soon as her thirst was quenched she turned over, face upwards. Above her, the sky. Pale blue. Her *dupatta* caught in the wind, flew upwards, and covered her face. She gazed up at the sky through it. Her eyes were heavy with sleep.

. . . She was running to catch a train. Why were all the roads made of mountains and deep gorges? A deep fear arose within her, as if someone was chasing her. She heard horse hooves. Horse hooves, in the middle of the town? She reached the railway station. She hung on to the metal handle and climbed into the train. Her breath came fast. Even before she could sit down, they had reached the next station. When she looked out of the window, she saw her father sitting on a bench, a little distance away.

"Appa, Appa, how did you get here?"

"I'm waiting here, just for you."

"For me?"

"Yes." Her father straightened his glasses with one hand, smiling at her.

"But I can't get off, Appa."

"Why not?"

"There's all my luggage, Appa."

Appa smiled. He stretched out his hand towards her. His hand was still in that position when the train began to move.

"Appa, Appa. . ."

Suddenly, her father, who couldn't sing a single line in tune, mimed as if he were keeping time with a *sapplaakkattai*, and began to sing, jumping up and down. The song came from Appa's throat in the voice of her first music teacher, Ramachandra Bhagavatar. In the background was the sound of the vinai. Purandaradasa's Devarnama.

"*Naaneke badavanu, naaneke paradesi?*. . . Am I really destitute? Am I truly a wandering beggar?"

The railway station moved along with the train.

Ramachandra Bhagavatar was blind. He used to go from house to house giving singing and vinai lessons. When he first came to their house, Amma asked him, "Sing us a song." A streak of a smile spread across his pockmarked face. He tuned his vinai and began to sing, accompanying himself. "*Naaneke badavanu, naaneke paradesi?* . . . Am I really destitute? Am I truly a wandering beggar? I who have been gifted with that rare treasure, Purandaravittala himself, how can I be destitute? How can I be a wandering beggar?" It was a song composed in Sindhubhairavi raagam, a ragam that has dazzling highs and lows, twists and bends. But in this song there is no technical wizardry, only a straight and sliding path.

He always arrived on holidays, just when she had finished eating and was considering a nap. A young boy usually led him by the hand. Annoyed at having lost the chance of an afternoon nap, she'd shake out her skirt and sit down for her lesson. In loving tones he would ask her in Kannada, "Why are you so cross, amma?" All those memories and details fell, one on top of another, thud after thud, as mere words, reflections; linked, dissolved, floating. In pieces, fragment by fragment. Just as Appa sang, outside the window.

Appa, who had for so long been jumping about and singing, began to stumble like a blind man. The train gathered speed. The station had stopped in one place. Appa was a mere dot in the distance, his hands groping in the air. Only the song still sounded in her ear, "Naaneke, naaneke."

Her face pressed against the window bars, she stretched out her hand. "Appa, Appa . . ."

She heard a voice calling out, "Bai, Chendiyabai."

She woke up with a start. Rukminibai, Minabai, and Savitabai – all three stood there, leaning down and looking at her as she lay there.

"*Kai jaala* bai? . . . What happened?" asked Minabai.

She sat up then.

They said they had been searching for her. They wanted to invite her to their homes. Their families and husbands had gone elsewhere. All four of them walked along together. Chenthiru had not quite recovered from her dream. It was as if she were still in an extension of it.

Savitabai's house had more space than the others. So they went there. Savitabai switched on the lights. She opened the back door.

Her house was spotless. To the right side of the single room there were two trunks. In the left-hand corner were an oil stove and a firewood hearth. The back door was half open. Beyond, there were banana trees. Clothes drying on bushes. Minabai and Rukminibai ran to their own homes to bring various things. They returned in a short while. By that time, Savitabai had lit the stove and made tea. All four sat down facing each other, and drank the tea. When she asked what they were celebrating, they said it was nothing special, that they tended to get together now and then, just like this. Savitabai teased Minabai and Rukminibai, saying it was very rarely that their husbands left them and went anywhere, here or there. Their sons and daughters were all married, they were grandmothers. Even so, their husbands always held on to them, wherever they went, she teased.

"Be quiet," Rukminibai chided, affectionately. She removed the lid of a small aluminium dish she had brought with her. Fish pieces spread with masala, yellow and red. Savitabai lit the firewood hearth, placed a shallow pan on it, and poured in some oil. Minabai went up to it and began to fry the fish. Savitabai sliced onions and chillies and put them together on a plate. Rukminibai lit the kerosene stove once again and put the chapati griddle on to heat. She took the millet-flour dough which Minabai had brought with her, rolled out pieces of it, placed these on the griddle, and began to cook them, frequently dipping her hands in water, and patting them as they baked. It fell to Chenthiru to grind the thuvaiyal. While she ground it, she watched Rukminibai who was humming a song under her breath. When she strained to listen, she realized they were the words of the saint, Bahinibai, "*Arré sansara, sansara.*" Life is like a griddle on which you are cooking *baakri*; it is only after you have burned your hands that you get your baakris, the song went. The rhythm of the song was completely in accordance with the pace at which Rukminibai was making the baakris.

When it was all done, Savitabai pulled out a tray, on which a dough of wheat flour mixed with oil lay covered with a cloth, and placed it in the middle of the room. She took out the *puranam*, a filling of mashed *channa* dal, jaggery, and coconut. The fragrance of cardamom filled the air. As if they were well rehearsed at this task, all four began to pat out the *puranpolis*, dipping their fingers in oil every now and then. Savitabai briskly fried them in batches, as they were patted out. The smell of roasting coconut and jaggery pervaded the room.

Savitabai arranged all the puranpolis in a neat pile and covered them. The other two went quickly into the backyard. She could hear water being drawn from the well. Chenthiru wiped her hands on a towel and stood up. The other two returned, wiping their faces with their sari-ends, which had been pulled tightly and tucked in at the waist. Savitabai went toward the back door. Minabai drank a tumbler of water. Before Chenthiru could have a drink, Savitabai had returned. When Chenthiru went to the back of the house, Savitabai came with her to show her the privy. By the well was a bucket of water, and a piece of soap on the parapet of the well. She splashed the cold water on her face, again and again. When she squeezed the soap, spread its lather all over her face and splashed it with water once more, she felt cool, comfortable. She wiped her face with her dupatta and looked ahead, where the banana trees, the shrubs, and the neem tree in a corner, were all like outlines in the dark. "Chendiyabai. . ." The invitation came from the house.

Inside, all three of them had knotted their hair back tightly. Tattoo marks shone on the forehead and chin of their well-scrubbed faces. They all stretched out their legs, and leaned back against the wall, relaxed and easy. As soon as she sat down with them, Minabai set the plate of fried fish in the middle. Rukminibai took a couple of bottles out of a bag. "Palm-toddy," she said.

The other two women put the glasses out.

"Is Chendiyabai used to drinking palm-toddy, though?" Rukminibai asked.

There was palm-toddy on the night they went to the Murud-Janjira Fort. They had gone with their friends and their children, in two cars, to Alibagh. And from there to Murud-Janjira. The fortress was right in the middle of the sea, a fortressed island, once in the possession of sea-pirates. The boatman hurried them into the boats which they rowed towards the fort. They reached it in two boat-loads. Right around the ruined fort were heavy chains, looking like mountain pythons. The boatmen urged them to look around the fort as quickly as possible, and return swiftly. One boat left for the mainland, Tirumalai and the children having given the fort the hastiest of glances. Within the next fifteen minutes, when the rest of the party tried to climb into the other boat, the sea had become turbulent. They were only rowing boats. Beneath the surface were huge rocks. The boatmen feared to put out to sea. At first they waited and delayed, but eventually they said they could not risk it and would wait until the morning. She and Tirumalai's friends went and sat in the central part of the fort. The boatmen brought them the fish they had kept aside to take home, and Steven made a small hearth of three stones, lit a fire, and roasted the fish. Lankesh brought out a bottle that he had bought from the men. Palm-toddy. Annamalai and he poured it out into the plastic cups they had in their bags. Kaarmegam helped his Chitthappa, and handed the cups around. The fish, roasted to a turn without any masala whatsoever, melted in the mouth. The palm-toddy, which she was tasting for the first time, travelled in many directions in her head, and made her fly. Above them, the sky was a pitch-black magician, who had tied up all the stars. Lankesh took out his mouth organ. He was a fan of S.D. Burman, Manna De, and Pankaj Mallik. He began to play S.D. Burman's song:

Sunu mere bandhu re. . . e sunu mere mithuva. . .
sunu mere saathi re. . .

Listen, my friend, listen my beloved,
listen my companion. . .

A song of the boatmen. A folk song. It made them feel as if they were sitting together, swaying in a boat. Steven and Kaarmegam began to whistle and sing Beatles songs. The toddy, S.D. Burman, and the Beatles went to her head, making her quite intoxicated. She lay back on the floor and sang one of Annamalai's favourites, "A tiny, tiny, nose-drop; a red-stone. . . encrusted nose-drop. . ." Then, a lullaby in Nilamabari for Kaarmegam who came and leaned against her. Her voice, touched by the toddy, went slipping and sliding. Songs, conversation, until daybreak.

The sea had calmed down by early morning. The boatmen came and summoned them. On the opposite shore, Tirumalai waited anxiously. A weariness, from having waited the whole night, was apparent on his face. A sleepless night. His eyes were red.

"Tirumalai sir, your wife is back from the pirates' fort, safe and sound," Lankesh's wife said.

When they told him about the toddy and the fish and the music, he asked his brother, "What, Annamalai, did you actually give your sister-in-law some toddy to drink?"

"Yes, Anna, hereafter you should give her a drink every day. It's then that her singing voice really comes into its own."

Tirumalai laughed with him.

After that one occasion, now once again, fish and palm-toddy.

"Yes, I'm used to it," she said in reply to Rukminibai.

A cool breeze blew. Rukminibai filled their glasses. When she bit into her fish and drank a mouthful of the toddy, her throat burnt. Then, gently, gently, like a smoke-cloud, a sense of intoxication rose in her head.

"That song that Rukminibai sang was one of Bahinibai's, wasn't it?" she asked.

"Yes, it's always Rukminibai who will sing at any of our organized struggles. She'll sing Bahinibai's songs, but she also knows the songs that mock the government officials."

Even as they talked, Rukminibai raised her voice and sang the same Bahinibai lyric, loudly. When the song was over, Minabai said, "It is Rukminibai who sings, and Rukminibai who settles our quarrels."

'What quarrels?"

"It's nothing," Rukminibai hastened to explain. "Minabai's granddaughter's husband deserted her. She was then four months pregnant. As soon as a baby boy was born, he wanted to claim him. I questioned him properly, in front of all the people."

"What did you ask him?"

"Look here, I said, the vessel is ours and the milk is ours. Just because the man gave a drop of buttermilk to turn the milk into curd, can we be expected to hand over the whole pot of curd to him, I asked."

"What did you say? Just because he gave a drop of buttermilk..." Chenthiru put her glass down and began to laugh.

They laughed with her.

After that, when they had eaten the millet-flour rotis with the thuvaiyal, both her stomach and her heart felt full. When she got up to wash her hands, she hit her head on the edge of the roof, with a sharp "ping." At the very same moment, she heard vinai music. It is said that at the seventh stage of meditation one can hear the music of the vinai. Could there be a seventh stage of intoxication, too? Once again, the music.

"What is that, Savitabai," she asked.

"*Biin*," said Savitabai. On the other side of the waterfall, there was an *ashramam*. Apparently, an *ustad* lived there. People called him the Sufi Baba. He was said to be somewhat like Sai Baba of Shirdi. Sometimes, he stayed here for two or three months at a stretch. He played the instrument. Sometimes, they went to hear him.

Even after they had washed their hands and lain down to sleep, they could hear the vinai play.

On the table in the guest house, the camel-yellow notebook lay open. The pages that had already been filled were ruffling in the wind.

———

Rama's sister, Shanti, kept on pestering her. "What did Ravana look like? Why can't you draw a picture and show me?" Sita's ability at drawing was well known. At last one day she agreed to her plea, took a piece of paper, and drew on it with a brush. After she had done his arms and legs, his entire body, and when she was just about to embark on his face, Rama entered the women's rooms. After an instant's confusion, she hid the picture under the long end-piece of her sari. The picture with the unfinished face was right there, under her sari. Sita was in distress, unable to move. She could not tear up the picture until Rama had gone, could she? As she was serving him his meal, Shanti mentioned the picture. "Some people here think of Ravana the whole time," she began, and went on and on.

The journey by chariot happened very soon after that.

———

Mid-day. It was the usual time for Lava and Kusa to come home for a meal, after their morning archery exercises. She laid her stylus down. The boys came in a great hurry and ate the food she served on their leaves. As she watched them, she imagined how her life would have turned out if they had both been girls. Would she have allowed them only to pick fruits and flowers, and play at home? She didn't think she would have done so. She would have brought them up, too, as women warriors. Nobody would have been able to kidnap them and carry them away.

A shadow fell over the threshold. It was Rama standing there. Lava and Kusa began telling her that they had met him in the forest; that he had asked them who they were; that they had said their mother's name was Sita, but they didn't know who their father was. They said it was possible he had followed them home. "Good," said Sita. "Your father's name is Rama. He is the king of Ayodhya. He's standing in front of you now." Without a moment's hesitation, they leapt towards their father. The kingdom was their father's, wasn't it? Had they been girls, they might have stood close to their mother. They might have looked upon a father who abandoned their mother in the forest with suspicious eyes.

Rama began to plead with her. Could Sita not understand his position? Did she think he lived happily without her? As he spoke on and on, she wondered, with a terrible pain, why the earth could not split open and draw her inside. She refused his plea with firmness. She said her journey lay in a different direction. After that she felt as if the earth had indeed split apart and she had gone within, somewhere far, far beneath.

As soon as they opened their eyes at break of day, Savitabai made tea without milk or sugar and gave it to them, piping hot. The other two set off for their own homes.

She had not forgotten the vinai music she heard during the night. Chenthiru began to walk in a southerly direction from the waterfall. After she had gone some distance, she saw four or five small hut-like dwellings. The door of what looked like the principal hut was open. She went in, softly.

On a thick mattress, spreading from one end of a facing wall to the other, were three *rudravinai*, left uncovered. Next to them sat a man, about sixty years old, with a vinai on his lap. White-bearded. He wore a chequered lungi about his waist. A kurta over that. He was fine-tuning the instrument, adjusting the pegs and bringing his ears close to the strings.

As soon as she went in, he spoke to her familiarly in pure Hindi,

"Come here, beti. Listen to this. Tell me whether it is in tune or not."

As if she had spent her entire life listening to the pitch of a vinai every day, she went up, listened carefully, and said, "It's just right."

She sat down in front of him.

"Everything comes down to sruti, getting the pitch right, doesn't it?" he asked her. "We speak of *sur*, being in tune. Who then is an *asur*? Not someone with crooked teeth and ten heads, but one who is ignorant of sur. A-sur. Because such a thing as sur isn't resonating within them, they run away with themselves, without subjecting their impulses or their strength or their direction to any discipline. They are not reined in by their sur."

She nodded.

"The pitch must come right, holding everything in tune. All of us are a-sur. Seeking after the right pitch."

"Is it such a difficult thing, then, to be in tune?"

He laughed.

"It's not a thing to be held captive, is it? It's like a wave. Even when you think you have overcome it and are riding on its crest, it can collapse beneath you. It can rise up again in a gigantic billow. It can turn into nothing but foam when it comes close to you. It will come together, and dissolve. Come and go. Drown you. Fling you right away."

His very words sounded like the sea.

"Can you sing?" he asked.

"A little. Carnatic music."

"Mm. Sing something. Sing in your Sankarabaranam."

Softly she sang the opening lines, the *pallavi*, of the Sankarabarana *varnam*.

"Mm," he said. Then taking the vinai on his lap, he pressed down on the *daivadam*, the sixth note, as if he were flicking a nerve. Then he played several cadences. Then once again that note, as if plucking at a nerve. Dani. . .

"This is the Bilaval raagam from Dhrupad," he said. She stooped at his feet and pressed her head against the edge of the mattress. Dani. . . dani. . . dani. . . It ran through her body like electricity.

"What is it you want, beti," he asked, his hand pressing upon her head.

"I don't know," she said, without looking up. "Even when I think I understand, I haven't really understood at all. As soon as I think I understand, I lose it all."

"That's how it is," he said, patting her head.

She lifted her head and sat back. "I've left Mumbai and come away."

"Each of us has just two choices. One is to renounce, the other is not to renounce. Why do I play this instrument? Why do you listen to it? Because we haven't yet understood what is renunciation and what is not."

"I cannot breathe in Mumbai."

"Mumbai can follow you here. And the forest too can go with you to Mumbai."

She looked into his eyes.

"That's how it is," he said. "Bilaval was a favourite raagam of my *Mataji*'s. Whenever a dove cooed outside our window, in the narrow lane off the crowded Mohammad Ali Road, she would say it was doing *riyaaz* – practising the Bilaval. Sometimes, she would hear the dove's voice above the roaring of a bus or a train. "A perfect Bilaval," she would say. She died here last year, in this very place. She was eighty years old. It was springtime when she died. She used to struggle all night because she could not sleep. At earliest dawn, by four o'clock, she would take a chair and sit outside. Opposite her, the mango grove. Around five o'clock, she would call out to me, "Jalaluddin! Ei, Jalaluddin! Come here. The koel is singing the Bilaval." She'd tell you exactly the notes it was singing. "A perfect

Bilaval," she'd say, rejoicing. She could hear the Bilaval, wherever she went, in all places."

He ran his fingers over the strings. A waterfall of sounds.

Some lines from a song she had learnt a long time ago, at school, came to life in her mind. In sound-shapes. In magical Sindhubhairavi.

"Like the unrestrained wind. . ." those low bass notes.

Outside, a sunlight which would not torment. Ustadji began the alaapanai, the preliminary free rendering of the Bilaval.

"Like the ocean that has seen the moon. . ." long, ascending cadences. Ustadji's students gathered quietly inside the room. They sat down, surrounding him. Again and again, there came the plucking of the rudravinai's strings, like the plucking of one's nerves.

"Like a cascading waterfall. . ." the notes reached a high point and poured downwards.

Ustadji continued to play.

"Play the music on the flute of life. . ." the notes returned to their path after their wild wandering.

The koel which sang the Bilaval called out from the mango grove. Dani. . . dani. . . dani. . .

The koel sings everywhere. The koel's song is transformed into the tune the listener wishes to hear.

She rose to her feet and began to walk towards the guest house.

———

Nobody was willing to accept Sita's decision. They said it was not proper to refuse to go, when the king of Ayodhya himself came to take her back. What was her goal, after all? What was she seeking? Then there were Hanuman's long appeals. The denunciations of the rest of them. She could not recover from her sense of having gone somewhere beneath the earth, somewhere so deep that nobody could reach her.

She rose to her feet and looked around the cottage. This time it would be a total renunciation. A lone journey which left behind all those who were known to her, those who spoke lovingly, who dispensed advice. A journey that would be long, that would go very deep.

The more she walked, the more the forest seemed to extend. She crossed the river, went past a waterfall, and walked on; saw the deer drinking at a small stream, was shocked by deer-eating tigers, delighted in the sight of baby elephants running alongside the herd, encountered nights through which owls' eyes glowed, observed the shimmering of green leaves as the sun's rays fell upon them, was surprised by the leaping of monkeys from branch to branch, their young clinging to their bellies. She walked on. Eagerly. Wearily. She rested.

And again she walked.

Their meeting took place early one morning. A time when not even the sound of birds was to be heard. The sun was hidden, secretive in the skies. Far away, she saw a small hut. The dim light of a lamp flickered through it. The sound of a musical instrument came to her, tearing the darkness. As she came nearer and nearer, she recognized it as vinai music. A tune that she had surely heard at some time. As she came yet nearer, the music bound her in its melody. The door of the hut was open. She looked inside. Someone who looked like a *tapasvi*, living a life of austerity, was playing the vinai. When she asked whether she was disturbing his practice, he said no. He had been waiting for her, he said. "Don't you know me? I am Ravana."

Startled, she stepped back.

"I thought you died in the war..."

"This life is full of magic, is it not? When Rama demolished everyone in my palace, there was one bodyguard left. He pleaded with Rama to spare his life. And he then prayed that a friend of his should be returned to life. Rama did so, and told them both to flee before Lakshmana appeared. When they said they no longer had the strength to run, he gave them wings. They changed respectively into a kite and a parrot, and flew away. This is a story that people tell. Could I not be that parrot that has been flying about in these forests? A parrot waiting for that moment when he would meet Sita once more. A tired old parrot."

"Even now, this infatuation? I have seen so many tragedies. My life has been like a game of dice in which I am a pawn. I am tired. I am weary. I am more than forty years old."

"It is then that a woman needs a friend. To support her when she is distressed by her changing body. To serve her. To encourage her. To stand at a distance and give her hope."

Sita sat down on the floor.

Ravana went on, "I have never refused to give my friendship to anyone. Before the battle began, Rama wanted to perform a puja. There were only two people in the world who could have conducted the puja for him. One was Vali. The other, myself. Rama had killed Vali with his own hands. So I was the only one left. He sent an invitation to me. I went to him. I did the puja as he desired. I blessed him and invoked his victory."

Sita addressed him by name for the first time. "Ravana, words make me tired. Language leaves me crippled. I am fettered by my body."

Ravana smiled. "The body is a prison. The body is a means of freedom," he said. "Look," he said, showing her his rudravinai. "A musical instrument that was created by imagining what wonderful music would sound if Parvati's breasts, as she lay on her back, turned into gourds, and their nipples attached by strings. It is an extension of Devi's body. You lifted Shiva's bow with one hand. You should be able to conquer this instrument easily. Will you try?"

"Will you teach me?"

"I did battle for you once, and lost. Would I deny you music? I will be your guru and give you lessons every day. Let the music break out of the vinai and flow everywhere in the forest. Don't think of it as an ordinary musical instrument. Think of it as your life, and play on it. Here."

He lifted the rudravinai from his lap and stretched it out towards her.

"Leave it there on the ground," said Sita.

"Why?"

"It is my life, isn't it? A life that many hands have tossed about, like a ball. Now, let me take hold of it; take it into my hands." So saying, Sita lifted the rudravinai and laid it on her lap.

Wrestling

The milk was at the right heat, comfortingly warm. She added palm sugar and a mere touch of pepper to it. She brought a flask and poured it in. It was needed every time. As soon as the music ebbed away and the applause rang out, he would turn slowly towards her. The way he moved his head was deeply engraved in her mind. A thick neck with folds of skin just beneath the jawline. A thin chain clasped about it. His entire neck drenched in sweat as he finished singing. A red silk shawl just touching his shoulders. A shawl that Kripananda Varrier had once draped about him. He would turn his head towards her and raise his eyebrows just a little. At once she would hand over the *tampura* to a disciple, and pour the milk from the flask into a silver tumbler. She would say softly, as she held it towards him, "It was wonderful."

"Mm," he'd say.

He'd drink the milk. And always, every time, there would be something slightly wrong.

"You could have put in less *kalkandu*, couldn't you?" Or, "Should you put in the pepper by the handful?" Or, "Not quite warm enough." And so on, and so on.

He would grumble in a low murmur. But the *sishya* would hear, plainly. He'd look at her from the corner of his eye. The expression on her face never changed, though. "Yes," she'd answer, accepting it all.

As they returned home in the car, he would take her hand gently. He'd mention a particular raaga alaapanai, or a song, *swaraprasta-aram*, or *niravel*, and ask, "Did it come off all right, Shenbagam?"

It wasn't enough just to murmur, "Mm."

"Was it the way Ayya taught it?" he would keep on at her.

On some days she stayed silent. She'd look out of the window. She'd stare at the streets, the houses, the passers-by.

"Tell me," he would insist.

At that day's concert there might have been a small mistake which no one else had noticed. When it was pointed out to him, his face would fall.

"Of course. You'd notice, wouldn't you? After all, you were Ayya's favourite sishya, weren't you," he'd say, piqued.

His resentment would last until they reached home. Then, at once, his mood would change. He'd play a game of carom with the children. At supper-time he would lap up the garlic-flavoured *rasam* with relish. Later at night he would caress her gently. He'd take the tampura on his lap and begin to strum it.

"You sing, Princess," he would say.

He would make her sing the very sequence where he had made a mistake that evening. While she sang, he would moan, "Amma,

Amma." Sometimes, he would hit himself on the head with the tampura. "Don't kill me di, you wretch," he'd cry out. Sometimes, he would call out to his father, "Ayya, Ayya."

Then came that endless pacing to and fro. From one end of the verandah to the other. Sometimes, if she chanced to wake up during the night and open her eyes, he would still be walking up and down on the verandah. Softly, she would walk up behind him and touch him. At once he would reach behind him with his arms and clasp her to him. She would stand there, her face and breasts and shoulder pressed against his back. Sometimes, after a while, he would walk back with her and lie down by her side, holding her close. And at times they would make love. He would put all his efforts into bringing her to a climax, making sure that she was satisfied, asking her again and again. But at other times, he would spread his mat on the verandah and lie there by himself. He would keep on humming the song he asked her to sing. In the morning his army of disciples would turn up. And surround him.

"Anni, Annachchi needs some warm water." "Anni, Ayya is asking for coffee." "Anni, some pepper rasam for Annachchi." The requests came to her continuously. He used his students like a screen behind which he disappeared. If she confronted him directly, he would not look at her. But by the evening, the crowds would melt away. His usual jokes and teasing would begin. This always went on like a kind of game. But a game without a referee. A game without set rules; a game which the players themselves were not aware of playing. A game in which there was neither victory nor defeat. A game in which winners became losers, and losers winners.

Ayya's portrait hung in the reception room of their house, garlanded. Kadirvel Pillai was "Ayya" to everyone who knew him. He was a performer who came of a long and renowned line of Isai Vellalar, steeped in the knowledge of their art. He used to say that when his mother danced, wearing her diamond eardrops, an *addigai* studded with rubies about her neck, her eyes touched with collyrium and her lips stained with betel juice, all of Kumbakonam was ravished and entranced. As a boy, he had seen her dancing through the streets, when the deity was taken out in procession. He used to say about that occasion, "I remember that the street was quite wide, Shenbagam. Even today, I can picture Amma in her arakku-red sari and green choli, dancing the *navasandi kavuthuvam* at the crossroads. Men walked on either side of her, carrying gas-lit lamps on their shoulders. There were such crowds there! And it seemed to me then that as Amma danced along the street, it grew wider and wider."

Many years later, when he went to visit the place, the same crossroads with gutters on either side seemed altogether to have shrunk and narrowed in size. He used to say that without the adornment of Amma's dance, the street was shown up in all its nakedness.

Ayya's mother, Kanakambal, went all the way to Chennai to see Gandhi, taking the young boy with her. Crowds had gathered along Chennai beach, wave upon wave. She stood for several hours there, her hands gripping Ayya's shoulders as he stood in front of her. She didn't say much on their way home by train. But the next time she danced she wore a plain hand-woven khadi sari. When the temple administrators admonished her for it, she put them in their place, saying, "Ask me which shastra says I must only wear silk! I am not just a street-acrobat, ayya. I'm a woman with sensibility, who eats salt with her food." Later on, when she came to know Ramamirtham Ammaiyaar well, she went with her to many meetings of the Self Respect Movement. By the time Ayya was ten years old, except for Vakil Govindaraja Mudaliar, the coming and going of other men to their house ceased. Mudaliar was a fine Tamil scholar. During the evenings, he would chant verses from Tevaram and Tirupugazh to different *raagams*, Ayya sitting beside him. It was then that Ayya's musical training began, on a regular basis.

Amma's dance performances became more and more rare and finally ceased altogether, when the law banning the dedication of devadasis to the temple was passed. It didn't seem, at that time, as if she took much notice of it. She led a busy and cheerful life teaching Ayya the subtler points of music and holding many vigorous discussions with his gurus. Mudaliar, though, would still ask her on some evenings to dance to a particular song, interpreting it through her *abhinayam*. He had already made his will, arranging for Kanakambal to have whatever she needed by way of land and property. The evening that a messenger came to tell them that Mudaliar had died of heart failure, Kanakambal stood for a while quietly, leaning against a pillar. Their lifestyle did not change. They continued to live in relative comfort. Ayya was perhaps seventeen or eighteen at that time.

Mudaliar and Amma had once taken a photograph of themselves at a studio in Kumbakonam. Mudaliar sat up straight in his chair, his hands spread over its arms on either side. She stood behind him, slightly to one side, her arm just seeming to graze the back of his chair. Her other arm hung by her side. That picture was hung in the left hand corner of the narrow corridor running the length of the main room of their house. Kanakambal did not move it. When her health failed her later, and when she was bed-ridden, her eyes roamed about all the time. It was perhaps the photograph she looked for, Ayya thought, the photograph which she would have glanced at constantly as she went up and down the corridor. But instead she beckoned him and asked him for the box that held her salangai, her dancing bells. As soon as he brought it to her, she lifted the bells and laid them against her side, as one would a baby, stroking them so that they chimed faintly, making a sound as soft as a baby's whimper. The next morning she died. Ayya spoke about his mother as if he were telling a story. The photograph which Mudaliar and she had taken together hung in his room, still.

———

When Shenbagam was about five years old, her mother brought her to Ayya. After her father died, her mother had made a living by cooking for several families. Her Amma loved to sing. She always hummed the Bhupalam raagam in the mornings and the Nilambari in the evenings. But life did not afford her the opportunity to study music properly. She never failed to attend a *kachcheri* at the temple. All Shenbagam's own memories of those early years were deeply associated with music. When the knife-grinder called out "Knives sharpened" and then laid the knife against the whetstone, its "kr kr" would seem to her to have its own melody and rhythm. She'd call her mother and tell her so. Then, her mother would seat her on a wooden stool, oil her hair, place a *chombu* of water in her hands, and begin to massage her scalp. She, meanwhile, would paddle her fingers in the water, making a splashing noise, "salak-palak." Paddling her fingers twice towards herself and four times on the opposite side, she would ask, "Amma, guess what song this is?"

"Who can tell, di?"

"Don't you know, Amma? It's '*Vara vina*.'"

"Oh, all right."

"And this? Salak, salak, salak, palak, palak, palak."

"I don't know, go on with you." Amma would rub her head hard. "'*Orumaiyudane ninadu*,' Amma. Can't you tell?"

Amma would burst out laughing.

Everyone in town knew about Ayya's music and his character. One day, Shenbagam's mother took courage in her hands and brought the child to him. Ayya came out and sat down on the *thinnai* in the verandah, and asked her, "What is it, amma?'

"You must teach this girl music."

"It won't work out, amma. Send the child to school. Let her study there and make her way. Music means hard work. You have to give up your life to it. Impossible for her to do, amma."

Ayya went away inside.

Amma didn't leave, though. She kept on standing there. When he came out, two and a half hours later, Ayya was taken aback.

"Haven't you gone yet? What is this, amma?"

"Please teach her music. Let her stay with you here. Let her be like your own daughter."

Ayya looked at Shenbagam. She could still remember the clothes she was wearing that day. A checked, green cotton *paavaadai* with a black border. And a yellow blouse with puffed sleeves. Amma had combed her hair back, and then taken a bunch to one side, tied it with a ribbon and encircled it with flowers. No chappals on her feet. She stood with her legs planted firmly apart, and stared back at Ayya.

"Let's see, sing me a song," he demanded.

Amma had primed her well before bringing her. At that time, Ayya had written and set to music a song in which Sita, as a young girl, asks who, in reality, are her parents. It was a moving, melodious song in Anandabhairavi, beginning, *"Bhumi yen thaai endraal. . .* If the earth is my mother. . ." Ayya himself had sung it in the temple, twice. She sang that song as she stood there, her arms folded. Looking straight ahead, she sang, making no movement at all with her body. Ayya was silent for a moment after she finished. Then he said, very tenderly, "Come here."

She went up to him swiftly. He lifted her up and sat her next to him on the thinnai. He stroked her head. Then he looked up at her mother. Before he had finished speaking to Amma, she was fast asleep, her head on his lap.

He used often to talk about it, later on. "You put your head on my lap and fell asleep, as if you had somehow arrived at the very place to which you were destined to come."

After that began the unending music practice. Ayya's son Shanmugam was four years older than she was. She was made to sing with him. Within two months her mother went away to Delhi to cook for a south Indian family. She sent money regularly from there. She came to visit her once a year. She'd ask Shenbagam to sing to her, then. And she lived until the time of Shenbagam's own first kachcheri. In every other way, she grew up as if she were Ayya's daughter; and Ayya's wife became her mother. Nagammal had a fine knowledge of Tamil literature. So one could say that she learnt music from Ayya and literature from Nagammal.

Ayya needed his drink, a whole bottle of it, every evening. He would sit down to it either with his musical friends, or by himself. It was during those sessions that he told his stories, passed on gossip, tried out the latest lyrics. It was at such a time, too, that he spoke about his mother.

But it was with Shanmugam that all her singing, her talking, her quarrelling, and her peacemaking took place. Shanmugam tended to be rather lazy. He took his daily practice very casually. He was offhand at lessons, as if to say, "My Ayya's music is mine by right; who else can claim it?" He seemed to be under the impression that his father's talents had already entered him through his very blood, and without any effort on his part. So he never exerted himself. When she and the other pupils woke up at four in the morning and began their voice-improving exercises, Shanmugam never joined them. And as if to prove that such disciplines were not necessary to it, his voice flowed abundantly, like a clear stream.

Ayya began to teach her to play the vina, since she needed to learn to play an instrument as well as to sing. He never allowed her to do such kitchen chores as chopping vegetables or cleaning vessels. He said her fingers would become worn out. If Nagammal was ever unwell, he never expected his own pupils to do the household chores. He managed everything himself, with the help of Shanmugam. She was never allowed to do anything other than to lay the banana leaves for meals, and to bring drinking water. He looked after her fingers to that extent.

"She is going to become really lazy," Shanmugam would grumble. "Why don't I start learning to play the vina as well? Then I won't have to do any of these chores either, will I?"

"Why do you try to compete with her, da?" Ayya would ask him.

When Ayya wasn't looking, Shanmugam would give her a knock on the head. Or he'd pull her plait when she was singing, and make her lose her concentration. It was a great game for him to watch her face all twisted up as she wept. All the same, it was he who climbed up the mango tree to pluck the fruit, who brought green cucumbers from the garden, who stole jaggery and coconut from the kitchen during the afternoon when Nagammal was asleep. All for her.

She was somewhat scared on the day she came of age. She went and stood by a window in one of the rooms at the back of the house, all alone. She was aware of a heaviness in her thighs. Would they isolate her for three whole days? Would she be allowed to sing? To touch her vina? To read the books in Ayya's room?

She also remembered her mother who was somewhere far away, in Delhi. Amma had spoken to her about all this on her last visit. She had left a cotton half-sari with Nagammal before she went away, a sandalwood-coloured one, with a print of purple flowers. The same one that she wore now as she stood there. But she must sing! She must play the vina! She must take the fat books in Ayya's room and place them on her lap like kittens, and riffle through their pages.

Ayya came there after a while. She started to cry when he walked straight up to her and laid her head against his chest saying, "My dear Princess." Heaven knew how he intuited her state of mind. "You are anxious, aren't you, whether you can sing, or play the vina, or touch books?" he asked.

She nodded.

"Silly girl! What connection is there between this and all that? Who told you to come and stand here all by yourself? Anyone may touch books or the vina whenever they please. Come out now." He took her hand and led her out of the room. He spoke to Nagammal, who was busy at her work, "Nagu, don't tell her to keep away from the others. You know I don't like that sort of thing."

"Of course," said Nagamma, smiling at her. "I didn't tell her. She went away by herself. She wouldn't come out, however much I asked her."

He spread out a *jamukaalam* in the front room and handed her the tampura. He summoned Shanmugam and all his other pupils. They sang together as usual. They also noticed she was wearing a half-sari. And so this event too flowed into all the other events of her life, causing no sudden rupture.

When Ayya chose her out of all his other pupils to sing with him at a kachcheri for the first time, there was some resentment on Shanmugam's part. He accompanied them to the concert, but he did not sing. He assumed that Ayya had arranged it that way, deliberately. Just two days earlier, someone had come from elsewhere, one afternoon, to invite Ayya to give a performance. Shanmugam had invited him to sit on the thinnai, and then disappeared inside and forgotten all about him. When Ayya emerged two hours later, the gentleman was still sitting there. Seeing Ayya, he greeted him respectfully, and mentioned that he was very thirsty. As soon as Ayya realized that he had been waiting for two hours, he stormed inside and shouted out, "Shenbagam!"

Shenbagam, who had been sitting in Ayya's room, looking at some books with Shanmugam, heard the anger in Ayya's voice and came out.

"Did you call me, Ayya?"

"What is this, amma, do you just ask a man to sit down in the thinnai and forget about everything else? He's come all this way in the midday heat. Shouldn't you ask him whether he wants anything to eat or drink? What were you so busy about, in there?"

Shanmugam came out then, and said, "It was I who asked him to sit down, Ayya. I'm afraid I forgot about him. It didn't strike me that it was going to be an important kachcheri. Judging from his clothes, I'd say you are not likely to get more than half a coconut out of it."

Ayya took the towel off his shoulder and flung it at him. He went inside and brought out a chombu of water and a platter of fruit and snacks. He placed it on the thinnai, saying, "You must forgive me. My son forgot to tell me you were here." He agreed to sing at the kachcheri.

After the man had left, Ayya came inside and said to Shanmugam, "A musician ought never to be arrogant, da." Shanmugam didn't reply. He merely looked at Shenbagam, raised his eyebrows and curled his lips.

It was for that very kachcheri that Ayya chose Shenbagam, out of all his pupils, to accompany him. He made her sing together with him, and at the end of the programme, he asked her to sing a couple of *kirtanai* on her own. The concert took place in a small village. They had just completed laying a main road, and it was in celebration of this that the concert was held. Apart from the microphone, and the small lights surrounding them, there was no other evidence of electricity being used there. None of the lamps shed a garish light. If anyone stood up and walked away carrying a battery-operated torch, its circle of light entrapped a few white shirts, or brightly coloured saris and cholis, or the cheeks of babies pressed against thighs, as they lay fast asleep. Between the audience and the performers on stage, a bridge was established within the very first minutes. Crossing it again and again, the two could touch each other. When Ayya had finished, there was no applause at all. Then, an old gentleman came forward and said, "Ayya, we have sat here this evening, spellbound by your music. I am now in my eightieth year. I have no idea whether there is such a thing as another birth or not. But if there should be such a thing, then I pray that I should be born a child in your household. I want to go on listening to your music." Then, having learnt about Ayya's usual ways, he held out a bottle towards him. Ayya did not refuse it. But from the presentation platter that held his fee, he took only the half coconut, saying, "Please buy some sweets with this money, and give them to those children who never cried or made any trouble tonight."

That night, as their bullock cart went slowly along the road that wound its way among fields and woods, Ayya said, "Shanmugam, don't think I asked Shenbagam to sing tonight in order to punish you in any way. There is no connection at all between this and what happened the other day. Shenbagam has outstripped the rest of you and gone a long distance ahead. She has worked that hard."

After that Shanmugam began to practise fiercely, like a demon.

Ayya began to make arrangements for Shenbagam's *arangetram*, her first public performance. It was held at a school in their town, on a modest scale, without much flourish. He did not forget to invite her mother. But Shenbagam had a secret that would take Ayya by surprise at the arangetram. She had composed a *varnam* describing a peacock dancing amidst a dense forest, set it to music as a *raagamalikai*; and she sang this in place of the usual invocation to Vinayakar. It contained her own signature in the line, "*Kadirvel Nagamiruvar magal Shenbagam manam magizha*... That the heart of Shenbagam, daughter of Kadirvel and the two Nagams, may rejoice." As soon as they returned home, Shanmugam asked, "Isn't it a sign of arrogance, Ayya, to sing without praying to Vinayakar?"

"No, da. Hers is the pride of knowledge. You need that too, da," said Ayya.

Amma deeply appreciated that special signature and its reference. Her name was Nagavalli. When Shenbagam invoked the two Nagams, she bound herself to her mother once again. It was as if it made up for all those years of cooking in other people's houses. But she wasn't there for Shenbagam's next kachcheri.

Shenbagam was invited to give at least five or six kachcheris in a year. Meanwhile, Shanmugam too began by singing together with Ayya, and then went on to take the stage alone and to give his own solo concerts.

One couldn't say at what instant exactly the deep bond between them became established. Perhaps, without their ever realizing it, it had been burgeoning deep within them. When Ayya spoke to her about getting married, she never said a word. "You mustn't marry a man who will stop you from giving performances," he said. "He must respect your music." Neither did she reply when he asked her whether he should look for a bridegroom from her own community, or what he should do. Shanmugam intercepted her in the corridor as she came away from this conversation.

"Shenbagam, how can you even think of looking for a bridegroom elsewhere? You've got to marry me."

An intense happiness rose up within her. Quickly she went up to him and held him tightly. She stroked his bare chest with her face.

When they told Ayya about their wishes, he did not reply to them immediately. Nagammal, however, hugged her with joy. Then Ayya said to Shanmugam, "Why don't you let it be for a couple of years? What's the hurry?"

"Now that it's been decided, why should we put it off?" Shanmugam asked in his turn.

"Let her grow up a bit," Ayya said.

For a couple of days, Shanmugam and she went around with long faces. After that Ayya agreed to fix their wedding date. Then two months passed as they touched and learnt each other, astonished and delighted each other. They were overwhelmed by their joy, wave upon wave. Not a single new song was practised. During the third month, she had an invitation to do a kachcheri in a different town. After she had accepted by telegram, she decided on her programme, and then sat down with Ayya to discuss it. He suggested a few changes. He promised to teach her a couple of new pieces.

While they were eating, Ayya told Shanmugam about the new pieces, and suggested they learn them together. Immediately Shanmugam asked, "Is Shenbagam going to give concerts?"

"What do you mean? What else is she going to do? Cook?" Ayya asked sharply.

"No, Ayya. But why should she go rushing about everywhere? Let her sing as much as she wants to, at home. These concerts will only exhaust her. Leave me to do the running around. Let her rest at home."

Ayya continued to eat without saying a word. Later, when she went into his room with his drinking water, he spoke to her brusquely. "Go on, go on. Run your household. Have your babies."

She stood there quietly. Her eyes filled.

"Why are you crying, wretched girl?"

"Will you teach me the new pieces?"

"We'll begin tomorrow. Go on," he said, without anger.

He never stopped teaching until he died. The outside world claimed that Shanmugam was the true heir to his music. Awards, degrees, presentation shawls, and citations kept on coming to him. The days when he and Shenbagam sang together gradually faded away. Along with the concerts came the pomp and show of success. Shanmugam entered the huge world of acolytes and sycophants as well as of true artists. Shenbagam lived with him. She stood close by him. From where she sat behind him, she handed him his milk. But somewhere, at a place invisible to the eye, they continued to be as wrestlers, locked in their struggle.

—•—

"Anni, could you give me some hot milk, please, with turmeric powder in it?" asked Somu, the sishya, coming into the kitchen.

"Why, aren't you feeling well?"

"I coughed a couple of times, Anni."

The bangles were still on his wrists.

It happened about three years earlier. While Shanmugam was away from home, Somu pestered her to teach him the varnam she had composed, and Shenbagam did so. He sang it at a small function a little later, citing her as the composer. By chance, a famous *vidwan* happened to be in the audience. He had made it an unswerving rule that no woman should be on stage with him while he performed. Apparently he had ridiculed the boy later, saying, "What is this, appa, you've started to take lessons from a woman, have you? Do one thing. Get a couple of bangles for your wrists."

"Bangles won't be a problem, Anna. Look, I can get a pair straight away," Somu replied. And he went off in haste to the jewellery shop and returned, wearing a pair of silver bangles. Later, Shanmugam scolded him for showing up the vidwan in that way. But Somu refused to remove the bangles.

As Somu was drinking his milk, another pupil came in haste to tell them that Rangasami had arrived. Within the next instant, Rangasami himself walked right inside the house.

"Shenbagamma, a terrible mistake has happened," he said in consternation.

Shenbagam came out of the kitchen into the main room asking, "Why, what's the matter?" She invited him to sit down, and sat down herself.

"I've been out of town for a whole month. I fixed Shanmugam Anna's concert date, and then went away. I asked the man working under me to arrange for the orchestra. He's somewhat new to all this and doesn't understand all the conventions. Not realizing what he was doing. . . he's gone and engaged women artists. . . Both the violinist and *ghatam* player are ladies. What shall we do?"

"When it comes to music, what does it matter whether the artist is a man or a woman, sir? In our Ayya's family, the women played all manner of instruments, mridangam, *kanjira*, everything. Even in those days, when they used to say that it was not necessary for women to sing raagam, *taanam*, and *pallavi*, the women of his lineage would sing raagams, and even go on to *swarams*. This is our Ayya's son. He won't say anything. Please go ahead." With these words of comfort, she sent him away.

Meanwhile Somu stood by, fingering his silver bangles. Shanmugam climbed on to the stage, his brocaded shawl glittering, greeted the audience, and sat down. A look of surprise crept across his face as his eyes swept over the accompanying artists on either side of him. By this time, Rangasami began to introduce the musicians.

Shanmugam began his first song, and paused for a moment at the point where Somu could join in with him. But just then Somu appeared to be looking elsewhere and not paying attention. A second time, Shanmugam contrived to pause, creating an opportune moment for Somu to join in; but the boy did not seem to notice. A split second later Shenbagam leaned towards the mike in front of Somu, repeated the line that Shanmugam had just sung, and joined in with the melody. Her eyes blazed into his, as Shanmugam turned towards her, startled. Her entire face was illuminated as she smiled. A huge applause rang out from the audience. Shanmugam looked at her as if he had been caught in a tight hold and wrestled to the ground at a totally unexpected moment. In an instant, Somu took away the tampura from her hands and moved the mike in front of her. Shenbagam led into the next line herself.

Perhaps Shanmugam was perspiring in spite of the air-conditioning in the room. He removed the shawl that was draped around his shoulders, laid it aside, and began to sing with Shenbagam.

A Rat, a Sparrow

When she turned around in her sleep and opened her eyes, the rat's face was right next to her cheek. And when she screamed out loud, leapt to her feet and stood there shuddering, the rat too, startled by her scream, jumped on to the window and sought shelter there. It lifted its nose and stared at her as if to say, "How you terrified me with your scream!" Every time it tried to move, she screamed again. Finally, it sat right where it was, motionless. And she stood frozen in front of it, staring at it all the time.

It is difficult to be friendly with rats. Most particularly so with this one. It must surely have been this one. A rat which tended to eat up only the autobiographies in the top shelf of her bookcase. Because the covers of the autobiographies had been nibbled completely at random, their titles stated starkly, *My His* or *My Autobiog* or *My St*. As for one of them, entitled *The Autobiography of a Donkey*, only the Donkey remained. When you looked up at it, beneath the smiling photograph of the author, you could only see the word "Donkey" in boldly-inked letters. Although many people might have thought the word appropriate to the author, one could not say whether they would have wanted it to be left to the rat's judgement in the end. It struck her that even if the author had called himself a donkey in false deprecation, he might object to its being emphasized in quite this way.

It was because of this that as soon she heard the sounds "krk, krk" the following night she flashed her torch along the top shelf. The rat was sitting on the autobiography, and had begun nibbling its way around the "Donkey." It looked down at her. It seemed to her that it was laughing. Her tongue rolled into a scream. Her friends, knocked out after their customary Saturday celebrations, woke up. They chased after the two-inch-long rat. It scuttled into the bathroom. Paramvir followed it inside with a coconut-frond broom, and locked the door behind himself.

"Param, don't kill it. Just make it faint."

"It's just two inches long. Do I know how to hit it so that it just faints?" he replied from within.

"If, after thou hast given it chase, it still does not die, what wouldst thou do?" asked Susan in pure Tamil. She was from Paris. Paramvir's girlfriend. She had attended a three-month intensive course in Tamil, and was here to do some research on female deities. According to her, Lakshmi sitting at Mahavishnu's feet and stroking them was not an indication of being dominated by him; she was only instilling in him the energy and strength he needed to succour the world and to create whatever was necessary. When asked why someone with so much energy should not stroke her own feet and take on Vishnu's work herself, she said, "Thou givest me cause for laughter." Now she stood there exclaiming "Aiyako" in response to the loud noises of Paramvir's battle with the rat inside the bathroom.

Paramvir emerged, with the rat lying prone on the coconut-frond broom.

"It's only fainted," he reassured her. He let it go on the street below, and then returned. The caretakers of the building were somewhat disturbed by the sight of a Sardarji with his hair bound up, coming downstairs at one o'clock in the morning, carrying a rat on a broom. The next day, they avoided looking directly at her.

Just as she had fallen asleep peacefully, assuring herself that when the stunned rat opened its eyes, it must surely have walked off into a world without autobiographies, here it was again, sitting right next to her cheek.

But was it the same rat? When it recovered from its swoon, did it come straight back here? Or was this one its mate?

Many people had forewarned her that the big city was full of rats and bandicoots. Because it was artists and intellectuals who told her this, it was reasonable for her to assume that they were referring metaphorically to the human inhabitants here. Besides, when she and Amulyo spent their very first night in this city in a flat which belonged to Gita and Sukhdev, with its single room, its kitchen smelling of mustard pickle, and sweaty clothes hanging up on the line, the rat-image had struck her as particularly appropriate. The kitchen was really like a rat-hole. And it was on that night that she had her dream.

Skyscrapers on all four sides, like mountains. Narrow streets. If you enter a building looking for a place to stay, they turn into rat-holes where you cannot even stand upright. Everywhere there are people lying either on their backs or on their sides, sitting with their heads on their knees, talking together, laughing. A woman returns home from her office. Very casually she enters her rat-hole. Voices, as if from heaven, tell her of the comforts of their flats. . . When she tries to take hold of a rope in order to raise herself up conveniently, it turns out to be a rough, abrasive rat's tail.

She must have called out in her sleep. She opened her eyes. Amulyo was peacefully asleep. He was one who was truly blessed with the gift of sleep. She shook him awake.

"Amul, Amul!"

"Ha. . ." he said, waking up with a start.

"Amul, I had a dream."

"Mm."

"A frightful dream, Amul. I went cold all over."

Amulyo sat up and drank from the water bottle. He poured some water into a glass and gave it to her. When she had drunk it, he said, "Tell me."

When she finished describing the dream, he laughed.

"How do you manage to dream in such beautiful images? It's complete with symbols and everything. And for all that, you don't even agree with Freud."

She hit him on the stomach. "You are a goonda, a loafer. You are a Kumbakarnan who sleeps all the time. You are a rascal." A blow accompanied each epithet.

He lay back, still laughing. She climbed on top of his stomach, her legs on either side of him, and took up the posture of the Destroyer of Demons.

Amulyo caught hold of her raised hand. Very gently. Her eyes filled. Tears came too, to his eyes.

He glanced at the shelves above them, blackened with smoke; at the aluminium vessels that could be discarded at any time they chose to pack up; the kerosene stove; the roach-powder scattered at the edges of the walls; the kitchen drain only ten feet away. Then he looked at her and was silent.

She touched his navel gently.

"It was only a dream, Amul," she said.

She remembered the spacious backyard of her grandmother's house in Coimbatore. Certain images are inextricably linked with certain places. Her image of her Paatti was inseparably linked with that house. Paatti who had borne children from the age of thirteen. Paatti who had cooked vegetables and stirred halva in great big pans. Paatti who had told stories from the Ramayanam as she massaged her puny grandchildren – including herself – with castor oil, firmly, firmly. Paatti with her tongue like a whiplash. Whose every word had stung.

Animals always surrounded Paatti, like the cattle which stood about Krishna, enchanted by his flute.

One hot summer afternoon, Paatti woke up with a start. She went to the backyard. A monkey sat on the wall behind the well, making the most frightful noises.

"What's the matter, da?" asked Paatti.

"Urr," it replied.

"Paatti, don't go near it Paatti!" she and her cousins, Chithi's children, called out.

Paatti looked at the monkey steadily. Then she went to the room next to the bathroom where the firewood was stacked, and brought an empty coconut shell. She dipped it into the water trough and filled it. She went towards the monkey and held it out, full of water. It grabbed the coconut shell from her and drank it down in a single breath. Having drunk three times from her shell, it leapt away, swirling its tail.

"It was thirsty," said Paatti.

The house was full of black and white and brown cats. At least a dozen of them. After a row of children had eaten their meal, followed by the men, when Paatti stretched out her leg and sat down to eat with the women, the cats would come, swarming about her.

"Miaou," one would say.

"It wants an *appalam*," Paatti would translate.

They were cats which had acquired a palate for appalam, *rasam*, rice, roast potatoes, and so on. She would give ghee-rice to a cat that had just survived the delivery of a litter of kittens. When the morning milk arrived, the cats too had their share.

"Would you like to keep a cat?" asked Amulyo.

"Mm. No. What about you? You keep a dog at home, don't you?"

"It's really wrong to keep animals locked up in these cage-like places," he said.

"Children too," she agreed.

After the rat-dream, there had been other rat-*darsanams*, manifestations. Rat legends. Rat experiences about which Sukhdevand

Gita told them. As she watched a cinema show, munching popcorn, Gita had felt a sharp nip at her foot. The very moment after she shook her foot and looked up again, Sukhdev was shaking off his foot, too. When both of them looked down, they saw a huge bandicoot running away. Both their feet were bloodied. Several injections later, full of righteous indignation, they had approached a journalist friend and asked him to make a report about it. He, however, had shed a patient smile and informed them about the experiences of the cinema critic of their paper. For some reason, this woman had missed the preview meant for the press, and went instead to the cinema theatre where the picture was being released publicly. As she was writing her notes, she felt her *dupatta* being pulled. Apparently, she took no notice of it, but held her pad against the armrest of her chair, and went on busily making her notes. When the lights came on for the interval, she bent down and saw a rat on her lap! When she stood up and screamed, the other spectators calmly watched the rat running away and commented, "Such a lot of fuss, just for a rat!" Then someone sitting next to her told her an elaborate rat joke. There was a girl who learnt judo. She learnt karate. She learnt *kalaripayittru*. One day, she saw a rat running across her kitchen floor. She screamed out loudly and climbed on to a chair. He cackled loudly, "ke-ke-ke-ke," as he told her this.

One does not know whether a bandicoot ever bit his feet.

She knew a story about a Rat Prince. Once, there were three princes. Two of them chased one away from the land. After many trials and tribulations, he meets a princess. When she kisses him, he turns into a handsome prince. When she grew up a little, she added a postscript to the tale. The Rat Prince became a handsome Human Prince after the kiss. The princess, though, became a rat. What a wonder! No prince came forward to kiss her. Not even the Rat Prince.

After Gita and Sukhdev had gone abroad for a year, they had taken over the flat and this rat had come to do battle with them. Often, there is a particular symbol which stands for a big town. Just as the Big Apple stands for New York. It struck her that only one symbol could possibly stand for this city: a Rat. Rat city. Rat people. People who stayed as rats, even after a kiss. There might be a whole history behind this rat cowering by the window. It might be a rat which was bored with many yugas of life as a rat, weary after eating so many autobiographies; it might be hoping to change after a kiss from her.

She got up and pushed the window shutter outward with a long rod. The rat sprang up and ran outside.

When Amulya returned home from his trip the next day, she told him all about the rat. He suggested they buy some rat poison. She thought that this was, after all, a literary rat. It shouldn't die in agony. There were any number of ways to die other than by poison. Come to think of it, she had a nonsense *ula*, a song of praise, in her possession. It was an ula composed in praise of a Tamil Nadu leader. In fact, one sect of the now-divided party had circulated a rumour that this ula had been sung to the leader hours before he died, and that there was definitely a connection between the poem and his immediate dispatch to the hospital. She thought that if this rat ate the ula, it would certainly die. But would it die without writhing in agony? She wanted to laugh.

"Why, do you have a book that will put an end to it or what?"

"Look here, don't make fun of Tamil. All your books are rotten ones which even a rat won't eat."

"What's this, a 'linguistic state' dispute?"

"Well then, should any idiot who can't even pronounce 'zh' make fun of Tamil? What's all this Tamil, anyway? It's Tamizh, Tamizh. Say 'zh.'"

"Zh," said Amulyo, pronouncing it perfectly.

"Is it enough to say it just once? Say after me: *Vaazhaippazham vazhukki kizhavi nazhuvi kuzhiyil vizhundaal.*"

"Look, I didn't get a sleeper, so I've sat up all night. Why can't you teach me Tamizh – see, I said Tamizh – after I've had a cup of tea at least?"

They said that this was a city where all sorts of people lived. But it was clear that several among them were marked off as Madrasis. There was a certain friend of Amulyo's. As soon as he saw her, his mouth would grimace a little. "*Namaskaram* ji," he would say, grinding away, with the idea that if you added "-am" to a word, it became Tamil. "*Sambaram*, rasam, tea-am, coffee-am, puri-am, *chappati*-am. . ." he would say in a rapid volley, and then ask in a drawl, "*Kya* ji?"

After he had done this a couple of times, she questioned him, full of concern, "Vijay, you poor man, have you had this speech defect since you were a child? Is there no way to correct it? How you have to struggle to speak!"

Vijay was taken aback. He stumbled, "No, no. This is. . . Madrasi. . ."

"Oh, I see. I was feeling sorry for you all these days. You see, we don't speak like that at all."

Vijay looked at Amulyo as if he were seeking help.

"Well, Vijay, what will you drink? Tea-am?"

"Tea," he answered in a subdued voice.

There was another friend who insisted on telling jokes after **having** downed three pegs of rum. "I'm going to act like a Madrasi," he proclaimed loudly. Before the others could stop him, he had turned himself into a Madrasi. He rolled back his shirt sleeve. He pretended that there was a leaf in front of him, scooped up a handful of food and sucked at it with a loud hiss. Another scoop, another hiss. Then a series of rapid movements as if he was shovelling the food into his mouth. Finally, he thrust out his tongue and licked off both the inner palm and back of his hand. He laughed at his own performance. Nobody else laughed with him.

Vijay went up to him and whispered something. He looked at her and said, grinning away, "It was only in fun. I like the temples in Tamil Nadu very much. Then dosa, vada, idli," he drawled, stressing the "d."

"*Saniyane*," she said, meaning, You wretch.

Only Amulyo understood what she said. He gave the friend his bag and sent him on his way. When Vijay left that day, he didn't say, "Namaskaram ji," but gave her a hug and said limply, "Good night."

She was in a sudden frenzy. She wanted to embrace the plantain-leaf seller in that part of the city where most of the Tamil people congregated. When she heard a certain Tamil accent, she felt as if the Tambaraparni had burst its banks and come flowing towards her. Dosai, idli, rasam, *idiaappam*, and Chettinad chicken curry seemed to her like the very staples of life. Suddenly at night, or in the afternoon, or in a crowded bus or train as she was wiping away her sweat, a long-forgotten song would come to mind, sharp as a lightning of pain. She heard the Kaavadichindu song her grandfather used to sing in the terrace at night, looking at the stars and pacing about with his legs held apart,

> *This rotten body is of use to no one –*
> *like a broken sieve, oh parrot,*
> *always it brings pain.*

That frenzy held her in its grip until she reached the Tamil library. There, when she saw the brightly coloured book covers, all of them portraying women either on their backs or lying prone, her legs began to buckle.

It seemed that the overseer of the library would never take his hand out of his *veshti*. Heaven knew what buried treasure he had there. As soon as he clapped eyes on a woman, his hand went into hiding. He spoke vociferously about Tamil culture, gesticulating with his other hand.

"We are safeguarding a whole culture, amma. For the sake of Tamil, I've had stones thrown at me." He displayed a bald patch on his head. "We are making great efforts to have a statue of Bharati placed outside here, and another of Tiruvalluvar. I've also put forward the idea that we should cover all the walls here with *kural* couplets. As soon as you walk in, a kural should catch your eye immediately. It should hit your eye. Say you've just come in. You see a kural right in front of you:

She who worships none other than her husband as her god
Says "Rain" and instantly the rain falls.

What do you think of that, amma? Your hair would stand on end, wouldn't it? You'd be thrilled. We must praise our women, amma. We have competitions at singing kural, *tevaram*, and all that. If women win, we don't give them prizes at random. We might give them a pedestal oil-lamp. Or we might give them a book about the role of women in Tamil culture." He leaned towards her. "It's simple, amma. Our entire culture is in the hands of women, amma."

His voice revealed his tranquillity at having given over Tamil culture into women's hands. She thought to herself, if his hand were ever to emerge from its own cultural search, then some of Tamil's cultural burden might be placed there too.

Outside, just by the door, a singer attached to the Sabha, where all south Indians came to learn various arts, was talking away.

"They've got rid of me. Did you know that?"

"Is that so? And why?"

He rapidly undid the buttons of his crisply starched shirt and displayed his bare chest.

"I don't have a sacred thread."

—•—

The two of them bought an extremely potent poison. They smeared it on bread and placed the pieces in corners of the room. She put one piece behind *The Autobiography of a Donkey*. Heaven knew which particular piece of bread it ate. It lay dead, modestly, in a bag made of soft blue material. She felt a shock. Would it have suffered a lot? Might it have been in agony? Certainly, it had tormented them. Wrecked their sleep. Ruined their books. It died alone and in agony, in the blue bag. Amulyo went and shook it out on the seashore.

This rat would not act in obstinate resistance like the one they had once seen. One evening at the beach a man had walked ahead of them, carrying a rat trap. The tiny rat peeped out of the trap, squeaking. He placed the trap facing the sea and opened its door. It saw the sea in front of it and was paralysed. It refused to come out of the trap. Squeaking aloud it clung to the bars. The man who had brought it there tilted the trap. He shook it hard. He banged at it. The rat obstinately refused to come out. Not knowing what else to do, the poor man settled down by the trap as if in penance, waiting desperately for it to come out. When they left the beach and turned around one last time, the rat still had not come out, and he still sat there waiting, so that he could take the trap home. It didn't seem as if the rat appreciated the man's obstinacy either. Both man and rat trap were silhouetted against the fading light of the sunset. In front of them, by the horizon, apartment blocks rose, like mountains.

Some days after all this, there was the advent of the sparrow. Standing in the balcony which could only accommodate one person comfortably, she looked down on the rubbish heaps below and the children sitting there defecating; then turned her gaze towards the old theatre opposite. An old Hindi film was showing there. The balcony doors stood open, perhaps to compensate for the breakdown of the electric fans. Through the heavy black curtains a song sung by Mukesh for Raj Kapoor came floating towards her. It was then that it fell, brushing against her shoulder. Startled, she moved, leaned down, and saw that it was a sparrow. A baby sparrow. One wing was broken and crooked. Inside its beak, its mouth showed, red as a berry. She was afraid to touch it. She filled an ink-filler and dropped water into its mouth. It opened its eyes. She carried it inside on a piece of cardboard and laid it in a corner. At night she covered it with a net basket.

When she lifted the basket in the morning, the sparrow shrieked. It circled about, calling out "ki-ki-ki." It tapped the ink-filler with its beak. Before she could recover from her shock, two birds alighted on the balustrade of the verandah parapet. Swiftly they flew down, and thrust little worms into the baby sparrow's mouth. With little relishing squeaks, it swallowed. Then it snuggled down once more.

In the afternoon, flying lessons began. One of the sparrows flew up and down, down and up; first slowly then rapidly. As soon as it stopped, the other one took over. The baby sparrow rose to its feet, raised itself into the air with its crooked wing, then fell. Until five in the afternoon the parent birds went on trying, incessantly. The baby sparrow gave up its attempt at flying and began to walk about. At last, the parent birds left the baby sparrow in her safekeeping, and flew away. The older birds came back for some days, but disappeared after that. The little sparrow could not fly further than five or six feet. It made its home against the first iron bracket of her book shelf. Unlike the rat which laid siege to the books stealthily in the middle of the night, this sparrow cast its droppings all over the books on that side, in broad daylight. One day, she knelt in front of it and sang, "Sparrow, little sparrow, do you know what has happened? My husband has gone away and not yet come home." The sparrow squeaked "kerk," making its protest clear. It was greatly attracted to red things. It shed its droppings most generously on books with red covers. When they came in late at night after a long time away, as soon as they opened the door, it called out sharply from the corner of the book shelf, expressing its disapproval loudly.

When she opened the window nearest the bookshelf, it immediately went and perched against the bars. As she gazed out at the buildings covered in factory smoke, standing out against a background of stench and noise, it was the little sparrow in the foreground that caught her eye. A sparrow that opened its jewelled eyes and looked outward.

When she rested her head against the window bars, and everything behind the curtain of rain turned into shadowy lines, the sparrow perched next to her. She narrowed her eyes and looked sideways, and the sparrow filled her vision. Behind it, the ash-coloured city extended. Like a city that was placed upon its head. Like a crown.

One day, after she had stood for a moment with her head against the window, eyes closed, she opened her eyes again to find the baby sparrow gone. She searched throughout the flat, calling out, "Kutty, Little One!" She came out into the verandah, calling loudly, "Kutty," when it peeped out from a hole in the outside wall of the apartment building. She could just catch a glimpse of its broken wing. As she stood there wondering anxiously how to save it from the clutches of a kite, or an eagle, or a vulture, it rose gracefully upward and then flew back into the hole. Another time it rose upward, demonstrating that it could fly. A third time, while Amulyo and she stood watching from the window, it rose high into the air, flew up and down harmoniously, and then disappeared into a tree that stood at a distance of fifty feet. There were several other sparrows there.

As far as the eye could see, there were long rows of buildings, with no space in between. Unrepaired walls, displaying their cracks. Curving lines of cement covering some of those cracks. Some walls tarred over, to prevent rain water from seeping through. Many-coloured clothes hanging on hooks extending from the verandahs. Green leaves sprouting from flowerpots on window sills. The city lay like a rakshasa, displaying all this. And in the branch of a tree that had somehow struggled its way up in the midst of it all, a little sparrow.

———

And then one evening, a little later, this happened. Street lights and shop lights and neon advertisements had all come on. The street was an ocean of traffic. Roaring double-decker buses; autorickshaws with their incessant noise as they wound their way in and out; impatient scooters and cars. An absolute deluge of noise. Amulyo entered the traffic stream, ran, shoved, pushed, and reached the other side. She got halfway across the street, and was stuck on the stone barrier, one foot wide, that divided the street into two. Amulyo stood on the other side, beckoning with his hands, "Come over." All around her, huge advertisement lights flashed, without even a foot's interval in between, assaulting her eyes. A red double-decker bus, with violent blue, yellow, and green lettering rushed past, practically scraping her back. Terrifying vehicles, stopping, screeching, and then overtaking each other. She sprang forward a couple of feet, then fell back again, frightened by a furious black car. Car horns practically squealed into her ears. Her face, her neck, her armpits, and her thighs were all streaming with sweat. And then a woman came next to her, holding a couple of empty fish baskets at a slant. She caught a whiff of smell from the baskets. With the one hand which was free of the baskets, the woman caught her by the waist. Holding her baskets high up to stop the traffic, the woman dragged her along. As soon as they reached the opposite verge, the fisherwoman left her at Amulyo's side and went on her way.

As she stood gasping for breath on that pavement covered with spittle, waste, cigarette stubs, vendors, and gutters, a place where all the city's noises seemed to gather and overflow, he suddenly appeared in front of them. In the city's language, he was a *bevda*, a drunk. The city behaved with kindness towards bevdas. If they stretched themselves out to sleep in buses or in trains, nobody shook them awake. "Bevda *hai*. . . He's only a bevda," they would say, and walk past, excusing him. Once, a bevda boarded a bus at midnight and obstinately refused to buy a ticket from the conductor. He stood there, shouting in Hindi, "Drink, drink, drink; drink in the evening, drink in the morning; drink at day, drink at night; drink, drink, drink." The conductor himself bought the man a ticket. The bevda said, "Wake me up at the temple," crashed down and slept. There

161

were temples all along the way. A wayside shrine to Sai Baba every ten feet. At which temple should he be woken up? "Poor old bevda," said the conductor.

The bevda came near her, and she realized he was middle-aged. When he was just about ten feet away, he slithered down, gently and in slow motion, on to the pavement. Nobody took the slightest notice. They just started walking around him.

He tried to get to his feet as she and Amulyo went up to him, but failed. He held out his thumb and forefinger, two inches apart, and smiled radiantly, saying, "It just got a bit too much." They helped him to his feet and made him sit up, leaning against a wall. "Are my chappals on my feet? Place them in my hands. Otherwise, these rascals will snatch them and make off." He hugged the chappals as soon as they were in his hands, and closed his eyes. A peaceful smile on his face.

When they reached the bus-stand, they joined the long queue. She leaned against the lamp-post nearby and started to laugh. A second later Amulyo joined in. They could not stop laughing.

River

It was Upen who had the idea. Crowds were jostling at the bus station. There was no place at all to sit out the next six hours. She thought she would retch and die if she heard that Tamil film song, interrupted in the middle by a kind of cough, just once more. A knot tightened at the pit of her stomach.

"Taru, the river flows close by. Why don't we go there?"

Taru thought about it. She didn't know much about rivers. She had been ten years old when she was shown the water flowing at the bottom of a small square hole and told, "This is the source of the river Kaveri." At that very instant a leech had attached itself to her thigh. When they had burned it with a cigarette and pulled it away, the blood had come spurting. She remembered the blood. Somewhere in the depths of her mind the notions of river and blood became one. But in no other way was she moved by rivers.

She had seen rivers when travelling on trains, far below; sometimes as narrow as the cord tying back her hair; at other times spreading like a many-headed Ravana. The rivers she had seen were glimpsed through the iron bars of the windows of her railway carriage, or flashing intermittently upon her eyes as the train rattled past the iron supports of bridges.

Their forms had been incomplete.

They were magical blue lines, but also sometimes brown as the bed of sand beneath, or water-weed green, or gutter-black and covered in soap suds. It seemed impossible to link all these images into the notion of a river.

"What do you think?"

"Very well. Come on."

When they reached the river bank, there were very few people there. A few men were swimming in the distance. Five or six women were washing clothes nearby. The river was dark grey, with touches of blue. They sat on its bank.

She looked at those women. They were laughing at something or other. Laughing, they beat their clothes against the stones, again and again. One of them was rubbing a piece of turmeric against a small stone. The glass bangles she wore moved up and down, rising and falling. She scraped off the ground turmeric and smeared it upon her cheeks, her feet and into her armpits. She dived into the water with a little leap, and lifted her head about a foot further away. Again she dived in, and reappearing still further away, lifted both hands high up and shook away the water from her hair sideways, starting from just above her ears. Very slowly. As if she had any amount of time to spare.

Taru watched the river flowing about the woman's waist.

"Taru, shall we go into the water?"

Upen stood ready to go in, having changed out of his clothes.

"You go in first."

He went a bit further, climbed in, walked along parting the water with his hands, and then began to swim.

The river flowed on, drawing to itself all that was going on, in it and about it, like a sannyasi, without being troubled or fragmented. That steadfastness seemed to loosen all the constrictions within her.

Women of the epics must have stared at the river water, having set afloat upon it small bamboo baskets carrying their babies. They had trusted the river as they set down their baskets upon its water, giving them a firm, thrusting punch with their hands. And as the baskets floated away upon it, the river too had changed its form. It was no longer just a river but the waters that supported life. The waters of the womb. The water upon which the tiny foetus floats. The river was but an extension of the same waters, into the world outside.

She looked at the river.

It seemed to offer protection. One could dare to put one's trust in it.

She opened her bag and took out a lungi. She tied it to her chest and removed her clothes.

She placed her feet in the river. When she was waist high in the swiftly running water, her feet began to tickle. Fish! They were biting her feet. She shrieked; then laid her head back and laughed out loud. Swiftly she dipped under and rose. She walked on, parting the water and splashing. The river spread out over her. She kicked her legs out again and again and began to float. When she lay back and looked up, the sun's rays shone right into her eyes. Again she wanted to laugh.

Trisanku

It occurred to her that the most difficult thing to accept about oneself was one's own mediocrity. There was nothing more terrible than having to live with that for the rest of one's life.

When she stood in front of her professor, asking a question, and quick as a flash, he exposed her with his reply, a sense of her own mediocrity would press back her tongue against her cheek, mocking her. She had a great desire to sit in the professor's room; to talk to him at length about the historical period he had researched; to point out the flaws in his arguments, sifting and separating them out; to become the teacher's teacher. But if she ever even mentioned a book which she had just read, he would immediately tell her about the article that had followed it.

Her mediocrity troubled not just her, but her professor too. It was put about that on the day she finished her thesis, 15 August, he had remarked to another professor, "My independence day. Anjana has finished her thesis." What hurt her even more was the occasion when he tossed aside the five pages of much rewritten material she had handed him, declaring there was nothing more he could do with it. He had then put pen and paper in her hands and told her what to say, without so much as leaving out a comma or a semicolon or a full stop. He had declared finally, "Now you have written it unassailably."

Sometimes she asked herself whether her timidity was because she was a woman.

But that couldn't be true.

Newly joined women students got to their feet without the least hesitancy in seminars of up to thirty people, asked the most ordinary questions, chewing gum the while, then turned to their neighbor to light a cigarette and casually blew out the smoke while awaiting the answer. Such self-confidence shocked her.

If she commented, "That professor is a genius," they answered her with contempt, taking it all for granted, "Who, he? Not bad. Spoke a lot of rubbish yesterday." She was envious of that kind of arrogance. She too would have liked to possess such hauteur.

But she could only tremble and bow low.

Had her father, an upper-division clerk, allowed the dog-like treatment he had received from his officer to pervade each rat-hole of a room of their tiny house off the Mavalli Circle in Bangalore, passing it on with his very looks, his breaths, his sighs, his words? Had she grown up breathing it in?

Deeply embedded in her mind was a picture of her father touching his officer's feet and crying out, "I am a family man. I have children. I'll never touch the money again." She had felt as if she had been forcibly stripped naked. A sense of being disgraced and humiliated had been born in her then, as if spittle from the onlookers fell upon her naked and ugly body.

She wanted to hit back in her turn.

All she could manage was an attitude of deference, bowing and bending, begging to be given the blow. When her father's officer picked her up in his car one rainy evening, and then asked her in Kannada, "What will you do now if I kiss you," she could not rage with the fury of Kannagi. She could only stare ahead, tears streaming down her face, thinking with fear of all the pregnant heroines she had read about, and of the inevitable tragic fate approaching her. As soon as she reached home, she went into the two-foot-wide bathroom, felt herself all over, and wept silently for her lips which had been bitten and her breasts which had been kneaded in return for the money her father had stolen long ago. Had the simple food that she ate, the curry leaf chutney and the plain tamarind *rasam* taken the fight out of her? She knew that her individuality had become like a dulled knife, and she herself was deeply troubled and tossed, like a puff of smoke, like a shred of floating cotton.

A stray wind's blowing that pushed her into her research on foreign policy.

Because she had a scholarship, her father was not put to any expense. Just once, he had said, "Why don't you get a job, my dear? At least it would help the family." She had looked at him with eyes full of longing, and pleaded, "Please, Appa, let me study. I don't wish to marry." He had never said anything after that.

It seemed that it was only her sort for whom everything was a huge mountain which made one either stagger with weariness, or press on with severity. When others skimmed through Toynbee and tossed him aside, she could only speak her opinion after thinking it over ten times. Even in her method of study there was some dogged quality which made her plod on until her back broke. Sometimes her programme of further study seemed to her not unlike the grades and promotions that a clerk seeks. Yet she hated with all her heart the thought of herself being such a clerk, a stenographer, a typist. She could only accept, to some extent, that somewhere in the depths of her mind there was this clerk-like quality.

The very thought of a life spent in going to work every day by electric train, reading either the *Vikatan* or *Kumudam*, gossiping about one's aunt's son or the clipped moustache next door, saving money each month for a foreign-made nylex sari, was bitter to her.

She wanted all her abilities to flower fully and completely, to take some god-like universal form, and for herself to be able to investigate and understand her innermost self. But there didn't seem to be any way to achieve this.

Every example of her limited knowledge created a kind of fear mixed with shame within her. If she dared to take a single step beyond her natural timidity, she felt a weariness, a lassitude, a total helplessness worse than that experienced by a whipped slave.

That was why she was so deeply wounded by what she took to be an April Fool's Day joke when Narasimha Rao said to her, "I love you." One evening she had come out of the college library, and started off in the direction of the bus stop, wiping her face firmly with her handkerchief as she went. Narasimha Rao had stopped her.

"Shall we have some coffee?"

"Oh, but I have to go as far as the Mavalli Circle."

"I'll drop you off on my motorbike."

"Did you want to talk about the term paper? I'm afraid I haven't finished mine yet."

"No, I didn't want to talk about that."

He ordered espresso coffees and then said quietly, "I love you very much."

It was the first of April that day. Her face tightened. "Can't you play your April Fool jokes on someone else? Here I am, minding my own. . ."

"Don't be an idiot," he said. "I'm telling you this in complete seriousness." When he took hold of her hand she got up quietly. She was wearing a brown handloom sari with a narrow yellow border, most inappropriate in that sophisticated restaurant. In the deliberately dimmed light her brow and cheekbones and chin glistened with an outbreak of sweat. Piteously she said, "I want to be somebody." Her throat choked.

He couldn't understand.

She sat down suddenly and did something that women do not usually do when they know they are loved. She dropped her head upon the table and wept, the deep sobs almost stopping her from breathing.

That was the end of such matters as love.

As soon as she finished her M.A. as an accredited student of Bangalore University, she registered herself to research into Hoysala art.

Although he had no connection whatsoever with her chosen

subject, she had to register under Professor Basavayya, and the research proceeded under the supervision of one of the other lecturers. It struck her that Professor Basavayya suffered from an extreme sense of inferiority. It was said that when he was in America, they treated him as a black among the other blacks. It was also said that when he was a poor student living in a Harijan hostel, he had been forced to marry the hostel warden's daughter because of his indiscreet behavior on some occasion. His wife was seven years older than he was. This was another black mark against him for people to point out. When American professors visited the university, he behaved towards them like a dog with its tongue hanging out. And they, too, treated him like their black slave, patting him and hectoring him by turns. He could never utter a single word in public without having to stop because of the onrush of spittle in his mouth. And before he could struggle through his stammering to explain himself, the other professors would have attacked him with their words and ripped him apart. At those times, there seemed to be no difference between the Harijan who was prevented from touching the well water in a narrow-minded village and this man here. In those educated surroundings, they attacked him with great finesse, but also with a mad rage, secretly declaring, "See, you have been uplifted indeed!" She sometimes thought that that face with its swollen cheeks would one day become distorted with tears.

Professor Basavayya had one means of escape. He liked young women. Anjana had not known this.

Once he had asked her to come on a Sunday, to collect an important book that she needed. His room was above the library, and had to be reached by going up a spiral staircase. She went. The professor told her that the book was in the cupboard. While she was looking for it, he came up from behind and pressed her hands against the wall. For an instant she had the terrible feeling that she would faint. But pulling herself together, she began running down the spiral staircase. The professor's steps followed.

Downstairs the library was locked. She attempted to raise a howl of distress. Frightened by this, he flung open the door saying, "Hogu, go away." She fled.

The trees, the grass, everything seemed gigantic, rising up high to attack her. Her breath came in long broken sighs.

After this she began to hate Hoysala art with a deep hatred. She might have informed the other students, torn away Basavayya's disguises, and sought protection for herself. She didn't do it. She assisted in short research projects lasting from six to eight months, spending the rest of her time staring at the yellowing walls of her home.

Then she read in the papers about a research institute in the north, which had been set up for work on international relations. She was invited for the selection examination and interview.

Her mind was an empty blank. A complete and utter blank. A stagnant pool in which no memory would appear. Even so, she went.

The general knowledge paper.

Who or what are the following:
Liaqat Ali Khan
Angola

Bhagat Singh
Tej Bahadur Sapru
Martin Luther King
Phnom Penh
Chile

1. What is your opinion about Gandhi's part in the
   Independence struggle?

2. What are the underlying precepts in the foreign policy ad-
   opted by the US towards the Arab states?

3. Some historians consider that the Russian revolution is an
   unfinished revolution. Why?

The letters flew about in front of her eyes like so many flies. Who
was Liaqat Ali Khan? A sitar player, like Vilayat Khan? Couldn't
be. This is an institute for international relations. Bhagat Singh was
a name that rang a bell. A hockey player? All Singhs were certainly
brilliant at games. She couldn't attempt a single one of the essay questions. All she could remember about Gandhi was his loincloth and
his toothless smile. She calmed herself. She said to herself, "Anjana,
you have passed your M.A. in the first class. You have studied about
all this in some fashion. Think. Think." Her brain swirled in confusion.

She came out.

"Gandhi was a bourgeois. The people that he trained to take over at Independence were capitalistic aristocrats with half-baked humanitarian values."

"I wrote that American Jews were an important factor in the consideration of American relations with the Arab States and Israel."

"Oh, I wrote of all that as a part of Soviet and American relations."

There were others discussing their answers in faultless, fluent English. She began to feel as if her legs were sagging weakly from the knees, like torn off pieces of cloth.

A peon summoned her to one of the lecturers from the department in which she had requested a place.

"Well, how was the general knowledge paper?"

"I could not answer a single question."

"You are an M.A. first class, aren't you?"

"Mm."

"What have you been doing, this past year?"

"I have been assisting in various research projects."

"Oh, well, never mind. Make sure you do well in the interview. The professor will be there."

"I'll try."

The personal interview. There were ten people there. One of them had her general knowledge paper in his hand.

"You have a good sense of humour," he said, looking at the other professors who were there, and winking.

She went red in the face.

"You say you want to do some research on Jews. Why?"

"They have suffered a great deal. They have been oppressed."

"More than the Tamil people?"

"Sorry. What was that?"

"Oh, come on Dr. Tripathi, don't confuse her."

He laughed.

"What were the changes in the political divisions of Europe after the Second World War?"

"One part came under Russian influence."

"Were there no other changes in these parts?"

"No."

"Not even in Yugoslavia?"

"No."

At this point another professor agreed about her good sense of humour.

"What journals of international relations have you read?"

"I can't remember."

"Any relevant books?"

"I can't remember."

"Please take your time. Tell us slowly, without getting nervous."

"No. I really cannot remember."

The professors looked at each other.

"Very well, you may go."

The professor of the department she had applied to accepted her, saying that she possessed a basic intelligence. (Or it may be doggedness.)

She started on her research. Here too, there was a fierce, animal-like competition. It was considered that a true intellectual would publish ten research papers in five years. The research students were caught up in the rat race, working with the haste of rats making for their holes, sometimes to the extent of sacrificing their integrity. Haste. . . haste. . . haste. . . There was no place for her there.

Ten years of hard work, disappointment, yearning, discouragement, lack of confidence, unemployment, lack of money, longing for love, bitter realization of her own limited knowledge. After that, her doctorate.

Even to this day she continued to be fearful, fearful, fearful of everything. Had she been an Egyptian slave in an earlier era, one who had been flogged? A black slave who had been too frightened to open her mouth and sing in cotton plantations? Had she been one of those Jewish women standing in front of the gun, eyes in a trance of fear? How was it that she was overwhelmed by such fear? It chased her like a serpent determined on revenge. As soon as the professor walked into the room and said, "What news," her tongue would cleave to her palate with fear. When she read out her research paper in seminars, fear made her voice tremble. Her uncertainty was such that her professor had to help her out if there were outsiders asking difficult questions.

She had been away from town for a few months, and had just returned for the beginning of the new academic year. She went into the professor's room. One of the lecturers from the department was also there.

"Professor, after hearing you speak yesterday, students from other departments have been speaking very highly of our seminars," the lecturer was saying.

"We'll ask Anjana to read a paper. Those illusions will soon disappear. They both laughed.

The professor had spoken in jest. All the same, she felt attacked. But she laughed, too, as if in agreement.

There was another seminar being held on that day. An overseas visitor was to speak at it. She determined that on that day she would speak out.

As soon as he had finished, she said in a ringing voice, "Professor, I don't agree with you."

Silence.

. . . She pointed out the cracks in the professor's middle-of-the-road exposition. She ripped apart his argument by referring to a couple of examples from recently published articles. She sensed the words pouring out of her without hesitancy or confusion, like a great flood that tears down a dam; words spreading all over the room, hanging everywhere. Her mouth burst open like a cave, and like animals coming out in a rage, the words sprang forth furiously to assault the ears with the speed and swish of whiplashes.

The overseas professor was totally taken aback. In a low voice he asked, "Who is this woman?"

"My student," said her professor. . .

When, still dripping and floating about in that joyous pride, she lifted up her head with a smile, there were voices, questions, replies, and laughter all about her.

"Since there are no further questions, the discussion is at an end," said the professor.

Yet another seminar was over. She rose to her feet, leaving her words to hang about like dead snakes filling the room with their stench.

The professor looked at her, twisting his lips in a grimace.

She thought that while she sat in the open fields with heavy eyelids, back bared to all passers-by, it was impossible to reveal anything freely, without fear or shame. Not even tears.

Trisanku is the King of the Ikshvaku clan who wished to perform a sacrifice which would enable him to ascend bodily into heaven. The celebrated sage Vasishta refused, declaring it to be impossible, and Vasishta's sons condemned him to become a chandala for his presumption. The sage Viswamitra, to whom he next applied, made it possible, and Trisanku finally rose into heaven. Here, his entry was opposed by Indra and the other gods, until it was finally agreed that Trisanku should hang with his head downwards, and shine among some stars newly called into being by Viswamitra.

Journey 3

As soon as the summer began, Amma would start planning the food-offering to Mariamman. When she began announcing twice a day, like a news broadcast, "It's absolutely burning hot. We must make a food-offering to Mariamman," Mythili would start to get excited. Because this short excursion was a special annual event. It always took place soon after the school holidays began. A little tour undertaken just by Marudayi who worked in their house, Marudayi's daughter Minakshi, and Mythili.

The Mariamman temple was at the Majestic. Amma undertook all the preparations for the offering, but would never go to that temple herself. Marudayi interceded on their behalf and worshipped Mariamman who prevented diseases like smallpox. "She is their deity, you see," Amma would explain to Mythili. Amma herself went to the temple of Kannika Parameswari at Malleswaram's 8th Cross Road. On each of the nine days of Navaratri, Kannika Parameswari was offered a different adornment. Turmeric, sandalwood, *kum-kumam*, *javanti*, jasmine buds, orange sections, *kadali* bananas, *kanakambaram* flowers, and finally a silk sari. Crowds surged in the temple at evening puja time. Amma usually took Mythili with her. When the screen parted to reveal the goddess in all her adornments, Amma would be transported. Folding her hands, she would begin to sing softly, "*Amba, ninnu nera nammidi*. . . Mother, in you I have faith." But it seems that the goddess who received all these adornments didn't have the power to prevent smallpox. Only Mariamman, who wrapped a bright red cloth about herself, daubed herself with kumkumam, and had huge staring eyes, had that power. And there had to be a Marudayi to act as a messenger from them to that Mariamman.

The preparations for the offering would begin with the question, "Marudayi, have you had your cleansing bath yet, this month?"

Once the discussion about Marudayi's state of ritual purity came to an end, a date was set for the food-offering. On that particular day, Marudayi would turn up at their house at earliest daybreak. She would finish all the household chores at top speed and have a bath under the tap in the backyard. She'd call Minakshi who was usually running around the extensive back garden planted with oleander, southernwood, and *kasi-thumbai* plants, and mango, jackfruit, plantain, papaya, and drumstick trees. "Ei, Minakshi, come here," she'd call out, and give her a bath too. Minakshi had curly hair. It spread out, flaring, before falling down her back. Marudayi would pour water over it, add *shiyakai* and scrub hard, while Minakshi screamed and screamed. She'd hold her firmly between her thighs and bathe her, while the little girl struggled to free herself, shouting, "Let me go, Aya, let me go." Sometimes Mythili, who was watching from the back door, would be called and bathed too.

After her bath, Marudayi went into the empty garage to change her sari. There were some saris which she kept only for special occasions, such as the bright green Chinnalampati sari with the imitation zari border, or Amma's old blue silk with its red border which almost hit you in the eyes, or else a glowing yellow handloomed cotton with black checks. She emerged from the garage wearing one of these with the same black blouse with red spots which went with all of them. She'd have fastened a *paavaadai* on to Minakshi – red with yellow dots, or purple with green stars – beneath her navel. The blouse above the paavaadai always stood a little short of her waist. Mythili often stood by the door to the backyard, waiting for the moment when Marudayi would emerge from the garage, with wet hair, her face covered in turmeric, and a big kumkumam spot on her forehead, holding Minakshi by the hand. In the back garden full of mango trees and plants, the very first rays of sunlight just beginning to glint, Marudayi would stand, looking like a woodland sprite. Next to her, Minakshi with her curly hair fanning out about her, a tiny sprite.

A big earthenware pot to cook the *pongal* offering. Another pot containing the rice, jaggery, coconut, bananas, and banana-leaf. Amma would have kept everything ready. By this time, Mythili too would have had her oil massage and bath, been dressed and adorned. She would stand next to her mother, her wet hair loosely plaited in order to allow it to dry, wearing her favourite green paavaadai, with a black velvet choli. Hers was a "bodice-paavaadai." The bodice was attached to the skirt and concealed the waist. She used to pester her mother, demanding a *naadaa* paavaadai, which tied around the waist with a string, just like Minakshi's.

Because Mythili and Minakshi were going with her, Amma would tell Marudayi not to take the bus. She gave her the fare for a *jutka*. Every year the return fare by jutka went up, from twelve annas to a rupee, a rupee and a quarter, and so on, until it was as much as two rupees on their last journey. Amma always added some small coins to the jutka fare. For Minakshi and Mythili to buy sweets.

Every time she said to Marudayi, "Marudayi, you won't take the child to *that side*, will you?," emphasizing *"that side."* When she said "the child," she meant Mythili. Apparently the other child, Minakshi, was at liberty to go to *that side*.

Marudayi would declare, "I won't do anything like that, 'Ma." *That side* was a place to be relished. A place that also aroused fear and excitement. A place where roosters, their screams rising and falling, or sheep calling out "me-e-e-e" as they were dragged along, were sacrificed, skinned in an instant, and cooked. A place where she and Minakshi stood with clasped hands, their eyes wide, their mouths gaping open. A place where the two of them walked about, asking each other about pain, blood, and death. Sometimes they would get piping-hot chicken pilau on sewn-leaf plates, the chicken meltingly soft, with cinnamon, clove, and pepper. Mouths watering, they would blow and blow on the rice, and then eat it.

When there were so many buses going to the Majestic, it didn't seem right to Marudayi to take a jutka. On their very first journey, just as soon as they had turned around after waving goodbye to Amma and the baby, Marudayi asked, "Shall we go by bus, Mythili?" After that, it became their regular practice.

All three of them would set off along the street leading to the Pillayaar temple. The bus stop stood on the main street, before they reached the temple. It was right in front of a shop with a placard announcing, "Ganesh Butter Stores." They could see the proprietor seated there, sometimes. He looked as if he himself had consumed all the butter in the shop. When her *athai* came to visit them from Trichur, she taught Mythili little songs. She taught her to dance, too. One of the songs she taught her went, "*Aanatalaiolam venna taraameda, ananda Sri Krishna, vaay mudukku. . .* We'll offer you as much butter as an elephant's head, joyous Sri Krishna, shut your mouth. . ." Every time she tried to imagine a person who ate as much butter as an elephant's head, the proprietor of Ganesh Butter Stores would come to mind, holding a flute. As she approached the bus stop, her walk took on the rhythm and tempo of a dance sequence her athai had taught her, where she entered the stage from one side singing "*Aanatalaiolam*," swinging her arm like an elephant's trunk.

When he saw them, the proprietor would ask, "Off to the Mariamman temple?"

Aanatalaiolam, aanatalaiolam. . . the tune and the rhythm running through her head, "Yes," she'd say.

"Come here."

Aanatalaiolam, aanatalaiolam. . . She'd go up to him, with Minakshi. He'd pick up two small packets and give them to the girls. Aanatalaiolam, aanatalaiolam. . . "Thanks, maama."

As they waited for the bus to come, they licked the butter. Until the bus arrived, "Aanatalaiolam, aanatalaiolam" filled the mind.

They had made a pact that on the outward journey, Mythili would have the window seat, and that Minakshi was entitled to it on their return. As soon as they reached the temple, Marudayi would make a hearth out of three stones and begin to cook the pongal. The two girls would hold hands and wander about, taking a look at Mariamman now and then. Once the offering was made, they would eat some of it, distribute the rest, and then leave. Amma had made it clear that they need bring home only the kumkumam *prasadam*.

It was only after this that the money saved by taking the bus rather than the jutka was squandered – in the shops spread all around the temple, loaded with hot, spicy fried peanuts smeared with chilli and turmeric; jujube fruit; ripe tamarind; parrot-nosed mangos; and sweetened balls of gram. Everything went into their stomachs. After that came sweet, sticky *javvu mithai*. The mithai-man held the sticky mass on a long stick. He could make whatever you asked from the sweet stuff – elephant, cat, peacock, rabbit, or deer. A rose-coloured sweet. The more one licked at it, the sweeter it tasted. Sometimes they bought glass bangles and put them on. As they licked away at the sweet, the bangles jingled up and down. Then came the journey home. As they got off the bus, lime sherbet from the corner shop, with ice-cubes afloat.

When they reached home, the kumkumam prasadam was handed over to Amma. And Amma would place the kumkumam on the foreheads of all three of them, saying, "Mariamma, keep us safe, di, Amma."

After that, the cross-questioning session would begin, starting with, "Where did you pick up the jutka?"

On the days that the proprietor of Ganesh Butter Stores had seen them, Marudayi would say, "We went by bus to Mallechpuram Circle, Amma, and found a jutka there." On other days, she'd answer that they found one at the 8th Main Road corner, or even at the next street. In every case, though, the jutka man would not have had time to turn into the 8th Main Road on the return journey. He was a man in a terrific hurry, insisting on dropping them off at the corner of the road and making off immediately. What sort of jutka drivers are these, Marudayi would complain.

"You haven't eaten any rubbish, have you, only plain sweets?" Amma would ask.

She and Minakshi would shake their heads vigorously in denial. Sometimes, even as they did so, their stomachs would be rioting. The spicy gram and ripe tamarind and javvu mithai would all be in collision inside them. Belching from the lime sherbet, she and Minakshi would run towards the toilet in the back garden. And so the journey to the Mariamman temple would end. Every time.

———

When her younger brother was four years old, he insisted obstinately on going along with them. On that occasion, Amma gave Marudayi the round sum of three rupees. As soon as they came out of the temple, Marudayi bought them javvu mithai, and as they were licking their elephant, rabbit, and deer, she said, "Mythili, there's a Tamil film running at Central Talkies. Shall we go?"

"M. . . m," Mythili murmured in assent.

Thambi was primed to reply properly to Amma's catechism. He learnt to repeat correctly, in telegraphic style.

"How did you get to the temple?"

"Jutka."

"What did you see there?"

"*Mari saami*."

"What did you eat?"

"Pongal."

"And what else?"

"Orange drops."

There was a huge crowd of women waiting for the afternoon show at Central Talkies. When Marudayi had bought six-anna bench-seat tickets, taken them to the toilet, and then ushered them inside, the film started straightaway. Because they were seated so close to the screen, they had to crane their necks upwards to see. The faces on the screen looked gigantic. In a very short time, it became apparent that the hero was up to something wicked.

"Corpse of a fellow," the *maami* next to them cursed.

"You're in for an evil time, da. Your wife is a chaste woman, da, a *pattini*," another woman put in.

"Look at your face and your chin! You'll go to hell," Marudayi commented, cracking her finger joints.

After the interval, just when they had finished their ice-lollies, and the film started again, Thambi began to whimper that he wanted to go to the toilet. Marudayi led him outside. When she came rushing back, she asked the neighbouring maami, "What's been happening, maami?"

"I tell you, this lecher has gone and fallen for that whore of a woman," the maami answered.

"Look at the way the slut is showing her teeth. Her mouth is wide and her cunt is wide," said Marudayi.

In the end, the man who had done wrong returned to his wife, and the audience roared its approval, "That's right, come to your senses, now!"

They came out, caught their bus, and arrived home. As usual, Amma touched their foreheads with kumkumam, and then asked, "Where did you find your jutka?"

Out of the blue, Thambi announced in his shrill voice, "Amma, we went to the cinema." Then he added, loud and clear, "A lecher fell for a whore. That slut's mouth was wide and her cunt was wide."

After that the excursions to the Mariamman temple ceased. Amma began to set aside some money in a yellow cloth for Mariamman. And with many prayers that Mariamman should not get angry, nor mind that the money was going into the safekeeping of the modest Kannika Parameswari, the offering was deposited in the hundi of the Parameswari temple.

Whenever their numerous uncles and aunts came to visit them, Mythili had the chance to see many films such as *Guna Sundari*, *Kanavane Kankanda Deivam*, *Tuukku Tuukki*, and *Manohara*. But without Marudayi's and the other women's special commentaries, her heart was not in it.

Parasakti and Others
in a Plastic Box

Spreading out some rice mixed with ghee on the windowsill, and giving it a sharp tap with the back of her spoon, Amma called to the crows in Telugu, "Krishna, *raa*." What was so special about Telugu remained a mystery. Though Dhanam's father was transferred often, and to such different places as Assam, Ahmedabad, Orissa, and Bangalore, Amma's language to the crows never changed. Even in faraway Assam, the crows came flocking to her, as soon as she called, "Krishna, raa." Perhaps crows are united in this matter of language. Amma had taught this very same language signal to everyone who was close to her. Even Dhanam's younger brother Dinakaran's American wife's child by her first husband called out to the crows, "Krishna, raa," whenever he came to India. The windowsill her base, and scorning all border disputes, Amma had established for herself a world where crows recognized no difference among states and nations.

Yet, sometimes it seemed to Dhanam that although it appeared to encompass only these small things – a drop of ghee, a spoonful of rice, and a windowsill – Amma's space wasn't just contained there. She imagined that the tapping of the spoon against the windowsill drew to it everything that happened outside that window, too. It would seem to her that her mother's space wasn't confined to a single identifiable shape, but was ever spreading outward.

Dhanam's elder sister Bharati's marriage had taken her to America, and then ended in divorce. Bharati was devastated by this. She was greatly distressed; overcome by panic, fear, and shame. Every time she took a step, she felt as if there was no firm ground beneath her feet. Amma agreed to their father's plea, boarded a plane, and went to her daughter's aid. Ten days later, a long letter arrived from Bharati.

Dhanam, Amma has arrived here. Two days after she came, the inland airline company on which she travelled telephoned, harassing her to accept a contract to make wild-lime pickle for them. Apparently, Amma declared it at the customs' examination. They must have tasted it as a check. As if this weren't enough, on the fourth day, when I came home from work, I saw that she had just finished stirring up some *paal-kova*, which she had made out of a couple of litres of milk. When I asked her about it, she said that she had seen three pregnant women in the neighbourhood. The paal-kova would be good for their health. Then she dragged me along with her, explained to them that these were milk-sweets, pointed out that they contained saffron, and left me to enlarge on the many wonders wrought by saffron for both mothers and children. (Amma has brought a small container of high-quality saffron with her. She hasn't explained, to date, why she felt obliged to bring it. It's exactly like the lack of answers to questions about the wild-lime pickle.) Now I'm terrified that these women will invite her to be present when they give birth.

There's plenty of sunshine here. I can guess that Amma's hands are itching to make *vadagam*. Do you remember how, in Bangalore, she used to wear a hat against the sun, and squeeze out vadagam? How she used to leave us both on guard, with an open umbrella tied to a stone beside us, to frighten away the crows? Do you remember how we used to imagine that we were like Valli and her friends when they were chasing the birds away, in that old play from Independence times, "*Valli's Wedding*;" and how we used to sing, "O white, white storks"? What Independence struggle did we see; what after all did we understand by "*aalolam*"? It was that song that Amma taught us, wasn't it, that went, "You sparrows who come from elsewhere, who squat upon our land and peck at our fields, despoiling India..."? How furious we used to get as we sang those words! Even today, it seems to me, if Amma were to make vadagam, we could sing the same song with the World Bank and the International Monetary Fund in mind.

My window here doesn't have a sill. I've put in a wooden attachment, though, to hold flowerpots. Amma lays out rice there, and calls, "Krishna, raa" every day. How can there be crows here? But from the second day, the squirrels began to arrive. Now, as soon as they hear the sound of the spoon tapping, they turn up, big as bandicoots. Amma's friends. Even amongst these, she's looking out for a couple of pregnant ones. Maybe she'll mix an herbal potion into their rice, who knows? When I think about it, it seems to me that this coded language in which Amma speaks to crows and squirrels is actually one which binds the earth and sky together. In a strange way, it's like *vajram*, cementing us together and keeping us from withering away.

Amma hasn't asked me a single word about Kumarasamy. Nor has she spoken about the divorce. She carries on with her own business, making mustard seasonings, fragrant with ghee. If I am gazing out of the window, she nags at me to come and grind a chutney in the blender. Or, she will explain to me at length how a *poriyal* of finely chopped banana flowers, when soaked in buttermilk and cooked with a well-ground masala of onion, ginger, cumin seeds, and coconut, is very good for the health. How is this information useful to me here, in this town, where banana flowers are not to be found? But all the same, Dhanu, the backyard of Paatti's house in Coimbatore spreads out in my mind. How many banana trees stood there! In the front courtyard, by the threshold, there were traveller's palms with fan-shaped leaves. Do you remember that photograph of the two of us, sitting on the *thinnai* there? I can see it even now, my narrow face, hair combed flat, plaited with a fibre ribbon and taken over my shoulder; all my teeth showing in a grin. I often wonder about the eucalyptus sapling that we planted together before Thaatha sold the house, and whether the present owners have let it grow and not cut it down.

When I asked her to come and take care of me, I never imagined she'd create all these jobs for herself with the speed of a whirlwind. In a street close by, where they sell Indian groceries, there's a shop run by a Tamil. Amma has had a couple of conversations with him already, about Tamil Nadu politics. She is trying to break up the everyday routine and discipline that I need so much for my work. She irritates me no end. She makes me yell, "Amma, leave me alone!" All the same – you won't believe this – I've gained a whole kilo in just these ten days.

Day before yesterday, when I came home Amma was singing "*Dikku theriyaada kaattil*. . . In the forest where I cannot find my way." After expanding on the line, "Flowers like fragrant embers in the heart," when she came to the words "Weary of limb I sank down to the ground," Dhanu, I leaned against the door and wept. You sang that very song at school, at the Bharati song competition, wagging your head and shaking your two plaits, this way and that.

We went to visit the Sivanesans, who work at the University here, at their home. During the conversation, Amma discovered that Tilakam Sivanesan's mother was her childhood friend Shenbagam from Vilaatthikulam. It seems

Shenbagam's family were very much involved with the Self Respect Movement. Amma then sang the Bharatidasan song she used to sing with Tilakam's mother, "Rise up, you noble Tamil women, like many moons in a single sky! Arise and make good the humiliation to your finest heritage, the Tamil language!" Tilakam was completely overwhelmed. It seems that her mother died when Tilakam was still a child. She was so moved, and kept saying over and over again that she had not known all this about her mother.

"All the same, my mother has kept her belief in God," I told her.

"Amma, do you go in for elaborate *pujai* and all that?" Tilakam asked.

"I've only brought four idols or so in a small plastic box," Amma said in reply.

When you open Amma's plastic box, you'll find a small Amman, a Sivalingam, Ganapati, Murugan, a baby Krishna on all fours, and some other gods. I really don't know, Dhanu, whether she has come here as a woman on her own, or whether she has rolled up the whole world and brought it with her in her bag.

———

Once Bharathi was connected again to the squirrels, to the minutiae of her neighbours' lives, to food tasting of salt and tamarind and chilli, and to the Tamil songs that she had totally forgotten, their mother returned home. It was only later that they realized that she had actually met and spoken to Kumarasamy. Some members of his family came one day to bring back various pieces of jewellery, silver vessels, and such things. Amma served them an elaborate meal and sent them on their way. When Dhanam asked her, "Why, Amma, did you ask them to return all this, then?" she retorted, "All this belongs to Bharathi, doesn't it? Didn't we give it to her for her own use?"

Nobody spoke about Kumarasamy after that. A couple of years later, when Bharathi came home, having married a Gujarati, Amma gave her the jewellery. She sold the silver vessels, and gave her the money, to spend in India.

———

As Dhanam watched her mother calling to the crows, Amma turned round and came towards her.

"Have you eaten, Dhanam?"

"I ate a dosai at the restaurant before I came. I didn't actually plan to come here. That's why."

Amma sat down to eat. Once she had begun eating, Dhanam asked her, "What have you decided, Ma?"

Amma was quiet for a while. A month had gone by since Appa died. The owners of the house kept on asking for it to be vacated.

"Tell me, Ma."

"What can I say? Your father left me in this state. How much I nagged him to build our own house! He always said, "Why do we want such a headache." Now he has left me to struggle alone, without a place of my own..."

———

"Why do you say that, Amma? You must stay only with Bharathi and with me. You can go occasionally to Dinakaran, if you want to."

"That's a fine thing. When you yourself are having such a difficult. . ." she dragged the words out, hesitantly.

Dhanam's husband Sudhakar had tried to set up a business, and had overreached himself. There had been a huge loss, to the extent that all their savings were gone. It was this that Amma meant.

"That's nothing, Amma. I will take you home and look after you," Dhanam told her.

"I didn't say no, now, did I? Do I need a mansion or a palace, after all? Rice for one meal, rice-water for the next, that's it. It is love that is important, di."

"Don't all your things have to be packed?" asked Dhanam.

"What things do I have, di? I'll just put my four deities into a plastic box, and be ready to leave."

But it was only when Dhanam and Sudhakar came to help her pack, having taken a couple of days' leave, that certain matters became clear. Everything that Amma possessed had a story: the shiny, dark red stone with stripes which she had picked up in Haridwar before Bharathi was born, the frying pan that she had bought for eight annas when Bharathi was just one year old, the tiered standing-lamp with her name, Kumuda, etched on it, which had been presented to her when she visited her parents for the first time after her wedding. She went round and round the house in vain, unable to decide what to keep and what to throw away. It didn't look as if she would get rid of anything, easily – not the chest of drawers with a mirror that she had brought away after Paatti died, nor the dolls that Bharathi,

Dhanam, and Dinakar had stored away, nor the bound volumes of serialized stories, nor the green trunk full of letters, nor the recipes for Siddha medicines and the cookery notes that she still collected. Like the rakshasa who would die if you crushed the bee that was hidden in a small box and placed in the hollow of a tree across the seven seas, Amma's very life was buried in each and every one of these things.

Dhanam and Sudhakar made a few quick decisions. For the time being, they rented a car-shed that was not in use, two houses away, and deposited all Amma's things there, carefully. And after that, Amma came to stay in Dhanam's house with seven or eight pieces of luggage – including the plastic box – and her vinai. That vinai had been packed with care every time Appa was transferred. A vinai that had been bought for Amma in Andhra, when she was only six years old. A vinai carved out of dark wood. She had made a cover for it out of an old sari, to keep it free of dust. There was not enough space in Dhanam's house for it to lie horizontally as it should. They had to lean it upright against a wall, supported by a piece of wood.

Amma looked for a suitable place, in Dhanam's atheistic household, to open her plastic box. In the end, the box with Amman and the other deities climbed on to one of a set of shelves intended for books, which they had fixed behind a door.

—•—

One evening, a week later, Dhanam sat close to the table at a window writing a letter, while watching the parrots as they alternately flew about or settled down on the fruit tree outside.

—

Bharathi, Amma has come to my house now. But she is not at peace. There isn't the fuss and excitement of preparing meals every day, here. Until he can decide on what to do next, Sudhakar is mostly at home. Some bread and an egg, and his meal is done. At the most he'll make a *kichidi* with rice, dal, and vegetables all cooked together, and eat that. The regular cooking is only for Amma. A couple of times she tried to insist that Sudhakar should eat. Then one day I said to her, "Amma, Sudhakar will cook for himself whatever he needs. Leave him to his own ways. We must allow each other that much freedom, Ma."

"Is that what you call freedom? I can't understand it," she fretted.

As soon as she arrived, she was anxious to make all those things like *rasam* and *sambar* powders before the monsoons set in. Now, look, within one week, all these powders are ready in my house. And there are still three months to go before the beginning of the rains! Day before yesterday she went and bought a quantity of limes, chopped them up, and made salt pickle and hot pickle in two separate lots. Ginger *murabha* and ginger pickle have also been prepared. Because of something that I said casually during the course of conversation, she went out in the hot sun, bought a lot of greens, which she has now cleaned and kept ready. She thinks that we have to do so much thinking for our jobs and such, so she has boiled up some oil with hibiscus flowers in it, for massaging our heads. In anticipation of Sandhya's holidays from the Rishi Valley school, she has made fried snacks and packed them in a tin. Meanwhile, all sorts of divisions have been established in our house: good water (which Amma has collected) and ordinary water (which we have collected); vessels in which meat and eggs have been cooked, and vessels in which they have not; Amma's plates and our plates.

Of course, the plastic box for the gods is quite a small one. But within three days, this matter of Amma's *pujai* has expanded, spilling along the wooden plank beneath, accompanied by a brass pot, a plate for the camphor offering, a decorative *kolam* pattern, incense sticks, sandalwood paste, *kumkumam*, and flowers. Her jobs in connection with the gods keep on increasing: scrubbing them with tamarind and bathing them; offering them milk and raisins; dressing Amman in different skirts and *davanis*, and decorating her with sandalwood and kumkumam. The little girl from next door is roped in, because the milk and raisin *prasadam* needs a recipient. Then, because the little girl's mother's sister-in-law doesn't have any babies, Amma has to prepare a Siddha medicine for her. When Lingamma's husband, from the house opposite to us, has a headache, she'll grind up a mixture of dried ginger and pepper in milk, at nine o'clock at night.

Amma's gods can be contained in a small plastic box, it is true. She can pick up that box and fly wherever she chooses. But in order to return, she needs a place which contains the brass vessels etched with her name, Kumuda; her teakwood cabinet; her bureau with its wire-mesh doors; a place with windowsills. A place with a jasmine bower and a snake-gourd vine; a place where her vinai can be laid as it should be, horizontally. She might sing that Thevaram which begins, "Forsaking all other attachments, on your sacred feet alone my mind is intent." But Amma is one who is deeply bound to the earth. Even though she might float free like cotton wool, she'll always feel the need to touch the earth again. Certainly, she could stay either at my house or at yours. But it is bound to be hard for her. She'll tell a thousand little lies: this one to hide that, that to hide this. It's not just that Amma needs a place to live; she must reign indisputably in that space. Because Amma isn't just an individual, she's an institution. Her need is not simply a small space in which she can keep her plastic box. The pity is, she is wandering about seeking after a realm of her own. And if you and I wish to do so, we could give it to her. The jewellery that you and I possess were all given to us by Amma. If we were to sell these, we could give her house back to her. The owners are still trying to sell it. Dinakaran can send her a fixed amount each month. In a couple of months, Sandhya will finish her schooling and come home. She is eager to go and stay with her Paatti. So with many long-term schemes such as learning English so that she can talk to your children, embroidering *salwar-kameez* sets that Sandhya can wear to college, giving music lessons, planning her autobiography, grafting roses, and setting out spinach plots, Amma will live happily in her own house.

When she had finished writing, she looked up to see her mother seated in the easy chair, gazing out at the street. The green parrots had ceased their restless flying about and were quiet, hidden among the leaves.

Wheelchair

She knew at that moment that she must go away from that place at once. It was not because she took fright at the sight of blood. But it became clear to her that this blood that was being shed was in no way within the permitted bounds of justice. When those first few drops appeared, singly and so unexpectedly that for an instant she almost fainted with the shock, and then began to flow rapidly, spreading crimson over his forehead, and eyes, and nose, and mouth, she knew with certainty that she must make an end that very day. All her quarrels, her arguments, the misgivings that she had hitherto justified, her disaffections and fears, rose up like demons clad in red, standing like a rearguard behind that blood.

She walked away.

The boy from the thatched corner shop saw her and asked, "Tea, didi?"

She nodded and sat down. Nambiar and Meena, who were already there, looked up and came to sit by her, asking, "Has the struggle finished so soon?"

"No. I didn't feel very well. I came away."

"Headache?"

"Mm."

"It strikes me that these headaches and monthly pains all reflect the enforced repressions of the lower middle class. Look, Meena doesn't suffer from any of these things. Do you know why? She has no obstacles by way of money worries. Isn't that so, Meena?

Reasons. Reasons. Reasons. For headaches, for constipation, for facial pimples, for hiccoughs.

Everything had to be subjected to the rules of logic, researched in depth, analysed with the whole weight of one's knowledge; broken down, separated into tiny glass containers, their reasons written on labels and pasted on. . .

She thought of herself as a much-used legal file, the edges bent and crumbling with much fingering. Written on its front cover would be: Hitha, a representative of the lower middle class. Characteristics: given to mental struggles because of insecurity, tending to be emotional and to be emotionally dependent.

"Well, Hitha, am I right?"

Nambiar had studied at Oxford. It was given out that when he went there, he had taken with him ten suits tailored to his measurements. He returned wearing pajamas and kurtas. At the university, he was one of those most enthusiastically on the Left. He only smoked bidis. At times he would even be seen in torn kurtas. The only attributes he was unable to abandon were his Oxford mannerisms and his Ambassador car. He spoke with a bidi in his mouth, but his tongue could only manage an English "r." He found it impossible to learn to speak either Malayalam or Hindi. But he fully believed that he could convert the working-class people of Kerala to his way of thinking through his bidis and kurta-pajamas alone. He spoke with emotional fervour of the time when he himself converted to the Left:

"I was walking in Paris on a bitterly cold winter's evening. I had gone there for the vacation. There was a little girl, without shoes, her feet red with the cold, heels cracked and chapped, wearing scarcely any warm clothes, picking up pieces of coal in the snow. I couldn't bear the injustice of it. I joined the Left that very day.

Hitha asked him once, "Is there less poverty in the lanes and slums of India than in Paris, or what? Or does the lack of snow make it an easier life here?"

Nambiar became angry. He called her an anti-intellectual. Another time he castigated her saying she was a bourgeois who accepted everything and wandered about holding on tight to her own security. It was on that occasion that he told her about the Indian village he had seen for the first time.

"I was sitting outside, in the garden. The tap was just next to me. A woman came by, she might have been a servant. 'Open the tap, please,' she said. 'Why can't you do it yourself?' I asked her. 'These people are Brahmins; I am a Harijan woman,' she replied. Look at the restrictions of caste, Hitha. I couldn't stand it."

"That's existed for a long time, Nambi. It has been there many years before you went to Oxford, and it's still there today."

"Ah, we have to dig very deep down, to uproot such superstitions, to throw them away and bring about change."

"You sit tight in your chair. There will be others to do the digging, and while they are about it, to uproot the likes of you."

"You are trying to humiliate me, Hitha. I accept it only because you belong to the Party. I know you are only a bourgeois, going about seeking security."

"And you?"

Nambiar was not without his own mental struggles. He had freed himself from his class boundaries with difficulty, and managed to fall in love with the daughter of a clerk who lived in one of those little houses that had to be passed when one went from one part of the university to another. He was holding forth one day in his broken Hindi, giving a detailed account of the horrors committed in Vietnam by a capitalistic United States, when she used the end of her sari to wipe her baby brother's nose. Suddenly his stomach turned. He suffered great remorse because of his feeling of revulsion. But at the same time, he could not deny that it was much easier to be in love with Meena, whose father possessed lakhs. She had the time, the intelligence, and the opportunity – all three – to think about independence and to try to experience it to the full. It was easy for her to unite herself with Marxist principles. She had no difficulty in understanding the horrors of Vietnam, the problems of black Americans, the harijan struggle, class war, and even the reasons for hating her own class. Nor was she unaware that spending thirty-five rupees for a Peter Pan bra or fifteen rupees for a pair of panties could be at variance with those same Marxist principles. It was not difficult to be in love with someone who argued that to be aware of one's own inconsistencies was actually a victory for Reason.

The tea arrived.

"Hey, Hitha, what are you thinking about?" asked Meena.

"Nothing." The tea felt warm to her throat.

"Have you quarrelled with Gautam?" Meena was laughing.

"Nothing like that."

"What's happened then?"

As she was asking the question, Gautam came in, in a great hurry. Tenderly he placed a hand against her fingers which were pressed around the teacup.

"What's the matter, Hitha, why did you come away so suddenly? Are you not feeling well? Headache? Mm?" he asked in Tamil.

"A headache," she said in a low voice.

He drank a mouthful from her cup. "Right," he said to her, "I'm off. You go home straightaway. Don't bother to cook a meal. We'll see to things after I get home." Then he left on his own, saying to Meena and Nambiar, "You two stay here."

Nambiar, who had understood what Gautam had said to her in Tamil, commented, "Gautam needs your support even in this small struggle."

It seemed to her that it would have been better if it had not been so. She had a sense that all the work she had done among the students in the past two years as his inseparable companion, and her total belief hitherto that there was nothing else she could have done, was today laid bare at the very roots to the swing of a hatchet. She experienced a pain as if all her nerves reverberated from such a swinging blow. It was as if that pain caused fissures and cracks in her from which all the doubts and disagreements that for so long she had firmly suppressed now crawled out like crabs, making her whole body shudder as they walked all over, pressing their claws into her.

"Okay, Hitha, you'd better go home. You really look as if you are ill," said Meena.

Hitha rose. She handed the boy some money.

"Okay," she said and began to walk away.

If she walked all the way, it would take her half an hour to get home. Never mind. This was one thing about her that Gautam genuinely admired. Her stamina. Her good health, which, like a lightning conductor, absorbed all physical pain. He was astonished by her thighs, her calf muscles, her arms – all as firm as rolling pins. Such sturdiness, he would say, was the birthright of her class. As for him, he was torn to pieces every time he got an attack of asthma. His was a delicate body. He only got illnesses that required expensive medication. "Diseases appropriate to the moneyed class," he would say, laughing. He'd take her hand and say, "These are sturdy fingers."

"No. These are fingers that have been put to use," she would answer, pointing to the scars acquired from grinding flour, and to the fingertips worn down from scrubbing vessels.

She was used to confronting troubles and obstacles without having to formulate complex strategies; without having to refer to guiding doctrines. Because she knew very well about hunger, shame, reproach, and contempt, she tended to oppose injustices with nothing but a blind emotional fervour, an intense rage.

Once Gautam said to her, "You can't achieve anything single-handedly. Doesn't it ever strike you that you need my help?"

At that time she was both studying and working. Kishori Lal

was an office boy at her place of work. He did not get the health certificate that he required, to comply with the office rules for employment. The reason given was that he was underweight for his age. She had seen Kishori Lal's house. It was in Panchkuyya Street, by the sweepers' lane. It had seemed to her that the pervading smell of faeces was not conducive to anyone's gaining weight in that area, except, perhaps, for pigs. It struck her as an unbearable wickedness that a system which did not make it possible for a boy to attain the weight appropriate to his age should then make that a reason for dismissing him from work. She fought for the boy.

It was at that time that Gautam asked his question.

"No. I'll only get crushed within the confines of a party. Just leave me to fight my battles on my own."

Not only was she defeated, she lost her own job as well. Then at last she realized that it was not a matter of Kishori Lal alone. What she had to oppose was not merely the brother who hit her with his shoes, and the sister-in-law who ordered her to scrub vessels until her very fingers seemed to burn away. It wasn't even possible for her to believe any longer that her father, who had put all his desires, longings, disappointments, and hardships into one wheelchair, the one in which he would one day end his life story, was the one and only example of life's injustices. He was only a means of introducing her to them. The bitterness and hatred that her brother had awakened in her as he opened the creaking padlocked door at eight one evening and pushed her out even while her wheelchaired father watched with ash-covered eyelids and paralysed gaze; the fire that was lit in her belly during that night of distress – it was because of these things alone that she had battled thus far. She admitted as much, to Gautam.

Then she was unemployed. She accepted the generosity of Gautam's married friends, a room to live in, food to eat; with the same commitment with which she worked for her exams she united herself with Gautam's politics. But she was not without doubts that niggled at the back of her mind.

After they had attended seminars such as that on "The responsibility of students in a changing society," after those debates on social consciousness, equality in education, and consciousness raising, after the discussion that continued over beer with Agarwal, Prasad, and Nambiar in Gautam's room, when at last she lay down alone on the terrace under the stars, questions would gleam in her mind.

Is this really what I want?

After she and Gautam had decided to live together, the question raised its head many times.

"Agarwal has no right to talk about peasants and agricultural methods."

"And why not?"

"He hasn't even met a peasant farmer. He doesn't even know that most peasants still use a wooden plough. When I tell him so, he gapes at me with his mouth open, the idiot."

"So what? Is that such a huge flaw in him? This is your whole problem. You think everything should be perfect, without the tiniest fault. Do you think it will be Agarwal who is actually going to transplant the rice? He will be an expert at theory. He will be the one to make policies."

"Perceiving India from Delhi alone?"

"Are you being sarcastic?"

"No, Gauta. Sometimes I have the picture in my mind of a frightful cultural island. Everybody is sitting around, continually talking about American democracy and Russia's unfinished revolution and about the Chinese revolution, and about factories and factory workers. Amongst themselves and for themselves. They slap one another on the back. If one of them exclaims that blood must flow and that the revolution has got to come, ten of the rest praise him and pour him a whisky. At first they speak out because they have something to say. Later they continue because they like the sound of their own voices. In the end they begin to believe that what they say is the actual truth. You can hear the sound of their voices everywhere, like the howling of dogs, reverberating like drumbeats."

"Hitha, can't you hear how incoherent you sound?"

"I'm not playing a game, Gautam. Sometimes, there is a real battle going on inside me."

"Madness."

If she were to explain to him about this morning and begin an argument, he would put it aside in the same way. For him, it was only a strategy for self-preservation. A mere strategy to attack a man in a wheelchair as soon as they realized they were only ten individuals and that the people opposing them numbered over thirty. A mere strategy to beat them with cycle chains as soon as they gathered round the disabled man, and to run away. She knew very well how the conversation would go.

"When the entire royal family was committed to the guillotine at the end of the French Revolution, do you think it was rose water that they sprinkled about? It is blood that needs to be spilt," he would say in his fluent English.

"Gauta, he was a cripple. This was no strategy. It was a crooked path we took."

"I don't do my work in order to gain a certificate from you, Hitha."

"But why can't you understand what I say?"

"Because I am not one of your humanitarians who kiss orphaned children and believe that the world can be changed through love. I am a revolutionary. It's that language alone that I understand."

"What I'm saying isn't humanitarianism. I'm saying that you can't turn an unjust act into a just one by referring to the revolution."

"It is all part of the same thing. I do not wish to say any more."

She had realized that Gautam's sense of "justice" was not one that he had formulated by himself, but rather one whose bounds had been set by others. It was similar to the way he had acted in the business over Mahesh.

Mahesh's father was an important lawyer based in Lucknow. A believer in nonviolence. Mahesh was nonviolent in Lucknow and a revolutionary in Delhi. He had been close to Anandi for three years. When the nonviolent father raised objections about her caste, the revolutionary immediately accepted them. There were a few lakhs implicated in those objections anyway. It was Hitha who had wandered about with Anandi to prevent the birth of an heir to the revolutionary.

"This is really base, it is making use of a woman," she had said. He had replied, "He's one of us. We can't give him up."

"Do all the rotten things he does become just simply because of his service to the revolution? There is no difference whatsoever between a revolutionary and any other man when it comes to treading upon women."

"You are confusing the issue by bringing in the question of women's freedom."

"Where's the confusion? It is all perfectly and absolutely clear. We used to be conned in the name of motherhood, compassion, womanhood, chastity. And now too we are cheated in the name of modernity, freedom, and the revolution."

"Enough, Hitha. Where has your brain gone? I will not betray Mahesh. Leave it now. It's not our business."

That's how that affair ended.

She was home. She unlocked the door, went in and fell upon her bed. For a few minutes, she had the feeling that she had become a material object in the room, like the chair, the table, the bed; the four walls narrowed about her, becoming a coffin bearing her as she gradually grew rigid.

She had been born through an accident, in the days before there were contraceptive pills. She had felt rejected by all those around her. By her mother first of all. Then by her brother and sister-in-law.

She needed love with a huge hunger. Gautaman had never understood this. Whether it was because in his family they had showered him with money in place of love, she did not know, but both her love for him, and his friendship for her were like necessary weaknesses that he merely endured.

On one occasion, when they were together, at a most intimate moment of lovemaking she had asked him, "Do you love me?"

He had freed himself and turned away. He had made her sit up. "Why have you asked me this question now?"

"I just felt I had to ask you."

"What's the difference between you and the heroine of a two rupee novel? It is possible for you to think about the revolution. You have been able to accept a relationship like ours without any difficulty. Then how can you ask such a question?"

"Are we together only to help to bring about the revolution? Then you could be with anybody else, couldn't you?"

"Desire, love, compassion – these are all bourgeois diseases."

"Are they not going to exist after the revolution?"

"After the revolution there will be justice. There will be honesty. There will be work. There will be equality."

"No, Gauta, there will be this too. Surely an important goal of our revolution is that love and friendship should change altogether from being mere words for cheating and using each other. Not to kill all feelings. The revolution is to make us more human; not to turn us into castrated creatures."

He got up with a quick sound of disgust and lit himself a Charminar.

216

In the darkness, the cigarette ends glowed. One, two, three, four, five Charminars. When at last her eyes, weary from watching, began to close, he shook her awake.

"Hitha, in what sense can I say the words, 'I love you?' There is no value attached to those words as we use them ordinarily. If I use them for a different meaning, then I have to understand that first. And if I say them now, what certainty is there that they won't be mere words in order to use you, for the comfort of this one night? Mm?"

What he said seemed true enough. She was thoroughly confused.

She used to be very fond of Pankaj Mullick's Hindi songs with their Bengali resonance. That voice seemed to her to throb with life, and at the same time, to suggest the moment of death, and of life's departure. She was not unaware of the falsehood inherent in those love songs. Yet there were times when she could really enjoy them.

She was immersed in those songs one day when Gautaman came in with Meena, Nambiar, Agarwal and two others.

"Turn that off, Hitha." Gautaman said the words casually and went to fetch the glasses. Nambiar took the bottles out of his bag. Hitha felt as if she had been slapped hard. As if he hadn't respected her as a woman. She didn't move to switch off the record player.

"Hitha, turn off the record."

"I want to listen to it."

The emphasis in her voice made him look up in some astonishment. Meena and Nambiar exchanged glances.

"Why don't you stop listening to all this sentimental nonsense?"

"Why don't you stop flying to your Chivas Regal? Why don't you stop your upper-class habits, talking revolution and drinking whisky?

Meena hung her bag on her shoulder. "Well, Gautam, don't you think it is time for us to go?"

Gautam's face tightened.

He said, "Don't, Meena," and rushing to the record player, pulled out the plug and flung it aside.

For a second, Hitha was totally taken aback by his rage. Then to his complete surprise – why, hers too – she took a couple of strides forward and kicked aside the bottles. Her foot was pierced by a splinter of glass. Blood flowed, mixing with the alcohol, seeming to burn through her.

The rest got up and left. She sat down in the midst of the spilt alcohol, surrounded by splinters of smashed glass, put her head on her knee while her foot bled freely, and began to weep. He stood there and looked at her and then walked out. She wept for a long time.

When Gautaman returned in the evening, the room had been tidied up completely. There was a rather large bandage on her foot. When she hobbled to the door to let him in, he glanced at the foot briefly and then came in without a word. He sat down on a chair.

She began to spread some old newspaper on the floor in order to put down the dishes of food.

"I am not eating, Hitha."

She lifted her head with fury. "What is the difference between you and an average husband? He beats his wife, goes off to his gambling and comes home after eating at a restaurant. If he's rich, he'll drink at his club before coming home. At home he'll remain aloof and stiff so that his male pride isn't diminished in any way. What revolution are you capable of?" He went and lay down without speaking to her.

Sadness welled up within her. She, who had mocked him for being like an average husband, had actually expected, like any average wife, that he would pacify her with something that she liked: with gifts such as jasmine flowers, *jilebis*, gin. Yes, she had indeed limped rather obviously when he came in. She hadn't quite imagined the crudity of a dialogue that began, "I behaved like an animal, Hitha, forgive me," and "Nevermind, it's the hands that hit that also embrace." But she knew that her expectations were of that order, all the same. She fell asleep that night, pierced by thoughts of the contradictions that remained with her and the ordinariness that characterized them both.

She thought about their relationship with a kind of surprise mixed with fear.

Who was Gautam?
    A revolutionary?
    A reactionary?
    A research student?
    A student leader?
    A clever son who managed to differ in his principles from his father without causing hostility?
    Her lover?

Who was Hitha?
    A research student?
    A camp follower of the revolutionaries?
    A bourgeois looking for security?

A woman expecting some kind of freedom?
A soul yearning for love?
Gautaman's intimate friend?

Everything inside her seemed fragmented, incomplete. She needed completion. Perfection? Was there such a thing?

She shut her eyes tightly to avoid the cloud of smoke which choked her.

Why did Gautaman stay with her? She knew that at first, he and Meena had been very close. Was it because she was saturated in the kind of experience he couldn't even begin to imagine? Was it because his relationship with a lower-middle-class girl would push all his own class weaknesses into the background and become the most important thing about him?

And she? What satisfaction did she get out of the relationship? Was it his passion, his intensity, his idealism?

Gautaman's father was a high-ranking official in the United Nations. He usually lived in the US or in other countries abroad. Whenever he came to Delhi, Gautaman would go to see him, wearing somewhat different clothes than his usual ones, and taking her along with him. They usually met at the Oberoi Intercontinental or the Hotel Akbar or the Hotel Ashoka. Hitha was a kind of representation of Gautam's total opposition to his father principles. When they were preparing to meet him for the first time, Hitha realized that Gautam was somewhat nervous.

"Why, Gauta? Are you afraid of what your father will say about us?"

Gautaman shook his head, denying it. Very hesitantly he spoke. "You won't get cross, will you, if I say something?"

"No."

"The place we are going to is a sophisticated setup. It's my uncle's house. Will you try, when we are eating, not to gobble your food?"

She felt absolutely attacked by him.

Her sister-in-law had practically killed her by withholding food from her. When she was working, for the first six months she had cooked and eaten enough for two every single day. Her tongue would salivate even while she was cooking. Sometimes she would fall upon the food as soon as it was ready, without changing her clothes or bathing, even at times, without brushing her teeth. It was only after – breathing hard, her forehead breaking into a sweat – she had swallowed the first five or six mouthfuls that she would become tranquil. Even now the intensity of that hunger was somewhere within her, like a dog held on a leash. Her enjoyment of food was something that was accepted among her group of friends. Although they were slightly contemptuous of the fact that she ate three times as much as Meena, and that when she ate, it was always single-mindedly, without letting her thoughts spill on to anything else, nevertheless they accepted it with generous hearts.

She had been making *aviyal* in the kitchen when Gautaman brought her a research article to read.

"What possible pleasure can there be in cooking? This shows that what you actually crave is an ordinary married life. What difference is there between you and other women?" he snapped at her in annoyance.

She screamed back at him, "I don't choose to do things by considering that if I do I will be different or that if I don't I will be like everyone else. By cooking food, I don't become like everyone else. Nor does someone who stops cooking suddenly become different, either. These are all external things, anyway. Like Nambiar drinking beer and wearing torn kurtas. Like Meena going about for a few days without a bra. Even their smoking cigarettes is just to show they are different. It's not as if they have a real desire to smoke or anything. My difference is not in these things. It's inside me. If I want to, I'll drink gin. I'll smoke. It's not to make some sort of statement."

He had just flung the article on the bed and left.

That night, after they had both read the article, he said, "I was not in a good mood this evening."

After a short silence, she told him about her hunger. She told him about the plain rice and *rasam* and wild-lime pickle her sister-in-law had given her. "While you were pushing away your untouched cutlet and apple, I was spreading my mat and lying down, my belly aching with hunger. It ached even after I had cooked and eaten properly for six months, because I wasn't used to eating well."

Without a word he laid her face against his chest and she had thought that this particular problem would never rise between them.

Then when he asked her that question on the day when they were about to visit his father, she stared at him blankly.

"Are you ashamed of me?"

"Che, che. Nothing like that," he said and took her along with him.

But in that big house, her chest heaved, leaping up and down like an uncontrollable frog, putting her in a state of terror. Her feet became entwined in the carpet. Gautam's father greeted her normally enough. The uncle's butler brought her a strange-tasting liquid which he called lime juice. The uncle, noticing the state of her face, said, "This is not made by squeezing limes. Who can keep running to the market every day? We get our bottled lime juice from Sicily once every six months."

"What is your research on?"

"Latin America."

"Oh, have you studied Spanish? I have been in that part of the world."

"Mm. I'm learning Spanish."

"Hablas español?" he asked suddenly.

"Un poco," she answered instantly, starting to sweat. His father seemed satisfied with her knowledge of Spanish with those two words. She began to suspect that his knowledge of the language, too, was confined to the same two words.

During the conversation, he ascertained through discreet enquiries that she was a brahmin woman. The meeting was more or less satisfactory.

Because she tended to imagine everything in an excessively dramatic style, this meeting seemed to her to be totally insipid. She had expected him to be shocked by their relationship, to protest about it. In her family too, it had been the same. She had rehearsed many logical arguments in her mind to explain why she did not wish to marry, and went to her father expecting a veritable earthquake. She looked at his paralysed body lying there and said, "Appa, I do not wish to marry." He murmured, "Mm?" in a weak voice and turned aside, trying to make himself more comfortable. She had almost felt cheated. She felt the same now.

"What do you think of my father?" asked Gautam.

"I feel a bit scared when I think of him."

"Nonsense. You are not scared of me, are you?"

"Sometimes," she said quietly.

"Idiot," he said, clasping her about the waist.

But it was true that an indefinable fear branched out from her mind every now and then.

There was the fear at the level of feelings. A fear that, even though she was so close to him, she could be attacked by small things; that part of her mind which had already been pierced through with lances, which was already bruised, could bleed easily if pressed, wounded by his inconsistencies.

Fear took other forms too.

When she gave assent to such principles as the equal distribution of wealth, and began to study them in depth, it was her lack of preconceptions that helped her to read with clarity and sharpness, without either confusion or mixture of other colours, with the engagement of her whole mind. But this had not been expected of her. What was asked of her was acquiescence, acceptance, and obedience – these three alone.

A silent howl tore at her lower belly every time Ammukutty Menon began a speech with the words, "According to our long standing revolutionary principles. . ." At each meeting she felt a ball of fire striking at her vocal cords and urging her, "Speak, shout out, roar." Finally she did just that.

Hitha shouted, "The revolution needs to be repeated again and again, but in different forms. Stagnation cannot be strength. Self-examination, purification, more and more analysis, clearing out the weeds that have branched out within us – without these there can be no growth. To ask permission of a group that has stopped growing is like giving the appropriate rites to a dead man."

Gautaman put his arm around her shoulder and took her out forcibly.

In the coffeehouse she burst out in English, the veins in her neck swelling, "Gauta, you don't understand my confusions. A fire starts burning in me every time I come to a meeting. Every single person there has an address in one of Delhi's richest, choicest areas. They make me feel humiliated. Anybody who joins the Party is respected only according to his class. Nobody gave Nambiar a job to do in translation, or in the trade unions, or at grass roots level. He got to the top ranks of the Party organization without having done any work. You too are the same. I'm respected because I am with you. How can you claim to be free of class-consciousness?"

"There's a difference between actual practice and your book learning. Don't talk nonsense, Hitha."

This incident happened again and again in various guises. Mrs. Menon summoned Gautaman and asked him to speak sharply to Hitha. Self-control and discipline were important, she said.

Hitha replied, when Gautam reported this to her, "A buffalo hide is important."

It sometimes seemed as if their principles were actually like drugs that were necessary, that injected some enthusiasm into their lives which were otherwise without complexities, which faced emptiness. Sunday revolutionaries, they were.

Were they all frauds? *Then, in that case, am I genuine*, Hitha asked herself.

Confusions crowded in upon her before she could understand where and which corner they came from. They moved in front of her eyes, like carcasses that were rotting away, broken up, shapeless, blackening. Before she could define each shape and name it, it moved, changing form.

Her temples ached as if from the pain of hammer blows.

The door opened.

Gautaman came in. He came to sit by her, asking, "How are you, Hitha?"

She sat up and said, "Only a headache."

"Shall I make some tea?"

"No. It is cooler this evening. Shall we go and sit on the hill? It should be pleasant there."

"Come on then," he said, and went to wash his face.

They locked the room and began to climb the little hill opposite their house.

"We had a hair's-breadth escape today. All ten of us could have been beaten up."

Hitha said nothing.

"What is it, Hitha? Haven't you got a reply?"

She took his outstretched hand and said, "Gautam, I have so far agreed with all your actions, whether I objected to them or wanted to reject them or otherwise, arguing that they had to be done in order that a further good should come about. But today it strikes me for the first time that what we are doing and the goals we claim for ourselves are actually miles apart." Before she could go on, he interjected, "Please, Hitha, you often get these attacks of doubts. You know that this is what we must do. It is also what we can do."

"Are you certain of that? Even about beating up a cripple in his wheelchair?"

"That was a strategy, Hitha. What else could we have done at that moment?"

"I seem to remember that you and the other boys with you wore beards. You could have taken the beating. I was prepared to do so as well."

"Nonsense."

They were silent for a time. Then Hitha said quietly, "I have lost my belief in this. Yes, I have a genuine desire to do something. I can't live with only the illusion of doing something. I want to get inside myself, to ask questions, nag, shake myself free of the mud and mire in which I am stuck, and to wash myself in floods of water. I am terrified by the masks and disguises implicated in the work we do."

"Did you remember your father when you saw the wheelchair? Did you get frightened by the blood it was necessary to shed in order to complete our job? Are you going in for nonviolence?"

"Those are not my fears, Gautam. My fear is that when that day comes, when blood really has to be shed, when truly a gun is being held out for justice, it will be pointing at you and your friends. My fear is that it might be that I will be holding that gun."

He was completely taken aback.

"Are you calling me a fraud?"

She shook her head. Then she said softly, in English, "If you and your friends are frauds, then who is genuine? My question is, where are those true revolutionaries? Yet they must be around somewhere. They must be there, without belonging to any organization, with real ideals, with anger and a passion for justice as their only companions.

"What's this, a lecture?"

Hitha smiled at him and said, "I have decided to go."

Gautam opened his mouth to protest against that, to argue with her, but he was silent.

They reached the top and sat down.

Hitha stared ahead, holding back the confusions in her mind: whether she was doing the right thing, what she must do next, whether she should accept the security of Gautam's simple rules after all, and repress all those opposing questions.

In all those empty nights to come, would she yearn for Gautam's comforting hand upon her breast, the feel of his fingers stroking her nipples, adding pleasure to her slumber?

When Gautam got his attacks of asthma and muttered her name, who would be at his side?

She climbed on steadily, treading on each question.

She was overcome with weariness at the thought that she had lost forever the security of accepting everything with closed eyes, that from now on she must walk through paths which she herself had to clear of stones and thorns. At the same time her backbone stiffened. Tears gathered slowly under her lashes and began to run down. She stayed still, allowing them to flow for the time being.

A Thousand Words, One Life

When Kamakshi found herself pregnant for the third time, she was somewhat shaken. She did not know at what impulsive moment, during which upsurge of emotion, her womb could have received the seed.

The Second World War was going on at the time. There was severe rationing. Life in Bombay afforded them little chance of savings. A household managed by carrying bags of wheat to the Panjabi family that lived three floors above them and receiving their rice in exchange. It was a life which avoided scarcity. A life that avoided luxury too. There were no objects in their house which were in the least bit showy. She wondered if this third pregnancy was itself an unnecessary luxury.

She tried various potions during the next two months: green papaya, powdered sesame seeds, crushed henna leaves dissolved in water. The foetus was like a stone, unmoved by any of this. After a while, she gave up all such attempts. But a fear lurked in the corner of her mind: In what shape would this foetus finally arrive, having resisted all attempts to shift it?

Her father wrote from Coimbatore. She had a fragile body. She would find it very difficult to manage this pregnancy as well as taking care of her two older children. She should return to her parents' house in Coimbatore, as early as her sixth month. Her husband gave his consent. The eldest child, a boy, was just coming up to his Christmas holidays. The school authorities agreed that it would not matter greatly if he could not attend classes for a month or so. The second, a girl, was a chatterbox. She came away, having informed her teacher, "My Amma is going to have a baby. I'm going to Coimbatore with her."

Her younger sister Gauri also arrived in Coimbatore, from Chennai. She too was expecting her third. Kamakshi's father had only recently been transferred to Coimbatore, from Kovilpatti. The house was in R.S. Puram. It was a quiet place, without a fly or crow to be seen anywhere near. The next house was a short distance away.

As soon as she arrived in Coimbatore, she felt a huge relief. Her older two played with Gauri's children, in the garden or in the street. After herself and Gauri, there were eight other younger siblings. The last of them, a little sister, was only three. The house was animated and lively, full of all the children.

Their mother was full of care and concern for Gauri and Kamakshi. She would massage them gently with oil and give them baths. She would make Kamakshi lie down and spread out her long hair upon a basket upturned over a vessel of smoking frankincense. Gauri's hair was short. Their mother would make her sit up and untangle it with her fingers. Even at her relatively young age, their mother always had a *tevaram* on her lips. She was always singing softly, "*Kaadalaagi kasindu kannir malgi,*" "Melting with love, eyes brimming" or "*Mandiramaavadu niiru,*" "Magical is the sacred ash." As Kamakshi lay there, leaning her head against the frankincense basket and gazing up at the ceiling from which the huge rings of the swing were suspended, she could not feel at all the weight of her stomach. She felt as if she were an *apsara*, floating in a world of smoke. It was as if Bombay and its severe regulations, and all the attempts she had made to abort the baby, belonged far away, in a distant world.

Her husband was adamant that the baby should only be born in a hospital. He was terrified of a home birth after hearing about an incident which happened in a household nearby. Customarily, the much experienced older women in the family took charge of any childbirth themselves. The barber's wife would come only to cut the umbilical cord. Or if the women knew how to do it, they would attend to that business as well. Kamakshi's great-aunt Rajammal was a woman who had delivered many babies. She could do everything. She bought clean new razor blades with her own money, and kept them in a small brass box. She would set off with her brass box, at whatever time she was summoned, and to any family that needed her. However difficult the delivery, she wasn't frightened. Once when she arrived at one of the hutments, she found the baby in a breach position. Without hesitating a moment, Rajammal Paatti put her hand through the birth passage and turned the baby.

As soon as she had cut the umbilical cord she would set off home. The family would attend to bathing the new mother themselves; in some households the washerwoman did it. As for Rajammal Paatti,

233

she went her way, after advising them to splash plenty of hot water on the young woman as they bathed her, and reminding them to bind her stomach tightly with strips of cloth. After every delivery, whoever the girl, she had a bath as soon as she returned home, and then sent to the new mother a small brass box full of the special *legiyam* that she made, from time to time, and stored away. Even if a midwife attended to the actual delivery, people turned to Rajammal Paatti for the legiyam.

But the irony was that Rajammal herself had no children. Nobody had ever seen a smile on her husband's face. He never addressed Rajammal by name. "Ask that barren prostitute to come here," he'd say. The story went that just once, when he was sitting in the *thinnai* playing cards with his friends and summoned her loudly in this way, she came outside, placed a *kuuja* of coffee and four silver tumblers near him, and asked, in front of everyone, "Who is the barren one here, you or I?" She stood quietly, asked her question, then went inside in haste. It seemed that after that, he stopped talking to her altogether.

Rajammal came to Kovilpatti from Satyamangalam, to attend on Kamakshi, for her two earlier deliveries. But now, Rajammal wasn't there. One day she delivered a baby in her usual way, came home, sent the legiyam and fell asleep. She never woke up. The baby girl she delivered last was named Rajammal in memory of her. Every child she touched became part of her dynasty. If a man creates his dynasty through his seed, how many families does a woman create through those she touches in this way? Families that are not confined by the direct relationships of caste, religion, blood, status. In

Satyamangalam, a girl named Rajammal must be running about. Would she remember Rajammal's touch? The touch of those hands which held her even before she reached this earth? Would she remember any of that? How can we say which of the events that make up history are remembered, and which forgotten? History is made up of so many silences.

Kamakshi's eyes would close as she lay there, head against the frankincense basket, lost in her thoughts. But her mother would insist on waking her up. "You mustn't fall asleep after an oil massage and bath. You will get a headache," she'd say. She would wake her up, plait her hair for her, loosely, and bring bowls of hot *rava-kesari* for both the young women, made with milk and semolina and dripping with ghee. Later, she and Gauri would sit on the thinnai and chatter away as they picked stones out of the rice, or chopped the vegetables.

It was during those times too, that they often talked about the terrible event which made them both agree to the decision that they should have their babies only at the hospital.

Their parents heard about that incident a couple of months after they settled in Coimbatore. An old woman who lived a few doors away spoke to their mother about it. When the old woman's second daughter, who lived in a neighbouring town, became pregnant, her mother-in-law and she attended to her delivery. Neither of the older women realized that the girl was carrying twins. When the girl's labour appeared to continue, even after the first baby had been delivered, this lady voiced her suspicion that there might be yet another baby in the girl's womb. But the mother-in-law proceeded to bandage the girl's stomach tightly, proclaiming firmly, "There have been no twins in our family, ever." The child's death poisoned the girl's entire body, and she, too, gave up her life.

"We killed our girl ourselves, amma. The life inside her was not able to come out. We went and bound up a life that was about to be free. It was only when the bandages were loosened that we realized what had happened. After that, by the time we rushed her to the hospital, before mother and child could be separated, both died." The old woman repeated her story to their mother several times, lamenting loudly. It might have been an error that happened very rarely. All the same, the very thought of it made them shudder from the depths of their stomachs. Rajammal Paatti's gently warm hands weren't there to give them courage. So it was that they decided it must be the hospital for them.

It looked as if Gauri and she would go into labour more or less at the same time. Her third child decided to arrive at a time when their father was on tour. She had just had her evening meal, washed her hands, and popped a betel into her mouth when she felt that stabbing pain at the middle of her back. Six years had passed since the birth of her second. She had forgotten the pain. For a second she was shocked, and then she realized what it was. Before she could call out to her mother, there it was again. Her mother was taken by surprise, just a little. Then, she called the gardener, Velucchami, and sent him off to fetch a rickshaw. She decided that Velucchami's wife Mutthamma should keep Gauri company. As soon as the rickshaw arrived she helped Kamakshi into it, and climbed in after her. The rickshawman left for the hospital, pulling the vehicle gently and without haste. Yet each turn of the wheel seem to go right across her waist. Her mother's cheek, smelling of turmeric, was close to her face. There was no movement along the street. Streetlights shone here and there. When she leaned her head against her mother's shoulder, and looked upwards, she could see the moon very clearly. A journey that felt endless. It would always stay in her mind, she reflected.

As soon as they reached the hospital, her mother asked the rickshaw to wait, and went inside with her. She made Kamakshi lie down on a bed. The hospital was dusty and full of rubbish. Mosquitoes swarmed about. The doctor who examined her pronounced that she would give birth only the next day. Kamakshi told her mother to go home, and to return in the morning. Her mother found the hospital uncongenial. She decided to go home.

At about four in the morning, the pain became much more forceful. In the delivery room, the nurse spoke sharply to her, for no reason at all. She had moaned softly, without even raising her voice. At once the nurse fell on her. "What's all this moaning and groaning for," she rapped out. At about four-thirty, as she thrust her neck and head back and gave a strong push, her gaze fell directly on the window; a single star filled her eyes. The baby fell against the crook of her thigh, bringing it warmth. The words, "A baby girl" sounded, as if from afar. In an instant there was a loud cry. Then she sank into oblivion.

When she came to, briefly, she could see that both she and the baby were covered in a white sheet stained with shit. She called out softly to the nurse and said, "Please change this sheet." Once more she was overcome by weariness.

In the morning her mother arrived with piping hot *kanji* made of *rava*. As Kamakshi drank the kanji, her mother examined the baby.

"Kamu, she is the very same colour as your sister-in-law."

"As dark as that?"

"It's as if her whole body is covered with moles. Just take a look."

"Amma, please see if her arms, legs, ears, and everything are all in place."

Her mother's face darkened. "Why? Did you go take some sort of potion?" she asked.

When she nodded, her mother said, "You wretch. . ." and proceeded to stroke the baby's fingers, her limbs, the flaps of her ears, and all her body. Nothing wrong whatever.

"Nothing at all wrong, Kamu."

"Thank goodness for that much. If there were something wrong, and being a girl at that, where could I have gone and knocked my head?"

"What does she lack? She is going to be exactly like her maternal grandmother."

"I'll give her the same name as you," Kamakshi said, Ranganayaki.

"Today is Friday. An auspicious day. You are going to become very wealthy through her." She added the good fortune of Friday to the name.

Sriranganayaki.

The name was shortened to Nayaki, even before Kamakshi

brought her home. Nayaki did not care for her mother's milk. She refused stubbornly to drink it. She lay silent, while the boy baby, born to Gauri the following week, screamed through the night. If she was given a bottle, she drank the milk. Otherwise, she didn't make the slightest noise. Sometimes, Mutthamma would carry Nayaki to her home at the bottom of the garden. Mutthamma had a two-month-old baby. For some reason, whenever Mutthamma picked up Nayaki, Nayaki would develop a sudden desire for milk. She would turn her head towards her breasts and begin to whimper for milk. Sometimes Mutthamma would feed her own baby at one breast, and give her other breast to Nayaki, who by this time would be clamouring and throwing her limbs about. When she was done, she would lie there, quietly smiling. Once Kamakshi came to the bottom of the garden to see. "Mutthamma," she said, "Nayaki doesn't care for my milk, she likes only yours." As long as they stayed in Coimbatore, Mutthamma fed Nayaki at least once a day.

After three months, her father put them on the train to Bombay. There were twenty-five packages including *appalam*, various spice powders and prepared condiments. Gifts from the bridal home, sent by her mother. A Singer sewing machine. ("You have given up music, now at least keep this. What is in the heart has to come out in one form or another. Otherwise, you'll just go mad.") That was put in the luggage van. Her father accompanied her as far as Arakonam, and helped her to change trains. A telegram had already gone off to Bombay.

The train arrived in Bombay. She couldn't see her husband. Fear seized her heart. All the same she began to think hard as to how best she should reach home. First of all she made the older boy and girl climb down from the train. She placed the three-month-old baby in the boy's arms and told him to hold her very carefully. She made the girl stand close up to her brother. The little girl, for her part, also put an arm around the baby.

Then, with the help of a coolie, she brought down all twenty-five pieces of luggage. She ran to the luggage van and collected the sewing machine.

She came outside the station with everything, and negotiated the fare home, on two Victoria coaches. They arrived home, the bigger pieces of luggage with herself, the baby, and the little girl in one coach, the boy and the rest of the luggage in the other. The total fare came to a rupee: eight annas for each coach.

When they reached home, she found that her husband was just about to set off to his office. The telegram had never reached him. He was totally surprised by her arrival. All of them went inside.

Nayaki arrived, too. She was laid in a corner. The husband did not pick her up in his arms. That night he complained: she was dark-skinned, she was not chubby; she was a girl. He did not say that they should take the baby to a studio and have her photographed. Neither did Kamakshi think of it. Her return to a life of coping with wartime shortage left no time for anything else.

When Kamakshi's younger brother visited them in Bombay, Nayaki was already four and sucking her thumb ceaselessly. Her brother insisted stubbornly that he should take the child to a studio and have her photographed. He claimed that she looked exactly like the film star Nargis. So Kamakshi made a beautiful dress for the child. The Parsi woman living next door subscribed to a women's weekly which came from London. Kamakshi borrowed the magazine and copied one of the children's dresses modelled there. A cotton material, patterned densely with flowers. It had a full skirt and a bib front, with decorative shoulder straps which crossed over at the back. A white blouse with puff sleeves. When she wore it, Nayaki was as pretty as a doll. She had tightly curling hair.

In the studio photo that her uncle arranged, Nayaki looked straight ahead of her, slightly bewildered. She looked a little shy as she stood there, the thumb she always sucked held together with her forefinger, in a circle.

At the age of four, Nayaki loved her thumb above everything. Because it had been sucked constantly, it looked somewhat pale and was worn smooth at the knuckle. As soon as anyone spoke sharply to her, that thumb would be popped into her mouth. She would sit down and lean against the wall, finger in her mouth.

She first began to draw with a slate pencil. She made many pictures using the coloured crayons belonging to the Bengali woman who lived next door. She would lay a blue oil crayon against white paper, press it down, and roll it across. Waves would form across one part of the paper. As soon as she finished, she would go and show Kamakshi her picture. Kamakshi would very likely be fast asleep, tired out from her morning's chores. The two older ones would have just gone back to school after their midday meal. Sometimes, she would glance at the pictures and say wearily, "Yes, yes, now off you go." The paper would be tossed in a corner, and end up on the dust heap. Nayaki would go off and draw another picture.

On the advice of her mother, Kamakshi began to massage Nayaki's stick-like limbs with castor oil before bathing her, in the hope of strengthening and filling them out. She would smear oil all over the child and then massage her firmly. There would be a Ramayana story at the same time, to stop her from crying. Always it was the story of the birth of Rama.

"A Gandharvan came out of the fire-pit bringing a silver bowl full of milk *payasam*. He gave it to all three of them: Kausalya, Sumitra, and Kaikeyi. So all three of the queens drank that payasam. After that, some days later, a baby came and lay down in each of their stomachs."

"Amma, did you too drink payasam, Amma, before I came into your stomach?"

"Payasam? Of course I did."

"Out of a silver bowl?"

"Of course. It was a beautiful silver bowl. You know the bowl in which I place flowers for the puja? That very same one."

It was a finely worked bowl. Creepers rose from its base and spread all over it, covering it with flowers and leaves and fruit.

"Mm. And then?"

"You know, I drank that payasam? It was a payasam in which the milk was boiled down and boiled down. A payasam in which the rice and the milk were so well mixed and mingled, it melted in my mouth. I drank it and drank it and made you grow. Then I went to Coimbatore."

By this time she would mix the *shiyakai* and place it on the child's hair. Nayaki had to shut her eyes tightly to stop the shiyakai from falling into them. Coimbatore would begin to take shape within her closed eyes.

Amma would describe the hospital: a palace such as the one where the sons of Dasaratha were born. A hospital that had just been built, brand new. A building as freshly white as tumbai flowers. Inside, the walls covered in pastel colours. New iron bedsteads. Shining white sheets. Window curtains patterned in tiny flowers in rose and violet. Nurses and doctors all in white, like angels. At dawn, Nayaki was born, surrounded by these angels. The auspicious goddess of the family was born.

Nayaki would emerge from the bathroom, a towel wrapped around herself, given new life. In her imagination, a princess.

———

She pressed the red button, and then said to Nayaki, "Go ahead." The journalist was interviewing artists in order to write about their life and art.

Nayaki began, "I was born during the Second World War. . ."

———

Everything had to be contained within a thousand words. Artists, after all, once they started speaking could go on for ever. So each was allowed a thousand words. Only a thousand words. Nayaki had spoken about her birth and how her mother had described the hospital to her, imagining it to be a palace; she told it as a story. She said that

243

although her mother was not an artist by profession, she was indeed an artist. She said that the story of her birth was a good example of the selectiveness of memory, and how the events selected by the memory become changed. She ended that section with the words, "I never tried to find out what that hospital was really like. Nor did I enquire about any of the other details. It is not that I cannot face the truth. But that imaginary version is my mother's gift to me. It has the warmth of the fine fibres lining a bird's nest. A safeguard. I can't tell whether she told it for that reason. And it isn't important anyway. Because we live this life through the real and the imagined, memory and forgetfulness."

That section alone went on for over ten minutes. Once transcribed, it would run to two or three pages. The journalist, who went about her task meticulously, wrote down only her date of birth and pressed the button to fast forward the tape.

The Calf that Frolicked in the Hall

It felt cold to the touch. Like a wet kiss.

It wasn't that difficult to contact Kadir, who lived in the United States. He had written her a long letter in the past year, soon after Udayan's untimely death. He wrote that with Udayan's death, something within him died too.

A kind of distaste threaded through everything Udayan did. She used to tease him, saying that of the *navarasas*, he was the hero of the *bibhatsa rasa*, the disgust mode. One of his younger brothers had committed suicide, for no apparent reason. He had not been in contact with Udayan for several years. This brother lived in a narrow lane, in a single room occupied by four other men. There wasn't even a rope in the house for him to hang himself with. Nor was the ceiling of any height. Udayan's younger brother, on the other hand, was six foot two and a half inches tall; he strangled himself with great difficulty, using his own *veshti*. Kadir recalled, in his letter to her, Udayan writing to him about this incident. "They sent me to bring home the body of a brother who had completely distanced himself from the family. Just as I was about to set off, my younger sister said to me, 'He came to me out of the blue last month, and borrowed some money. He said it was for a gas stove. If the stove is in his room, please bring it away.' I brought away my brother's body, and I didn't forget to bring the gas stove too. I trust that day was a joyous one for my sister." So Udayan wrote.

Kadir said, in his letter to her, that Udayan was a man who had experienced an extreme alienation. Alienation perhaps was a phase in most people's lives. But for Udayan it was his entire life.

When she telephoned Kadir, it was that letter she remembered. A handwritten one. When she rang the telephone number he had given, Kadir himself picked up the phone. The very first sentence which came from her lips was about Udayan. She couldn't believe a whole year had gone by. "I keep remembering him all the time, Kadir," she said. "I too," he agreed. He said, in English, "He had in his hand a very long thread which held me to the years we spent together. His death snapped that. I was tugged back forcibly, and fell upon those years."

There was a silence after that. In the United States, silences are not allowed during a telephone call. But in order to speak after twenty-five years, silence was indeed necessary, after that initial exchange. Memory can move very swiftly. Words do not possess the same swiftness.

A senior official in a bank cannot allow time to freeze, however. "And then? And then?" he pressed her.

And then they decided on a time to meet, and a place.

The early nineteen seventies. A time when some relationships came to an end suddenly. One relationship had lasted for six years. He was a married man. She fell easily into the web of stories he wove: his wife was an invalid; his intellectual thirst tormented him; his loneliness was his sorrow. It took all of six years to tear that web apart. And it was a small mouse that tore it. A mouse that cleverly brought her out – she who was caught in a spell and unaware of the web. She called him mouse, a man with a slight frame and a long face. "If I'm a mouse, then you are a cat. A cat that holds me in its mouth," he would say. She could not swallow the mouse. He would not let her swallow him. When she opened her mouth one day, he leapt away to his hole.

They were relationships that did her no damage. During the six-year relationship, her musical wings began to spread. That was when she was allured by Begum Akhtar's rendering of ghazals. Bhimsen Joshi, who could take a single line and create a whole world, found a permanent place in her house. Vaisnavite and Saivite bhaktas sat cross-legged comfortably, in her heart. The two-year relationship was different. It was a relationship closely involved with the world of jazz, the Beatles, Joan Baez, and Bob Dylan; a relationship that introduced her to ganja. It reached a high point one night at about two o'clock, when she was somewhat stoned on ganja, conscious of Louis Armstrong's trumpet music rising like white smoke pervading everything.

One year she came to Chennai from Jamshedpur, for a training session. She was staying with a friend, before moving into the Working Women's Hostel on Poonamallee High Road. She had just arrived that morning. She met Udayan that very evening. When the bell rang, it was she who opened the door. He stood there with a big snake gourd dangling from his hands. He lifted it high, shook it from right to left and announced loudly in English, "Today it's going to be a linga-puja meal in this house." Her friend and his wife laughed and told her not to pay him any attention.

He invited her to eat at his room in T. Nagar the next day.

His was a small, tile-roofed room at the back of a large house. Books everywhere. He was not in any regular employment. Sometimes he worked; sometimes he didn't. The feast consisted of *sambar*, *poriyal* and *appalam*; that was all. As soon as they had finished, he told her, "My friends and I have begun a new journal. I need to go and meet them."

"Shall I come with you?"

He looked at her, as if he were taking in her sleeveless choli for the first time. "We'll see. The elders in that family are a bit old-fashioned. I'm not sure whether they will let you in their house. What are my friends going to say, besides? Let's see."

He left her standing outside the compound wall and went in. That was Kadir's house.

Kadir came out at once and invited her in. He berated Udayan.

The room in the front verandah was Kadir's. Cover designs for the journal were scattered all over his desk. It was a struggle to make out its name, *Thedal* (Quest). The letters making up the name wandered all over the page.

"What do you make of them," asked Kadir.

"They look as if they're staggering about, drunk to the gills," she said.

"Where have you brought her from?" Kadir asked Udayan. Laughter then.

—————

In Kanchipuram, that night, they sat up for a long time, in the front *thinnai* of Amudan's house. Arangannal had left for his home. The lights had been put out in all the houses around. They could hear, only intermittently, small noises from different houses, and the occasional sound of a passing vehicle.

It was a while since *Thedal* had ceased to appear. They shared a feeling of inexplicable helplessness: a sense of closure and lack of closure, of structure and lack of structure, of order and utter disorder. Inexplicable emotions that fell apart, however much they tried to string them into words. Each of them was silent.

—————

Kadir came to the house where she was staying, in order to pick her up. His face seemed to have hardened, a little. His eyes had lost their light. She searched for the compassion of poetry she once found there.

"Why do you look like that?"

"I'm looking to see if you have changed."

"And have I?"

"That's how it strikes me."

"Life here is a rat race. You cannot manage if you don't change. But don't worry; it's only a superficial change."

"Where are we going for dinner?"

"Only to my house."

"I hope that hasn't caused a lot of work."

"What work? It's already prepared; I only have to reheat it in the oven and serve it."

"No cooking?"

"Only during the weekend. There's no time during the week."

"Was Shirley working today?"

"Shirley is not at home. She's gone to California on office work."

"Children?"

"How will they not be at home? They are eager to meet their father's old girlfriend." Then he laughed.

"Why do you laugh?"

"You called them children, that's why. The boy is twenty. He's studying at Syracuse; he's here just for this week. The girl is eighteen; she's going to college right here."

"Do they speak Tamil?"

"How will they speak Tamil? I can't talk Tamil to Shirley; only English, American English."

"Then with whom do you speak Tamil?"

"It comes to me in my dreams. I wrote a few poems suddenly, last year."

"Poems? You?"

She laughed.

He laughed with her.

At first they subjected every word and action of hers to an intense critical scrutiny, as if under a microscope. There was Udayan's sarcasm on the one hand, Kadir's analysis on the other. There were two others. They were from Kanchipuram, and were punch-drunk on Marxist-Leninist ideology. These two were the theoretical supports for *Thedal.* They had set aside their real names and given themselves the pseudonyms Arangannal and Amudan. Their love of books bound these four together. Even in the densely occupied Ranganathan Street, it seemed they were in a remote island of their own as they read and discussed Camus, Sartre, and Pablo Neruda. There were debates on T. Janakiraman, Indira Parthasarathy, Mauni, and Asokamitran. They described themselves as travellers and tourists of literature. They declared they were not devotees who would undertake literary pilgrimages to Madurai, Tiruvananthapuram Tirunelveli, Nagercoil, and Delhi. They were not prepared to go to the Literary Temples of Chennai, and prostrate before the icons there; they were only prepared to meet these deities when they circulated in the outside world. Only Coimbatore Kumarasamy, who shared with them all his experiences and thoughts, and supported them entirely, received their whole-hearted respect. Several issues of *Thedal* saw the light of day only after his forceful touch.

It was with him alone they were prepared to discuss, fight, and make peace. Kadir used to say, laughing, that you could enjoy a profound friendship with Kumarasamy only if you stopped talking to him.

Intent on analysing her, they took apart, piece by piece, her dress, her words, her attitude, her ideas. She couldn't bear it. Once, when she went to Bangalore for another course in her training, she wrote a letter to them. "You look at me as if I belong to some strange species. It really troubles me. I could speak, read, debate with you. But it can happen only if I'm one of you. Otherwise I will always be an outsider. Just a spectator."

The letter brought a result. On the day she returned from Bangalore, Kadir and Udayan were at the station. Flowers held in their hands. Smiling faces. They accompanied her all the way to Poonamallee. They waited while she had a bath, and then took her to a restaurant for breakfast.

"What's so special, dear friends?" she asked.

"No more cold war. Hereafter it's all cordiality," said Kadir.

The good relations continued on every occasion she came to Chennai thereafter.

In the darkness of the thinnai they were all shadowed outlines. "In the nineteen seventies, only an alienated middle-class young man stands as the symbol of Tamil youth," she began. He was present in every story or poem which appeared in *Thedal*. A young man who was unemployed, scorned by his own family, who returned home late in the evening to eat the cold buttermilk-rice and lime pickle left for him in the corner of the kitchen; who lived with the sorrow of Being, and other such sorrows. Or else he was a young man trapped in a permanent job which his heart rejected and which gradually sapped his life; caught up in the aridity of daily life. He ate. He rushed to work. On Sundays he soaped his clothes and washed them. He even got married. Then he published a book and proclaimed his life of detachment with the words, "This recently married man likes saffron, the colour of renunciation." He was a young man who could neither break free of his family, nor live with them. The umbilical cord was still around his neck. Besides all this, he possessed a craze for literature. More, a craze for poetry.

———

It didn't seem likely that she would meet Kadir again, after that dinner. The conversation, somehow, didn't get anywhere. It went in many directions – literature, politics, culture – appeared to delve further, but fizzled out eventually. Before the marks were made, they were erased. His son and daughter conducted themselves very politely. Nothing could be faulted in the food, hospitality or conversation.

All the same. Something was discordant. The ascending and descending scales were all in perfect order, only the tune would not take shape. Besides, there was the cold.

After she had said her goodbyes, there was some kind of superficial conversation between them as he drove her home. Suddenly, after she had climbed out of the car, he came up behind her and wrapped a thick shawl around her. When she looked at him in surprise, he wore a smile such as she had not seen throughout the evening. Just as she crept into the comfort of her blanket that night, the telephone at her bedside rang. When she picked it up, wondering who would telephone her at that time of night, Kadir's voice sounded.

———

"Have you gone to bed?"

"Yes, just now."

"You weren't happy with this evening's programme, were you?"

She was silent.

"Hey, it's a huge gap, twenty-five years."

Her throat choked as she said, "Yes."

"You are able to melt instantly, like snow. That's your strength. It's all easy for you. For me, it takes a while. I have to wander through many different spaces, before I can even begin to meet you. Don't you know that? Sleep well."

"You too."

"I have some work I must finish. I can only go to bed after that. If you can't sleep, you must call me at any time. All right? I'm here. I'm not about to go anywhere."

She put out the light and slept instantly and very soundly.

—•—

Every time she came to Chennai, as soon as her work was done, she would set off directly to the bank where they were employed. All the way back on the electric train from Beach station to Mambalam, they'd talk and laugh and joke noisily. When they reached Kadir's house, Udayan would be waiting there. Arangannal and Amudan would go to their own room and join them later. Theirs was a small thatched room built on the terrace of a house. Arangannal described such rooms as urban huts.

The first thing they did when they reached Kadir's house was to look at the post. Kadir's mother worked in a firm, and she usually arrived home a little before they did. Just as soon as Kadir changed into his veshti, her invitation would come from within, "Here, come and take your tea." Kadir would go in and return with the tea.

By the time Kadir's father came home, Arangannal and Amudan would have joined them. They'd make off to the terrace then. They worked furiously inside the thatched area. Udayan's blunt criticisms cut in now and then. Once, she declared that a poem Arangannal had translated contrived to upturn language itself, and started to read it out at the top of her voice. He tried to snatch it out of her hands, she ran away, while the rest rocked with laughter. In Kadir's mother's words, "The whole of Mambalam was shocked to see such misbehaviour."

It seemed that many years ago, Mambalam had been utterly shaken by Bhuvana of the corner house, who married for love. Kadir's mother gave them several instances to prove that Mambalam had been brought to the same state of shock now. When these words reached Kadir's father's ears, they came coloured by his mother's code of conduct. The older man, for his part, had no doubt at all that literature, music, painting, and dance were all strongly linked to impropriety. Now, Kadir's father was not in the least concerned about her propriety, or lack of it. But the argument, "The boy will be ruined," struck him forcibly. He told Kadir to behave in a less obtrusive manner. A long lecture followed, Kadir reported.

For some days following this, they met in Arangannal's room. Or else at Udayan's. Once the pillars of propriety belonging to the houses along Kadir's street, so shaken by witnessing their horseplay, were firmly in place again, they returned to Kadir's room.

The conversation continued into the night, as all other sounds died away.

So are women not bothered by questions about Being and Nothingness, Udayan and Kadir asked her.

Of course a woman reads Camus too. She reads Sartre. She also reads the *Tirumandiram*, Akka Mahadevi, and the Sufi poets. But when the entire family is engaged in creating the head of the household, a man, she has to find the nooks and crannies where she can create herself out of the evidence of her own being. It is because she continually asks herself philosophical questions concerning Being that she is able to redeem herself and come outside from the grave-pit of daily living. She lives in a world full of symbols. "Why are you at the window?" is the question underlying her life. The window is the symbol of the world outside. Her freedom lies outside the window. Both the running stream and the stagnant well are her symbols, too. Symbols of death. Words such as "I'll fall into the river or well and die" are the sounds of her language-world. She is always denounced, finally, as a prostitute.

"Fine. All this is mere breast-beating. Are you saying that women are sacrificial lambs, then? I can hear songs like 'If you are born a woman, this world must always be sorrowful' playing away in the background," Udayan said.

She denied it. A woman is aware of both the heaviness and the lightness of Being, she said. Sometimes, Non-being is itself her

Being, she said. Sometimes she is when she is not. At other times, even when she is, she isn't.

———

The shawl that Kadir gave her was snug and warm against the chill American winter. The telephone sounded each evening. Kadir spoke to her. Gradually his voice grew warmer, gaining in warmth like a hearth being lit. When she remarked on it, he said nothing is ever lost forever.

It seemed as if her American trip was one long car journey. She made several trips with Kadir. Sometimes Shirley came too.

Sometimes they talked about some of the incidents that had happened during the twenty-five-year interval. Once when they were travelling along a seemingly endless highway, he asked her about one such incident. "Amma wrote once. She said you visited her after Naomi was born; when she was about a year old. She said you had brought a silk *paavaadai* for the child."

"True. I'd gone to Chennai on some work. Udayan gave me the news. I went to Nalli, bought the silk skirt-material and took it to your mother. She returned it saying you wouldn't dress the child in silk clothes."

"She was right. We didn't put her in silk clothes."

"I came outside with the silk. It was terribly hot. Your mother went back inside. You remember the mango tree in front of your house? It had been chopped down. Only the base of the tree was left standing. I went and sat on it. You know how, when the sun is very bright, there is a sudden dazzling white that strikes across the eyes? I felt just that. Nearby they had erected a pump-set with a tap. I pumped up some water and washed my face. I drank some water, drenching my clothes. It felt suddenly as if in all of that great city of Chennai, there wasn't a single door I could knock on, Kadir. Udayan was somewhere in Tambaram. Amudan and Arangannal had lost touch with me entirely. I had continued to read everything that was published, but there was no way I could knock on the door of a writer and say, "I came to discuss literature with you." Everything, everything lay within limits and bounds. Except for myself."

"And then?"

"I walked out of your compound, found a small stall, and drank a bottle of soda. I looked at the newspaper hanging there and found out what pictures were running at which air-conditioned theatre. I went to a comfortable air-conditioned theatre and bought a balcony seat. I fell asleep even before the titles finished appearing."

She laughed.

"What did you do with the silk material?"

"You won't believe me if I tell you."

"Go on. Tell me."

"When the picture finished, I walked all the way back to the hotel where I was staying. There was a wayside shrine along the way. Some Amman shrine, Bhadrakali or Esakki. All stone and *kumkumam*. I draped the silk over the idol."

"What colour was the silk?"

"Dark blue, patterned with stars."

A warmth and closeness sprung up between Kadir and herself, very quickly and naturally. On one occasion, as she arrived in Chennai, she was overcome with tiredness. She just could not go to the bank, as usual, to meet all of them. Neither could she bring herself to go to her hostel.

She decided to go directly to Kadir's verandah room, which was also the Thedal office. Udayan was there already, correcting proofs. As soon as she got there, she spread out a mat and lay down.

"Hey, what's happened?" he asked her.

"Udayan, please go and buy me two cups of hot tea and a Baralgan."

"Why, what's wrong with you?"

"Nothing. Stomach ache. It's what happens every month." Udayan took the flask and ran.

She drank the tea, took the pill, and lay curled up.

By the time Kadir and the rest arrived, her stomach churned with pain compounded by the tea. She went to the toilet adjoining the room, and threw up. After that, she began to feel a little more settled.

Later, when she had washed her face, they set off to the printing press. Kadir didn't take his eyes off her while she sat there.

That evening, when they had accompanied her to the hostel he asked, "Does it ache a lot?"

"No. Not so much now," she told him.

"Will you come tomorrow?"

"Yes, I'll come."

"You know something? You know how I've got used to your coming to meet us in the evenings – when you weren't there today, I had a sudden dread. Then when I came home, you were lying there, all curled up. I was really frightened then."

She held her hand out to him. "Hold my hand, please."

He hesitated a second, then took her hand in his. Slowly he tightened his grasp.

———

Stars lay in clusters against the Kanchipuram sky. As for the sky, it was that dark blue which Bharati's songs mention. After their initial conversation, they were all silent for a while. Then Udayan began again.

"It's true, nothing is clear. You can't hold on to anything. Even during the Independence struggle there were journals which held firm beliefs. They had forceful names, *Ezhuthu*, Writing; *Manikkodi*, Banner. Now, even the names of the journals show a lack of goals: *Vanampadi*, *Vaigai*, *Yatra*, *Kaatru*, *Padigal*, *Chuvadu*, and so on. . ."

"Don't generalize," said Kadir. "There is still *Visvarupam*. Also *Kollipaavai*. *Darsanam*. *Gnanaratham*."

"But are any of those names forceful, though? *Visvarupam*, Cosmic form; *Darsanam*, Vision; *Gnanaratham*, Chariot of wisdom. . . And what about us? *Thedal*! Quest! What quest?"

"Great, Udayan, you've started on your *ninda sthuthi*, have you, berating the deity on his failings?"

"Udayan's sarcasm, Thanjavur style," she put in.

"That's right. I'll be sarcastic, you be abrasive."

"This is good," remarked Amudan. "Sarcasm and abrasiveness. You could describe the clash between critics and writers in those terms."

For the first time that evening, there was a sense of the ice melting.

During another car journey, he asked about her family.

"Didn't Udayan give you any news about them?"

"He might have done. I can't remember."

"After we all went our different ways, I didn't return to Chennai very often. I had my work in Jamshedpur. Within two years, my father died. Do you remember my younger brother, Mukund? Just as soon as he got himself a job, he insisted he would only marry a certain girl who had been in college with him. And immediately, at that. She was a fine girl, too. One day the two of them were going somewhere on their scooter, when a truck crashed into them. She died there and then, on the spot. Mukund suffered a severe blow to his spine. He is completely paralysed from his waist down. Now he can only go about in his wheelchair. My younger sister Gita is here, in the US. You saw her yesterday, didn't you? She spoke to you, didn't she?"

"Was that Gita? I didn't recognize her at all."

"It's ages since you saw her. As soon as I said I was coming to this conference, she insisted stubbornly I should stay with her."

"Didn't your mother come with you?"

"Amma isn't alive now."

"Is it because of Mukund you've stayed single?"

"That's one reason. But it's not the only one. I now run the company that Appa started. We have a big house in Jamshedpur. I can't abandon all that. I have a network of good friends. It isn't as if being single leaves me wanting in any way. Gita's second daughter lives with me and goes to school in Jamshedpur."

"But isn't love necessary too, in one's life?"

"How can it not be? But it doesn't last forever, it's something that comes and goes. Sometimes it's a delight when it happens. Sometimes it's a delight when it leaves. If it's there, it's a sadness at times. At times, if it isn't there, it's a sadness too. Don't imagine I haven't been sad, Kadir. Sometimes I am deeply, deeply sad. But even that's a comfort, too. Call it a kind of privilege."

"Do you recall what Udayan used to say? He'd ask, 'What's an unfulfilled love? What exactly has to be fulfilled?'"

"True. Once, when a friend of his married the girl he loved, he remarked, 'Poor man, his love hasn't been fulfilled.'"

"He had a way of plunging into seriousness, even when he was joking. Once we were on a bus together. Suddenly he turned to me and said, 'If there weren't love, nobody would have talked about death.'"

"In the end, he left us without telling us what he thought about death."

"I can't understand why he made that decision."

They sank into their own thoughts after that. The car moved on steadily.

One evening there was a huge, jostling crowd near the T. Nagar bus station. All of them were there, part of the crowd. The occasion was the unveiling of a statue of Periyar. The statue was still covered in its wraps. Next to it a high stage had been erected. In a little while, K. Viramani arrived. The crowds broke into cheers when the wraps were removed. In his speech, Viramani enunciated the Gayatri Mantra, giving each word a special emphasis. This was how brahmins say it, he told the crowd; Periyar was a man who opposed brahmins, he trumpeted. The speech was punctuated by clapping, whistling, and frequent cries of, "Well said."

She had never heard Periyar speak. She knew of him only through the books she had read. Nor had she ever heard a speech such as this. She felt as if she were participating in a historic event. She too clapped her hands enthusiastically. She screamed with the rest of them. They were standing very near the stage. During a magical moment when she was shouting gleefully, she had the sudden illusion that the Periyar statue came alive and looked steadily at her. She leaned her head on Kadir's shoulder.

After the crowds had dispersed, it seemed to them they had been witnesses of history in the making. They walked along, all of them hand in hand. Because it was very late by then, they all lay down to sleep on the terrace floor. Nobody else was at home that day, in Kadir's house. They talked for a long time, gazing at the mango tree's branches high above them, and the moon, and the night sky.

About the Self-Respect Movement and the stagnancy of its current policy. They discussed the unveiling of the Periyar statue, debating whether it was a symbol of rationality, or an icon of someone newly deified.

Long after she had fallen asleep, sometime later that night, she felt Kadir's hand on her. That first kiss, soaking wet, went on for a long time. They lay there for a long time, seizing at each other's lips. His lips, cold at first gradually began to burn. "Hamma," he moaned from time to time.

—●—

When they finally finished talking and went inside, a tiny calf stood in the *kuudam*, the central hall of the house. The cow had calved that evening, even as they arrived in Kanchipuram. It stood there now, its legs still trembling. With its large wet eyes, the calf stood there like a small white fawn.

When she touched it, it gave a shudder. After they had finished dinner and were setting off to the thinnai, Amudan's mother had said, "I've left the calf in the hall. It might gambol about in the night. You'd better warn the girl. I don't want her to be scared." Amudan hugged it, and stroked it for a while. From its stall in the backyard, the mother cow called for its young, "Mma." "She will keep calling like that. But if we let her have the calf, she'll pretty nearly lick off its skin." The calf nuzzled against him.

—●—

Kadir had to go to Syracuse on some business of his. He thought he should look up his son at the same time. She too had some relatives in Syracuse whom she needed to visit. They decided to go there by car. The arrangement was that after the Syracuse visit, she would go on to New York, and return home from there.

It was their farewell trip. Kadir didn't say much. After a little while, when the car had begun to run at a steady pace, she began.

"Kadir, I need to tell you something."

"Go on, tell me."

"Udayan and I were living together for ten years. It was after that, he died."

He turned his head sharply, and looked at her.

"For some reason, he didn't want me to tell you. It all happened unintentionally. He was working at one thing or another, desultorily. He began many things. Never finished them. Once he told me, "If only I could find an evening job, it would suit me down to the ground. Then I could read all day, and work in the evenings." I found him such a job in my own company. I even arranged accommodation for him. A couple of months later he said, "The night shift doesn't suit me at all, I can't watch the stars." Again I found him a daytime job. In time, he was bored with that as well. He grew very close to Mukund, meanwhile. He would come and talk to him for a long time, every evening. He stayed on and ate with us. We used to look forward to his arrival, every evening, Mukund and I. One day I went up to his room and invited him myself, to move in with us. He came without standing on any ceremony. He moved in as naturally as if we had been living together for many, many years."

"Did Arangannal and Amudan know about this?"

"I think they must have known. Udayan continued to go to Chennai from time to time. He might have told them. But they had broken off any contact with me, so I didn't know. He only hesitated to tell you."

Kadir was silent. When they had gone a little further, he stopped the car at a petrol pump, and went in to buy two freezing-cold ice-cream cones. They began to eat them, as they sat in the car. He finished his quickly and started the car again.

Still eating her ice cream, she turned and looked at him. His hair was cropped close to his head. It was beginning to go grey at the back. His neck appeared very long. She stroked the back of his neck, very gently.

———

Once when she was returning from Chennai to Jamshedpur, Kadir and Udayan came away with her. The three of them travelled around many cities together. Finally, they returned to Chennai together. Kadir and she were at a stage when their relationship was at its most intense. The stage when you want to be inseparable at all times. His parents were deeply upset by this. A tense atmosphere filled the house. Arguments went on every day. Udayan and the others did their best to protect the two from becoming too frustrated. All the same, she was hurt by his parents' stubborn opposition towards her. At the same time she was tormented to see how pained he was by his parents' taunting. She wished that they could return to the carefree days of old when they selected poems for *Thedal*; when they sat together on the steps of the printing press in Mylapore, waiting for the proofs; when they woke up at dawn and hurried out to watch the sunrise; when they travelled on the electric train in the evenings; when they went to the same picture seven or eight times in order to critique it properly; when they attended literary conventions as a group.

On that occasion, when she was returning to Jamshedpur, Kadir looked miserable. "Do you really have to go?" he asked her. As the train began to move, he held her hand and pleaded, "Come back soon." She wrote him a long letter soon after she reached home. That letter was to be the cause of a great disaster.

The letter which came from him made no mention of the one she had already sent. Soon after that, when her father returned home from his office one day, he asked her, "Did you send Kadir a letter recently, amma?"

"Yes, Appa. Why?"

"His parents seem to have intercepted and read it. It seems they have a relative here, in Jamshedpur. They sent the letter to him. He turned up at my office today and shouted at me in front of everyone, amma."

She felt her face redden.

"I'm sorry, Appa. Did you retrieve the letter from him?"

"He refused to let me have it."

Everyone in Jamshedpur knew that man, Swaminathan. He was an astrologer. He made predictions. He also took on the responsibility for all the pujas, festivals, and celebrations among the Tamil people in town. He took charge of collecting all donations and giving accounts. It was said that when his mother died, the first thing he did was to send his wife to remove the jewellery from her body.

One day he actually turned up at their house. It was a direct attack.

He made for her mother, "What is this, Amma, have you no idea about bringing up a girl properly? The boy is an utter innocent. It seems she hangs on to him like a *pisaasu*, and wanders about everywhere with him. It seems the whole town is laughing at them."

He turned to her. "Get on with leading a decent and correct life. Leave off enticing the neighboring boys. I'll see to it that you won't be able to hold your head up in this town. Just watch it."

"You get out of this house, first of all," her mother told him, driving him out.

The letter went into the hands of every Tamil family in Jamshedpur. It reached all of them, but never Kadir. Eventually, it must have ended up among the waste paper in some Tamil household.

She had revealed all her doubts in that letter, all the anguish she felt.

"Of course I need you, and the closeness of you. That kiss on that terrace is still wet on my lips. The touch of your hand on my smoldering body does indeed set it aflame. But it seems to me that as far as I'm concerned, our meeting has happened too late, whereas on your part, it is too soon. I have travelled many miles. You, though, are still within the womb of your family. You don't quite know how to come out of it. But you have to make your way outside, first of all. You can find a life of your own only after that.

I feel as if I am being tied down, hand and foot.

Sometimes I wonder if these feelings which well up within me and my body belong to an instant that will simply float away."

It was as if everything was blasted apart by an earthquake. When the Emergency was declared by the central government, Arangannal made the decision to follow the politics of the extreme left. Amudan sought to change his job. Kadir asked for a transfer and went to Chandigarh.

After the storm died down, Kadir left for the United States. They planned that before he went away, they would all go down together to Amudan's house in Kanchipuram.

⟶

They spread their mats and lay down to sleep. The early part of the night went by silently. Then the cow called out a few times, "Mmaa." She heard the creak of the swing in the kuudam, as it moved. Noises of the calf, running about. Kadir lay on a mat within an arm's reach. He slept with his arms crossed over his chest. She wanted to reach across and touch him. But she pushed away her desire. Let all that remain truly at an end. When she had fallen asleep at last she felt that wet roughness against her cheek. She shivered. When she opened her eyes, she saw the calf bending over her with wondering eyes, licking her cheek. As if it were gentling her. Its tongue felt cold against her cheek. Like a wet kiss.

⟶

Kadir's letter arrived a few days after she returned home.

I don't know why Udayan hesitated to tell me that you were living together. It gives me great satisfaction that he was with you for ten years. I still feel his loss. He might have thought that he never achieved anything in his life. But what have others achieved, other than the achievement of staying alive?

I continue to live in this country although I find fault with its politics and culture. But I don't have the will to return to India either. I think this will be a lifelong struggle for me.

You have your feet firmly planted in some place, somewhere. As for me, I feel as though beneath my feet there is nothing but air. I am cursed, like Trisanku, neither to hold firm, nor to fall. Do you remember a poem by Atmanam, which says, what I need is a place where I can be. It strikes me it was written for me, or for people like me who cannot put down substantial roots.

I think one day I will die during a car journey on an American highway. You might come to hear of it. Or you might not.

On our last car journey together, you stroked the back of my neck with fingers that had been holding an ice-cream cone. Thanks. I shivered at that moment. That touch felt cool. Like a wet kiss. . .

Even before Kadir's letter arrived, she had written to him in detail about Udayan's death.

I don't know entirely, why he made that decision. But I can make a guess. About a month before Udayan's death, Mukund's health worsened greatly. He could not even get out of bed. Udayan was with him constantly. One night, when he was in great pain, Mukund apparently asked him, "If anything happens to me, don't abandon Akka. Stay with her." Udayan was stunned. Apparently he wept and said, "Mukund, I am not capable of taking on any sort of responsibility. I am only a vagabond, a bird of passage. Please don't threaten me."

Do you remember that painting by Edward Munch? A face frozen with terror. I saw that look on Udayan. A look as if he had gazed upon death, close up. One evening, when I came home, I found him looking for Sampath's novel, *Idaiveli*, Interval.

Even when he invited me to visit his sister's house in Bangalore, with him, he hadn't decided anything, I believe.

Perhaps he might have thought about it. In his diary, there was only a quotation from *Tirumandiram*. There was only that.

"If a kuyil lays its eggs
in the nest of a crow

the crow rears its chicks
tirelessly, in good faith.
Even so,
without movement, without direction,
without cause or reason,
as if in delusion
the body is cared for."

The second day after we arrived in Bangalore, he fell into the well in the back garden of his sister's large house. Someone screamed, and before I could reach him, he had been lifted out. I went to him, lifted his dripping hand and laid it against my cheek. It seemed then as if he was still alive. It felt cold. Like a wet kiss. . .

Journey 1

The bus stood there as if it were a heaven-sent vehicle, meant just for her. A brand new one. It had a single seat next to the driver. It was parked some distance away from the other buses. They said it would leave in about fifteen minutes, but as yet there were no passengers. Making sure she had her ticket with her, she climbed in and sat down in the single seat. She had let several buses go by for the sake of that particular seat. At least on her return journey she wanted to travel without anyone bothering her. She wanted to sit well away from the other passengers. These were people who expected her, if she only opened her mouth, to lay out her entire life before them. This single seat was going to be her line of defense. Nobody was going to get past it. Any stripling Abhimanyu attempting such a thing would be felled immediately. She sat there, making her plans as if they were strategies in preparation for war. Because she had taken no such precautions during her forward journey she has suffered inordinately. And so her lap had been drenched by a child's urine, the shoulder of her choli had been dribbled upon by a sleeping and exhausted woman, her sari *pallav* stained by tobacco juice borne across from the front seat by the wind. She had not set out prepared for all this. She had been exposed to torment because she had no safeguards; no protective armor at all.

The morning had begun well enough. Because she slept against a window opening eastward. She had been touched by the sun's very first needles of light. As she opened her eyes slowly, the rays of light were like long threads, extending from the ball of red cotton behind the distant neem tree. When she shut her eyes again and faced the light, her eyes were flooded with red. Then when she turned away from the light, closing them with her hands, they filled with peacock-green. By the time she had done this four times, her body had accepted the world. And prepared itself to move about in it.

She could hear the water pump being worked downstairs. Must be Valli. She had asked Valli to come quite early and pump up some water. She had to go to Tiruchi that day. She had already sent word to the person whom she was to meet there. After Valli had pumped the water and cleaned the house, she bought some idli and dosai from the *appam*-stall woman at the corner of the street, ate her share, and then left. When asked, "What do you want from Tiruchi, Valli?" Valli had retorted "Are you likely to bring me the *prasadam* from the hill-top Pillayaar?"

Valli knew well enough she would not go to the temple. So she too had just smiled, and said nothing.

She had her bath and put on her mango-colored tie-dyed sari with a black border, and a choli of black handloomed cotton with fine yellow checks. Valli, however, did. "It only looks good that way," she

would say emphatically. In all these matters, it was Valli who organized her life. Valli had taken over the burden of these day-to-day
decisions and left her the neem tree, the koel which nested there, the
street, the sky. Gifts made over to her by Valli.

That morning, because she aimed to reach Tiruchi in good time,
she climbed into the first bus that was ready to go, and went and sat
by the window, on a seat meant for two. Just as the bus was about
to depart, a couple climbed in, with their baby. The husband wore
a stiffly starched shirt. A crackling new silk *veshti*. The wife wore
a blue silk sari, blindingly bright at that early hour, with a red border. Golden motifs covered the entire body of the sari. Her wet hair
was heavy with flowers. Her neck was over-crowded with jewellery.
Her gold-worked choli, stretched tightly across her body, was wet in
large patches under her arms. The baby was in her arms, of course.
Soon after they boarded the bus, when it was clear that there was no
possibility of their sitting together, the wife came and sat next to her.
The woman then placed the child on the thigh nearest her, so that
he faced her directly. For some reason, perhaps to announce to the
whole world that he was a male child, he had been dressed only in
a chocolate-colored shirt covering his upper half. Now, in rhythm
with the speed of the bus. The baby began to stretch his ankleted feet
towards her waist and lap.

The woman petted him and said, "Don't make trouble, Kannan."

Perhaps he melted when she called him "Kannan" so fondly; at
any rate, the little darling braced his feet comfortably against her
waist and began to pee. Startled as she felt the dampness over her

waist and hands and said, she said sharply, "See to your child, will you?"

The woman said casually, "Oh, you've gone and wetted her sari, you naughty boy!"

She spoke in anger, "What is this, amma? Can't you hold the baby properly in your own lap? I'm on my way to Tiruchi on business. Can I turn up like this, in a wet sari?"

"What's happened, amma?" asked the old woman seated behind them.

The mother answered, "She's shouting because the baby made her wet."

"What?" asked the woman in surprise. "If people are so refined as all that they should go about in a pleasure car. Who is asking them to travel by bus?"

She rounded on the old lady, "Is there some sort of law that if I come by bus I should let all the babies here urinate on my sari?"

"Why, *thayi*, don't you have any children yourself? Or, have you borne babies who never pee?"

Someone else glanced at her neck and put in, "Looks as if she isn't even married, anyway."

She argued loudly, "Why sir, where's the connection between this business and whether I am married or not? Why couldn't she bring the baby with a piece of cloth wrapped around him? Why should he wet other people's clothes? The baby's father is managing to travel with his shirt and veshti uncrushed, I see. But I have to suffer instead!"

The child's father, who had been swaying, half-asleep, now woke up, startled.

"What's the matter?"

"An elderly person said to him, "It's nothing. You carry on sleeping. An unmarried girl here is getting cross. What does she know about the joy of children?"

"Amma," said the old lady, touching her shoulder lovingly, "I tell you this. May the moment dawn when you too are touched by your child's urine. You'll have a baby in your own arms by next year, just see if you don't."

"You tell her out of your own mouth, *paatti*. Let good times come to her."

She turned away and gazed out of the window, afraid that were she to say anything more, they would find her a bridegroom and tie the knot between them there and then. She could not explain to them that she was indeed married, that her husband worked in a different town, and that she didn't believe in such outward symbols like a *tali*. In any case, all sorts of questions would be sure to follow, like "Why don't you have children?" It was while deep in such thoughts that she suddenly became aware of a certain weight and dampness at the shoulder of her choli. The woman had fallen asleep against her shoulder, the boy Kannan held firmly in her lap and facing forwards. Kannan's head too was drooping. Perhaps he had not allowed her to sleep all night. Or, she might have woken up very early that morning to wash her hair. By the time she had massaged in the oil and the *shiyakai*, her arm would have pretty nearly broken. Time would have passed swiftly while she bathed, then bathed, dressed, and suckled the child before donning her gold-worked choli. Perhaps she had set off after just a cup of coffee, as they were on their way to a temple or a wedding. As soon as there was a convenient shoulder – a shoulder wearing handloomed cotton, from which her head was not likely to slip off – the woman must have dropped off. When that shoulder was jerked, the woman sat up, wiping the dribble from the corner of her mouth. She glanced at the shoulder she was sleeping against, pulled out a handkerchief, and tried to wipe it.

"Forgive me, akka," she said.

By this time, Kannan too opened his eyes, and as if he had already determined upon his next plot, thrust the strap of her handbag into his mouth, and began chewing on it forcefully, with all four of his existing teeth. She freed her handbag from his grasp. Immediately he bent forward and fastened his mouth upon her watch strap. If this went on any longer, she might find herself singing "Thaye, Yasoda," she thought. It was while she was preventing Kannan's further attacks that the consecration by tobacco-juice happened. The old lady seated behind her noticed this and called out, "Who's spitting?" and patted her. As if she were saying, "Just you get married and you won't ever be bothered like this again."

As soon as they reached the Tiruchi terminus, she went into the changing room and retied her sari, turning it around and wearing the outer edge inside, hiding all traces of the journey. Seeking out a single seat now was by way of ridding herself of all the distress of the morning.

Other passengers began to board the bus. The driver took his seat. The vehicle had filled up. When there were just a few seconds before departure, someone came up to her and called out to her most compassionately, "Amma." She turned towards him as if about to ask, in her, "What is it, my son?"

"Won't you move over to the Ladies side?" he asked, pointing to the corner of a seat which already held three people. He was making a grave mistake. He was attempting to pierce through her line of defense. But this time she was ready.

"No, I will not," she replied with determination. He was somewhat taken aback, but went on, "Ladies shouldn't sit here, amma."

"Why, is there some rule to that effect?" she asked.

"There isn't a rule as such. But I usually sit here and go on chatting with the driver-*annacchi*."

"Well, I too intend to sit here and go on chatting to the driver-annacchi," she told him.

The driver looked at her in surprise. The man who had called out to her asked, "Are you travelling on your own?"

She nodded and turned away. "Leave it out, *ya*," said the driver, starting up the bus. His friend gazed all round the bus, as if he wanted to inform all the passengers about some scandalous happening.

Two stops later, an old woman boarded the bus, along with a ten-year-old boy. The woman sat down at the edge of a seat meant for three people. The boy stood nearby, holding on to the back of her seat. She turned slightly and looked at him. He was wearing khaki shorts. His much-washed T-shirt was unironed and carried the name of an American university on the chest. Perhaps, he had liked the symbol and bought it just for that. He stood there, watching the reflection of the street in the mirror in front of him. His hair was combed down smooth. Piercing dark eyes, fringed with long lashes. She moved along her seat a little, turned around and asked, "Thambi, would you like to sit down?"

He hesitated a moment, then came and sat down. The bus went on its way. A tiny bird with a black tail, yellow breast, and sharp beak seated on a telegraph wire grazed the eye and then disappeared. She and the boy saw it together. Then he turned and smiled at her. She smiled back.

"What's its name?" he asked.

She told him she didn't know its name, but that there was a book which told you all about the birds in India. She said that it explained about birds in each region. She told him about Salim Ali. She explained that it was his favorite pastime to watch birds through a telescope.

"Can I find that book?"

"Mm. It must be in your school library. Look out for it."

"Our school took us to Vedathangal. There were birds there which had come even from Russia. I wondered how they come from such a distance."

"Is that so?"

"Sometimes, I go with my father when he is guarding the fields; we sleep overnight there. Say, you suddenly wake up at two, two-thirty. If you look up you can see a crowd of seven or eight birds, white as white, flying quietly past. Sometimes, I even think I'm dreaming."

"Really?"

After a moment's silence, he said, as if he were sharing a secret with her, "I reared a squirrel, once."

"When?"

"When I was in the fourth. It had fallen under a papaya tree. I took it and put it in the cardboard box in which Appa's clock was packed, and I put a cloth underneath it. Amma fed it with a piece of cottonwool dipped in milk. Later I fed it with an ink filler. It drank up the milk and ran all over my arms."

"Mm."

"It died," he said, his throat choking.

"How?"

"I don't know."

"Did you make holes in the box?"

"Of course I did. How would it breathe otherwise?"

"Then how did it die?"

"I don't know."

As they were talking, they heard an uproar outside, "Stop the bus! Stop the bus!" There was a crowd of villagers out there. Some had stones in their hands. A cry was raised, "Chuck the stones at it, da!" The hands holding the stones went up.

Instantly she hugged the boy to herself, and leant down.

The driver stopped the bus in a panic, and climbed out.

"How dare you drive past, ya? You knocked over one of our people this morning and coolly drove off; now you think you can escape, do you? Are you likely to let you off?"

"Set the bus on fire, da!"

When the shouting and the outcry died down a little, the driver explained that his was not the bus they meant. And after a few others intervened to make peace, the bus was finally on its way.

The boy was still trembling slightly, all over. He leaned back against the arm she had placed on his shoulder. A little while later he fell asleep, his head laid back. There were still traces of fear on his face.

When she glanced at him, and then turned away to the right, the sun was sinking, floating in an orange sky. Cool circle of fire.

"Thambi," she said, waking him.

When he woke up with a start, she pointed to the sunset. "Look there."

He opened his eyes wide to see. She told him about an extraordinary sunset she had seen as a child in Karnataka, at a place called Agumbe. She told him how the sun seemed to take all sorts of forms as it sank, appearing to the eye as square, or oblong, or winecup-shaped.

"Truly?" asked the boy, in wonder.

The bus entered the terminus and came to a stop. The old man who had boarded the bus with the boy caught hold of his hand again and climbed down. She took got off the bus. The boy took the old lady's hand and began to walk towards the exit of the bus station.

When he reached the gate, he turned around and looked at her. In the gathering dusk, his eyes gleamed.

A Movement, a Folder, Some Tears

Charu's message came by email.

I haven't yet got rid of my jet-lag. When others are asleep,
I'm awake. When they are awake, my eyes feel heavy. Hence
this letter, written while the CD plays. The usual song.
Tamal's favourite, in Hindi:

Alone
in this city
  a man
seeking a living
night and day
seeking a nest...

You didn't even turn up at the airport. I waited until the
last moment. Every time someone passed by with cropped

hair, wearing a kurta, my heart leapt, certain it must be you. Sakina and you must have been together that day.

True, Sakina didn't say much as they travelled together on the electric train. Dark circles under her eyes. The fan where they stood wasn't working. Sakina's face was covered all over with sweat. She could never stand the heat at the best of times. In the swelter of May, she hung on to the chain in the crowded compartment, streaming with sweat. Her neck and shoulders – once burnt by fire, now swollen, twisted, scarred, changed in colour – were wet through. She didn't even notice when her face was gently blotted with her *dupatta*. Ten years ago, when she came home from the hospital after the event, she had said, "Look at my neck and shoulders! It's as if some strange creature is lying upon me. You said, didn't you, that a snake tumbled about your Sivan's neck? Now, I too have a snake around mine."

Exactly six months later she broke down. "They're here. They've come. They are throwing torches dipped in oil into the house," she began to scream as she ran about. A whole month passed during which she screamed and wailed and shouted. After that, gradually she quietened down. She wrote about that day for the psychiatrist, with complete lucidity.

"It was a Friday. Only Ammi and I were at home. Although it was December, the afternoon felt really warm. We had left the window open, to let in a little breeze. Ammi was asleep. I was reading a book. In the distance, I heard a cry rising to a crescendo. An outbreak of noises, screaming, roaring, clamouring. Suddenly, it had become a great deluge. Before I could get up, rolls of cloth smelling of kerosene thudded into the room. Following them came burning torches. I had a nylon dupatta about my neck. I hastened to throw it away, but it had become stuck. I prised it off and flung it. It fell on Ammi, who was hard of hearing, and still sleeping peacefully. Before she could get away, screaming, two more burning torches were on her. I fell down in a faint. When I became conscious, Ammi was beside me, a blackened corpse."

Her voice, recorded on a tape, spoke in English without a falter.

Doctor: Sakina, do you harbour any anger in your heart?

Sakina: (Laughs.) Doctor, when I heard the shouts of those crowds, I was reading Sahir Ludhianvi's poems. The poem that begins, "That dawn will break some day." The next instant I was burnt by the fire. Until I broke down, I felt no anger. Only despair. Now, I have a feeling I have saved myself from drowning in my grief. Now, yes, there is anger in my heart, Doctor. That is my support. My strength. My anchor. Have you been told to remove the anger from the minds and hearts of those who have been caught in these riots, Doctor? Don't do it. I'm going to keep this anger knotted up in my dupatta. I'm not going to scatter it away. I shall go about, hereafter, wrapped in it. Listening to it. Learning from it. I need that anger to help make sure it never happens again.

"Sakina, *tabiyat theek nahiin hai, kya?*. . . Don't you feel well? Did you take your blood-pressure tablets?"

"Mm," she said.

"Charu must have packed up all her luggage."

"Mm."

They didn't say anything more as they got off the train and made their way to Hutatma Chowk where the meeting was to take place. A small pandal had been put up there. There would be songs, speeches, and discussions until late evening.

At five o'clock, Sakina touched her shoulder and said, "I'll just walk up to Nargis Khala's house, and come back. We'll go to the airport together later."

But she hadn't come back even after the meeting was over at eight.

Nargis Khala said, when she rang her from a public telephone, "I've just heard the news about Sakina."

"What news?"

"Sakina fell down."

"What? She isn't hurt or anything, is she?"

Khala's voice broke. "She fell from above."

"From above? Has she broken any. . .?

Khala wept. "She fell from the seventeenth floor. . . From the terrace of the building where Iqbal Maamu lives."

She listened to all the details, and then hurried there. . .

Sakina's neck was broken. She had fallen on to the grass lawn. No dreadful sight of splattered blood. Her head hung down like a chicken whose neck had been wrung. Her body waited for the routine post-mortem procedure.

When she touched Sakina's arm, it felt cold. She stroked Sakina's neck. Gently she pinched her ear. Kissed her forehead. All the while, tears spurted from her eyes. A pain inside, as if she were being hit by a hammer.

At what moment did you decide to do this, Sakina? When you saw the grass far beneath you, what did you think? What came to your mind? Did you think, wretched girl, that if you fell, the grass would be soft beneath you? Did you place your foot on the hook set into the wall and climb on to the parapet? Did you stand right up there? Did you gaze at the mountainous buildings all around, reaching up to the sky? Did you see the ocean beyond the building, blue and flowing? Did you lift your arms and dive like a swimming champion? Or, did you slip and slide as you fell? Did you scream, *kannamma*? Did your voice dissolve away in the wind, *thangam*? At what instant did you die? When you touched the ground? On the way there? Or, had you died already, even when we travelled together this morning?

She continued to stroke Sakina's head.

What was it that shattered you? What defeated you? What came upon you in that instant's whirlwind and pushed you over? Was it what happened last month? Charu and you went to Ahmedabad to prepare a report. Charu's father's sister has a house there. An aunt who knew you from the moment you became Charu's friend. The same aunt who always looked forward to the vermicelli *payasam* you brought her at the time of Id. This time she refused to allow Charu and you inside her house. Her daughter and son-in-law stood at the doorway, blocking your entry. When Charu proclaimed loudly that the upstairs room belonged to her father, she was handed the key and told to use the outside stairs to go up. Charu and you stayed there for three days. There isn't a soul who has not read the report you two prepared. When Charu, you, and I were together on two different evenings, you spoke about a couple of things that happened.

First. The front door which Charu and you had to pass was sometimes ajar. When you glanced inside, once, the aunt's three-year-old grandson was playing with dolls. A small sword and shield, a few plastic dolls – these were his favourite toys. He sliced off the doll's arms and legs with his sword. He struck a blow even in that shiny place where the doll had no organ.

You called him to the door. "Kuber!" He turned round and smiled.

"Should you cut up the doll like that? Isn't it like a little baby?"

Tiny sword in hand, he came to the door, with shining eyes. "It's a Muchlim. I've killed it," he said, in his childish language.

"Kuber, Sakina *Mausi* also is a Muslim."

Still smiling, he stuck his toy sword into your stomach.

"*Jai* Cheeram," he said.

Second. There was a celebration in the temple at the street corner. Singing loudly and shrilly, Charu's aunt leapt up and down, calling on God's name. The devotional *bhajans* came out like hisses. At one stage, she and her bhajan companions whirled round in what appeared to be a frenzied dance, streaming with sweat, their hair loose, while the floor shook beneath their heavy tread.

When her aunt returned home, Charu called down to her, "Bua."
Her aunt turned her gaze towards the upstairs room.

Those were not Bua's eyes. In the fading twilight, lit by the
streetlamp's yellow light, they glinted like a wolf's eyes.

Now, Iqbal Maamu laid his hand on her shoulder. "Selvi Beti," he
said, patting her, consoling her.

The whole family came to the airport. Kalavati Mausi's son
sent a car and a driver. You won't believe it. Tamal's parents
were there. Tamal's son, Manush, had brought them. Amala,
Tamal's wife, too. She said she could understand at last my
relationship with Tamal for twenty-five years. She wished
me success in my journey towards further research. Tamal's
father stroked my head and blessed me. He said, "Who
knows whether we will still be here if and when you come
back; go safely and return safely." At that moment I wasn't
at the airport. I was on the train to Matunga. In 1993. To us
in the women's compartment, the bomb blast sounded only
like Diwali celebrations. That instant when the train stopped
and I peeped out with the others is still sharply etched in
my mind. It goes on extending, extending, extending in my
mind, like batter spreading out and out in a pan. Because of
the crowds, I had joined the women, while Tamal stayed in
the general compartment.

"There's been a bomb blast in one of the general
compartments." When I jumped down, went forward a little,
and pushed my way through the crowds, Tamal lay on the

ground. Both legs reduced to a blood-porridge below the knees. His chest covered in blood.

When I rushed to him, calling out "Tamal," I realized that for an instant he himself didn't know what had happened.

"What happened?" he asked. As he was carried into the ambulance, he raised himself a little and looked down towards his legs. He looked at me and folded his hands, as if to say, Save me from this. Next to him was an old Muslim man, covered in wounds. The games of History. Historical games. Nobody was with him. Some good people from the train helped me to take him and Tamal to the hospital. Tamal remained conscious until his name was registered.

"Tamal Mukherji," he said, without faltering. Fifty years of age, he said. His religion was Humanity, he said. There was no one to introduce the old Muslim gentleman.

The police investigation came from a strange and oblique perspective. "Did these two conspire together to place the bomb, or was it only one of them who did it?"

With the help of many people, I reclaimed Tamal's body and had it cremated in the crematorium attached to the hospital. Even when it was all over, the Muslim gentleman's family was wandering about, waiting for his body. His aged wife, who didn't have the least idea about the severity of the regulations, came to me and began, "Beti, if an accident happens when you are travelling by train, can you claim compensation? I have two daughters. I must get them married. It was to arrange for some money that he set out this morning." I stood there holding her hand. You will remember. We tried to claim compensation for her. We failed. Then we set up a fund and made a collection for her. All this came to mind, lit up as if by a lightning flash. And once again, as I write this.

Sakina put an end to herself. She was a lawyer. She was not unaware of the procedural confusions following such a death. It was not unknown to her that she should have left a letter. Surely her death could not have been predetermined. It must have been the result of an aberration, a sudden whirlwind attack, a wave of vivid emotion that overcame her. Attempting to lean over just a little, she must have tipped over completely. She suffered from blood pressure. She had received psychiatric treatment in 1992.

After Sakina's death was recorded in the police files, complete with all these explanations, in a language peculiar to government offices, her body was handed over. And buried.

Sakina had gone to collect a folder which was left in Iqbal Maamu's flat. That is what she said to him on the telephone. Soon after she arrived, she had a cup of tea, and went to the room where the books were kept.

The file was there, in an almirah. The door on the far side of the room opened on to the terrace. Fifteen minutes later, the caretaker of the building rang the doorbell and kept on ringing until the door was opened.

"A woman has jumped from the terrace of your..."

"Don't talk nonsense," said Maamu, "I'm alone in the flat..."

Before he could finish, he remembered Sakina's presence. He ran to the library. No Sakina. The door to the terrace stood open. The door of the almirah in which the file was kept had been unlocked. The lock and key together had been left on top of the almirah. Far below, Sakina lay, a crooked line. Her black dupatta was caught at the wing-tip of the topiary bird in the garden, and was swinging in the wind.

Running downstairs, laying her in his lap, weeping aloud. The neighbours supporting Maamu. . .

Again and again Iqbal Maamu described it all. His beloved niece. He had supported her throughout her legal studies. He had accepted all her decisions. He spoke of them repeatedly.

The almirah was still unlocked. He opened it, took out the folder, and gave it to Selvi. The cover bore the name of their organization:-Jagruti. Awareness.

When it was time for me to go in, a silence fell over all of
us. Then, the goodbyes. Choking throats. Tears in Ba's eyes.
Bapu wiping his eyes with his handkerchief. As I went in,
I saw my own reflection in the glass door. I was weeping. I
am weeping, I told myself. I have wept before, many times.
In the upper berth of a railway compartment. Waiting for a
train late one night at a railway station empty of humanity,
looking up at the stars. In a bullock cart, staring at the
animal's tail. In the bathroom of an airport. Sitting in the
corner of the upper deck of a bus. Driving at speed down the
middle of a road. So many leave-takings. So many farewells.

Another goodbye. Another bout of tears. In the glass door, a fifty-year-old woman holding on to her shoulder bag and setting off for further research. Long hair, uncut. Cheeks streaked with tears. I held on to the rubbish bins for support, and let the tears flow.

"Do you need any help?" A woman, a fellow-traveller, had stopped in front of me.

"No, thank you," I said, and walked on towards the inner door. Even now as I write this, at this instant when everyone is asleep and I'm awake, the tears flow from my eyes. It's as if a long era of which we were part, as makers of history, has now come to an end.

I can't understand it. I sometimes wonder if it's part of the tiredness which comes with the menopause. But I think I have never felt such weariness before. When did the body control us, ever? When did it dominate us? Were we ever afraid of it? We never even thought of old age. How would it occur to us to be concerned about old age with the example of Nargis Khala before of us? She has never stopped working for her organization has she, even though she is eighty-seven years old now, and crippled, besides? Whenever I think of Nargis Khala, I remember the sound of her typewriter – placed on the table by the window, so that she can look out – as she taps out a statement on human rights, or writes a letter to a newspaper about freedom of speech. Last month she told me she was considering buying a computer. I said,

"Don't, Khala. I can relate to you only with this typewriter."
She answered, "Can I keep from changing, just for the sake
of your illusions?"

I argued a lot with her that day. I shouted at her. "Just
be quiet, Khala. Why did people like you – people who
spent the best part of your lives with Gandhi, who fought
for Independence – end up later on in ashrams and small
towns? Why did you decide not to enter politics? If you had
given your country half the devotion you gave to Gandhi, the
politics of this country might have taken a different course.
Who asked you for your renunciation? In 1942, you marched
through all these streets without fear, like the queens of the
locality. How often have we been thrilled by the photographs
of your processions, you with your banners held high. Don't
provoke me. You, your khaddar, and your spinning-wheels.
You have all become mere symbols. Symbols which we hang
on walls or wear as fashionable clothes and caps. Useless,
marginal symbols. Cowardly symbols. Frivolous symbols.
You left us no other political heritage."

Perhaps, I spoke like that out of the emotional state in
which I returned from Ahmedabad. As I spoke, I went up to
her wheelchair and shook Khala. Khala didn't stop me. Then
I buried my head in her lap. She laid her hands on my head,
like a blessing.

The folder lay on the table. All the other books and papers from
the room were in cardboard boxes. The boxes still gaped open. The

schoolboy, who lived downstairs, and his two friends had offered to tie them all up. The arrangement was that they would be paid enough so that they could go watch a Hrithik Roshan film.

She asked Nandini that morning, "We have to vacate the room, Nandu. Could you take a day off? I can't, on my own. . ."

Nandini answered, "I have a lot of work at the office. Otherwise I would have helped. I have to go to Pune as well, on Saturday, for my work. Won't it do if you clear it next week?"

"The landlord insists. . ."

Nandini was embarrassed. She felt sorry she couldn't help. She knew Charu had gone to the United States, Sakina wasn't there anymore, Selvi was on her own. Because of this, she answered without annoyance or irritation, without barking at her mother. Otherwise, she certainly would have retorted, "Please, Amma. I work in a private company. This is not a government job from which I can take off as I please. Nor is it a women's organization where I'm allowed a day's leave if I have my periods, or my child sneezes, or my husband has a headache, if there is a feast or a fast. If we want equal employment with men, we have to be prepared to work with them on equal terms."

Sometimes, Selvi wanted to say in return, "It was we who laid the way so that you could find a job suited to your intelligence, earning an equal wage with men. We weeded the thorns from your path, removed the obstacles, made you aware of your rights." But such discussions had ceased between them, long ago.

Three years ago, Charu, Sakina, and she had finished some work in Dongri and returned home past one o'clock at night. They had all decided to go straight to Selvi's place, as it would delay them even more if they stopped to eat on the way. They rang the front doorbell until their hands ached, but to no effect. No signs of anyone inside. At last they woke up their neighbours, jumped across from their balcony to Selvi's, pushed open the door which was just closed, and went in. It was a fifth-floor flat. Quite a circus feat, leaping from one balcony to the next at one o'clock at night. They were desperately hungry. Used plates and empty vessels lay strewn all over the kitchen work-surface. In an instant Charu cleaned the work-top. Sakina began to make the dough for chapatis. Selvi put the potatoes on to boil. When she took out the already boiled dal from the fridge, Charu seasoned it with chopped onions, tomatoes, ginger, garlic, and green chillies. A piping-hot meal of chapatis, dal, and potato-sabzi was ready at two o'clock in the night.

Ramu was alive then. When she asked him angrily, the next morning, why he had not opened the door at night, he snapped back, "If you come home at twelve and one, I can't be expected to keep awake and open the door."

"Why, haven't I opened the door for you when you came back at three after a night out with your friends? Haven't I fed you?"

"I was tired. I fell asleep. So must you make such a song and a dance about it?"

"We had to jump across the balcony to get in. Sakina suffers from blood pressure. You know that, don't you?"

Charu and Sakina intervened, preventing the argument from growing worse.

Later, while they were having tea, Nandini turned up and Selvi asked her, "How could you have been so fast asleep? Didn't you hear us ringing the front doorbell?"

Nandini said, "Amma, I could hear quite clearly the way you were fighting early this morning. That is what is known as oppression. Goon. Go and write another book." Then, turning to Sakina and Charu, she added in English, "Isn't that right?" When Selvi explained to her friends what Nandini had said, their faces tightened.

Even though Ramu died in an accident, the relatives spoke as if it was all owing to her lack of care. "A good man. Half the time he made his own coffee, and drank it all alone... And for all that, it was his own choice to marry her..."

Yes. That happened twenty-five years ago. It still remained their complaint.

Nandini too had said, "You should have looked after Appa better, Amma. You were always running off to some procession protesting against dowry or rape or whatever. People who think like that should never get married."

At that time she had not had the strength to explain to her daughter that in their youth Ramu and she had belonged to the same group of friends, and that he had married her precisely because he admired her activism.

The landlord came and looked in.

"*Udya kali karnarna nakki*?... You'll definitely vacate the room tomorrow, won't you?"

It was an old-fashioned tiled house. As you climbed up the wooden stairs, there was a small room to the right. Their office for the past twenty years.

"Yes," she assured him, and turned away. The sharks of the building trade had their eyes on this house. It was in an area that had become popular among actors and the newly rich. The landlord had been muttering for the past two years about so many women coming here. When Muslim women came, he said, the house stank. As if the winds emanating from him were perfumed! Perhaps our own farts smell sweet to us. He said they stank because they ate beef. Having endured the many odours he expelled, lifting his thigh and contorting his body, they had no wish to explain to him about Vedic times.

He was concerned that they might ask for some compensation because they had rented the room for so many years. Sakina had said that before they looked for another place, they should really hold out for the money.

When she took up the folder – the folder with a purple cover – and placed it on her lap, it was as if Sakina was beside her. Snake-neck woman. She who knotted up her anger in her dupatta.

You were angry when I began to apply for research grants.
You shouted at me. You charged me with being a coward.
You said I was running away to hide. I accept all your
accusations. But my dear friend, I am also the woman who
saw her lover's legs reduced to a mess of blood. I didn't give

way then. I didn't run away. I stood. I opposed. I fought. These past ten years, I gave all my breath and being to the work of Jagruti. I immersed myself in music. How many Kabir *dohas* I sang, in how many places! Do you remember the devotional song, "Aaj sajan mohé," which begins,

Embrace me today, my love,
let this life reach fruition.
Heart's pain,
body's fire,
let all be cool. . .

Rising higher and higher, the song would go

Quench my thirst, Giridhara,
enchanter of my heart
I thirst from the very depths of my being,
I have thirsted for many generations.

When I sang the words "I thirst – I have thirsted," repeating them over and over again, didn't all three of us – you, me, Sakina – weep?

It wasn't just a thirst for human love. It was that unquenched thirst within us. We are people who continue to wander about with that thirst. Even now, when I say "from the very depth of my being," an ache like a cold wind enters my whole self. You must believe this. If I decided, in spite of that, that I had to come away, should you not understand that I had a strong enough reason?

Selvi, Kumudben Bua is not just my aunt. She became a widow at an early age, and came to live at our house with her young son. She gave me her unflinching support in all my decisions. She accepted Tamal. Just because Tamal loved fish, she allowed it to be cooked in her house. She called our house-dog "Arjun Beta" without any hesitation, and fed it the offering from her daily puja. After Arjun died, she gave the offering every day to a street dog, in Arjun's name. She was never held back by the requirements of ritual. She never allowed anyone to be held back in that way. It was she who taught me about humanity.

The first shock came when she refused to allow me inside the house in Ahmedabad. The look she gave Sakina was the second blow. The third whiplash was the change in her eyes that evening. There was a further blow which felt as if it ripped my flesh away. I never told you both this. Bua used to go out with other women from time to time. Always, when she returned, there would be a kind of energy in the way she walked. Once, on her return, I came face to face with her. She lifted her hand to stop me from touching her. Selvi, the stench of kerosene came from her hand. My whole body began to shudder. We left that very day.

I didn't say anything to anyone. That evening, when I was at home, Bapu said at the dining table, "The Muslims have learnt a good lesson." Ba added, "Let them all go to Pakistan." These people are all of my blood. The food stuck in my throat. How did this lake of poison come about? How could I have been so blind? Why did we never see the growth of this horror which was capable of dividing parents and daughter, brother and sister; which could come between all relationships?

Several little incidents appeared in a new light, suddenly. No one asking after Sakina for many days. Ba's simple puja of lighting her lamp becoming more and more complex over the last two years. A sticker on Bapu's car mirror, saying, "Say with pride, I am a Hindu." My sticker on top of that one, "Say with pride, we are human beings." Ba's comment when I bought a green sari, "Why did you go for this Muslim-green?" No longer buying bread from Mohammed Kaka's shop as we have done for years. Various conversations in relatives' houses. Small incidents, whose violence was striking, when added together. Each and every one had been a drop of poison. It felt as if the kerosene I smelt on Kumudben Bua's hand had pervaded our house.

A fear that this storm of madness might never cease, caught in my mind like a hook. It's a good thing Tamal died. He could never have borne this.

There's a little story in a Paulo Coelho novel. In a distant land there lived a wizard. He poured a drug that induced madness into the town well. The people drank it and began to go about as they pleased, in a totally crazy manner. When

the king tried to bring about laws to control them, they told
him to leave the throne. So the king decided to abdicate. The
queen, though, counselled otherwise. "Oh, king, don't give
up your throne. Come, let us also drink from the same well."
And as soon as they drank, they became like everyone else.
The problem was over. I was afraid there was no well left that
the wizard had not touched, Selvi. It was then that I decided
to leave the country. I did not have the strength to live with
this day after day. Today, I write this to you alone. It will take
me days to write to Sakina.

In the folder, there were notes for the Jagruti newsletters, descriptions of some of their events, details of women who had come to them for legal advice, summaries of discussions, details of arguments. Records that Sakina had collected and kept with care.

There was even a note on the occasion, in 1980, when they had cut their hair. She wrote, "On the dais, there was a debate going on about physical beauty. A professor-poet began by saying that the beauty of an Indian woman is signalled by long hair, big breasts, tiny waist, and sword-like eyes, and went on to sing a purana to long hair. Selvi and I exchanged glances. Since Nandu was born, Selvi scarcely has time to comb her hair. As for me, travelling constantly, long hair is a real burden. What's more, as the professor went on and on, gushing and melting about long hair, the trail of peacock's feathers, the spread of dark clouds, etc., everyone's eyes were on us. We went straight off and had our hair cut. We felt light-headed; head-strong no longer!

Selvi remembered it well. Those were times when they faced everything with an energy that said, "You can't define us. We will break your definitions, your commentaries, your grammars, your rules." They felt an urgency to defy everything. She and Sakina had gone to a Chinese beauty parlour and had their hair cropped close to their heads. When she went home, Ramu only asked, making no fuss, "Well Selvi, was it a pilgrimage to Palani or to Tirupati?" "Neither; it was to China," she told him. Lively times, those were.

There was a little notebook containing the songs they sang in the eighties, during their marches:

Don't surrender,
don't submit,
don't drown,
don't die.
We are the Revolution.
To all injustice we are the reply.

Charu always led the singing. All the rest joined in the chorus.

There was a copy, in the folder, of the sticker printed with the *Mandir-Masjid* song, which they had pasted on all the railway compartments after the Babri Masjid was demolished.

Temples, mosques, and gurudwaras
they divided from each other.
They divided the land,
they divided the sea.

Don't divide human beings
Don't divide human beings.

Charu had written a note on the occasion when Sakina was to give a speech at a meeting in a women's college near Churchgate during the Shah Bano case. The question of maintenance was being re-examined.

"They had announced that the meeting would be at six in the evening. When Sakina and I went there, there were many burka-clad women outside the college, carrying placards which said things like, "Shariat alone protects women," and "We will only listen to Shariat." I looked at Sakina. "There are two sides to everything, aren't there?" she remarked. There was a huge crowd in the hall. Sakina's lawyer friend, Shahid, sat down beside me. When Sakina began to speak, the burka-clad women rose up in a wave. They moved in on Sakina, shouting, "You are not a true Muslim. You don't know the Koran. You don't say your prayers. You are an enemy of Muslim women." When they insisted again and again, "Tell us, are you a Muslim or not?" Sakina became distressed, unable to move any further back. Her voice broke as she said, "I really am a Muslim. I have read the Koran. I know my prayers. Let me speak. . ." Shahid tried to restrain the man next to him who was jumping up and down, and said, "Why don't we listen to her at least?" The man yelled back, "Shut up, you are not a Muslim." Shahid replied, "I am, actually." The crowds became uncontrollable, and the police arrived.

"Shahid and I brought Sakina away through the back door. She was shattered. "This is going to be a huge battle, Charu," she said. "It begins with someone else giving me an identity."

Like a sequel to this, there was an incident in the house of Charu's relatives two years later. Selvi remembered it as soon as she read Charu's report.

The discussion had begun in an apparently lighthearted manner. "Every Muslim has four wives." Charu and she had interrupted to say that it wasn't true, and that in any case, many Hindus they knew had more than one wife. At this, Charu's uncle's son remarked, "Of course, Charu, you have to say that. It concerns you, after all. You are Tamal's *rakhel*, his mistress, aren't you?"

"Very well, let me be a rakhel, Sudhir. But how many wives did your grandfather have? And do you know the story of your great-grandfather? He scattered his seed all over Gujarat very generously. Watch out, there are several of his great-grandsons walking all over Gujarat, with the same features as you."

"All that is irrelevant. Selvi, have you read Tulsiramayan?"

"Why would I read Tulsiramayan? I've read Kambaramayanam, certainly. As Tamil Literature."

"Isn't Sri Ram your god, then?

"Life is my god."

"If I ask you whether you are a Hindu, can you answer Yes or No?"

"I can only say I was born into a Hindu family."

"Yes or No? Tell me that."

"Yes. No."

They didn't hit out. They didn't kick. But that was all. They roared. They thundered. They ridiculed. They spoke with contempt. When she refused to eat, they said, "Che, this is only a friendly discussion."

The interview with Nargis Khala was on green paper. An interview which all three of them had held with her. She had talked of her days during the Independence struggle, and had ended by saying, "You might ask me what I achieved in my life. I'll tell you a story in reply to that. A Zen master went away to live in a cave in a remote mountain. On his return, the king summoned him to the court and asked him to give an account of the wisdom he had attained. The master was silent for a while, and then he took out the reed flute that was tucked in at his waist, and played a cadence on it, very softly and sweetly; then walked away. Some things can't be said. They can't be wrapped up in words. If you ask me about my achievements, I will touch you with these hands. Hoping that through my fingers, the warmth of my experience will reach you. I will touch your heads with my hands. What else can I do? What do I know except that?"

How often had Nargis Khala touched her? Stroked her cheek? When Sakina and Charu returned from Ahmedabad and poured out their distress, she put her arms around both, embracing them. At that moment she looked like Jatayu.

"Broad views about life have shrunk into religions, and we have been turned into their symbols. They regard us as empty symbols. Symbols of a religion, a nation. We mustn't be trapped by that. In this war, let that be the ground of your contest. A ground that cannot be reduced to definition and detail."

"But what are our weapons, Khala? What, if anything, can be our weapons?"

"Only this," she said, laying the palms of her hands, wrinkled like withered leaves, against their cheeks. She smiled.

"Aunty, may we come in?" The two young boys were strikingly tall. A girl of the same age was with them. All three worked fast. When they stopped for a rest, halfway through, they danced to "*Bole chudian*" and "*Shava shava*." Then they returned to their work. All for the sake of Hrithik Roshan.

One of the boys said, "Our Baba told us Amir Khan is Muslim. We mustn't go to Amir Khan films. And we mustn't drink Coca-Cola."

"Really? Hrithik Roshan's wife is Muslim. Amir Khan's wife is Hindu. Don't drink either Coca-Cola or Pepsi. Your teeth will rot. Tell your Baba."

"I'll tell him," he said, hesitantly. He was afraid the money might not come into his hands.

As soon as they were paid, they fled, shouting, "*Thanda matlab* Coca-Cola."

It's night-time here. I'm sitting in a cyber centre, writing this. I'll tell you later why I'm here.

First, there is some important news. Sakina is dead. She fell from the terrace of Iqbal Maamu's seventeenth-storey flat and died. Her neck was broken. How much violence there has been in our lives! Tamal's death in the bomb blast. Ramu's death in the car accident. Now, Sakina's ill-fated death. These are violent times. We cannot redeem our lives until we have passed through them.

Sakina's death stabs at my heart even now. She was with me that day until early evening. She seemed a little weary. I was distraught because I could not understand why she told me she would go to Nargis Khala's house, but changed her mind and went to Iqbal Maamu instead. She was my friend from our school days. I agonized over why she committed suicide when there should have been so many more years of friendship ahead of us. I couldn't accept that it was suicide. Before she went she had said, "Let us go and say goodbye to Charu at the airport." I thought and thought about what could have happened between five o'clock and the moment of her fall; I retraced her steps again and again. Some things became clear to me.

The night before, she returned from her second visit to Ahmeda-bad. When she telephoned me, her voice didn't sound right to me. I insisted, "Come round to my flat at once. You don't sound good at all. I'm sure you haven't eaten at all properly." She came. I made her favourite soft rotis, and a potato, and bell-pepper curry. She ate. Later, as we lay down and talked, she told me about an incident that happened the previous evening. It was rather late when she reached the refugee camp. A young Muslim woman was walking in front of her, she said, one child on her hip, and another clutching her hand. She walked along, supporting both children, and managing at the same time to carry a bag in one hand. The tri-colour flag was stuck between her fingers and she was walking along, extending it in front of her. Like a protective shield. As if she were proclaiming, I too am a citizen of this country.

"I wept and wept, Selvi, when I saw this. Why has it become so necessary for just a few of us to have to do this? My Khala was a freedom fighter. My Maamu heads many charitable institutions in this city. My Ammi retired from an administrative post in a school. She died a blackened corpse. My father was a high-ranking official. Here am I, walking about with a snake-neck. That girl might have come from a similar family. Or she might have been one of India's many, many poor women. I couldn't bear to see her stumbling along with her children, her bag, and her tri-colour flag." She wept for a long time. She repeated again and again, overwhelmed by the thought, "The time has come when I have to establish that my Khala was this, my Ammi was that, and so on and on..."

She was devastated by the thought that the actions of her family – performed naturally and as a matter of course – had to be presented now as her credentials. She said, "Selvi, do you remember what Charu used to say? That when certain birds decide to die, they swallow many pebbles; then when they try to fly, they cannot because of the weight inside them. So they crash down and die. My heart feels so heavy – as if I've swallowed many stones."

"You go to sleep now," I said, patting her. She dropped off

like a child. But there was no cheerfulness in her expression the next day. Later, we stood together in the heat in Hutatma Chowk. She was participating in the hunger strike, besides. At first, she really must have set out for Nargis Khala's flat. Then, remembering we had to vacate the Jagruti office in the next few days, it could have struck her that she might as well collect the folder from Iqbal Maamu's flat since she was in that part of town. I conjecture all this from Iqbal Maamu's memory of his conversation with Sakina over tea, that last day.

It seems that while she was waiting for a taxi to take her to Iqbal Maamu's house, she met Nandini. She asked Nandini where she was off to. Nandini said to her, "Sakina Mausi, I have to tell you something. Keep away from Amma and me for a while. I hold a responsible position. I don't wish to be caught up in any kind of trouble. . ." This from the girl whom you and Sakina brought up. When she was a child, she thought of Sakina's Ammi and Khala as her grandmothers.

Already Sakina was a bird that had swallowed many pebbles. Nandini made her swallow a block of granite. It seemed Sakina just patted her on her back. Soon after she got to Iqbal Maamu's flat, she went and opened the book-almirah. I went to Maamu's flat myself, and made myself go through all her actions. The instant she opened the almirah, she would have seen the photograph of Ammi holding Nandini in her arms. Sakina must have been deeply moved.

I think she didn't take her blood-pressure tablets that day. She must have felt dizzy. She must have opened the terrace door, gone outside, and taken a few deep breaths. She might have remembered the topiary bird. She might have held on to the parapet wall, raised herself a little, and peered down. Empty stomach. Seventeenth floor. Suddenly her foot might have slipped. I believe that's what happened. She fell against the topiary bird, and then crashed to the ground. And that is how our Sakina met her end.

Now, please read the attachment I have sent with this message. Finish the letter later. When the girl who worked in Sakina's house had her baby, it was the fiftieth anniversary of Independence. Sakina wrote this then. I found it in the folder. I think she must have written it for us, all that while ago.

Attachment: For Roshni, a morning song.

A few weeks ago your mother invited me to your home to give you a name; to whisper it in your ear. In that tiny hut, where there was scarcely enough room to sit down, your mother had hung a cradle which she had bought for a hundred rupees. She had strung flowers around the room. She had bought a new frock for you. A couple of months ago I had seen you in the hospital – within three hours of your birth. You looked like a peeled fruit then! Now your face and your features were bright, radiant. When I whispered in your ear, like a secret,

"You are Roshni, you are Light," you swivelled your eyes round and gazed at me.

Every night, your grandmother, who gave up her share of a small piece of agricultural land and left her village to come and work in the big city and bring up four daughters in this slum colony by the seaside, will sing you to sleep with lullabies. As you grow up she will tell you stories to the sound of the waves until you fall asleep. Stories of kings and queens, stories about the devil, about valorous mothers and noble wives. At dawn, the calling of the *azaan* from the mosque will wake everyone, summoning them to prayers. I have heard that in the temples too, they sing the *tirupalli ezhucchi* to wake up the gods. Roshni, this is my azaan for you, my dawn song. To wake you up and keep you awake. This is the song of my generation. The generation that has lived through these past fifty years. A generation that wants to tell many stories, in many voices, in many forms. You will hear many tunes here. And there will be some discordant notes, too. Because it spans many years. It touches many lives. Lives which are similar, and very different. But do listen to it.

During these years, it wasn't easy to grow up, to live, to make the right choices in life, in education and work. Several of us, even now, keep changing those choices. We had to oppose the mainstream and swim against it, taking care not to be caught in the whirlpools. They told us many stories, too. They told us that for women, marriage was the most important thing in life. But we had also heard of the Sufi saint

Rubaiya, and of Meera. We knew about Bhakti. All the same, several among us were atheists, didn't believe in rituals, didn't accept that one religion alone was true. Even now, that is so.

From our childhood, the Independence movement and its ideals had merged into our lives. The men and women who had been part of it were our role models. Many of them lived among us. They came and spoke to us in our schools. You could say there wasn't a home without a picture of Gandhi, smiling. From our schooldays we learnt the song about Gandhi's life, which began, "*Suno, suno ae duniyavalo Bapujiki amar kahaani.*" When we were still in school, we saw the film *Jagruti* in which a teacher takes his pupils all over India and sings to them, "Take this earth, and wear it on your forehead as an auspicious sign. This is the land of our sacrifices." For our generation it became almost a national song. We were stirred by other Hindi songs, such as the one that went, "We have saved the boat from the storm and brought it safely ashore. Children, safeguard this land." We wept. There were some among us who had grown up learning the poems of the poet Bharati. Iqbal's lyric "*Sare jehan se accha*" rang out in every school. We learnt to sing Tagore's songs, "*Ekla chalo*" and "*Amar janmabhumi,*" making no discrimination against any language. In another picture Kabuliwallah, the hero, from Kabul, sings a song, remembering his country. "My beloved land, I dedicate my heart to you. You are my desire. You are my honour. I greet the winds that come from your direction with a *salaam.* Your dawns are most beautiful; your evenings most splendidly coloured." We used to apply these words to our own country, and weep. Of course, there were other labels amongst us – as Marathi, Kannadiga, Tamil, Telugu, Punjabi, Assamese, and so on. But for us who grew up in the years following Independence, the country as a whole was the important thing.

But these were not the only songs we heard. There were other sounds and voices. Proverbs, discussions, the voices of everyday life. Listen to some of them: Rubbish and daughters grow quickly. Women and cows will go where you drag them. Women and earth become fertile with beating. A woman learns by giving birth; a man learns through trade. A daughter is like a basket of snakes on the head. A leaking roof and a nagging wife are best abandoned. A woman's virtue is like a glass vessel. If a husband batters or the rain lashes, to whom can you complain? You may sit on any ground, you may sleep with any woman.

Sometimes, the older women in our homes, or travellers we met on journeys, sang yet other songs. Work songs, dirges, lullabies. Women spoke of their tribulations in such songs. Such sounds brought us down to earth from the idealistic heights where we were floating. I found some of those songs in books, too. One remains in my memory: it's a song by a widow who says she might have served society better had she bloomed as a flower on a tree and not been born a woman. The metaphor in the song refuses to leave me.

There was also something called national culture. Motherhood was at its core. A woman like Jija Mata. A woman who suckled her child with the milk of valour. Before our time, women had already left their homes to work for the country. They had accomplished extraordinary things. But we, who came after them, had to safeguard our homes. We were instructed that our duty was to reap the benefits of the previous generation, to listen without opening our mouths, never to raise any questions. Our responsibility was to create a home, set up a good family, learn what was useful to society. The advice to us was clear: Sit still. Otherwise you will rock the boat.

Our bodies grew heavy. We carried a heavy burden of stones that we did not choose to carry. I say all this, Roshni, with the clarity of hindsight. But at that time we were both clear and confused. We were not silent, though. Do you know, there is a Bengali proverb that says, No one can control a woman's tongue? So we never stopped talking. We spoke up through poems, stories, political essays, music, drama, painting; in many different ways. Many of us aimed for higher education. If you look at many family photograph albums, there will be one photograph of a young woman in a graduation gown, clutching a rolled-up degree in her hand. Wearing an expression of fulfilment. Head held high. A keenness in the eyes. I too have such a photograph. But it was also customary, as soon as this photograph was taken, to remove the graduation gown and take another photo which would be sent to prospective bridegrooms. I told you, didn't I, there were all kinds of pressures on our lives? It wasn't easy to deal with them. A woman called Subhadra Khatre has said, "It would be good to deposit one's femininity in a safe-deposit vault and move around freely in the outside world." She was an engineer of that time. She writes, "Had I been a typist, I would have picked up a job easily. As an engineer, they looked at me as if I were trying to usurp a man's place."

Until the end of the sixties we fought only within our own homes and our narrow surroundings. It was a battle to stop others from directing our lives. In 1961, the law against dowry came into force. We debated it in schools and colleges. There were some women in politics even at that time. But it was in the seventies that a serious networking among women with divergent views began through conferences, workshops, protest marches, and dialogues. We wrote many songs for our movement. We sang them. We raised our voices against price-rise, against dowry, against rape, against domestic violence, against liquor, and against the exploitation of the environment. We worked together and independently. We gained victory. We saw defeat. Sometimes, we were divided as activists and academics. But one thing we understood clearly. Just because we had similar bodies we did not need to have similar thoughts. The political atmosphere made some of us disillusioned with the movement. Some of us opted out. Others became isolated. They retreated into their shell, refusing to communicate. We became aware of one thing. We needed to learn humility. However much we celebrated sisterhood and love, there were still many demons within us such as jealousy, competitiveness, arrogance, insolence, hatred. Some of us emerged with renewed strength. Like so many Sitas who couldn't be banished to any forest. Like so many Rubaiyas who walked their own path, singing the stories of their own lives.

Roshni, Light, I have strung together for you fifty years of doubts, rebellions, battles, struggles. This is only a song. When I write an epic for you – and I will write it one day – I will speak of all this in detail. But don't think the song is complete. It is true that communal violence, caste wars, and human degradation have all dispirited us greatly. But our battle continues. We still raise our voices to safeguard rivers, trees, and animals. To safeguard human beings, above all. You will hear in this song, resonances of our joy, despair, disappointments, and exhilaration. Sleep well, Roshni. And when you wake up, let it be to the sound of our song. You and I and many others must complete it. For we believe that a song once begun ought to be completed.

Now read on.

As soon as I realized how Sakina's death had come about, I left for home. I waited for Nandini. When she returned, the questions I put to her confirmed for me what she said to Sakina that day. At once I telephoned Susie, who manages a working women's hostel, and booked a guest room there until further notice. I told Nandini to pack whatever clothes she might need into a single case. I told her I would send on the rest of her belongings later. Then I asked her to leave my house. She was shocked. She had assumed it was I who was leaving, and I think she was preparing herself for a histrionic farewell. She became furious. "Don't I have any rights in my father's house?" she demanded.

"The house is in my name. Your rights to it will come after me."

As she was about to leave she said, "Don't expect me to come to your aid when you fall ill and take to your bed."

I said, "I know how to live alone. And I know how to die alone. You can go."'

"How can people like you call yourselves mothers?"

"I count myself a real mother. Those others live with the illusion of motherhood," I said, closing the door.

I sent on all her belongings, including the computer. That's why I write to you from this place.

I have put all the things from the Jagruti office in the warehouse of a factory belonging to one of Iqbal Maamu's friends. A go-down without any windows. A go-down which never sees any sunlight. Someone belonging to another generation, perhaps one of the little girls we educated, like Roshni, might one day open the warehouse and let the sunlight stream in. We'll wait. Until such a time, we'll take up other kinds of work; little drops falling into the great ocean.

Sing a song for me, during a quiet moment there. "From the very depths of my being, I thirst." I shall hear those words. I send you, with this, some tears. Take them. Let me know when they reach you. Selvi.

She clicked on "Send," and as soon as she got the message "Sent," she disconnected. She rose to her feet, and paid her fee to the manager of the cyber centre. Outside the glass door a fine rain was descending.

"The first rains of June, madam," said the cyber centre fellow.

"Yes," she said.

She came outside, lifted up her face to the sky, and received the cool raindrops. In that instant, time stood still.

Some Deaths

The old man, the critic, appeared to me in a dream. He said there were drops of blood present in the last poem written by the poet who died recently. "I saw death there," he said. I had no objection to the old man appearing in my dreams. Except that he appeared without any clothes on. A pale pink body. His head and chest were all grey. The hair spreading above his male member was all grey too. His buttocks were shrunken, like a mouth without teeth which has fallen in. His genitalia hung down, aged. He struggled to sit down or to walk as if he held something tightly between his thighs. I don't know why my subconscious had chosen to call up this man's nakedness, when there were so many others whom I knew well, liked, loved, even desired.

He seated himself comfortably. Having delivered his opinion about the poet, he was silent. Then, after some time he began to talk slowly.

"I was travelling by electric train once. It was night. I was on the last train. The one-thirty train. There was only one light, in the corner of the compartment. It was dark where I was. It was only when the lights outside, along the route of the train, were reflected inside that some figures took shape, then dissolved. Occasionally the light from within the compartment spread in waves above the figures, unfolding like a carpet. Sometimes a sleeping head fell forward into the light and then pulled back into the darkness. As it pulled back, the Adam's apple seemed to be thrusting forward from the base of the neck. Light rays fell upon a few heads alone. The hair then seemed to wave about on its own, seeking the body. In a sudden flood of light, a nose-ring suddenly came alive, and seemed to float in space.

"A man got up from the corner of the lighted section of the compartment. He came to the area where it was half light and half darkness. On both sides were the two exits. He stood in the middle. 'I can't,' he shouted. 'I can't, any longer,' he shrieked out. Then he took four strides to the left and went outside the train. The train kept on going. It was a fast train."

A rocky mountain rose in front of my eyes. I said to the old man, "We were walking over huge rocks. Myself, Sudhir, and fifty-year-old P.C. Shah. The more we climbed, the more rocks there were. We passed a young couple and an old woman who were on their way down. The old woman's legs were swollen. But she smiled cheerfully. "*Nilakant maharaj ki jai*," she called out. The young man informed us that there was a tea-stall about a mile further along, and slightly lower than the mountain. We walked along, repeating to ourselves, the tea-stall, the tea-stall. When we grew tired, P.C. Shah urged us forward, calling out, "The tea-stall." There seemed to be no consistency in the way the path was laid out over the stones.

One step might be a mere inch in height. To reach the next you had to raise your leg as high as your thigh. Yet another could be reached only by crawling on all fours, like an animal. Water dripped under one of the rocks. A leaf had been rolled and pushed through the hole, forming a kind of a tap. When I had collected some water drop by drop in my cupped hand, and drunk it down, tongue pressing against my palm, I turned my head and saw it. A cow. Dead. Its belly was swollen. It had been in calf. Beneath its tail, the head of the calf could actually be seen. The moment of tightening. That instant when it was caught, even as it began to bump its way out into the world. Before I could reach out my wet hand to touch my cheek, a wintry fog spread over us with the speed of fire. It touched my nose with cold, a shiver reached my navel. I couldn't see the rocks any more, only the cow. Its tongue was blue, and very near."

We were silent.

I don't know why, but my father's legs suddenly came to mind.

All his strength was in his legs. He had a brisk way of walking. When he played badminton, he'd run up to the net in an instant, scoop up the falling ball and hit it back hard. They were legs that could run well, even though they weren't particularly long. Quite sturdy, without any curves; rather like pillars. Feet like winnowing trays: broad, sweeping, outspread. When he walked he would press down on the entire sole of the foot. As I had scrutinized those legs ever since I reached his knees, I could remember clearly even the dark green veins that ran along them.

He used to link his legs and feet with many things. If he got angry, his usual chorus was, "I'll kick out as hard as I can." He'd go on emphatically about "the ability to stand on one's own two feet." Even in that last letter there had been a reference to them.

"You say that your mother and I need not come there for another two or three years. I don't know whether I can hold out for another two or three years. I am now seventy. And I have trouble with hernia. I find it very difficult to walk about. You don't have to put yourself out in any way. Just give me foothold in your home, that will be enough. . ." My mother told me that after he had written this letter, he placed it upon his chest, lay back on the easy chair where he normally stretched himself out, and wept, each dry sob coming out like a growl.

They had built the funeral pyre carefully. But my father was a tall man. One foot stretched out a little way beyond the pieces of wood. When the fire spread elsewhere, it still left the pale skin of the sole untouched. Then a small flame stroked it. A plume of black smoke spread over it. Slowly, slowly, the foot blackened.

The old critic sat there at his ease. To make himself even more comfortable, he lifted his legs and placed them on the stool. One foot stretched a little way beyond it.

A Fable

It was about half past six when the pig came to talk to me. There might have been fifteen to twenty piglets in its down-hanging, sagging stomach. It had been rolling about in the gutter. Its back shone charcoal-black from the gutter waters. Underneath, its stomach hung in flesh-coloured lumps

"Look here, I need to talk," it said.

"Why have you chosen me?" I asked.

"Don't expect me to say all manner of things to the effect that I chose you because of your intelligent, brilliant eyes. As a matter of fact, I don't see any such light shining around here. See, I am a pig. Give me an opportunity to talk. I am frustrated by the slow passage of time."

Now I am not one who is taken in by flattery, but all the same these words seemed excessively egotistic. But before I could retort hotly, "Look, I don't have the time," the pig had sat down and lowered its stomach carefully, hanging piglets to one side.

"All right, talk," I said.

"I am doing just that," said the pig, as it laid down its large head.

"Nothing that I can hear."

"I talk silently," it said.

Now if it's one thing that I hate more than arrogant pigs, it's philosophical ones. I turned my head away with indifference.

"Just joking. People tend to think that words come out of the mouths of animals, dripping with wisdom. They let us run free in fables and moral tales. They expect us to come out with epigrams like, 'The grapes are sour.' As for me, I am a pig who is bored, tired, and weary from rolling about in rubbish heaps. I have no experience of anything to do with wisdom."

"Well then, what is it you want to talk about?"

"About the gate to your apartment block."

Ours was a block of apartments on two levels, with six apartments in all. Next to it, enclosed on both sides with barbed wire, stood an empty plot of land. Empty in mere name, that is. Actually, it was a free lavatory for the hut dwellers. And it was also a shelter and dwelling place for pigs. Beneath our windows, in the afternoons, you could sometimes hear a shriek that went *driiyo driiyo*. At once the pigs would start running. Sometimes, as you entered the lane near the top of the street, you could hear a blood-curdling yell, *ei, ei*. If you stopped, people would push you onwards, saying, "Keep going. They are slaughtering the pigs."

"Why? Why are they doing that?"

"Why do you think? To eat them, of course. Keep going."

There was a small square hole in our gate, just large enough to let a dog through. Several times, the pigs who had been chased would run through this hole and escape. There was talk of closing the hole.

"I like this escape hole very much indeed. I find I crawl through it most delightfully. When I am surrounded by barbed wire on all sides, it's a most convenient hole to crawl through. When I am running for my life, it's like heaven's gates opening in front of me. It strikes me that what every pig needs is a door it can crawl through."

I remembered the pet pig in Wodehouse's novels. The Earl's fat, rose-pink pig. The pig that won prizes in many competitions.

I spoke about it.

I also told it about pigs in America which were fattened in their sties and then slaughtered painlessly.

It agreed that it was a considerable privilege if one could die without pain. It didn't show that much interest in the question of colour. What did it matter to a pig doomed to die whether it was pink or black, it said. It wasn't even concerned about dying in order to be eaten by others. When I asked about this, it refused to speak, saying it wasn't in a position to raise objections. After that it was silent for some time.

"What do you think about death?" I asked.

"It's a huge rod," it answered. "A rod that is long and cylindrical, made of either iron or wood. If iron, one is stabbed to death from the seat through to the mouth. If wood, one is clubbed to death."

"How can you be so calm about it?"

"Nothing is gained by getting excited. Perhaps we should fight for the right to choose the manner of our death: by clubbing, stabbing, or electrocution. Unfortunately we pigs are not united."

"Why do you refuse to talk about a natural death?"

"What's natural about death? It is always enforced."

"O no, no. To mingle gently with nature, just as the leaf withers away from the tree..."

"Do me a favour. Please don't bring poetry into this. As it is, my life is as terrible as possible. I just couldn't bear poetry on top of it all."

"What's poetical about what I said?"

"You are separating blood from death. You speak of a death without bloodshed, a death like the beautiful withering away of leaves. But death is inseparable from blood. Whether you are actually spilling it externally, or whether it drains away within. You are trying to make death beautiful."

Accusation.

I first thought about death when I was twelve years old. Feet floating in air, I was reaching out to catch a ball. On that instant, just as I tossed my head back to look at that ball, on that very instant, the thought struck me like a painful shaft of lightning. I shall die. I ran in and buried my face against my knees and knew fear. My hands and feet, my face, my whole body seemed alien to me. As if they were hung on to me. I crawled deep within, seeking myself myself myself. Fear took hold of me. I searched in the ear hole and within the eye and between the teeth and in the pit under my arm. Where was I? I was sweating with fear.

After that, I allowed myself certain privileges. I did not wish to die in certain ways. I did not want to die in an accident. I did not wish to die in a sudden disaster, my body shattered and destroyed.

A death of protracted pain? I didn't want that either. After reading about the second world war, I did not want to die like the Jews in gas chambers. I did not want a death by nuclear explosion, as in Hiroshima. After Vietnam, I refused for myself a death by chemical weapons such as napalm. After I had learnt about other countries in Asia, Africa, and Latin America, I rejected in turn deaths by famine, floods, earthquakes; death in prison, death by hanging, death by gunfire. What was left was a beautiful death. A poetic death, merging into space. Without pain. Or wounds. Or blood.

I understood the pig's anger.

The pig rose. It went away, shaking its body from which the piglets hung.

Some days later, at break of dawn, wild shrieks could be heard. Four men were chasing the pig with their sticks. It ran in haste towards the hole in the gate. but it had forgotten that its body had grown even bigger than before. It got stuck in the passageway. Before I could get there, its blood poured out in great gushes. The piglets fell out, one by one, like dolls. When I approached, the pig recognized me. It opened its bloodshot eyes and said, "Please don't expect me to speak some rare truth about death. There is only one thing to say. We die."

The long rods drew nearer.

Fish in a Dwindling Lake

As usual, all travellers arriving at the huge Kashmiri Gate bus station were plunged immediately into a state of confusion. Would
her pre-booked ticket be valid? It wasn't possible for her to rush
about here and there with her luggage, all by herself. She wanted
desperately to go to the toilet, but couldn't go in, leaving her luggage
abandoned outside. She stood there hesitating, with shoulder-bag,
handbag, and a bamboo basket containing rose cuttings. Finally, she
left the basket outside and went in, carrying her bags. When she
came out again, the bamboo basket was still there, safe, a small boy
standing by, looking at it in surprise.

"Auntyji, is this yours?"

"Yes."

"Shall I carry it for you?"

"It's not at all heavy; I can carry it myself."

He stood there, watching her. She found an eight-anna coin from
her purse and offered it to him. He refused to take it. She explained
that she didn't like putting small children to work. He argued that

if she gave him eight annas when he had not earned it, that would make him a beggar.

"Very well, you can put me on my bus," she agreed.

Immediately, it felt as if she was being protected by a Black Cat patrol. As soon as she told him she was bound for a small town on the India–Nepal border, he started ahead of her swiftly, parting the crowds and almost swimming forward. In a short while they stood in front of the right bus. The person who had booked her ticket had informed her that the bus would be air-conditioned. As for this vehicle, it was covered in dust and looked like an actor whose make-up was in disarray.

The passengers, carrying their sacks and their huge trunks, were trying to load their luggage and fight their way into the bus, calling out at the top of their voices. She asked the conductor who was trying to cope with all these people, "Is this the AC bus?"

"No, it's not air-conditioned, but it's the bus you want," he replied, indifferently.

The small boy explained to her that this bus would stop in front of Anand Vihar in about an hour. There she must board the bus that would actually take her to her destination.

She asked whether the bus would stop conveniently for calls of nature. Certainly it would, the conductor told her. These would not be at proper toilets with running water. Instead, they usually stopped at deserted streets with an abundance of wild shrubs or tall trees nearby. Sometimes there wouldn't even be those to provide any privacy, only the darkness. On one occasion, on a dark night, the bus had stopped at an unknown wasteland. She was the only woman to climb down. It was blindingly dark. There seemed to be some sort of building, locked up, nearby. She wandered about a bit, searching for a private place, and came to a wall where she squatted down. When she rose to her feet, a lorry hastened past, spitting its light in her direction. As she looked about her during that brief moment, her heart beat fast. She was standing next to a pedestal which carried a statue of Gandhi. There he was, his staff in his hand, one leg in front of the other, as if he were stepping forward. In her head, she asked him for forgiveness, "Bapuji forgive me. You said: India would be truly independent when at last a woman, wearing all her ornaments, could go about freely in the middle of the night. You might have thought it important to mention ornaments specifically. We don't need a single ornament, Bapuji. We would be content if there were enough toilets for us, should we need to answer calls of nature, even at midnight. We'd be happy if there were toilets accessible in all the highways and chief places of independent India, so that women don't ever have to suffer, controlling themselves. Our bladders have grown weak from the strain of it. The urine, splashed freely by men, has made its mark on endless walls, starting from the temple wall; it's become a metaphor for freedom, indeed. The kings of long ago planted trees. They dug wells. They built inns and resting places. We don't know whether they established toilets. It seems to me this was our loss throughout the generations, Bapuji." Her imagined conversation with Gandhi had continued like this, during that journey. The small boy told her to climb in. He went in first and then called out to her. He had found her a window seat in the middle of the bus. He assured her there would be no problem with

333

changing buses. The basket holding the rose cuttings slipped under her seat easily. The boy laid her shoulder-bag along the luggage rail above her. She held out a rupee note towards him. He ignored it and asked, "Auntyji, don't you need some water?" She agreed she would, opened her handbag and gave him some money. He climbed out of the bus and ran. When he returned, he held in his hands a bottle of water and six bananas. Standing under her window, he held them out to her.

"Why the fruit?"

"You don't know, Auntyji, you'll get hungry. My village is right next to Mahendra Nagar," he told her, like one who had been sent on many journeys.

She pulled off two of the fruit from the bunch and gave it to him. He smiled as he accepted it. This time she handed him a five-rupee note. He hesitated a bit, but accepted that too.

The bus was filling up with foreign tourists, carrying heavy bags, and the usual passengers who were returning home. As the bus was making ready to start, the boy said goodbye to her. He called to her above the noises that the bus was making, "Auntyji, in those parts, when the sky is clear you'll see snow-covered mountain peaks in the distance..." The bus began to move as the wind brought this information to her.

It struck her that snow-covered mountain peaks, revealed when the skies were clear, were a good goal for this journey.

———

Journeys had become the symbols of her life. Journeys with objectives, journeys without; meaningful journeys, journeys made of necessity; journeys which were planned, but never happened; journeys which broke all decisions; journeys which had become rituals.

Her very birth was witness to her mother's final journey. She was the sixth child. After that, she became her elder sister's baby. When Didi married at the age of sixteen, and left her family on her *bidai* journey to her in-laws, she went with her, as part of her dowry. After that, her sister's husband, her Jijaji, became her new father. At intervals, she returned, to see her real father, elder sisters, and elder brother. In spite of Jijaji's disapproval, her father insisted on arranging a marriage for her as soon as she finished her schooling, claiming that he was ready for his own last journey. Her life seemed to be ruled by other people's journeys, indeed. She set off on her own bidai journey with a man who had a slight frame and dim eyes. Later it came to light that he suffered from tuberculosis. As soon as he set foot on his final journey, before everyone could say she must break her bangles and remove her kumkum, her Jijaji arrived and took her away. There followed many journeys as she pursued her further education. Journeys to do with her profession, first as a lecturer in Delhi, then as she rose to become a professor. Journeys undertaken after Didi died, to look after her children and to educate them. Journeys with Didi's youngest son, who had to have electric shock treatment for his psychiatric problems. Journeys with Jijaji when he had cancer, for radiotherapy. Journeys within the country and journeys abroad. A life threaded together by journeys.

After she retired from work, Didi's sons and daughters, who were now United States citizens, had demanded affectionately that she go and live with them in California, New York, Washington, and Boston. She had made up her mind to do so. And now, all of a sudden, she was bound on this journey. Entirely by accident.

The arguments and counterarguments between her and those Indians who no longer lived in India had lasted for a whole year.

"So what is so wonderful in India, Mausi, apart from dust and noise and crowds? Why don't you come and see what it's like here?"

"You won't have to roast in the sun nor be drenched in the rain. There will be a whole world within your home."

"You won't have to rush about for anything here. There will be no worries at all for you. This is a world which works at the touch of a button, without any problems."

"You've been here as a postgraduate student, haven't you? You know very well what it's like."

She had indeed lived in that world for a while. It was a world with many choices. Even when she tried to buy a sandwich, she had faced a number of choices. White bread or wholemeal? What sort of butter? With fat or without? Vegetarian or otherwise? What sort of salad or meat? Should they add gherkins or other relishes, or not? Grilled sandwich, or plain? Did she want cheese or not? After she had answered all these questions, there was the final one. Would she eat her sandwich on the premises or take it away?

Here life didn't have so many choices. Nor many buttons to press. It was only after she arrived at Delhi that she even came across a doorbell.

At home, in the village, their front door was always open. Women carrying their water pots home would often set them down and rest in their front verandah. They'd pack their mouths with betel leaves and call out to Didi for a chat. Drivers of horse carts would help themselves to water from the big earthenware pot there, and quench their thirst. One of them was a great singer of folk ballads. Once he had drunk some water, he'd summon all the children in their family and sing to them in his resounding voice. Once, a patron of arts invited him and his group to Paris. He went there, wore his colourful turban, raised his voice and sang loudly, and then came back. After that, he drove his horses as usual. If asked, "What was Paris like?" he answered casually, "Not bad. Rather big." There was no change in his lifestyle, apart from a picture of the Eiffel Tower in his cart.

Sometimes the cow, Kalavati, which had gone grazing, would come and stand at their front verandah. "Mma," it would call out to Didi. It had once eaten a few pages out of Munna's homework book. Jijaji scolded the child for leaving her notebook there. Now, many years later, in New York, Munna's son did his homework on the computer. How would a cow turn up there? Nowadays, the milk, yielded by nameless cows, arrived pasteurized, anyway.

Stories, all of them: the bridegroom arriving on an elephant; the camels padding across the desert sands; the annual camel races; the children dressed as brides and grooms, with laddoos or jalebis in their hands during Akkha Teej; peacocks spreading their dark green and blue feathers as they flew to the low-lying branches of the trees and sat there; comfortingly warm *razzais* made of old saris sewn together; saris knotted and dyed dark blue and indigo and red, the colours spreading as soon as the knots were undone and the saris shaken out. Stories, all of them, from beginning to end. Stories she told their children, and the children of friends and relatives. And the children assumed that they were tales of magic, like Harry Potter stories. Many of the heroes and heroines of those stories were no longer alive. But some of them were. The horse-cart driver still sang in the evenings, after his drink of toddy. The horse was no longer there, nor the cart. He told his grandchildren the tale of his journey to Paris. They were special magic tales to them. Some months ago, walking along a path dense with trees and bushes, she stumbled over a peacock which lay dead, obstructing her path, its feathers shorn. Was it magic or real? It was all magic; it was all true.

In this bus which tore through the night, sitting with her bamboo basket of rose cuttings together with unknown individuals, sacks, trunks, foreign bags, cloth bundles, cloth bags full of clothes, on this sudden and accidental journey, she didn't know what was real, what was magic.

———

A couple of days after she decided to live abroad permanently, she received a letter from Bimla Devi. It had been written on paper headed with the name and address of the Lok Seva Sangh which she ran. The letters were printed in saffron, on a white background. Bimla had written in her usual dark blue ink. She asked her please to visit, and to bring some cuttings from a rose nursery in Delhi when she came; she, Bimla, would be looking forward to her arrival. She had been a little surprised by the letter. It was now some years since she had lost contact with Bimla Devi. She had withdrawn herself after everyone began calling Bimla Devi "Mataji" and "Sadhviji."

Bimla had not shown any disapproval when people addressed her like this. Neither did she ask that she should be addressed thus.

Bimla Devi and she were classmates when they were at university. Later, for some time, Bimla taught history in the same college where she was employed. She was the first, in a family of agricultural labourers, to seek out higher education. Mid-brown skin. Long hair, combed flat. Eyes which darted about everywhere, like fish swimming around in a glass bowl. A dazzling smile. Strong arms and legs. A strong body, not afraid of toil. Because the two of them found it difficult to speak English fluently, they became roommates and friends. During her holidays, with Jijaji's permission, she went to stay with Bimla Devi's family. Although, by that time, they owned sufficient land, they worked on it themselves. She had never seen Bimla's father in laundered clothes. In her memory his legs were always mud stained, his face sweaty. Bimla and her mother worked in the fields and at home untiringly. They were constantly at work, weeding, carrying loads, cleaning out the cowshed, looking after their poultry, cooking meals. Besides, she would go to graze the goats, along with her brothers. The background music in that household was the jingling of Bimla's mother's green glass bangles.

She was not one who shirked hard work, either. Didi, too, was one who laboured hard and tirelessly. But there were servants in their house as well. When she visited Bimla's family, she was eager to join in with the others in their daily chores. She failed abysmally at the task of grazing the goats, however. She admitted to Bimla and her siblings that it was not an easy task to gather the herd together, nor to separate it into smaller groups. They tended to laugh at her. It seemed to her that even the goats joined in with that laughter. Only one small black kid clung to her side and comforted her.

After she started visiting Bimla's family regularly, she too picked up the habit of chewing tobacco. Bimla's mother always had a wad of tobacco leaves tucked inside her mouth. Bimla often said to her mother, "Maji, please don't go any further than the tobacco. Don't go and get her used to toddy as well. She shares a room with me in the college. . ." When Bimla's father came home in the evenings, tired out, he had a drink of toddy. He sat in the backyard, next to the cowshed, and drank his toddy. Her mother, too. Sometimes, her brothers joined them, squatting down and drinking. They usually had their drink away from the house, at the toddy shop. Only occasionally did they gather together in the backyard, squatting together. They avoided drinking inside the house, or in front of Bimla. Beyond the cowshed, there was a rose garden covering an acre of land. The toddy drinking took place there, when she and Bimla went out on their evening walks. When they returned they would just glimpse their backs, turned away.

It struck her, sometimes, that the rest of the family treated Bimla with a special respect. The others in the village – including those who were well off, and belonging to higher castes – appeared to speak to her with deference. When she asked Bimla about it, Bimla laughed it off. She spoke to everyone with ease, touching them. At college, once, when the daughter of a lowly employee was taken into hospital after a suicide attempt, Bimla spoke to the father, putting her hand on his shoulder to comfort him. He broke down then, and began to weep. He held her hand and wept aloud. Sometimes, the college lecturers spoke to Bimla about personal matters. Bimla never gave anyone any advice. She never preached any dogmas. She never attended any rituals or pujas in anyone's homes. Yet she seemed to attract everyone in some way which was other than materialistic or mundane. She gave out a sense of comfort. Once their college mates had joined together to make up a farce about Bimla's special nature, which they acted out at one of their evening celebrations. Bimla just laughed at that too.

Once she was sitting with Bimla's mother, cleaning a chicken and cutting it up. When she thought about it later, that short conversation, and the background to it, returned to her mind like a scene in a play. Preparations for their midday meal were going on in the kitchen. The wheat flour had been kneaded and set aside. Dal was bubbling on the firewood hearth. Sliced onion, potato, and other vegetables. The chicken pieces had been marinated in curds. A smell of mingled onion, garlic, and ginger. Rays of light fell through the small window of the kitchen with its low, thatched roof. The cow-shed could be seen through the window, outside. Bimla was cleaning it out. That was when she asked her the question, "Maji, when will Bimla get married?"

"Bimla? We'll see," said her mother, as if it were not a matter of concern.

She thought perhaps that Bimla's mother hadn't liked her asking this question. But in a while the answer came, "If ever Bimla wants a family or a marriage, then we'll arrange it."

"Why, doesn't she want to get married?"

"It doesn't seem so. Let's see what Swamiji Maharaj will say."

The conversation came to an end as the marinated chicken pieces dropped with a sizzling noise into the earthenware pot with its hot oil seasoned with cinnamon, clove, and fennel seeds.

———

They took Swamiji Maharaj by his hand and led him to a seat in the front of the house. He was blind, and bare-bodied, except for the small piece of cloth wound about his waist.

"Whose house is this, tell me."

"It belongs to Madangopal Misraji. He has a hundred acres of land."

"The land will be the land's. How can it be his?" He laughed aloud.

They brought him a small water-pot full of water. "Please talk to us, Swamiji Maharaj."

"It was terribly hot. A fiery heat that burnt the body. Later, the rain fell. Not a rain with blustering winds, but a rain that fell in straight strands. A rain like a shower of flowers. That was when it came and clung to my legs. I lifted it up. A puppy. It licked my face. This Govind told me it was black and white. It was he who named it Kalu. However many miles I walked, it would follow me. At nights it would sleep, rolled up against my feet. People began to call me 'The Dog Maharaj.' Now there's no dog. Just the Maharaj." He laughed again.

"Please, Swamiji Maharaj, say something that will be useful to us in our lives."

"Something useful?"

———

"Yes, perhaps something from the Bhagavad Gita. . ." "The Bhagavad Gita? What do I know of the Bhagavad Gita? I am a wanderer, a constant traveller, a vagabond and gadabout. I drink water anywhere, eat everywhere, sleep and wake up wherever I please. I said I was thirsty; this Govind brought me here."

"In that case, why don't you come to my house too," a shrill voice piped up.

Swamiji Maharaj turned in the direction from where the voice came. So did the others. A five-year-old girl with her satchel of books, leaning against a pillar, her hand at her waist. A girl who should not have stepped into houses belonging to people such as Misraji.

Swamiji Maharaj smiled. "Oh, you are here, are you, little girl? Come here and take my hand."

She came running up and took his hand. She slung her satchel across her shoulder. Before anyone could stop him, the blind man followed as she pulled him along.

They were stunned when they saw him. Where should they ask him to sit? What should they give him to eat? A portion of the cattle shed in Bimla's house was cleaned and tidied. He sat down there.

"Maharaj, what should we give you to eat? We have cooked beef in this house today."

"Beef, is it? You eat and enjoy. Have you made rotis?"

"Yes."

"A couple of rotis and a squashed onion will be enough for me."

343

An onion was squashed by hand, seasoned with salt and pepper, and laid on top of hot rotis. They gave him this. He ate with relish, and slept soundly in the cattle shed. He stayed with them for fifteen or twenty days.

———

The people of those parts wanted a temple. Swamiji Maharaj was not interested in that. He arranged for them to gain ownership of the fallow land lying beyond the cattle shed, which lay unused. He went here and there and brought them the rose cuttings. He instructed them to plant the roses. Roses came up in the land which had been thought unusable. A cooperative farm for rose cultivation began to take shape, gradually expanding into other businesses such as manufacturing attar and making rose garlands and bouquets for shrines and *dargahs*. A small hut was raised for him, right next to the rose garden.

Those who once called him "Dog Maharaj" now began to call him "Rose Maharaj" instead. He still walked on his journeys.

———

These were all supplementary stories told about Swamiji Maharaj. Stories everyone told, with embellishments, or otherwise. He had said he knew neither magic nor magical spells. For those who came to him, refusing to believe this, he dispensed neither sacred ash nor kumkum. He could walk. For the sake of the rose garden. For the sake of educating the poor. A small piece of cloth around his waist. A face obscured by a white beard. Blind eyes. A loud laugh.

———

Bimla's mother had told her in detail about the event that took place a couple of days after he moved in with them. It was dusk: that time of day when all the cows were returning home. The air was full of the call of birds flying home to their nests. At this time, people would gather to see Swamiji, in the hut they had put up for him. That day too, some people were sitting in front of him. As soon as Bimla came running up with her satchel of books and stood by the front door, he was aware of her arrival. He spread his hands towards her and said, "Come." She set down her satchel and ran up to him. He stroked her hair and kissed her forehead. Then he leaned down and spoke softly into her ear. Just one second. Her expression registered shock and surprise. Then, gradually, her face began to blossom like a flower. As soon as he moved his head away from her ear, five-year-old Bimla hugged him and kissed his white-bearded face. Swamiji Maharaj gathered her tightly to his heart.

When she asked Bimla about that incident once, she didn't get an answer immediately. Some of them used to sleep on the terrace, in the heat of the summer. There were charpoys there, for that purpose. That evening they both lay on their beds there, gazing up at the sky. When she asked her question, Bimla continued to look at the sky intently, as if her gaze were piercing through the stars. Then she said softly, "I'm not sure I can explain it clearly..."

"Why? Can't dimwits like me understand, or what?"

345

She laughed. "No, it isn't that," she said in a low voice. "But language has its limits, doesn't it?"

There was silence for a while.

"Kumud, what he spoke in my ear can't be contained in words. First it was like the buzzing of a bee. Then the rustling of running water. After that, the sensation of a great flood on which I floated like a cork, weightlessly. Then the sensation of hurtling back and forth on a swing, and then gradually, very gradually coming to a stop and climbing off. The way you feel after those games we play, holding hands and whirling round. A feeling of unbounded, unlimited love flowing within me and stroking me, like the milk pouring down in consecration over the temple images. . ."

She fell asleep as Bimla went on with her description.

She, too, met Swamiji Maharaj on one occasion. She had no particular desire to meet him. In fact she shunned all so-called *swamijis*. When Roop Kanwar lay beside the corpse of her husband and set fire to herself, many of her college lecturers had taken out a procession to protest against the superstitious belief in sati. Without exception, all the swamijis who were interviewed on television had declared, "Women who go out on these processions are immoral. They have relations with more than one man." They were all there, complete with their matted locks, their sacred ash and sandalwood paste, bald heads and religious forehead-marks. Even though a very few such as Swamiji Maharaj had supported them, on the whole she avoided all religious sages.

Once Didi had insisted she accompany her to see the head of a religious mutt from the south of India. The people at the door had asked them a hundred questions about their caste and sub-caste, and found out that Kumud was a widow. Immediately they said, "We can't give you permission to go in; if he sees widows he will have to fast." She had never before seen Didi so furious. "It would be a good thing if he were to look at her and then fast. We're leaving. Tell him to eat. . ." she had said, and gone home. Later she had fought with Didi, attacking her for believing in swamijis.

When Didi was at the point of death, she had asked, hesitantly, "Please will you ask Bimla to come." Bimla did come. She was still teaching at the college in those days. Didi's eyes filled as soon as she saw her. "Bimla, Beti, I want to die in my sleep," she said. Her face was twisted in an unbearable pain. Bimla began to stroke her forehead. In a while Didi had fallen asleep. Bimla never left her side. At about half past four the next morning, Didi's breath fell away, gradually. All the wrinkles on her face had disappeared, as if they had been smoothed out. At once Bimla had her bath and prepared to leave. She said she was going to Rishikesh with Swamiji Maharaj.

It was ten or fifteen years after this that she herself met Swamiji Maharaj. Didi's youngest daughter had finished her studies in the United States, and had decided to marry an American. Her fiancé's family believed that India was a country full of snake-charmers, elephants, and tigers. They imagined it to be a country where the food was hot and spicy, the women dark and voluptuous, wearing brightly coloured clothes; the country of the Kamasutra and of the great sages, but also a country riddled with poverty, disease, and beggars;

a land that could delight in many different ways. The bridegroom wanted to arrive in procession, riding on an elephant, and did so, amidst delighted cries of "Ohs" and "Ahs." As she stood watching the procession, a sob rose in her throat, like a sudden stroke of paralysis. Before she could understand it, more sobs followed. Her eyes filled. Jijaji, who was doing an errand nearby, noticed her and came up. "Well, Kumud, your girl has grown up, hasn't she? Hereafter she too will set up a home, a family. . ."

She nodded, quietly.

He looked at her again, and said, "What is it, Kumud, what has happened?"

Like a flash of lightning, the words which had been formulated at some time, somewhere, came out of her, shocking her. "Jijaji, you could have arranged another marriage for me, couldn't you? Why didn't you do it?"

Jijaji was utterly shaken. She was forty years old at the time. "You. . . you. . ." he stuttered in confusion. He put his arm around her shoulder and hugged her. Her eyes were blinded with tears, preventing her from seeing the bridegroom arrive in elephant procession.

During the course of a conversation, later on, she had told Bimla how, for that instant, her own words had taken her by surprise.

The next time Swamiji Maharaj was in town, Bimla insisted that Kumud accompany her to the place where he was staying. During those many years, Swamiji had set up Lok Seva Sanghs in several places. Adjacent to each ashram, but outside it, there was a rose garden, and a small hutment for him to stay. He had come to stay in Delhi, with a social worker. Kumud had gone with Bimla, at last, after she invited her several times. A number of people had gathered there to see the Swamiji. A couple of men who had failed in their Civil Service exams had turned up, saying they wished to become *sannyasis*.

"Then why don't you do it?"

"Training. . ." The word was dragged out.

"Training? Can you stand hunger? Can you endure disrespect? Are you able to sleep in a space of two square yards? If you can, you are certainly a sannyasi."

"Initiation. . ."

"If a hand is placed on your head, that is an initiation. Do it yourself."

They had come prepared to renounce the whole world, and now stood aside, a little disappointed.

A woman, a singer, was eager to sing to him. He asked her to do so. The Mira bhajan that the woman sang seemed to echo her own state of mind at the time. She felt as if pushed down to the lowest possible state in life.

The woman sang, *"Hey Govind, Hey Gopala, ab tho jivan haari, I have given away my life now."*

When she sang this, Kumud felt herself choking. Her throat ached as if a thorn were stuck there. She felt ashamed. That this should happen at a place where she knew no one other than Bimla.

Swamiji looked in the direction from where the voice came and said, "It was that Mira alone who was able to lose her life. Beat it as you will, it always bounces back, like a ball that returns to the hand. It is not so easy to give away your life."

She went and made her obeisance to him and left.

People like him would never understand. It wasn't spirituality that she needed at that time. A husband with a robust body at the right age. One or two babies who grew and hung heavy in the womb, and in due time pushed, shoved, and tore their way past the birth canal, covered in blood. Or even three or four babies. Breasts running with milk. It was all part of the body. The body was the only truth she knew. It was the body alone that was left, even as she went beyond the body. She needed an oar to begin that crossing. She needed a boat and a boatman. Her body was the river. It was itself the shore. It was the hunter and the hunted; the path and the goal.

———

After that came the rise in her career at college. Her worries about Jijaji's health and of her care of him. So the years went past. A distance grew between Bimla and herself. Bimla came when Jijaji died. She was the same old playful Bimla. All the same, as she entered the house it seemed to Kumud that a flame of fire had walked in. Bimla wore a saffron shawl draped over her customary pale-coloured handloom cotton sari. Later Kumud thought it had been the sorrow of that moment and her eyes swollen with tears that had exaggerated her vision of Bimla.

Later still, many people asked her, "Do you know Mataji Bimla

Devi?" "Is Sadhvi Bimla Devi a close friend of yours?" "Is it true she embraces everyone she meets?"

Gradually, she lost contact with Bimla, after that. Occasionally she received a postcard from her, with brief news such as which town Bimla was visiting, and when. And now, this letter. Kumud didn't get a place on the train. Neither was there a direct train which would take her to her destination. This novel bus journey was the result.

———

The rains had failed that year. Everywhere along the way, she saw a withered green. Everywhere, a land that was thirsty. When she reached her destination, she was told she must travel some distance by rickshaw in order to reach the small town where she was headed. Asking the way at small shops scattered here and there, she finally reached the place where the Lok Seva Sangh was located. She went up to a man who stood at the doorway, and said she was Bimla Devi's friend. Immediately she was shown into a small reception room and asked to sit down.

In a little while, she heard Bimla calling her by name, "Kumud." And then she was there in person. She had grown very thin. At once Kumud rose to her feet, went up to her, took her by the hand and embraced her. "How did you know it was I? You must have so many people coming to see you."

"But he told me it was my friend. And aren't you my only friend," she said. She smiled.

"Here are the rose cuttings you wanted. I bought them from the

———

same rose nursery that you mentioned. But this bus journey has broken my back, I tell you. There were potholes and dips all along the bus route. We were well and truly flung about."

"Come. Come and have a hot bath. I've kept some really good tobacco just for you. We'll talk later."

As they came out of the room Bimla said to the man they encountered, "Sukhbir, your rose cuttings have arrived. Look, she's brought them."

"Oh, very good," he said, walking on.

Her health had been failing for some months, she said. It seemed she had begun to get better only recently, and very gradually. She hadn't recovered fully as yet. A common friend of theirs, Urmila, had told her about Kumud's intention to leave the country forever and live abroad. She spoke as she lay on her bed. She said her spine hurt. From time to time, her face was bathed in sweat. Even as Kumud wiped Bimla's face with a towel tenderly, hot words came out of her mouth. As if she were continuing with an argument which started somewhere, at some time, she asked, "Bimla, in the end it is this pain that is the truth. Isn't that so?"

"It too is the truth."

"You always denied the body. Now, see, all that is left is the body."

"Who denied the body?"

"You. You did. I lost mine because of the decisions made by all kinds of others. But the body alone is certain. The truth. You denied this truth. The body's urine, shit, blood; its desires, hunger, and thirst are all truths."

"It isn't quite like that, Kumud," Bimla said gently. "The body has several aspects to it. Its appearance, its everyday functions may seem to be common experience, but the truth of each individual body will be different from anyone else's. The body is indeed an anchorage. But each body casts anchor in a different sea. Everything external – trees and plants, creepers, forests, beasts – all of it is the body. Only the body. Without the body, there is nothing. Everything is through the body. You can keep on stretching the boundaries and limits of the body. It will accept everything, contain everything. It will be able to mingle with everything."

Once more her face was bathed in sweat. Kumud wiped it away.

She explained why she had invited Kumud to come there.

She arrived at this mountain village some years ago, entirely by chance, she said. A conference on spirituality was to be held at a small town nearby, to which several women had been invited. People from different groups were expected to participate: a great number, including Catholic nuns, Sufis, Jains, Parsis, Sikhs, people like Bimla, people who insisted on harmony amongst religions, activists. Bimla was travelling with some nuns, in two or three compartments. At about half past eight, after they had finished dinner together, a young nun left for her own compartment. It was only a couple of hours later that they realized she had never got there. Terrified, they

353

looked everywhere for her, and found her at last, fallen down in the bathroom. She had been raped. All over her body were scratched with a razor-blade, the syllables "Om," "Om." They had written their religion on her body. It lay there, a symbol of the violence that religions are capable of. The conference took place against the backdrop of this tragedy.

They concluded that the only weapons they had against such madness were education and good health. To create healthy bodies and healthy minds. Many among them were skilled in these two fields. On their way back, she stopped at this village for a couple of days. She wanted to start a school here. To build a hospital. Swamiji Maharaj was at the last stage of his life, at that time. He told her she had made an excellent decision.

"So who is likely to come to this school then? There are only about fifty houses in this village, I think."

"There are several villages hereabouts. There might even be children coming across the border."

"Very well. You summoned me here because of your dream school. What about your hospital?"

"Why, there's Sukhbir. He's a doctor."

"Really? And there was I, thinking he was the gardener." Bimla laughed.

"Look here, Bimla. Why don't you travel around to cities here and there, giving your sermons? Go abroad. Travel the world over and talk about your thoughts and the lifestyle you believe in. What is there for you in this place? Only ignorance and corruption, and a life lacking enough money to do what needs to be done. Why should you be confined to India? And in this village which doesn't even appear on a map of India."

"Kumud, did you see the book Ira Pande wrote about her mother, Shivani? It describes how Shivani went to visit her elder sister, who was failing in health. Shivani asked her, You have a house in a pleasant setting in the hills, why can't you go and live there instead of staying in this place. The answer her sister gave her is the same answer I should give you."

"And what was that?"

"You read it yourself. Or ask Sukhbir; he'll tell you." Bimla closed her eyes.

When the lake dwindles, the birds fly away,
seeking their nests elsewhere.
Yé Rahim! Fish lacking wings,
where can they go?

A poem by Abdul Rahim Khan-e-Khana, who lived in Akbar's time.

"In that case, Sukhbir, they are fish to be pitied. Fish that will die when the lake dwindles away."

"No, not so. Fish that believe that the rains will come. Fish that are not afraid to die. Fish that wait for the lake to fill again. Fish that have become one with the lake. . ."

———

Dreams. Mere dreams. They were trying to entangle her in those dreams. But she was a free bird. The four people she had raised were all living abroad. She had a room in each of their homes. If she grew tired of one home, she would be welcome in another. She need not be imprisoned in any one of them. Bimla and Sukhbir may have very good reasons for their plans here. Sukhbir had studied medicine at a foreign university, and had worked in a big hospital in India on his return. One evening, when he was driving his car very fast, he crashed into a family, and all of them died instantaneously: husband, wife, and two children. One of the children was a baby in arms. Shocked, he stopped the car and rushed towards them. The woman, holding the baby to herself, called out with her dying breath, "Ei, you sinner, you destroyed my entire family." The verdict at the court proved favourable to Sukhbir. But those eyes filled with panic at the moment of death, chased after him. "Ei, you sinner, you sinner..."

He took refuge with Swamiji Maharaj. During the first four years, he planted all of the Lok Seva Sangh rose nurseries, and cared for them. Four crore roses for four lives. Four Years. Then he established hospitals at all branches of the ashram, and appointed appropriate staff. He said that even now, he saw those eyes on some nights, accusing him. He was past sixty now. When she asked why he had not gone away and worked elsewhere, he said that no country had a border that would prevent those eyes from following him. They were eyes written upon his body, he said. He never stopped laying out rose gardens.

But Kumud was not held fast by anything. There was nothing that pulled her to itself.

Sunk in thought, she had walked some distance. Nothing was

cooling to the eye. The mountains were at a great distance. During her bus journey, she had glimpsed, now and then, spotted deer, and peacocks with their tails outspread, even though there was no sign of rain. Here there was nothing at all.

A barbed-wire fence stopped her from going any further. Beyond it, a pond. A little girl stood at its further shore. Bare-bodied, except for a small skirt about her waist. A stick in her hand. She too was like that as a little girl. Didi could not cope with all the children. Kumud would run off towards the fields, a stick or a doll held in her hand. She'd sit under the shade of a tree and think of the photograph of her mother which hung in their home. What had her mother been like? Was she as loving as Didi? But Didi never had any time. Everything was done in a hurry. Bathtime was a rush. Making the rotis was a rush. Serving the food was a rush. She had to go to school, didn't she? When Didi returned home in the evening, there were more constraints. It wasn't possible for her to sit on Didi's lap. But her mother must have had lots of time. Her mother would have laid her on her lap. Stroked her hair. Hummed a song to her in a low voice. At the thought, tears would gather in her eyes.

Grasping the barbed wire in her hands, she wept. The tears came, in great sobs. In an unfamiliar town, in this unknown place, these tears in the presence of a barbed-wire fence. The pond was witness; the little girl the spectator. She felt someone touch her hand. The little girl was standing next to her, on the other side of the fence. Her hair had been plaited in five sections. The plaits stood out, like sticks.

"Mausiji, why are you crying?"

"Some dust in my eyes. How did you get here?"

"The pond isn't deep. I waded across."

"Don't you have school?"

"Our house doesn't have a door."

"I asked why you haven't gone to school."

"That's what I'm telling you. Our house doesn't have a door."

"Where's your house, then?"

"Over there. Quite far off. Now Mataji is going to build a school for us. I can come and study there in the evenings. Babuji and Maji will have come home by then, won't they?"

"So who's at home now, in your house?"

"Dada's there. Otherwise the dogs will come and upturn all the food. We don't have a door to our house, you see."

A girl who couldn't go to school, who safeguarded a house without doors from prowling dogs.

"What's your name?"

"Chunari."

"Would you like to go to school?"

"I want a notebook, pencil and everything."

"And then?"

"Mausiji, I know lots of stories. I want to tell them all to the teacher. Mataji promised us. She'll build a school."

She crawled underneath the fence and came beside her. "Mausiji, do you know this? You can walk all the way to Nanda Devi from here."

"Is that so?"

"Yes, and after that, if you walk and walk and walk a long, long way, you'll see the Panchuli Mountain range. There are five mountains in all. The five Pandavas made a hearth out of all five mountains and cooked their food."

"When was this?"

"Before they went up to heaven."

"Who told you all this?"

"I just know it by myself."

"Very good."

A cool breeze blew. A couple of raindrops splashed on Chunari's cheek. Then they fell on her head too. It began to drizzle.

"Rain, rain," sang out Chunari. She too, wanted to sing aloud.

Chunari had been laughing, chuckling, and snorting. Suddenly she stopped. "I must go," she said. "Dada will scold me."

She was just about to step forward and crawl under the fence, but turned round and came back. "Mausiji, please don't cry."

"No, I won't. I won't cry."

"When Mataji builds her school, you too will get a pencil and notebook and everything. You mustn't cry."

"I won't."

She crawled beneath the fence, and in an instant had crossed the pond and reached the other side, scattering water and drenching her skirt. Running, she disappeared.

Kumud stood there until she was drenched to the skin. The rain water seeped through her, with the chill wind. She felt as if she had been scoured clean. The barbed-wire fence she held, the withered trees accepting the rain, the pond which lay there like a thirsty mouth opening, Chunari with her little skirt, the small boy who had bought her bananas in that crowd-tossed bus station, anticipating her hunger, the snow-covered mountain peaks he said you could see when the skies cleared – everything entered her body and came out again, spreading, spreading everywhere and taking universal form. Her body diminished into a dot – a single dot among the several that were all strung together.

———•———

It was evening. Bimla Devi sat in an easy chair by the window, her eyes shut. The pale pink light of dusk fell on her face. Her spine must have ached. She grimaced very slightly, now and then. She looked as if she had lived through many centuries. As if she was beyond age. As if she had achieved eternal life.

"Bimla," she called, gently.

She opened her eyes and smiled.

Kumud went and sat next to her. "Does it hurt a lot?" she asked.

"Rather a lot."

"Bimla, the rains have come," she said.

"Yes. We have been waiting anxiously."

"Bimla, we can put up fences behind the ashram, and make a thatched shed. It will house the first five classes. We need to order from Bareilly, or some other town, blackboards, chalk, notebooks, pencil, textbooks, and everything. Bimla, we must have book bags, mustn't we? And then, Bimla, would it be possible to give the children a cup of hot milk every day?" Her voice seemed to echo. Bimla was peacefully asleep, holding on to Kumud's hands. She was breathing evenly.

———

Yellow Fish

High summer. Already the sand feels hot. It will not hold its wetness. Away, to the left of the shrunken sea and spent waves, the sand
spreads like a desert. Yet the eye is compelled by the sea alone. Now
the white boat has arrived. This is the forerunner. Its appearance is
the signal that the fishing boats are returning. It floats ashore like
a swan, swaying from side to side. Far from the shore, bright spots
begin to move. The fisherwomen make ready to welcome the boats
ashore. Bright colours: blinding indigo, demonic red, profound
green, assaulting blue. They stand vibrant against the white boat
upon a faded blue and ash-grey sea.

Now it is possible to see the other boats. Walking further, quite
close to the boats, you may see the fish filling the nets. Bodies and
hands darkened by the salt wind, the men will spread their nets and
start sorting the fish the minute the boats come in. Now the fish
splash into plastic troughs, round eyes wide open. The unwanted
ones are thrown away. There is a general murmur of tired voices, rising for a split second, then falling. Black hands. Brown wood of the
boats. Between the meshes of the nets, white-bellied fish. Crowding

near, the colours of the saris press upon the eyes gently, but firmly. Painted troughs. Dry sand. An extraordinary collage of colours, on the shores of the wide-spread sea. A composition that imprints itself on the mind and memory.

A yellow fish is thrown away on the sand.

Of that palest yellow that comes before the withering and falling of leaves. It has black spots. As I stoop to watch, it begins to shudder and leap. The mouth gasps; gasps and closes. It shudders and tosses on the hot sand.

The men carry on sorting their fish quickly and efficiently. That mouth closes; closes and opens, desperate for water.

Like Jalaja's mouth.

Too hasty infant Jalaja. She pushed and bumped her way out into the world. Her name had already been decided. She who rises from the waters. Lotus. Jalaja. They had to put her in an incubator. I stood outside that room constantly, watching her. Her pale red mouth. Her round eyes. Sometimes she would open and close her mouth, as if sucking.

The ashes which Arun brought back from the electric crematorium were in a small urn, a miniature of those huge earthenware jars of Mohenjodaro and Harappa. Its narrow mouth was tied with a piece of cloth.

"Why is the mouth closed?"

"What mouth?"

"The mouth of the urn. Open it."

"Anu. It contains only ashes."

"I want to see. Open it."

"Anu."

"Open its mouth. That mouth. . ."

Loud racking sobs. The cloth was removed to reveal the urn's tiny mouth.

The ashes were in this very sea.

The sea is at some distance. The yellow fish leaps hopelessly towards it. Its mouth falls open, skyward. Lifted from the hot sand, it falls away from the fingers, heaving and tossing. It falls away again from a leaf with which I try to hold it.

A fisherboy is on his way back from splashing in the waves. He comes when I summon him in Marathi, "*Ikkade yé.*" "Come here."

"Will you throw this yellow fish back into the sea?"

A quick snort of laughter. He grabs the fish firmly by its tail and starts running towards the sea. I run after him. He places it on the crest of an incoming wave. For a moment it splutters, helpless, like a drunk who cannot find the way home. Again it opens its mouth to the water, taking it in. Then a swish of the tail fin. An arrogant leap. Once again it swishes its tail and swims forward. You can see its clear yellow for a very long time. Then it merges into the blue-grey-white of the sea.

Archipelago would like to acknowledge
the generous involvement of The Yali Project
and Aditi: Foundation for the Arts.

YALI